Meadow Brook

by

Mary Jane Holmes

Double 9
BOOKS

Meadow Brook
by Mary Jane Holmes

Copyright © 2024

All Rights reserved.

ISBN: 978-93-63057-15-9

Published by

DOUBLE 9 BOOKS

2/13-B, Ansari Road
Daryaganj, New Delhi – 110002
info@double9books.com
www.double9books.com
Tel. 011-40042856

ABOUT THE AUTHOR

American novelist Mary Jane Holmes is well known for her widely read novels and short tales from the 19th century. She was raised in a low-income household and was born in Brookfield, Massachusetts, in 1825. Her work was renowned for its emotional and romantic tone and often addressed issues of love, family, and social status. In her lifetime, she wrote more than 60 books, demonstrating her prodigious talent. Despite Holmes' writing being well-liked during her lifetime, it went out of favor in the years after her death in 1907. Scholars and readers alike, who value her contributions to the romance novel genre and her insights into 19th-century American life and society, have lately shown a renewed interest in her work.

CONTENTS

TO MY MOTHER,

Who, more than any one else, will be interested in a story which has in it so much of my childhood and early home,

THIS WORK

is affectionately dedicated by her Daughter

MARY.

PREFACE

In this story of Meadow Brook there is, I am aware, nothing very startling or wonderful; but it has the merit, at least, of containing more truth than books of the same character usually possess. From this, however, the reader is not to infer that I have made myself the heroine; for though the early home, the childhood, and childish experience of "Rosa Lee" are mostly my own—while more than one whiskered young man will recognize the little girl of thirteen, at whom he once made faces from behind his desk as the "schoolma'am"—the similarity extends no further.

The fickle Mr. Clayton and his haughty bride, the unfortunate Herbert, the disappointed Ada, the proud Southern planter, and the gentle, bright-haired Jessie, are intended to represent different varieties of American character, and are such as many of us have met in our intercourse with the world. For my portrayals of Georgia life, I am indebted to a friend, who recently spent two years in that State, and whose graphic descriptions of what she there saw have been to me of much service.

Believing that the world loves better to read of the probable than of the improbable, I have tried to be *natural*; and if, by this means, but one friend is added to the number I now possess, I shall feel that my labor has not been in vain.

M. J. H.

Bockport, N. Y., 1857.

CHAPTER I
CHILDHOOD

Far away among the New England hills stands a large, old-fashioned farmhouse, around whose hearth-stone not many years agone, a band of merry, noisy children played, myself the merriest, noisiest of them all. It stood upon an eminence overlooking a broad strip of rolling meadow-land, at the extremity of which was the old grey rock, where the golden rod and sassafras grew, where the green ivy crept over the crumbling wall, and where, under the shadow of the thorn-apple tree, we built our play-houses, drinking our tea from the acorn saucers, and painting our dolls' faces with the red juice of the poke berries, which grew there in great abundance.

Just opposite our house, and across the green meadow, was a shady grove, where, in the spring-time, the singing birds made their nests, and where, when the breath of winter was on the snow-clad hills, Lizzie, Carrie, and I, and our taller, stronger brothers dragged our sleds, dashing swiftly down the steep hill, and away over the ice-covered valley below. Truly, ours was a joyous childhood, and ours a happy home; for never elsewhere fell the summer's golden sunlight so softly, and never was music sweeter than was the murmur of the dancing water-brook which ran past our door, and down the long green lane, losing itself at last in the dim old woods, which stretched away to the westward, seeming to my childish imagination the boundary line between this world and the next.

In the deep shadow of those woods I have sat alone for many an hour, watching the white, feathery clouds as they glimmered through the dense foliage which hung above my head, and musing, I scarcely knew of what. Strange fancies filled my brain and oftentimes, as I sat there in the hazy light of an autumnal afternoon, there came and talked with me myriads of little people, unseen, it is true, but still real to me, who knew and called them all by name. There, on a mossy bank, beneath a wide-spreading grape-vine, with the running brook at my feet, I felt the first longings for fame, though I did not thus designate it then. I only knew that I wanted a name, which should live when I was gone—a name of which my mother should be proud. It had been to me a day of peculiar trial. At school everything had gone wrong. Accidentally I had discovered that I possessed a talent for rhyming; and so, because I preferred filling my slate with verses, instead of proving on it that four times twenty were eighty, and that eighty, divided by twenty, equalled four, my teacher must needs find fault with me, calling me "lazy," and compelling me to sit between two hateful boys, with warty hands, who for the remainder of the afternoon amused themselves by sitting inconveniently near to me, and by telling me how big my eyes and feet were. I hardly think I should now mind that mode of punishment, provided I could choose the boys, but I did then, and in the worst of humors, I started for home, where other annoyances awaited me. Sally, the housemaid, scolded me for upsetting a pan of milk on her clean pantry shelf, calling me "the carelessest young one she ever saw," and predicting that "I'd one day come to the *gallus* if I didn't mend my ways."

Juliet, my oldest sister, scolded me for wearing without her consent her shell side-comb, which, in climbing through a hole in the plastering of the schoolhouse, I accidentally broke. Grandmother scolded me for mounting to the top of her high chest of drawers to see what was in them; and to crown all, when, towards sunset, I came in from a romp in the barn, with my yellow hair flying all over my face, my dress burst open, my pantalet split from the top downward, and my sun-bonnet hanging down my back, my mother reproved me severely, telling me I was "a sight to behold." This was my usual style of dress, and I didn't think any one need interfere; so, when she wondered if there ever was another such child, and bade me look at myself in the glass, asking if "I didn't think I was a beautiful object," my heart came up in my throat, and with the angry response that "I couldn't help my looks—I didn't make myself," I started through the door, and running down the long lane to the grape-vine, my favorite resort, I threw myself upon the ground, and burying my face in the tall grass, wept bitterly, wishing I had never been born, or, being born, that the ban of ugliness were not upon me.

Mother doesn't love me, I thought—nobody loves me; and then I wished that I could die, for I had heard that the first dead of a family, no matter how unprepossessing they had been in life, were sure to be the best beloved in the memory of the living. To die, then, that I might be loved was all I asked for, as I lay there weeping alone, and thinking in my childish grief that never before was a girl, nine summers old, so wretched as myself. And then, in my imagination, I went through with a mental rehearsal of my own obsequies, fancying that I was dead, but still possessing the faculty of knowing all that passed around me.

With an involuntary shudder, I crossed my hands upon my bosom, stretched my feet upon the mossy bank, and closed my eyes to the fading sunlight, which I was never to see again. I knew they would lay me in the parlor, and on my forehead I felt the gentle breeze as it came through the open window, lifting the folds of the muslin curtain which shaded it. Throughout the house was a deep hush, and in my mother's voice there was a heartbroken tone, which I had never heard before, and which thrilled me with joy, for it said that I was loved at last. Then I thought how lonely they would be as day by day went and came, and I came no more among them. "They will miss the little ugly face," I said, and on my cheek my own hot tears fell as I thought how Lizzie would mourn for me in the dark night time, weeping that I was not by her side, but sleeping in a narrow coffin, which I hoped would be a handsome one with satin hangings, as I had seen at the funeral of a rich neighbor's fair young bride. I did not want them to strew my pillow with roses as they did hers—for I knew they would not accord with my thin, plain face. In the distance I heard the sound of the tolling bell, and I saw the subdued expression on the faces of my school companions as they listened breathlessly, counting at last the nine quick strokes, which would tell to a stranger that 'twas only a child who was gone.

Then came the funeral, the roll of wheels, the tread of many feet, the hum of voices, the prayer, the hymn, in which I longed to join, but dared not for appearances' sake, and then, one by one, they stole up for a last farewell, lifting my baby brother and bidding him look upon the sister he would never know save by the grassy mound where they would tell him she was buried. I knew when Lizzie bent over me by the convulsive sob and burning kiss which she pressed upon my lips, and divining her inmost thoughts, I fancied she was wishing that no harsh word had ever passed between us In my heart I longed to tell her how freely I forgave her, but ere I had time to do so, she stepped aside, while an older, a wrinkled hand was laid upon my forehead, and my aged grandmother murmured, "Poor little Rosa, far better that I should die, than that she, so young, should be laid in the lonesome grave."

Instantly the dark grave loomed up before me, so dark and dreary that I shrank from being put there. I could not die; I was afraid to sleep with the silent dead. I would far rather live, even though I lived unloved forever. And then, softly in my ear, a spirit friend whispered, "Be *great* and *good*— get to yourself a name of which they shall be proud—make them love you for your deeds, rather than your looks, and when, in the future, strangers shall ask concerning you, 'Who is she?' let it be their pride to answer, 'My daughter,' or 'My sister.'" Older and wiser heads than mine would have said it was Ambition, which thus counselled with me, but I questioned her not of her name. I only knew that her words were sweet and soothing, and I treasured them in my heart, pondering upon them until I fell asleep, unconscious that the daylight was fast declining, and that the heavy dew was falling upon my uncovered head.

Meantime at home many inquiries were being made concerning my whereabouts, and when, at last, night came on, and I was still away, my oldest brother was sent in quest of me down the long lane where I was last seen by Lizzie, who had attempted to follow me, but had desisted through fear of being called a *tag*. I was just dreaming that the trumpet of fame was sounding forth my name, when, alas! I awoke to find it was only brother Charlie, making the woods resound with "Rosa Lee! Where are you? Why don't you answer?"

Of course I was disappointed,—who wouldn't be?—and in a fit of obstinacy I determined not to reply, but to make him think I was lost—then see how he'd feel! But on this point I was not to be gratified, for failing of finding me in the lane, he made straight for the grape-vine, where he stumbled over me as I lay, this time feigning sleep, to see what he would do. Seizing me by the shoulder, he exclaimed, "You are a pretty bird, scaring us out of a year's growth. Mother'll scold you well for this."

But he was mistaken, for mother's manner towards me was greatly changed. The torn pantalet and the chewed bonnet-strings were all forgotten, and in the kindest tone she asked, "If I were not cold, and why I went to sleep on the grass." There were tears in my eyes, but I winked hard and forced them back, until Lizzie brought me a piece of custard pie (my special favorite) which, she said, "she had saved for me, because she knew how much I loved it."

This was too much, and sitting down in Carrie's little chair, I cried aloud, saying in reply to the oft-repeated question as to what ailed me, that "I didn't know, only I was so glad."

"Hystericky as a witch," was Sally's characteristic comment on my strange behavior, at the same time she suggested that I be put to bed.

To this I made no objection, and pushing aside the pie, which, to Lizzie's disappointment, I could not eat, I went to my room, a happier, and I believe, a better girl; so much influence has a kind word or deed upon a desponding, sensitive child. That night I was tired and restless, turning uneasily upon my pillow, pushing Lizzie's arm from my neck, because it kept me from breathing, and lying awake until I heard the long clock in grandma's room strike the hour of twelve. Then I slept, but dreamed there was a heavy pain in my head, which made me moan in my sleep, and that mother, attracted by the sound, came to my side, feeling my pulse, and saying, "What ails you, Rosa?" "There was nothing ailed me," I said; but in the morning when I awoke, the pain was still there, though I would not acknowledge it, for scarcely anything could tempt me to stay away from school; so at the usual hour I started, but the road was long and wearisome, and twice I sat down to rest, leaning my forehead upon the handle of my dinner basket, and wondering why the smell of its contents made me so sick. Arrived at school, everything seemed strange, and when Maria, the girl who shared my desk, produced a love-letter from Tom Jenkins, which she had found on *my* side of the desk, and in which he made a formal offer of himself, frecks and all, I did not even smile. Taking my book, I attempted to study, but the words ran together, the objects in the room chased each other in circles, the little Abecedarian, shouting the alphabet at the top of his voice, sounded like distant thunder, and when at last the teacher called for our class in "Colburn," she seemed to be a great way off, while between her and me was a gathering darkness which soon shut out every object from my view.

For a few moments all was confusion, and when at last my faculties returned I was lying on the recitation bench, my head resting in the teacher's lap, while my hair and dress were so wet that I fancied I'd been out in a drenching shower. Everybody was so kind and spoke so softly to me that, with a vague impression that something had happened, I began to cry. Just then, father, who had been sent for, appeared, and taking me in his arms, started for home, while Lizzie followed with the basket and my sun-bonnet, which looked sorry and drooping like its owner. At the door father asked of mother, who met us, "Where shall I put her?" but ere she could reply, I said, "On grandmother's bed."

And there, among the soft pillows and snowy linen on which I had often looked with almost envious eyes, and which now seemed so much to rest me, I was laid. Of the weary weeks which followed, I have only a confused recollection. I know that the room was darkened as far as possible, and that before the window at the foot of the bed, grandma's black shawl was hung, one corner being occasionally pinned back when more light was needed. After a while it seemed to me that it was Lizzie, instead of myself who was sick, and the physician said she had a fever, which had been long coming on, but was undoubtedly hastened by her sleeping on the wet grass in the night. And so we all trod softly about the house, speaking in whispers, and lifting the door-latches carefully, while Lizzie, with my cap and night dress on, lay all day long in bed, never speaking, never moving, except when the long clock in the corner struck off the hour; then she would moan as if in pain, and once when somebody, who looked like Lizzie, but was still I, Rosa, stole on tiptoe to her side, with a bouquet of flowers, which Maria had brought, she put her arms around my neck, and pointing to the clock, whispered, "It keeps saying 'She's dead'!—'She's dead'!—She's dead!' Won't you tell it to be still?"

Then we knew that it disturbed her, and so the old clock was stopped, a thing which grandma said "had not been in fifty odd years," except the time when grandpa died, and then, with the going out of his life, the clock itself ran down. All the night through the lamp burned upon the table where stood the vials, the Dover powders, and the cups, while Lizzie, with her great blue eyes so much like mine, wide open, lay watching the flickering shadows on the wall, counting the flowers on the paper bordering, wondering if there ever were *blue* roses, and thinking if there were that they must smell as the dinner did beneath the chestnut tree.

At last, when the family were wearied out with watching, the neighbors were called in, and among them our schoolteacher, who seemed to tread on air, so light and noiseless were her footsteps; and Lizzie, when she saw how kind she was, wondered she had not loved her better. Then came other watchers equally kind with Miss Phillips, but possessing far less tact for nursing; and even now I have a vivid remembrance of their annoying attempts "to fix me so I'd be more comfortable." Was I lying in a position satisfactory to myself, I must be lifted up, my pillows shaken, turned over, and my head placed so high that my chin almost touched my chest. Did I fall into a little doze, I must rouse up to tell whether I were asleep or not, and did I get into a sound slumber, I must surely wake enough to say whether I wanted anything.

Again, I fancied that another beside Lizzie was sick, for in mother's room, contiguous to mine, there was a low hum of voices, agoing in and out, a careful shutting of the door, and gradually I got the impression that Jamie, my beautiful baby brother, was connected with all this, for I heard them talk of scarlet fever, and it's going hard with him. But I had no desire or power to ask the why or wherefore; and so time wore on, until there came a day when it seemed that the reverie beneath the grape-vine was coming true. There was the same roll of wheels, the tread of many feet, and through the closed doors I heard a mournful strain, sung by trembling voices, while from afar, I caught the notes of a tolling bell. I was much alone that day, and once, for more than an hour, there was no one with me excepting grandma, who frequently removed her spectacles to wipe the moisture which gathered upon them.

From that day I grew worse, and they sent to Spencer for Dr. Lamb, who, together with Dr. Griffin, held a council over me, and said that I must die. I saw mother when they told her. She was standing by the window, from which the black shawl had been removed, for nothing disturbed the little girl now, and the window was wide open, so that the summer air might cool the burning head, from which the matted yellow hair had all been shorn. She turned pale as death, and with a cry of anguish, pressed her hand upon her side; but she did not weep. I wondered at it then, and thought she cared less than Lizzie, who sat at the foot of the bed, sobbing so loudly that the fever burned more fiercely in my veins, and the physician said it must not be; she must leave the room, or keep quiet.

It was Monday, and a few hours afterward, as Sally was passing the door, grandma handed her my dirty, crumpled sun-bonnet, bidding her wash it and put it away. Sally's voice trembled as she replied, "No, no, leave it as it is, for when she's gone, nothing will look so much like her as that jammed bonnet with its chewed up strings."

A gush of tears was grandma's only answer, and after I got well, I found the bonnet carefully rolled up in a sheet of clean white paper and laid away in Sally's drawer. There were days and nights of entire unconsciousness, and then with the vague, misty feeling of one awakening from a long, disturbed sleep, I awoke again to life and reason. The windows of my room were closed; but without, I heard the patter of the September rain, and the sound of the autumnal wind as it swept past the house. Gathered at my side were my father, mother, brothers, sisters, grandmother; and all, as my eye rested upon their faces, I thought, were paler and more careworn than when I last looked upon them. Something, too, in their dress disturbed me; but, before I could speak, a voice which I knew to be Dr. Griffin's, said "She is better—she will live."

From my mother's lips there broke another cry—not like that which I had heard when they told her I must die—but a cry of joy, and then she fell fainting in my father's arms. I never doubted her love for me again, but in bitterness of spirit, I have many a time wept that I ever distrusted her, my blessed mother.

The fourth day after the crisis I was alone with Lizzie, whom, for a long time, I importuned to give me a mirror that I might see myself once more. Yielding at length to my entreaties, she handed me a small looking glass, a wedding gift to my grandmother, and with the consoling remark, that "I wouldn't always look so," awaited the result. I am older than I was then, but even now I cannot repress a smile as I bring before my mind the shorn head, the wasted face with high cheek-bones, and the big blue eyes, in which there was a look of "crazy Sal," which met my view. With the angry exclamation, "They'll hate me worse than ever, I'm so ugly," I dashed the mirror upon the floor, breaking it in a thousand pieces. Lizzie knew what I meant, and twining her arms about my neck, she said, "Don't talk so, Rosa; we love you dearly, and it almost killed us when we thought you couldn't live. You know big men never cry, and pa the least of all. Why, he didn't shed a tear when lit" — —

Here she stopped suddenly, as if on a forbidden subject, but soon resuming the conversation, she continued, "But the day Dr. Lamb was here and told us you would die, he was out under the cherry tree by our play-house, and when Carrie asked him if you'd never play there any more, he didn't answer, but turned his face towards the barn, and cried so hard and so loud, that grandma came out and pitied him, smoothing his hair just like he was a little boy. Brother Charlie, too, lay right down in the grass, and said he'd give everything he'd got if he'd never called you 'bung-eyed,' nor made fun of you, for he loved you best of all. Then there was poor Jamie kept calling for 'Yosa'" — —

Here Lizzie broke down entirely, saying, "I can't tell you any more, don't ask me."

Suddenly it occurred to me that I had neither seen nor heard little Jamie, the youngest of us all, the pet and darling of our household. Rapidly my thoughts traversed the past, and in a moment I saw it all. "Jamie was dead." I did not need that Lizzie should tell me so. I knew it was true, and when the first great shock was over, I questioned her of his death, how and when it occurred. It seems that I was at first taken with scarlet fever, which soon assumed another form, but not until it had communicated itself to Jamie, who, after a few days' suffering, had died. I had ever been his favorite, and to the last he had called for me to come; my grandmother, with the superstition natural to her age, construing it into an omen that I was soon to follow him.

Desolate and dreary seemed the house; and when I was able to go from room to room, oh! how my heart ached as I missed the prattle of our baby-boy. Away to the garret, where no one could see it, they had carried his empty cradle, but I sought it out; and as I thought of the soft, brown curls I had so often seen resting there, and would never see again, I sat down by its side and wept most bitterly. The withered, yellow leaves of autumn were falling upon his grave ere I was able to visit it, and at its head stood a simple stone, on which was inscribed, "Our Jamie." As I leaned against the cold marble, and in fancy saw by its side—what had well-nigh been—another mound, and another stone, bearing upon it the name of "Rosa," I involuntarily shuddered; while from my heart there went up a silent thanksgiving, that God, in his wise Providence, had ordered it otherwise.

From that sickness I date a more healthful state of mind and feeling, and though I still shrunk from any allusion to my personal appearance, I never again doubted the love of those who had manifested so much solicitude for me when ill, and who watched over me so tenderly during the period of my convalescence, which was long and wearisome, for the snows of an early winter lay upon the frozen ground, ere I was well enough to take my accustomed place in the old brown schoolhouse at the foot of the long hill.

CHAPTER II
THANKSGIVING

Thanksgiving! How many reminiscences of the olden time does that word call up, when sons and daughters, they who had wandered far and wide, whose locks, once brown and shining with the sunlight of youth, now give tokens that the autumnal frosts of life are falling slowly upon them, return once more to the old hearth-stone, and, for a brief space, grow young again amid the festive scenes of Thanksgiving Day. To you, who, like me, drew your first breath among the New England hills, and who have strayed away from your early home, in the busy world in which you are now mingling, comes there not occasionally pleasant memories of the olden time, when with eager haste you hied you back to the roof-tree which sheltered your infancy? And though, perchance, the snows of many a winter may have drifted across the graves of the gray-haired man you called your father, and the mild-eyed woman who bore the blessed name of mother, can you not recall them to mind, as when with tears of joy and words of love, they welcomed their children home, thanking God that as yet not one of their household treasures was missing? And if, after the lapse of years, there came a time when the youngest of you all was gone, when the childish prattle you loved so well to hear was hushed, when through the house was no more heard the patter of little, busy feet, when there was naught left of the lost one, save a curl of golden hair, or a tiny *shoe*, soiled and bent, but looking still so much like him who wore it once, that you preserve it as your choicest treasure: if, I say, there came to you a time like this, do you not remember how, amid all the social cheer, there was still an aching void, which nothing around you could fill?

But lest I make this chapter too sad, I shall not speak of our feelings as we missed our baby brother, for they who have lost from their fireside an active, playful child, understand far better than I can describe, the loneliness, the longing for something gone, which becomes almost a part of their being, although at times they may seem to forget. Children's grief is seldom as lasting as that of mature years; and hence it is not strange if I sometimes forgot my sorrow in the joyous anticipation of Thanksgiving Day, which was then to me but another name for plum puddings, chicken pies, meeting dresses, morocco shoes, city cousins, a fire in the parlor, and last, though not least, the privilege of sitting at the first table, and using grandma's six tiny silver spoons, with the initials of her maiden name, "P. S." marked upon them.

On such occasions my thoughts invariably took a leap backward, and looking at grandma's wrinkled face and white, shining hair, I would wonder if she ever were young like me; and if, being young, she swung on gates or climbed trees, and walked the great beams, as I did. Then, with another bound, my thoughts would penetrate the future, when I, a dignified grandmother, should recline in my arm-chair, stately and stiff, in my heavy satin and silver gray, while my oldest son, a man just my father's size, should render me all the homage and respect due to one of my age. By myself, too, I had several times tried on grandma's clothes, spectacles, cap and all; and then, seated in her chair, with the big Bible in my lap, I had expounded scripture to the imaginary children around me, frequently reprimanding *Rosa* for her inattention, asking her what "she thought would become of her, if she didn't stop wriggling so in her chair, and learn 'the chief end of man.'" Once, in the midst of my performance, grandma herself appeared, and as a natural consequence, I was divested of my fixings in a much shorter space of time than it had taken me to don them. From that day up to the period of my illness, I verily believe grandma looked upon me as "given over to hardness of heart and blindness of mind."

But I am wandering from my subject, which was, I believe, the Thanksgiving succeeding Jamie's death and my own recovery from sickness. For this occasion great preparations were made, it being confidently expected that my father's brother, who lived in Boston, would be with us, together with his wife, a lady whose reputation for sociability and suavity of manners was, with us, rather below par. She was my uncle's second wife, and rumor said that neither himself nor his home were as comfortable as they once had been. From the same reliable source, too, we learned that she breakfasted in her own room at ten, dined at three, made or received calls until six, went to parties, soirées, or the theatre in the evening, and seldom got to bed until two o'clock in the morning; a mode of living which was pronounced little better than heathenish by grandma, who had long been anxious for an opportunity of "giving Charlotte Ann a piece of her mind."

Mother, who was more discreet, very wisely advised her not to interfere with the arrangements of her daughter-in-law. "It would do no good," she said, "and might possibly make matters worse." Unlike most old people, grandma was not very much set in her own way, and to mother's suggestion, she replied that "Mebby she shouldn't say anything—'twould depend on how many airs Charlotte put on."

To me the expected visit was a sore trial; for, notwithstanding my cheeks and neck were rounder and fuller than they had ever been, my head, with its young crop of short, stiff hair, was a terrible annoyance, and more than once I had cried as I saw in fancy the derisive smile with which my dreaded Aunt Charlotte was sure to greet me. At last sister Anna, who possessed a great deal of taste in such matters, and who ought to have been a milliner, contrived for the "picked chicken," as she called me, a black lace cap, which fitted me so well, and was so vastly becoming that I lost all my fears, and child-like, began to count the days which must elapse before I could wear it.

Meantime, in the kitchen there was a loud rattling of dishes, a beating of eggs, and calling for wood, with which to heat the great brick oven, grandma having pronounced the stove unfit for baking a Thanksgiving dinner. From the cornfield, behind the barn, a golden pumpkin, four times larger than my head and about the same color, was gathered, and after being brought to the house, was pared, cut open, scraped, and sliced into a little tin kettle with a copper bottom, where for hours it stewed and sputtered, filling the atmosphere with a faint, sickly odor, which I think was the main cause of the severe headache I took to bed with me. Mother, on the contrary, differed from me, she associating it in some way with the rapid disappearance of the raisins, cinnamon, sugar, and so forth, which, in sundry brown papers, lay open upon the table. She was generally right when she made up her mind, so I shall not dispute the point, for, let the cause have been what it would, it was a very sick little girl which, the night before Thanksgiving, was put early to bed by Sally, who remarked, as she undressed me, that "I was *slimpsy* as a rag, and she wouldn't wonder if I had a *collapse*," adding, as she tucked the clothes around me, that "if I did, it would be mighty apt to go hard with me."

The next morning, just as the first grey streaks of daylight were appearing in the east, I awoke, finding, to my great joy, that my headache was gone. Rising upon my elbow and leaning far out of bed, I pushed aside the striped curtain which shaded the window, and looking out upon the ground below, saw, to my utter dismay, that it was covered with snow. To me there is nothing pleasant in a snow storm, a snow bank, or a snow cloud; and when a child, I used to think that with the fall of the first flake, there came over my spirits a chill, which was not removed until the spring-time, when, with its cause, it melted away: and even now, when, with my rubber boots, I dare brave any drift, not more than five feet four inches high, I cannot say that I have any particular love for snow; and as from my window I watch the descent of the feathery flakes, I always feel an irresistible desire to make at them wry faces, my favorite method of showing my dislike. On the morning of which I have spoken, I vented my displeasure in the usual way, and then I fell into a deep sleep, from which I was at last awakened by the loud shouts of my brothers, who, in the meadow across the road, were pelting each other with balls, occasionally rolling over in the pure, white snow, which they hailed as an old and well loved friend.

Not long after breakfast was over Anna, commenced dressing Lizzie and Carrie, and as she had herself to beautify before the arrival of the train which was to bring my uncle and aunt, it is not surprising that she hurried rather faster then was wholly agreeable to the little girls, who could see no good cause for such haste, even if Herbert Langley, my aunt's son and a youth of seventeen, was to accompany her. I, however, who was older, read things differently, and when Anna pulled Lizzie's curly hair, and washed Carrie's nose *up* instead of *down*, until they both cried, and when she herself stood before the glass a whole half hour, arranging just in front of her ears two *spit curls*, sometimes called *"beau catchers,"* I shrugged my shoulders, wondering if she thought a city boy would care for her.

The morning train from Boston was due about ten o'clock, and as Meadow Brook did not then boast a daily omnibus, it was necessary that some one should be at the dépôt in order to meet our expected guests. In New England it is almost an unheard-of thing for an entire family to remain away from church on Thanksgiving Day, but considering all the circumstances, it was, on this occasion, decided orthodox for us to do so, and accordingly at nine o'clock father and old sorrel started for the dépôt, which was distant about two and a half miles. Long and wearisome to us children was that waiting for his return; for stiff and prim, as starched white aprons, best gowns, and hemstitched pantalets could make us, we sat in a row like so many automatons, scarcely daring to move, lest we should displace some article of dress. In the best chamber, the room which Aunt Charlotte was to occupy, a cheerful wood fire was burning, and at least a dozen times did grandma go up there to see if all were right, now smoothing the clean, linen pillow-case, now moving the large easy-chair a little more to the centre of the room, and again wiping from the mirror some imaginary specks of dust.

As she was coming down the twelfth time, the sound of sleigh-bells took us all to the window, where, instead of the costly furs and rich velvet wrappings of Aunt Charlotte, we saw the coarse plaid shawl and dark delaine hood of Aunt Betsey, while at her side was the shaggy overcoat and sealskin cap of her better half, Uncle Jason. This worthy couple, good enough in their way, lived in Union, about nine miles from Meadow Brook, where, for the last ten years, they had been in the habit of spending Thanksgiving, without ever seeming to think it possible for them to return the compliment.

Although we had never seen Aunt Charlotte, we knew full well that there was nothing in common between her and Aunt Betsey, and after a long consultation it had been decided not to invite the latter, who, as it proved, did not deem an invitation necessary.

Uncle Jason was my father's half brother, and the stepson of grandma, who, the moment she saw them was actually guilty of the exclamation, "Good Lord! what sent them here?" Before any of us could reply, the door burst open, and the loud, boisterous laugh of Uncle Jason greeted our ears, intermingled with the squeaky tones of Aunt Betsey, who, addressing my mother, said, "How d'ye dew, Fanny. You pretty well? I s'pose you're lookin' for us, though you didn't send us no invite? Jason kinder held off about comin', but I told him 'twas enough sight easier to eat dinner here than to cook it to hum."

With as good a grace as she could possibly assume, mother returned her greeting, and then, taking her into her own bedroom, asked her to remove her bonnet, at the same time telling her she was expecting Uncle Joseph and Aunt Charlotte from Boston.

"Now, you don't say it," exclaimed Aunt Betsey, stopping for a moment in the adjustment of her cap, the fashion of which was wonderful, having been devised by herself, as were all her articles of dress. "Now, dew tell if that puckerin' thing is a comin'! How nipped up we shall have to be! I'm so glad I wore this gown!" she continued, looking complacently at her blue and white plaid, the skirt of which was very short and scanty, besides being trimmed at the bottom with two narrow ruffles.

With her other peculiarities Aunt Betsey united that of jealousy, and after getting herself warm, and looking round, as was her custom, she commenced with, "Now, if I won't give up—a fire in the parlor chamber. I s'pose Charlotte's too good to pull off her things in the bedroom, as I do. Wall, it's the luck of some to be born with a silver spoon in their mouth."

Grandma, who was the only person present except myself, made no answer, and after a moment Aunt Betsey continued, "Now I think on't, Miss Lee (she never addressed her as "mother," for, from the first, a mutual dislike had existed between them), now I think on't, Miss Lee, mebby Fanny meant to slight me."

"Fanny never slighted anybody," was grandma's reply, while her polished knitting-needles rattled with a vengeance.

"Wall, I guess she thought Jo's wife and I wouldn't hitch hosses exactly, but the land knows that I don't care the snap of my finger for her. I'm as good as anybody, if I don't keep a hired maid and have a carpet on every floor."

Here she was interrupted by the sound of horses' feet, and rising up, grandma said, "I guess they've come. Will you go and meet them?"

"Not *I*; I'm the last one to creep, I can tell you," was Aunt Betsey's reply, while grandma and I quitted the room, leaving her sitting bolt upright, with her feet on the fender and her lips pursed up as they always were when she was indignant.

Uncle Joseph, Aunt Charlotte, Herbert Langley, had all come, and as the latter leaped upon the ground and I caught a sight of his tall, slender figure, I involuntarily exclaimed, "Long-legs," a cognomen, which he ever after retained in our family. Shaking down his pants, he went through with a kind of shuffle not wholly unlike the Highland fling, ending his performance by kissing his hand to the group of *noses* pressed close against the window-pane.

"I shall like him," was my mental comment, as I turned from him towards the bundle of clothes which Uncle Joseph lifted from the sleigh and deposited upon the steps, and which we supposed to be our dreaded aunt.

"This is perfectly horrible," were the first words which issued from under the folds of her veil; but to what she referred I never knew.

We all knew and loved Uncle Joseph, and for his sake my mother conquered whatever of prejudice she felt towards his wife, who returned her cordial welcome with the extreme end of her forefinger, saying, when asked to sit down, "I'll go to my room immediately, if you please."

"Speak to the children first," suggested my uncle, and with a muttered, "It doesn't matter," the haughty lady bowed coldly to us, as one by one we were presented.

When it came my turn, her small, black eyes rested longer upon me, and the faintest derisive smile imaginable curled the corners of her mouth. I knew that either my cap or my face had provoked that smile, and with tears in my eyes I was turning away, when Herbert Langley caught me in his long arms, exclaiming, "And so, this is Rosa, the poetess, I mean to call you little 'Crop-head,' may I?"

He referred, I suppose, to a letter which I had once written in rhyme to my Uncle Joseph, but before, I could frame any reply, his mother said, scornfully, "Don't be flattered, child—Herbert calls everything poetry that rhymes. He'll learn to discriminate better as he grows older," and with a stately sweep she left the room, saying, as she reached the rather steep and narrow stair-case, "Dear me—how funny—it's like mounting a ladder."

While she was making her toilet we had an opportunity of learning something of Herbert, who, whether he were so or not, seemed much pleased with everything around him. Occasionally, however, I doubted his sincerity, for when Aunt Betsey was presented to him, he appeared quite as much delighted with her as with anything else, drawing his chair closely to her side, and asking her numberless questions about the best modes of making cheese and raising chickens, while all the time there was a peculiarly quizzical expression in his eyes, which were dark and very handsome, saving that the lids were too red to suit my ideas of beauty. To Anna and her *spit curls* he took kindly, and ere his lady mother made her appearance a second time he had put his arm around her twice, telling her she should come to Boston sometime and go to school. A rustle of silk upon the stairs announced the descent of Aunt Charlotte, and with her nose slightly elevated, ready for any emergency, she entered the parlor, where she was introduced to Aunt Betsey, who, courtesying straight down, "hoped to see her well," adding, that she "s'posed she'd come to the country to see how poor folks lived."

Falling back into the rocking-chair which Anna brought for her, Aunt Charlotte made no particular reply, save an occasional attack upon her hartshorn. Aunt Betsey, however, nothing daunted, endeavored to engage her in conversation by asking if "she knew Liza Ann Willcott, a tailoress girl, that boarded with a Miss Johnson, who used to live in Union, but who now lived in Boston."

Frowning majestically, Aunt Charlotte replied that she had not the honor of Miss Willcott's acquaintance, whereupon Aunt Betsey advised her to make it by all means, assuring her that "Liza Ann was a first rate girl, and that Miss Johnson was the best kind of a neighbor, always willin' to *lend*, or do a good turn" — —

Here, with a haughty toss of her head, Aunt Charlotte turned away and began talking in a low tone to Herbert, he being the only one who, she seemed to think, was at all worth noticing. It is strange how much constraint one person can sometimes throw over a room full. On this occasion, had an ogress suddenly alighted in our midst, we could not have been more silent or less at ease than we were with that Boston lady, sitting there so starched and stiff, her fat hands folded one over the other, and the tips of her satin gaiters just visible from beneath the ample folds of her rich silk dress. Even Uncle Joseph, whose genial nature usually shed so much sunlight over our circle, was grave and reserved, rarely venturing a remark, or, if he did, glancing at his wife to see if she approved it. Uncle Jason, who painfully felt his own awkwardness, sat tipped back in his chair against the wall, with his feet on the rounds, while his fingers kept time to a tune, which he was evidently whistling to himself. Glad were we all when finally called to dinner, the savory smell of which had long been whetting our appetites.

"What! dinner so soon?" said Aunt Charlotte, consulting her gold watch, which pointed to half-past two. "I don't believe I can force down a mouthful."

But, spite of her belief, she *did* manage to make way with the contents of her well-filled plate, which was passed back a second time to be replenished. So eager were we all to serve her that we partially forgot Aunt Betsey, who, after waiting awhile for a potato, at last arose, and reaching half-way across the table, secured one for herself; saying, by way of apology, that "she believed in looking out for Number One, for if she didn't nobody else would."

So incensed was she with what she termed our neglect, that the moment dinner was over she insisted upon going home, saying, as she bade us good-bye, that "when she went again where she wasn't wanted, she gussed she should know it;" and adding, while two big tears dropped from the end of her nose, that "she never s'posed she should be so misused by folks that she'd done so much for."

The sight of *her* tears brought forth answering ones from me, for, with all her peculiarities, I loved Aunt Betsey, and I remembered that when sickness and death were among us, she had left her own home to stay with us, ministering as far as she was able to our comfort. Many a night had she watched with me, and though she invariably placed the lamp so that its rays glared full in my face, though she slept three-fourths of the time, *snoring* so loudly as to keep me awake, and though at the slightest change for the worse in my symptoms she always routed the whole household, telling them, "Rosa was dyin' now, if she ever was," thereby almost frightening me to death, I knew that she meant well, and in my heart I liked her far better than I did my Boston aunt, who, after bidding her sister-in-law good-bye, went back to the parlor, saying to her husband in a tone loud enough for us to hear, "What a vulgar creature! Did you notice her hands? Why, they are as coarse and black as a servant girl's."

"And she's none the worse for that," interposed grandma, warming up in the defence of her son's wife. "She has now and then an odd streak, but on the whole she's better than they'll average."

After this, Aunt Charlotte relapsed into silence, which she did not break until she overheard Herbert proposing to Anna a ride on the morrow. Then she roused up, and while her little black eyes snapped, she said, "I am going home to-morrow afternoon, and so are you. Consequently, there'll be no time for a ride."

In a twinkling, Herbert's thumb and finger went up to his nose, a gesture which I did not then understand, but it struck me disagreeably, and had also the effect of silencing Aunt Charlotte, who made no further remark on the subject until they chanced to be alone, when I, who was in the hall, heard her say, "What can induce you to talk so much with that raw country girl? Your city friends would laugh well if they knew it."

Consigning his "city friends" to the care of the old gentleman supposed to preside over the lower regions, Herbert walked off in quest of the "raw country girl," by whose side he sat the remainder of the evening, talking to her so low that Lizzie whispered to me her private opinion that "they were courting."

The next morning Aunt Charlotte did not appear at breakfast, it being so much earlier than her usual hour of rising that she felt wholly unequal to the task. Accordingly, though we did not wait, the table did until ten o'clock, when, pale and languid, she came down, seeming much disturbed to find that Herbert had coaxed Anna into going with him to call on Aunt Betsey, to whom he had taken quite a fancy, and who had asked him to visit her "if he didn't feel too smart."

Darting an angry glance at her husband, she said, "How could you suffer it?" asking at the same time if there was a hotel on the road. Being told that there was one at Union and another half-way between that and Meadow Brook, she seemed more disturbed than ever, eating little or no breakfast, and announcing her intention of staying over that day, or, at all events, until Herbert returned. Seating herself at the window, she watched and waited, while the hours crept on and the clock in grandma's room struck four ere the head of "old Sorrel" was visible far down the road. Then with an eagerness wholly incomprehensible to me, she started up, straining her eyes anxiously in the direction of the fast approaching cutter. As it came nearer we all observed something rather singular in the position of Herbert, who seemed lying almost across Anna's lap, while she was driving!

"Merciful Heavens! it's as I feared!" was Aunt Charlotte's exclamation, as she sank upon the lounge, moaning bitterly, and covering her face with the cushion, that she might not see the disgrace of her only son—for Herbert was *drunk*!

Lifting him out, my father and uncle laid him upon the settee in the sitting-room, just where little Jamie had been laid, and my mother, as she looked upon the senseless inebriate resting where once had lain the beautiful, inanimate form of her youngest born, thought how far less bitter was *her* cup of sorrow than was that of the half fainting woman, who would rather, far rather, her boy had died with the dew of babyhood upon his brow than to have seen him thus debased and fallen.

The story was soon told, my uncle supplying all points which Anna could not. It seems that early in life Herbert had acquired a love for the wine and porter which daily graced his mother's dinner-table. As he grew older his taste increased for something stronger, until now nothing save brandy could satisfy the cravings of his appetite. More than once had he been brought home in a state of entire unconsciousness, for he was easily intoxicated, it usually taking but one glass to render him perfectly foolish, while a second was generally sure to finish the work. These drunken fits were always followed by resolutions of amendment, and it was now so long since he had drank that his mother began to have strong hopes of his reform, but these, alas! were now dashed to the ground. Unfortunately, Uncle Jason had offered the young man a glass of cider, which immediately awoke in its full vigor his old love for ardent spirits. Just across the road, creaking in the November wind, hung the sign of the "Golden Fleece," and in that direction, soon after dinner, Herbert bent his steps, taking down at one time a tumbler two thirds full of raw brandy. This made him very talkative and very affectionate, insomuch that he kissed Aunt Betsey, who, as soon as she could, started him for home. When the half-way house, called in opposition to its neighbor "Silver Skin," was reached, Herbert insisted upon stopping and taking another glass, which ere long rendered him so helpless that Anna was obliged to take charge of Sorrel herself, while her companion fell asleep, leaning his head upon her shoulder and gradually sinking lower and lower until he rested in her lap.

All that night he remained in the sitting-room, which in the morning presented so sorry and disgusting an appearance that when Aunt Charlotte for the hundredth time wished she had never come to Meadow Brook, our whole family mentally responded a fervent Amen. Herbert, when fully restored to consciousness, seemed heartily ashamed of himself, crying like a girl, and winding his arms around his mother's neck so affectionately that I did not blame her when she forgave him and wiped away her tears.

She might not have had much faith in his sincerity could she have heard his conversation with Anna, whom he managed to withdraw from the family to the recess of a distant window. Alone with her, his manner changed, and with flashing eyes, he charged it to his mother, who, he said, first taught him to love it by allowing him, when a little boy, to drink the bottom of the wine glasses after dinner.

"And if I fill a drunkard's grave," said he, "she will be to blame; but," he added, as he saw Anna involuntarily shudder, "it shall not be. I *can* reform. I *will* reform, and you must help me do it."

Anna looked wonderingly at him, while he continued, taking her hand and removing from it a plain gold ring, which grandma had given her on her fifteenth birthday, "You must let me wear this as a talisman to protect me from evil. Whenever I am tempted I shall look at it and be saved."

Anna hesitated awhile, but the soft, handsome eyes of Herbert Langley had woven around her a spell she could not break, and at last she consented, receiving from him in return a diamond ring, which he told her was worth two hundred dollars. When this became known to mother she very wisely insisted on Anna's returning it, and together with the note explaining the why and the wherefore it went back to its owner, who immediately replied by a letter, the contents of which were carefully kept from us all. The effect, however, was plainly visible; for, from the time of its receipt we lost our merry, light-hearted sister, and in her place there moved among us a sober, listless girl, whom grandma called foolish, and whom Charlie pronounced "lovesick."

Herbert's letter was soon answered, but when Anna requested my father to put it in the P. O. he refused, telling her "she should not correspond with such a *drunken dog*." Possibly it was wrong in him thus to address her, for kind words and persuasive arguments might have won her to reason, but now a spirit of opposition was roused—"Herbert was wronged—misunderstood"—so Anna thought, and the letter which father refused to take, was conveyed by other hands, a postscript longer than the letter itself being first added.

After this there was no more trouble. Anna wrote regularly to Herbert, who promptly responded; his missives always being directed to one of Anna's schoolmates, who was just romantic enough to think her companion *persecuted*! Gradually I was let into the secret, and was occasionally employed to carry Anna's notes to and from the house of her friend. I did not then consider the great wrong I was doing, but since I have shed many a bitter tear to think that I in any way helped to work my sister's ruin.

CHAPTER III
COUSIN WILL

If so far as the golden Californian land this book of mine shall reach, it may, perchance, fall into the hands of some who, from their number, can select the veritable hero, the "Cousin Will" of my story. If so, I would ask them to think as leniently as possible of his faults, herein recorded, for the moustached Will of California, whose generous conduct wins the love of all, is hardly the same wild, mischievous boy, who once kept our home in a perpetual state of excitement.

The tears were scarcely yet dried, which he had shed over his mother's coffin, when he came to us, and in one corner of his green, oval trunk, there lay a tress of soft brown hair, which he had severed from that mother's head. He was the son of my mother's only sister, who, on her death-bed had committed him to the guardianship of my father, asking him to deal gently with her wayward boy, for beneath his faulty exterior there lay a mine of excellence, which naught save words of love could fathom.

Without meaning to be so, perhaps, my father was a stern reserved man, never seeking the confidence of his children whose real characters he did not understand. It is true he loved us—provided for all our wants, and, as far as possible, strove to make us what the children of a New England Presbyterian deacon ought to be; but he seldom petted us, and if Carrie, with her sunny face and chestnut curls, sometimes stole up behind him and twined her chubby arms around his neck, he seemed ashamed to return her caress unless they were alone. Brother Charlie he looked upon as almost incorrigible, but if he found it hard to cope with his bold, fun-loving spirit, it was tenfold more difficult for him to tame the mischievous Will, whom scarcely any one could manage, but who, strange to say, was a general favorite.

It was night when he reached Meadow Brook, and I was in bed, but through the closed doors I caught the sound of his voice, and in an instant I experienced a sensation of delight, as if in him I should find a kindred spirit. I could not wait until morning before I saw him, and, rising softly,

I groped my way down the dark stairway to a knot-hole, which had more than once done me service when sent from the room while my mother and her company told something I was not to hear! He was sitting so that the light of the lamp fell full upon his face, which, with its high, white brow, hazel eyes, and mass of wavy hair, seemed to me the most beautiful I had ever seen. Involuntarily I thought of my own plain features, and saying to myself, "He'll never like me, never," I crept back to bed, wondering if it were true that homely little girls made sometimes handsome women.

The next morning, wishing to produce as favorable an impression as possible, I was an unusually long time making my toilet—trying on one dress after another, and finally deciding upon a *white cambric* I never wore except to church, or on some similar occasion. Giving an extra brush to my hair, which had grown out darker and so very curly that Charley called me "Snarly-pate," I started for the breakfast-room, where the family were already assembled.

"What upon earth has the child got on?" was grandma's exclamation as she looked at me, both over and under her glasses, while mother bade me "go straight back and change my dress," asking "why I had put on my very best?"

"Settin' her cap for *Bill*, I guess," suggested Charlie, who, boy-like, was already on terms of great intimacy with his cousin.

More angry than grieved, I went back to my room, where I pouted for half an hour or more. Then, selecting the worst looking dress I had, I again descended to the dining-room where Charlie presented me to Will, telling him at the same time "to spare all comments on my appearance, as it made me madder than a March hare to be called ugly."

"I don't think she's ugly. Anyway *I* like her looks," said Will, smiling down upon me with those eyes which have since made many a heart beat as mine did then, for 'twas the first compliment of the kind I had ever received.

Will had always lived in the city, and now, anxious to see the lions of the country at once, he proposed to Charlie a ramble over the farm, inviting me to accompany them, which I did willingly, notwithstanding that Charlie muttered something about "not wanting a *gal* stuck along."

In the pasture we came across "old Sorrel," whom Will said he would ride as they did in a circus, if Charlie would only catch him. This was an easy task, for Sorrel, suspecting no evil, came up to us quite readily, when Will, leaping upon his back, commenced whooping and hallooing so loudly that Sorrel's mettle was up, and for nearly an hour he ran quite as fast as his rider could wish. But circus riding was not Sorrel's forte, and he probably grew dizzy, for he at length stumbled and fell, injuring his fore foot in some way, so that, to our dismay, we found he was unable to walk without a great effort.

"*Je-mi-my!* Won't the old gentleman rare!" said Charlie, who was never very choice of his language.

Will, on the contrary, seemed more concerned for the horse, bringing water in his hat, and bathing the fast-swelling limb of the poor animal, who appeared to be grateful for the kindness. Charlie proposed that we should keep it a secret, but to this Will would not listen, and in a plain, straightforward way he confessed what he had done, and father, who saw that Sorrel was temporarily injured, forgave him, for he could not resist the pleading of Will's dark eyes.

This was his first day's adventure—the next one was a little different. Finding a cow in the lane, he tried the experiment of milking, succeeding so well that when at night Sally came in with her half filled pail, she declared that "Line-back was drying up, for she'd only given a drop or so." For this and numerous other misdemeanors Will also received absolution, but when on the second Sabbath after his arrival he and Charlie both were missed from church, whither they had started a full half hour before the rest of our family, father grew fidgety, holding his hymn book wrong side up, and sitting, instead of standing, during the prayer, a thing he was never known to do before. He was very strict in the observance of the fourth commandment, as indeed were most of the citizens of Meadow Brook, it being an almost State Prison offence to stay away from church on the Sabbath, or speak above a whisper until after sunset.

By the way, I think it a mistake, this converting the Sabbath into a day so much to be dreaded by the youthful, fun-loving members of the family, who are not yet old enough to see the propriety of having in reserve a Sunday face, as well as a Sunday gown. I would not have that sacred day profaned, but I would have it divested of that gloom with which it is too often associated in the child's mind. I would have everything connected with it as cheerful and pleasant as possible, and in these days of Sabbath schools and Sabbath school-books, it seems an easy matter to make it "The day of all the week the best." I well remember one rainy Sunday, when the whole family were obliged to remain at home, the younger ones reciting the Catechism to grandma, committing to memory and repeating to mother ten verses of the fifth chapter of Matthew, and then being compelled to sit up stiff and straight while father read to us a long metaphysical sermon, which he interspersed and lengthened out with remarks of his own, among which was the consoling one that "Heaven was one eternal Sabbath."

This was too much for Charlie, whose mind, instead of dwelling on the words of the good divine, was sadly wandering towards a nest of young white *pigs*, only that morning born. Turning towards me with a most rueful face, he whispered, "Darned if I'll go there. I'll run away first."

Of course I laughed aloud—how could I help it; and on my saying that "Charlie made me," we were both ordered from the room in disgrace, which latter we bore manfully—Charlie going straight to his pigs, while I stole up garret to a big candle-box, where, on one of my old dresses, lay sleeping six beautiful *kittens*.

But I am wandering from my subject, which was the time when Will and Charlie were missing from church, and when, to his utter astonishment, father learned that they had gone to the consecration of a Roman Catholic church, which had recently been erected a little out of the village, on an eminence, where its white cross could be seen from every point.

Against the Catholics as a religious denomination my father was prejudiced, and when he ascertained that his son, born of orthodox parents, and baptized in the orthodox faith, had not only run away to their church, but had also paid twenty-five cents, the price of admission, he was a good deal excited, and for a deacon showed considerable temper. It was, of course, Will's doings, he having coaxed Charlie to go by telling him of the wonderful sights there were to be seen.

At a late hour they came home, loitering around the barn a long time before they ventured into the presence of my father, whom my grandmother had somewhat appeased by telling him that "boys must sow their wild oats sometime, and it wasn't best to be too strict with 'em, for it only made 'em act worse," adding that "the Catholics were not the worst folks in the world, and they had just as much right to their form of worship as we had to ours." This in a measure mollified him, and consequently the two boys only received a long lecture, and were debarred the privilege of going to the village, except on Sundays, for three weeks, a punishment which annoyed Will exceedingly. But nothing could subdue him, and the moment the three weeks had expired he was as ready for mischief as ever. For a long time the coming of a Circus had been heralded by flaming handbills in red and yellow, one of which Will plastered onto our great barn door, from which conspicuous post it was removed by my father, who conscientiously turned his back upon men and women riding on their heads, declaring it an outrage upon all rules of propriety, and denouncing circuses and circus-going people as utterly low and vulgar. Thus from my earliest remembrance had I been taught, and still my heart would throb faster, whenever, with the beat of the drum and the sound of the bugle, the long procession swept past our door, and more than once had I stolen to the top of the hill, whence could be seen the floating banner and swaying canvas, watching from afar the evil I dared not approach.

Great, then, was my surprise, when, on the morning of the eventful day, Will suggested that Charlie, John, Lizzie, and I should run away in the evening and visit the "doings," as he called it. I was shocked that he should propose *my* going to such a place. "It was low and vulgar," I told him, "and no one went there but loafers and rowdies."

But he assured me that I was mistaken, saying that "some of our most respectable people attended;" and then he wondered "how I was ever to know anything unless I once in a while went to a circus, or a theatre, or something. It was perfectly ridiculous," he said, "for father to keep us so cooped up at home. Nobody else did so. There was Lawyer Smith's daughter, and Judge Brown's niece in Albany, who always went, and if it didn't hurt them, it wouldn't me."

Thus Will reasoned, persuading me at last; and just at dark, Lizzie and I, on pretence of going to bed early, went to our room, dressed ourselves in our best, I donning the white cambric, which I had worn on the first day of Will's arrival, and then when we were ready, got out upon the roof of the woodshed, which came up under our window, descending thence by means of a ladder which Will and Charlie brought from the barn. I had the utmost confidence in Will, and yet as I drew near the tent, and saw the rabble, whose appearance fully equalled my father's description, I wished myself away. Just then the band inside struck up, and giving my fears to the winds, I pressed forward, once involuntarily turning my head aside, as I heard a man near the door exclaim, "Deacon Lee's children, as I live! Is the world coming an end?"

Instantly my face flushed, for I felt that injustice was done to my father, and my first impulse was to exonerate him from all blame by explaining that we had run away; but ere I could do so Will pulled me along, and in a moment we were in the close, heated atmosphere of the vast arena, where were congregated more than a thousand people, of all ages and conditions. I was confounded, for it seemed to me that each and every one was pointing towards us the finger of scorn, and never since have I felt so wholly degraded and ashamed as I did at the moment of my first entrance to a circus!

We had been but a short time seated, when Will, who had divined my feelings, nudged my elbow, and pointing towards a group just entering, said, "See, there's 'Squire Talbot, his wife and daughter, Dr. Griffin, and lots more of Meadow Brook aristocracy. Now, ain't you glad you came?"

It was as he said, and as I saw the above mentioned individuals, some of them professors of religion, and all of them people of the first standing in town, I can scarcely tell how I felt. It was a sensation of mingled pleasure, bewilderment, and perplexity. Could it be that, after all, my father was wrong, that he was too strict with us, debarring us from innocent amusements, for if it were proper for members of the church to frequent such places, why was it not for me? *Now*, I can answer promptly that my father was right, wholly right, but I was puzzled then, and gradually I began to care less for being there, and to have less fear of what father would say when he found it out. I was growing very brave, entrenching myself behind the bad example of those who little suspected the harm their presence was doing. Father did not know the ways of the world, I thought, but after being enlightened by me, I was sure he would become a convert at once, and possibly at the next circus he would be in attendance, but from this last idea I involuntarily shrank, thinking I could never respect him again, were he guilty of such a thing.

I enjoyed it vastly, all except the riding of the girl, who I fancied had on her little sister's dress, and when *she* came out I looked for a place where to hide my head; but hearing the spectators cheer louder than ever, I cast furtive glances at those around me, discovering to my amazement that they seemed more delighted with her than with anything else; while, to crown all, I heard Will telling a young man, that "she was a splendid rider, that he never saw but one who could beat her, and that was a girl in Albany." Then turning to Lizzie, he asked if she would not like to ride in that way?

With an involuntary shudder I threw my arm around my sister, as if to protect her from what I felt would be worse than a thousand deaths. Gradually there was dawning upon my mind the suspicion that a circus after all was not exactly the school for pure young girls, and I felt that not all the wealth of the Indies could tempt me to fill the post that that rider did. Towards the other actors I was more lenient, thinking that if ever I joined the circus, I should surely be *the clown*, whose witty speeches amused me greatly, for I did not then know that they were all made up beforehand, and that what he said to us to-day he would say to others on the morrow. Mlle. Glaraine was just finishing up her performance by riding around the circle without other support than the poising of one foot on a man's shoulder, when who should appear but *our father*!

He had missed Will and Charlie from family prayers, and had traced them as far as the pavilion, where the fee-receiver demanded a quarter ere he would allow him to enter. It was in vain that father tried to explain matters, saying, "he never attended a circus in his life, and what was more never should; he'd only come for two boys who had run away."

The doorkeeper was incorrigible; "he'd seen just as honest looking men," he said, "who were the greatest cheats in the world, and if father wanted to go in, he could do so by paying the usual fee; if not, he must budge."

Finding there was no alternative, father yielded, and then made his way into the tent, scanning with his keen grey eyes the sea of faces until he singled out Charlie, who was so absorbed in stamping and hallooing at Mlle. Glaraine's leaping through a hoop, that he never dreamed of father's presence until a rough hand was laid upon his shoulder, and a stern voice demanded of him why he was there?

Perfectly thunderstruck, Charlie started to his feet with the exclamation of "Je-ru-sa-lem!" but before he could make any explanation father discovered Lizzie and me. 'Twas the first suspicion he had of *our* being there, and now, when he saw us, he turned pale, and reeled as if smitten by a heavy blow. Had he felled me to the earth it would have hurt me less than did the expression of his face and the tones of his voice, as he said, "You, too, Rosa! I never thought you would thus deceive me."

I began to cry aloud; so did Lizzie, and in this way we made our exit from the circus, followed by Charlie, John, and Will, the latter of whom, the moment we were in the open air, began to take the blame all to himself, saying, as was very true, that we never would have thought of going but for him, and suggesting that he alone should be punished, as he was the one most in fault. I thought this was very magnanimous in Will, and I looked up in father's face to see how it affected him, but the moonlight was obscure, and I could discover nothing, though the hand that held mine trembled violently. I presume he thought that in this case corporal punishment would be of no avail, for we received none, but in various ways were we made to feel that we had lost the confidence of the family. For four long weeks we were each night locked into our rooms, while for the same length of time we were kept from school, Lizzie and I reciting our lessons to our mother, while Will, Charlie, and John, to use their own words, "worked from morning until night, like niggers."

But the worst part of it all was the temporary disgrace which our act of disobedience brought upon father. A half drunken fellow, who saw him enter the tent, and who knew that we were there, hurried away to the village with the startling intelligence that "Deacon Lee and all his family were at the circus."

The news spread like wildfire, gathering strength in its progress, until by the time it reached us it was a current report that not only was father at the circus, but *grandma* too! This was more than the old lady could bear.

Sixty-nine years had she lived without ever having had a word breathed against her morals, and now, just as her life's sun was setting, to have such a thing laid to her charge was too much, and she actually worried herself into a fever, which confined her to the house for several weeks.

After this adventure it became a serious question in father's mind as to what he should do with Will, who kept our heretofore quiet household in a state of perpetual excitement. Nothing seemed to have the least effect upon him save the mention of his mother, and that for the time being would subdue him, but when temptation came, he invariably yielded, and Charlie, who was an apt scholar, was pretty sure to follow where his wild, dashing cousin led. There was scarcely any boyish vice to which Will was not more or less addicted, and "Deacon Lee's sons," who had often been held up as patterns for their companions, began soon to prove the old adage true, that "evil communications corrupt good manners."

John learned to handle an *oath* quite fluently, while Charlie was one Sunday morning discovered playing *euchre* with Will on the hay loft, where they kept their cards hidden. But all this was nothing compared to the night when both the boys were brought home so intoxicated that neither of them was able to stand alone or speak! They had been to a "raising," where the brandy bottle circulated freely, Will, as a matter of course, drinking from the beginning. Charlie, however, hesitated until they taunted him with "being afraid of the old deacon," daring him "to drink and be a *man*." Then he yielded, and with fiendish pleasure the crowd gathered around, urging him on, until he was undeniably drunk; after which they chuckled with delight as they wondered what the "blue Presbyterian" would say. We were sitting down to supper when they brought him home, and the moment mother saw him, she darted forward, exclaiming, "Is he dead? Tell me, is my boy dead?"

"Yes, *dead—drunk*," answered the man, with a cold, ironical sneer at her distress.

He was used to it, for of five noble sons who once called him their father, four slept in a drunkard's grave, and the fifth had far better have been there than the wreck he was. My father had risen from his seat, but at the words "he is drunk," he dropped upon the floor as if scathed with the lightning's stroke. You who think it a light matter—the holding of the wine-cup to the lips of your neighbor's child—you should have seen my father that night, as moan after moan of anguish came from his pale lips, while the great drops of perspiration stood thickly upon his forehead and about his mouth. The effect it had upon him was terrible; crushing him to the earth, and weaving in among his hitherto brown locks more than one thread of silver. Once when Charlie was with me, I heard him in the barn, praying that the promise of a covenant God might be remembered towards him, and that his son might yet be saved. Charlie's feelings were touched, and dropping on his knees at my side he made a solemn vow that never again should ardent spirits of any kind pass his lips; and God, who heard that vow mingled with my father's prayer, registered it in Heaven, and from that day to this, amid all the temptations which come to early manhood, it has been unbroken.

Not thus easily could Will be reached. His was the sorrow of a day, which passed away with the coming of to-morrow's sun, and after a long consultation, it was decided that he should go to sea, and the next merchantman bound for the East Indies, which sailed from Boston, bore on its deck, as a common sailor, our cousin Will, who went from us reluctantly, for to him there was naught but terror, toil, and fear in "a life on the ocean wave." But there was no other way to save him, they said, and so with bitter grief at our hearts, we bade adieu to the wayward boy, praying that God would give the winds and waves charge concerning him, and that no danger might befall him when afar on the rolling billow.

CHAPTER IV
THE SCHOOLMISTRESS

Of the many thousand individuals destined to become the purchasers of a copy of this work, a majority have undoubtedly been, or are still teachers, and of these many will remember the time when they fancied that to be invested with the dignity of a teacher was to secure the greatest amount of happiness which earth can bestow. Almost from my earliest remembrance it had been the one great subject which engrossed my thoughts, and frequently, when strolling down the shady hill-side which led to our schoolhouse, have I fancied myself the teacher, thinking that if such were really the case, my first act should be the chastisement of half a score or more boys, who were in the daily habit of annoying me in various ways. Every word and action of my teacher, too, was carefully noted and laid away against the time when I should need them, and which came much sooner than I anticipated; for one rainy morning when Lizzie and I were playing in the garret, I overheard my father saying there was a chance for Rosa to teach school.

"What, that child!" was my mother's exclamation, but ere he could reply, "the child" had bounded down two pair of stairs, and stood at his elbow, asking, "Who is it?—Where is it?—And do you suppose I can get a certificate?"

This last idea damped my ardor somewhat, for horrible visions came up before me, of the "Abbreviations" and "Sounds of the Vowels," in both of which I was rather deficient.

"*You* teach school! You look like it!" said my sister Juliet. "Why, in less than three days, you'd be *teetering* with the girls, if indeed you didn't climb trees with the boys."

This *climbing* was undeniably a failing of mine, there being scarcely a tree on the farm on whose topmost limbs I hadn't at some time or other been perched; but I was *older* now. I was *thirteen* two days before, and so I reminded Juliet, at the same time begging of father to tell me all about it. It appeared that he had that day met with a Mr. Randall, the trustee of

Pine District, who was in quest of a teacher. After learning that the school was small, father ventured to propose me, who, he said, "was crazy to *keep* school."

"A dollar a week is the most we can give her," returned Mr. Randall, "and if you'll take up with that, mebby we'll try her. New beginners sometimes do the best."

So it was arranged that I was to teach fifteen weeks for four dollars per month and *board round* at that! Boarding round! How many reminiscences do these two words recall to those who, like myself, have tried it, and who know that it has a variety of significations. That sometimes it is only another name for sleeping with every child in the family where your home for one week may chance to be—for how can you be insensible to the oft-repeated whisper, "*I* shall sleep with her to-night—ma said I might;" and of "ma's" audible answer, "Perhaps, *sis*, she don't want you to."

If "sis" is a clean, chubby-looking little creature, you *do* want her; but if, as it not unfrequently happens, she is just the opposite,——I draw a blank which almost every country teacher in the land can fill, merely saying that there is no alternative. We have got the district to please and we must do it some way or other.

Again, "boarding round" means a quiet, cozy spot, where everything is so pleasant and cheerful, where the words are so kind and the smile of welcome so sweet, that you feel at once at home, and wish, oh, how you do wish, you could stay there all the summer long; but it cannot be;—the time of your allotted sojourn passes away, and then with a sigh, if indeed you can repress a tear, you gather up your combs, brushes, and little piece of embroidery, to which some spiteful woman has said "you devote more time than to your school," and putting them in your sachel, depart for another home, sometimes as pleasant as the one you are leaving, sometimes not.

But of these annoyances I knew nothing, and when Mr. Randall came to see me, calling me *Miss Lee*, and when I was really engaged, my happiness was complete. In a country neighborhood every item of news, however slight, spreads rapidly, and the fact that I was to teach soon became generally known, creating quite a sensation, and operating differently upon different natures. One old gentleman, who, times innumerable, had held me on his knee, feeding my vanity with flattery, and my stomach with sweetmeats, was quite as much delighted as I, declaring, "he always knew I was destined to make something great."

Dear old man! When the snows of last winter were high piled upon the earth, they dug for him a grave in the frozen ground, and in the world where now he lives, he will not know, perhaps, that I shall never fulfill his prophecy.

Aunt Sally Wright, who, besides managing her own affairs, kept an eye on her neighbors', and who looked upon me as a "pert, forward piece," gave her opinion freely. "What! That young one keep school! Is Deacon Lee crazy? Ain't Rose stuck up enough now? But never mind. You'll see she won't keep out more'n half her time, if she does that."

Aunt Sally was gifted with the power of telling fortunes by means of tea-grounds, and I have always fancied she read that prediction in the bottom of her big blue cup, for how could she otherwise have known what actually happened! Ere long the news reached Pine District, creating quite an excitement, the older people declaring "*they'd* never send to a little girl," while the juvenile portion of the inhabitants gave a contemptuous whistle or so in honor of the school ma'am elect. Mrs. Capt. Thompson, who boasted the biggest house, handsomest carpet and worst boy in Pine Hill, was wholly incredulous, until she one day chanced to meet with Aunt Sally, who not only confirmed it, but also kindly gave her many little items touching my character as a "wild, romping minx, who was no more qualified for a teacher than for the Queen of England," citing as proof of what she said, that only the year before she had seen me "trying to ride on a cow."

Mrs. Capt. Thompson, who was blessed with an overwhelming sense of propriety, was greatly shocked, saying "she'd always thought Mr. Randall knew just enough to hire a child," and consoling herself with the remark that "it was not at all probable I'd get a certificate."

On this point I was myself a little fearful. True, I had been "sent away" to school, and had been flattered into the belief that I possessed far more book knowledge than I did; but this, I knew, would avail me nothing with the formidable committee who held my destiny in their hands. *They* were unbiased in my favor, and had probably never heard of me, as they lived in an adjoining town. But "where there's a will there's a way," and determining not to fail, I ransacked the cupboard, where our school-books were kept, bringing thence Olney's Geography, Colburn's Arithmetic, History of the United States, Grammars, etc., all of which were for days my constant companions, and I even slept with one or more of them under my pillow, so that with the earliest dawn I could study. Whole pages of Geography were committed to memory, all the hardest problems in Colburn were solved, a dozen or more of compound relatives were parsed and disposed of to *my* satisfaction at least, and I was just beginning to feel strong in my own abilities, when one Monday morning news was brought us that at three o'clock that afternoon all who were intending to teach in the town of S—— were to meet at the house of the Rev. Mr. Parks, then and there to be questioned of what they knew and what they didn't know. This last referred to *me*, for now that the dreaded day had come, I felt that every idea had suddenly left me, while, to increase my embarrassment, I was further informed that as there had the year previous been some trouble among the School Inspectors, each of whom fancied that the other did not take his share of the work, the town had this year thought to obviate the difficulty by electing *nine*!

One was bad enough, but at the thought of nine men in spectacles my heart sank within me, and it was some time ere I could be persuaded to make the trial. In the midst of our trouble, Aunt Sally, whose clothes on Monday mornings were always swinging on the line before light, and who usually spent the afternoon of that day in visiting, came in, and after learning what was the cause of my flushed cheeks, said, by way of comforting me, that "she didn't wonder an atom if I felt streaked, for 'twant no ways likely I'd pass!"

This roused my pride, and with the mental comment that "I'd *pass* for all her," I got myself in readiness, Juliet lending me her green veil, and Anna her fine pocket handkerchief, while mother's soft warm shawl was wrapped lovingly about me, and Lizzie slipped into my pocket the *Multiplication Table*, which she thought I might manage to look at slily in case of an emergency. On our way father commenced the examination by asking me the length of the Mississippi, but I didn't know as it had a length, and in despair he gave up his questioning.

Oh, how sombre and dreary seemed the little parlor into which we were ushered by the servant, who, on learning our business, looked rather doubtfully at me, as much as to say, "*You* surely can't be one of them?" In a short time the parlor was filled, the entire *nine* being there. Not one was absent, and in a row directly opposite, they sat, some tipped back in a lounging attitude, some cutting their finger nails with their penknives, while others sat up stiff and stern, the whole presenting a most formidable appearance. There were eight or ten candidates present, and unfortunately for me, I was seated at what I called the foot of the class. It seemed that the most of them were acquainted, and as I was almost the only stranger present, it was but natural that they should look at me rather more that I liked. My pantalets evidently attracted their attention, but by dint of drawing up my feet and pushing down my dress I hoped to hide my *short*-comings.

When, at last, the examination commenced, I found, to my great delight, that Geography was the subject introduced, and my heart beat high, for

I thought of the pages I could repeat and ardently longed for a chance to display! Unfortunately for me they merely questioned us from the map, and breathlessly I awaited my turn. At length the young lady who sat next to me was asked "What two rivers unite and form the Ohio?" I looked at her sidewise. The bloom deepened on her cheek, and I was sure she had forgotten. Involuntarily I felt tempted to tell her, but did not, and Mr. Parks, looking inquiringly at me, said, "Perhaps the next one can. Ahem!"

He caught sight of my offending pantalets, and thinking me some child who had come with her sister, was about to pass me by. But I was not to be slighted in that way, particularly when I knew the answer; so, with the air of one who, always at the foot, accidently spells a word right and starts for the head, I spoke out loud and distinctly "Alleghany and Monongahela," glancing at my father just in time to catch a nod of encouragement.

"The Nine" were taken by surprise, and instantly three pair of eyes with glasses and six pair without glasses were brought to bear upon me. For reasons best known to themselves, they asked *me* a great variety of questions, all of which I answered correctly, I believe; at least they made no comment, and were evidently vastly amused with their new specimen, asking me how old I was, and exchanging smiles at my reply, "Thirteen, four weeks ago to-day." One of my fellow-teachers, who sat near me, whispered to her next neighbor, "She's older than that, I know;" for which remark I've never quite forgiven her. Arithmetic was the last branch introduced, and as mathematics was rather my forte, I had now no fears of failing—but I did! A question in Decimals puzzled me, and coloring to my temples, I replied "I don't know," while two undeniable tears dropped into my lap.

"Never mind, sis," said one of the nine. "You know most everything else, and have done bravely."

I was as sure of my certificate then as I was fifteen minutes afterwards, when a little slip of paper was given me, declaring me competent to teach a common school. I thought it was all over, and was adjusting mother's shawl and tying on Juliet's veil, when they asked me to write something that they might see a specimen of my penmanship. Taking the pen, I dashed off with a flourish "Rosa Lee," at which I thought they peered more curiously than need be—and one of them, Dr. Clayton, a young man, and a handsome one, too, said something about its being "very poetical." He hadn't seen the *negro song* then.

The shadows of evening had long since fallen when we stopped at our door, where we found mother anxiously waiting for us. Very wistfully she looked in my face ere she asked the important question.

"Yes, I've got one," said I, bounding from the buggy, "and I'd like to be examined every day, it's such fun."

"Didn't you miss a word?" asked Juliet.

"Oh, I'm so glad!" cried Lizzie.

"Feel *big*, don't you?" suggested Charlie, while Anna inquired "if I'd lost her pocket handkerchief!"

CHAPTER V
PINE HILL

Ere long, exaggerated rumors reached Meadow Brook of the very creditable manner in which I had acquitted myself at the examination, whereupon Aunt Sally Wright was quite taken aback. Soon rallying, however, she had recourse to her second prediction, which was that "I should not teach more than half the summer out." Perhaps I wrong the old lady, but I cannot help thinking that the ill-natured stories concerning myself, which she set afloat at Pine Hill, were in a great measure the cause of her prophecy being fulfilled. Never before, to my knowledge, had she visited at Capt. Thompson's, but now she spent an entire day there, bringing back to us the intelligence that John Thompson, a boy just one year my senior, was going to stay at home that summer, as "Miss Cap'n Thompson hadn't no idee I could teach him."

Added to this was the comforting assurance, that "Cap'n Thompson was hoppin' mad because Mr. Randall had hired me in preference to his sister *Dell*, who had herself applied for the school." This, as I afterwards learned, was the secret of the dislike which, from the first, the Thompsons entertained for me. They had no daughter, but the captain's half sister Dell had lived with him ever since his marriage, and between her and their hopeful son John, the affections of himself and wife were nearly equally divided.

Dell Thompson was a proud, overbearing girl, about eighteen years of age, who esteemed herself far better than her neighbors, with whom she seldom associated, her acquaintances living mostly at what was called "the Centre" of the town. It seems that she had applied for the summer school, but remembering that she had once called him a "country clown and his wife ignorant and vulgar," Mr. Randall had refused her and accepted me. Notwithstanding that the people of Pine Hill generally disliked the Thompsons, there was among them a feeling of dissatisfaction when it became known that I was preferred to Dell, who, they thought, would have given *tone* and *character* to the school, for "it wasn't every *big bug* who would stoop to teach."

Of this state of affairs I was fortunately ignorant, and never do I remember a happier morning than that on which I first took upon myself the responsibilities of a teacher. By sunrise, the little hair trunk, which grandma lent me, was packed and stood waiting on the doorstep, where I had carried it, thinking thus to accelerate the movements of my father, who did not seem to be in any particular hurry, telling me, "he'd no idea that school would be commenced before we got there!" Grandma had suggested the propriety of letting down my dresses, a movement which I warmly seconded, but mother said "No, she did not like to see little girls dressed like grown up women;" so, in my new plaid gingham and white pantalets, I waited impatiently until the clock struck seven, at which time father announced himself ready.

"When will you come home?" asked mother, as she followed me to the gate.

"In three weeks," was my reply, as I bounded into the buggy, which soon moved away.

Pine Hill is not all remarkable for its beautiful scenery, and as old Sorrel trotted leisurely along, down one steep hill and up another, through a *haunted* swamp, where a man had once, to his great terror, seen his departed wife, and over a piece of road, where the little grassy ridges said, as plain as grassy ridges could say, that the travellers there were few and far between, my spirits lowered a little. But, anon, the prospect brightened, and in the distance we saw the white walls of Capt. Thompson's residence gleaming through the mass of evergreens which surrounded it. This, however, soon disappeared, and for a mile or more my eye met with nothing save white birches, grey rocks, green ferns, and blackberry bushes, until suddenly turning a corner, we came to a halt before one of those slanting-roofed houses so common in New England. It was the home of Mr. Randall, and it was there that I was to board the first week. In the doorway, eating bread and molasses, were his three children who, the moment they saw us, set up a shout of "somebody's come. I guess it's the schoolma'am!" and straightway they took to their heels as if fleeing from the presence of a tigress.

After a moment, the largest of them ventured to return, and his example was soon followed by the other two, the younger of whom, after eyeing me askance, lisped out, "Don Thompthon thays he ain't afraid of you; he can lick you like *dunder!*"

This was a pleasant commencement, but I smiled down upon the little boy, patting his curly head, while father inquired for Mrs. Randall, who, we learned, was sweeping the schoolhouse. Leaving the hair trunk, which was used by the children for a horse ere we left the yard, we again set forward, and soon reached our place of destination, which, without shade-tree or ornament of any kind, stood half-way up a long, sunny hill, commanding a view of nothing save the weathercock of Captain Thompson's barn, which was visible across the orchard opposite. We found Mrs. Randall enveloped in a cloud of dust, her sleeves rolled up, and her head covered by a black silk handkerchief.

"The room wasn't fit for the pigs," she said, "and ought to have been cleaned, but somehow nobody took any interest in school this summer, and I'd have to make it answer."

I didn't care particularly for the room, which, in truth, was dirty and disagreeable enough, but the words "nobody took any interest this summer," affected me unpleasantly, for in them I saw a dim foreshadowing of all that ensued. Father, who was in a hurry, soon left me, bidding me "be a good girl, and not get to *romping* with the scholars." From the window I watched him until he disappeared over the sandy hill, half wishing, though I would not then confess it, that I and the little trunk were with him. I was roused from my reverie by Mrs. Randall, who, for some time, had been looking inquisitively at me, and who now said, "Ain't you but thirteen?"

"No, ma'am," I answered.

"Wall," she returned, "it beats all how much older you look. I should s'pose you was full sixteen, if not more. But it's all in your favor, and I guess you'll be more likely to suit the deestrict, though they're afraid you haven't any government, and they're terrible hard to suit. So, if I's you," she continued, "I'd hold a pretty tight rein at first. I give you full liberty to whip my young ones if they don't behave. They know better than to complain at home."

Involuntarily I glanced at the clump of alders which grew near the house, and if they were somewhat diminished ere my reign was o'er, the "Deestrict" owed it to Mrs. Randall's suggestion. After sitting awhile, she arose to go, telling me "she should expect me at night," and then I was alone. I looked at my watch; it was half-past eight, and not a scholar yet. This was widely different from Meadow Brook, where, by seven, the house was generally filled with children, hallooing, quarrelling over seats, and watching eagerly for the first sight of "the new schoolma'am." Here the tables were turned, and "the schoolma'am" was watching for her scholars!

Suddenly a large bumble-bee came buzzing in, and alighted on a window opposite. Like Sir Thomas the Good, in the Ingoldsby Legends, I have a passion for capturing insects, especially whitefaced bumble-bees, and now I felt strongly inclined to mount the desks in pursuit of the intruder, but the thought "What if the scholars should detect me?" prevented, and, to this day, I have never known whether that bumble-bee had a *white* face, or belonged to the class of colored brethren! Ten minutes of nine, and I began to grow fidgety. I should have been more so, had I known how much is sometimes said about teachers not keeping their hours. Five minutes of nine, and round the corner at the foot of the hill appeared a group of children, while from another direction came others, shouting for those in advance to "wait," which they did, and the whole entered the house together. A few of the girls made a slight obeisance, while the boys laughed, and throwing down their books in a very consequential manner, looked distrustfully at me. My *age* had preceded me, and in many of these childish hearts there was already a spirit of rebellion.

Here I would speak against the impropriety of discussing a teacher's faults in the presence of pupils, who will discover them soon enough. Many a teacher starts disadvantageously because of some idle tale, which may or may not be true, but which, borne on the wings of gossip, reaches its place of destination, and is there thoughtlessly canvassed in the hearing of children, who thus become prejudiced against a person they have never seen, and whom they otherwise might have liked. In my case, the fault was *my age*, which had evidently been discussed in the neighborhood; for, on opening my desk, I found inscribed upon the lid, in a bold schoolboy style, "Rosa Lee, aged 13," to which was appended, in a more delicate hand, "Ancient—very!"

Taking my India-rubber, I erased it while my scholars were settling the matter of seats, which, strange to say they did without disputing. Then there ensued a perfect silence, and the eyes of all present turned inquiringly upon me, while, with sundry flourishes with my silver pencil, I proceeded to take down upon a big sheet of foolscap the names, ages, and "what studies do you intend to pursue?" of my pupils. After much talking and arranging, the school was organized; but the first morning dragged heavily, and when 12 o'clock came, and I drew from my sachel the nice ginger snaps which mother had made, the sight of them, or the taste, or something else, choked me so much that I was obliged to wink hard, and count the rows of trees in the orchard opposite twice, ere I could answer the question addressed to me by one of the little girls.

In the rear of the house was a long strip of dense woods, and wishing to be alone and out of sight of the sports in which I felt I must not join, I took my bonnet and wandered thither. Seating myself upon a mossy log, I tried to fancy that I was at home beneath the dear old grape-vine, the faintest rustle of whose broad green leaves would, at that moment, have been to me like the sweetest music. But it could not be. I was a schoolmistress—*Miss Lee*, they called me, and on my brow the shadows of life were thus early making their impress. Slowly to me dragged the hour which always before had been so short, and when at last I took my way back to school, it seemed that in that short space I had lived an age. Often since, when I have looked upon young teachers hastening to their task, I've pitied them, for I knew full well how long and wearisome would be their first day's labor.

As I approached the schoolhouse I saw that something was the matter, for the scholars were greatly excited, and with voices raised to the highest pitch, were discussing something of importance. Thinking that my presence would perhaps restrain them from such noisy demonstration$, I hastened forward, but the babel rather increased than diminished, and it was with difficulty that I could learn the cause of the commotion. George Randall was crying, while a little apart from him stood two boys, one of them apparently fourteen and the other twelve. They were strangers to me and instinctively I felt that they were in some way connected with the disturbance; and that the larger and more important looking was *John Thompson*, a surmise which proved to be correct.

It seemed that Isaac Ross, one of the new comers, had some weeks before selected for himself a corner seat, which, as he was not present in the morning, had been taken by George Randall, who knew nothing of Isaac's intentions, and who now refused to give it up. A fight was the result, the most of the scholars taking sides with George, while Isaac was urged on and encouraged by John Thompson, who, though not a pupil, had come up "to see how he liked the schoolma'am." As a matter of course an appeal was made to me, to know "if George hadn't the best right to the seat,"

Perhaps I was wrong, but I decided that he had, at the same time asking Isaac "if he were coming to school."

"I ain't goin' to do anything else," said he, glancing towards John, who, with a wicked leer at me, knocked off one of the little boys' hats and then threw it up in the air.

What would have ensued next I do not know, for at that moment Captain Thompson rode round the corner and called to his son, who, with mock deference, bowed politely to me and walked away. Disagreeable as Isaac Ross appeared in the presence of John Thompson, I found that when left to himself he was quite a different boy, and though he at first manifested some reluctance to taking another seat, he at last yielded the point, and for the remainder of the day conducted himself with perfect propriety.

On the whole, the afternoon passed away rather pleasantly, and at night, when school was out, I started for my boarding-place quite contented with teachers generally, and myself in particular. In passing the different houses which stood upon the road-side, I demeaned myself with the utmost dignity, swinging my short dress from side to side in imitation of a Boston lady who had once taught in our district, and whose manner of walking I greatly admired! From the window of Captain Thompson's dwelling I caught a glimpse of two faces, which were hastily withdrawn, but I felt sure that from behind the curtains they were scanning my appearance, and I remember lowering my parasol a little, just to tantalize them! But when at last I was over the hill and out of sight, oh, how glad I was to be "Rosa Lee" again, free to pluck the sweet, wild flowers, to watch the little fishes in the running brook, or even to chase a whitefaced bumble-bee if I liked.

About fifty rods from Mr. Randall's stands one of those old-fashioned, gable-roofed houses, so common in some parts of New England, and here, at the time of which I am speaking, lived Mrs. Ross, the mother of Isaac, or *Ike*, as he was familiarly called. I had never met the lady, but as I approached the house and saw a tall, square-shouldered woman leaning on the gate, I naturally thought that it might be she; and on this point I was not long left in doubt, for the moment I came within speaking distance, she called out, "How dy' do, Miss Lee—I s'pose 'tis? You pretty well? I'm Miss Ross, Isick's mother. He told me that he had some fuss about a seat that he picked out more'n a month ago, and thinks he orto have. I don't never calkerlate to take sides with my children, 'cause I've kept school myself, and I know how bad 'tis, but I do hate to have Isick git a miff again the schoolma'am on the first start, and if I's you I'd let him have the seat instead of George Randall, for mebby folks'll say you're partial to George, bein' that his father's committee-man, and I've kept school enough to know that *partiality* won't do."

As well as I could, I explained the matter to her, telling her I wished to do right, and meant to as far as I knew how.

"I presume you do," said she, "or I shouldn't a' taken the liberty to speak to you. I knew you's young, and I felt afeard you didn't know what an undertakin' it was to teach the young idea how to *shute*. The schoolma'ams have always thought a sight of me, and generally tell me all their troubles, so I know jest how to take their part when the rest of the folks are again 'em. Was Susan Brown to school? But she wasn't though, I know she wasn't."

I replied that there *was* a little girl present of that name, and my companion continued: "Now I'll give up, if Miss Brown has come round enough to send, when she was so dreadfully opposed to your teaching you've heerd about it, I s'pose?"

I answered that "I didn't know that any one had opposed me except Mrs. Thompson."

"Oh, yes," said she, assuming an injured look and tone. "Everybody knows about that, and there's some sense in their bein' mad, for 'twas plaguy mortifyin' to Dell to offer to teach and be rejected by Mr. Randall, a man that none of the Thompsons would wipe their old shoes on, and then, 'tisn't every *big bug* that will stoop to teach, for you know 'tain't considered fust cut."

"No, I didn't know it," and so I said, but she assured me of the fact, quoting as authority, both Mrs. Thompson and Dell, who, I found, were her oracles in everything. After a time I brought her back to Mrs. Brown, whose husband, she said, was gone to sea, and who had herself applied for the school.

"But between you and me," she added, speaking in a whisper, "it's a mighty good thing that she didn't get it, for she ain't the likeliest person that ever was, and nobody under the sun would have sent to her. Isick shouldn't a' gone a single day, for her morals is very bad. She used to belong to the Orthodox Church, but they turned her out for dancin' at a party, and when she lived in Wooster she jined the 'Piscopals, who, you know, let their members cut up all sorts—but, land sakes! how I'm talkin'! You must not breathe a word I say, for I make it a pint not to slander my neighbors, and if everybody minded their own business as well as I do, there wouldn't be so much backbitin' as there is. And that makes me think I've half a mind to caution you—but no, I guess I won't—mebby you'll tell on't."

Of course my curiosity was roused, and of course I said I wouldn't tell; whereupon she proceeded to inform me that Mrs. Randall was a very talkin' woman, and I must be pretty careful in her presence. "You can tell me anything you wish to," said she, "for I'm a master hand to keep a secret; but Miss Randall is forever in hot water. She and Miss Brown are hand in glove, and both on 'em turn up their noses at Miss Thompson and Dell, who never pretend to make anything of 'em. I'm considerable *intimate*, at the Captain's, and I know all about it. Dell is smart as a steel trap, and it's a pity she's took such a dislike to you."

"I don't think she ought to blame me," said I, "for I didn't know as she wanted the school" — —

"'Tain't that altogether," resumed Mrs. Ross, again speaking in a whisper. "'Tain't that altogether, and if you'll never lisp a word on't I'll tell you the hull story."

I gave the required promise, and then Mrs. Ross proceeded to inform me that Dell was jealous of me.

"Jealous!" I exclaimed. "How can that be?"

"You remember Dr. Clayton, don't you?" said she.

"Yes, I remember him, but what has he to do with Miss Thompson's being jealous of me!"

"Why," returned Mrs. Ross, "Dell's kinder settin' her cap for him, and I guess he's a snickerin' notion after her. Any way he comes there pretty often. Well, he was there the week after the examination, and told 'em about you. He said you was bright as a new guinea, and had better larnin' than half the teachers, and then you had such a sweet name—*Rose*—he liked it. You orto have seen how mad Dell was at you after he was gone. I don't b'lieve she'll ever git over it."

Here Ike called out that "the Johnny-cake was burnt blacker than his hat," and forthwith Mrs. Ross started for the house, first bidding me "keep dark," and telling me she hoped "I wouldn't be partial to Mr. Randall's children, for they needed lickin' if ever young ones did—they warn't brought up like Isick, who was governed so well at home that he didn't need it at school."

I was learning to read the world's great book fast—very fast—and with a slightly heavy heart I turned away, pausing once while Mrs. Ross, from the doorstep, called to me, saying, that "she guessed I'd better give Isick the seat to-morrow, seem' his heart was set on't."

I found Mrs. Randall waiting to receive me in a clean gingham dress and apron, with her round, good-humored face shining as if it had been through the same process with the long line of snow-white linen, which was swinging in the clothes-yard. The little hair trunk had been removed to the "best room," which was to be mine. The big rocking-chair was brought out for me, the round tea table, nicely spread, stood in the centre of the floor, and Mrs. Randall hoped I would make myself at home, and put up with her own rough ways if I could. To be sure, she didn't have things quite as nice as Mrs. Captain Thompson, but she did as well as she knew how. Dear Mrs. Randall! how my heart warmed towards her; and as I took my seat at the table, and she helped me to a larger slice of pure white honeycomb than I had ever before been allowed to eat at one time, I felt that I would not exchange her house for a home at Capt. Thompson's.

Without any intention of revealing what Mrs. Ross had imparted to me, I still felt a great curiosity to know Mrs. Randall's opinion of her; so, after a time, I ventured to speak of my having seen her, and to ask when and where she taught school. With a merry laugh, Mrs. Randall replied, "I wonder, now, if she's made your acquaintance so soon! She told you, I suppose, to come to her with all your troubles, for she knew just how to pity you, as she'd been a schoolma'am herself."

My flushed cheeks betrayed the fact that Mrs. Randall had guessed rightly, and after a moment she continued: "Her keeping school amounts to this. When she was a girl, a friend of hers who was teaching wanted to go away for *two* days, and got Miss Ross, then Nancy Smedly, to take her place, and that's the long and short of her experience. She's a meddlesome woman, and makes more trouble in the District than anybody else. She tried to make Miss Brown think she was misused, because we wouldn't hire her instead of you, who applied first, and for a spell, I guess Miss Brown was a little sideways, but she's a sensible woman and has got all over it."

I was about to tell her of the trouble between George and Ike, when she anticipated me by saying, "George says he and Ike Ross *fit* about a seat, and I've hired him to give it up peaceably, for if Miss Ross gets miffed in the beginning, there's no knowing what kind of a row she'll raise, and you are so young I feel kinder tender of you."

If there were tears in my eyes, they were not tears of grief, and if I was pleased with Mrs. Randall before, I liked her ten times better now, for I saw in her a genuine sincerity which convinced me she was my friend indeed. To be sure, she was rather rough and unrefined, but her heart was right, and in her treatment of me, she was always kind and considerate, making ample allowance for my errors and warmly defending me when she thought I was misused. If in every District there were more like Mrs. Randall, the teacher's lot would not be one half so hard to bear as oftentimes it is.

When I awoke next morning I heard the large raindrops pattering against the window, and on pushing aside the curtain, I saw that the dark heavy clouds betokened a dull rainy day. Involuntarily, I thought of the old garret at home, where on such occasions we always resorted, "raising Cain generally," as Sally said, and when, with umbrella, blanket-shawl, and overshoes, I started for school, I looked and felt forlorn indeed. Raining as it was, it did not prevent Mrs. Ross from coming out with the table-spread over her head, to tell me that "though she never warn't an atom particular, and never meant to interfere with teachers, as she knew just what it was, she *did* hope I'd give Isick the seat, and not be partial to George Randall."

I replied that "I'd see to it," and was hurrying along, when she again stopped me to know "what I'd got in my dinner basket that was good."

Afterwards I found it to be one of her greatest peculiarities, this desire to know what her neighbors had to eat, and I seldom passed her door that she did not inquire of me concerning the "kind of fare" I had at the different places where I boarded. When I reached the schoolhouse, I found George Randall transferring his books to another part of the room, at the same time telling Isaac "he could have the disputed seat if he wanted it."

With the right kind of training and influence Isaac Ross would have been a fine boy, for there were in his disposition many noble traits of character, and when he saw how readily George gave up the seat, he refused to take it, saying, "he didn't care a *darn* where he sat—one place was as good as another."

That day was long and dreary enough. Not more than half the children were there, and I found it exceedingly tiresome and monotonous, sitting in that hard, splint-bottomed chair, and telling Emma Fitch and Sophia Brown, for the hundredth time, that the round letter was "O" and the crooked one "S." The scholars, too, began to grow noisy, and to ask me scores of useless questions. Their lessons were half learned, and if I made a suggestion, I was quickly informed that their former teacher, Sally Damm, didn't do so. Even little Emma Fitch, when I bade her keep her eyes on the book instead of letting them wander about the room, lisped out that "Thally Damm let her look off;" a fact I did not dispute when I found that she had been to school all winter without learning a single letter by sight, though she could repeat the entire alphabet forward and back and be all the while watching a squirrel on the branches of the tree which grew near the window.

Before night a peculiar kind of sickness, never dangerous, but decidedly disagreeable, began to creep over me, and had it not been for the mud, I should probably have footed it to Meadow Brook, where alone could be found the cure for my disease. Just before school was out a little boy cried to go home, and this was the one straw too many. Hastily dismissing the scholars, I turned towards the window and my tears fell as fast as did the rain in the early morning.

"The schoolma'am's cryin,'—she is. I saw her," circulated rapidly among the children, who all rushed back to ascertain the truth for themselves.

"I should think she would cry," said one of the girls to her brother. "You've acted ugly enough to make anybody cry, and if you don't behave better to-morrow, Jim Maxwell, I'll tell mother!"

After the delivery of this speech, the entire group moved away, leaving me alone; and sure am I there was never a more homesick child than was the one, who, with her head lying upon the desk, sat there weeping in that low, dirty schoolroom, on that dark, rainy afternoon. Where now was all the happiness I had promised myself in teaching? Alas! it was rapidly disappearing, and I was just making up my mind to brave the ridicule of Meadow Brook, and give up my school at once, when a hand was laid very gently on my shoulder, and a voice partially familiar said, "What's the matter, *Rose*?"

So absorbed was I in my grief, that I had not heard the sound of footsteps, and with a start of surprise I looked up and met the serene, handsome eyes of *Dr. Clayton*, who stood at my side! He had been to visit a patient, he said, and was on his way home, when, seeing the door ajar, he had come in, hoping to find me there, "but I did not expect this," he continued, pointing to the tears on my cheek. "What is the matter? Don't the scholars behave well, or are you homesick?"

At this question I began to cry so violently, that the doctor, after exhausting all his powers of persuasion, finally laid his hand soothingly on my rough, tangled curls, ere I could be induced to stop. Then, when I told him how disappointed I was, how I wished I had never tried to teach, and how I meant to give it up, he talked to me so kindly, so brotherlike, still keeping his hand on my shoulder, where it had fallen when I lifted up my head, that I grew very calm, thinking I could stay in that gloomy room forever, if *he* were only there! He was, as I have said before, very handsome, and his manner was so very fascinating, and his treatment of me so much like what I fancied Charlie's would be, were he a grown up man and I a little girl, that I began to like him very, very much, thinking then that my feeling for him was such as a child would entertain for a father, for I had heard that he was twenty-seven, and between that and thirteen there was, in my estimation, an impassable gulf.

"I wish I had my buggy here," he said at last, after consulting his watch, which pointed to half-past five, "I wish I had my buggy here, for then I could carry you home. You'll wet your feet, and you ought not to walk. Suppose you ride in my lap; but no," he added, quickly, "you'd better not, for Mrs. Thompson and Mother Ross would make it a neighborhood talk."

There was a wicked look in his eye as he said this, and I secretly wondered if he entertained the same opinion of *Dell*, that he evidently did of her sister. At length, shaking my hand, he bade me good-bye, telling me that the Examining Committee had placed *me* and my school in his charge, and that he should probably visit me officially on Thursday of the following week. Like a very foolish child, I watched him until a turn in the road hid him from view, and then, with a feeling I could not analyze, I started for my boarding-place, thinking that if I gave up my school I should wait until after Thursday.

In the doorway, with her sleeves rolled up above her elbows, and her hair, as she herself said, "at sixes and sevens," was Mrs. Ross, who, after informing me that "it had been a desput rainy day," asked, "if I knew whether Dr. Clayton had been to Captain Thompson's?"

There was no reason why I should blush at this question, but I did, though my sun-bonnet fortunately concealed the fact from my interrogator, who, without waiting for an answer, continued, "He drove past here about fifteen minutes ago, and I guess he's been sparkin' Dell."

It must have been an evil spirit surely which prompted my reply that "he had been at the schoolhouse with me."

"How you talk! Isick never said a word about it!" was Mrs. Ross's exclamation, the blank expression of her face growing still more blank when I told her that he did not come until the scholars were gone.

"You two been there all sole alone since four o'clock! I'll give up now! I hope Dell Thompson won't find it out, for she's awful slandersome; but," she added, coming to the gate, and speaking in a whisper, "I'm glad on't, and mebby she'll draw in her horns, if she finds that some of the *under crust*, as she calls 'em, can be noticed by Dr. Clayton as well as herself."

Equivocal as this compliment was, it gratified me, and from that moment I felt a spirit of rivalry towards Dell Thompson. Still, I did not wish her to know of Dr. Clayton's call, and so I said to Mrs. Ross, who replied, "You needn't be an atom afeard of *my* tattlin'. I know too well what 'tis to be a schoolmarm, and have the hull Deestrict peekin' at you. So if you've anything you want kept, I'm the one; for I can be still as the grave. Did the doctor say anything about Dell, but he didn't, I know, and 'taint likely he said anything about anybody."

I replied, that he talked with me about my school, and then as I heard the clock strike six I walked along. Looking back, as I entered Mr. Randall's gate, I saw Mrs. Ross's old plaid shawl and brown bonnet disappearing over the hill as fast as her feet could take them, but I had no suspicion that her destination was *Captain Thompson's*! I did not know the world then as well as I do now, and when the next morning I met Dell Thompson, who stared at me insolently, while a haughty sneer curled her lip, I had no idea that *she* was jealous of *me*, little Rosa Lee, whose heart was lighter, and whose task seemed far easier on account of Dr. Clayton's past and promised visit.

Saturday night came at last, and very joyfully I started home on foot, feeling not at all burdened with the compliments of my patrons or the esteem of my pupils. Oh, what a shout was raised at the shortness of my three weeks, as I entered our sitting-room! All laughed at me, except my mother. She was not disappointed, and when I drew Carrie's little rocking-chair to her side, and told her how hard my head was aching, she laid her soft hand caressingly upon my brow, and gently smoothing my short curls, bathed my forehead in camphor until the pain was gone. Had there been no one present but our own family, I should probably have cried; but owing to some untoward circumstance, Aunt Sally Wright was there visiting that afternoon, and as a teacher I felt obliged to maintain my dignity before her prying eyes. Almost her first salutation to me was, "Wall, Rosa, so you've grown old since you left home?"

"I do not understand what you mean," I answered.

"Why, I mean," said she, "that somebody told me that Mrs. Green told them, that Major Pond's wife told her, that Mary Downes said, that Nancy Rice heard Miss Cap'n Thompson say that you told Dr. Clayton you was *sixteen!*"

I knew that the subject of my age had not come up between me and the doctor, but it was useless to deny a story so well authenticated, so I said nothing, and Aunt Sally continued; "They do say you thrash 'em round about right," while mother asked "who Dr. Clayton was?"

"Why, he's a young pill-peddler, who's taken a shine to Rosa, and staid with her alone in the schoolhouse until *pitch dark*," said Aunt Sally, her little green eyes twinkling with the immense satisfaction she felt.

Greatly I marvelled as to the source whence she obtained the information, which so greatly exceeded the truth; and considering that no one knew of the doctor's call but *Mrs. Ross*, it really was a wonder! She was proceeding with her remarks, when we were summoned to the supper table, where green tea had so good an effect upon her, that by the time she was blowing her third cup, she began to unbend, repeating to me several complimentary remarks which she said came from Mrs. Ross. By this I knew that she had Pine Hill as well as Meadow Brook upon her hands, and, indeed, 'twas strange how much Aunt Sally did manage to attend to at once; for, besides keeping her son's wife continually fretted, and her daughter constantly quarrelling with her husband, by her foolish interference; there was scarcely a thing transpired in the neighborhood in which she did not have a part. Not a marriage was in prospect, but she knew something bad of both parties; not a family *jar* occurred in which she did not have a finger. Not a man owed more than he was worth, but she had foreseen it from the first in the extravagance of his wife. But everybody in Meadow Brook knew Aunt Sally, and it was a common saying, that "her tongue was no slander;" so I did not feel as much annoyed as I otherwise should at her spiteful remarks, which continued with little intermission until dark, when, gathering up her snuff-box, knitting, and work-bag, she started for home.

The next day was the Sabbath, and if at church, I *did* now and then cast a furtive glance at the congregation, to see if they were looking at me because I was a "schoolma'am," it was a childish vanity, which *I* have long since forgiven, as I trust my reader will do. Among the audience was our minister's young bride, and when, after church, he introduced her to me, saying to her, "This is Rose, who, I told you, was only thirteen and teaching school," I felt quite reconciled to my lot, and thought that after all, it was an honor to be a teacher.

CHAPTER VI
DR. CLAYTON'S VISIT

Very slowly passed the days of my second week, for my mind was constantly dwelling upon the important *Thursday*, which came at last, and, with more than usual care, I dressed myself for school, sporting a pale blue and white muslin, which mother said I must wear only on great occasions. And this, to me, was a great occasion; and if, for want of a better mirror, I at noon went down to a clear spring in the woods, and there gave a few smoothing touches to my toilet, it was a weakness of which, in a similar way, many an older female has been guilty. On my return to the schoolhouse, I requested one of the larger girls to sweep the floor as clean as she possibly could, while two or three of the boys were sent after some green boughs to hang over the windows.

"I'll bet we are going to have company; I thought so this morning when I see the schoolma'am all dressed up," whispered one to another—and after a time, Jim Maxwell's sister ventured to ask me, not *who* was coming, but "how many."

With a blush, I replied, "Nobody but Dr. Clayton," wondering why his name should cleave so to the roof of my mouth! In a few minutes, the fact that Dr. Clayton was coming was known both indoors and out, and when I saw how fast John Thompson took himself home, after learning the news, I involuntarily felt as if some evil were impending—a presentiment which proved correct, for not long after school commenced, there came a gentle rap at the outer door, which caused a great straightening up among the scholars, and brought me instantly to my feet, for I supposed, of course, he had come. What, then, was my surprise when, instead of him, I met a haughty-looking young lady, who, frowning majestically upon me, introduced herself as "Miss Thompson," saying she had come to visit the school.

I had never before had so good a view of her, and now, when I saw how dignified she appeared, and that there really was in her manner something elegant and refined, I not only felt myself greatly her inferior, but I fancied that Dr. Clayton would also observe the difference between us when he saw us together. After offering her the seat of honor—my splint-bottomed chair—I proceeded with my duties as composedly as possible, mentally hoping that the doctor would come soon. She probably divined my thoughts, for once, when I cast a wistful glance over the long hill, she said, "You seem to be constantly on the lookout. Are you expecting any one?"

Involuntarily my eyes sought hers, but I quailed beneath their quizzical expression, and scarcely knowing what I said, replied, "No, ma'am," repenting the falsehood the moment it was uttered, and half-resolving to confess the truth, when she rejoined, "Oh, I thought you were," while at the same moment a little girl, who had been asleep, rolled from her seat, bumping her head, and raising such an outcry that, for a time, I forgot what I had said, and when it again recurred to me I thought it was too late to rectify it. It was the second falsehood I remembered telling, and it troubled me greatly. Turn it which way I would it was a *lie* still, and it smote heavily upon my conscience. Slowly the afternoon dragged on, but it brought no Dr. Clayton; and when, at a quarter of four, I called up my class of Abecedarians to read, what with the *lie* and the disappointment, my heart was so full that I could not force back all the tears which struggled so fiercely for egress; and when it came Willie Randall's turn to read, two or three large drops fell upon his chubby hand, and, looking in my face, he called out in a loud, distinct voice—"You're cryin', you be!"

This, of course, brought a laugh from all the scholars, in which I was fain to join, although I felt greatly chagrined that I should have betrayed so much weakness before Dell Thompson, who, in referring to it when school was out, said, "she supposed I wanted to see my mother, or *somebody*!"

The sarcastic smile which dimpled the corners of her mouth angered me, and when, at last, I was alone, my long pent-up tears fell in copious showers. It is my misfortune never to be able to cry without disfiguring my face, so that it is sometimes almost hideous to look upon; and now, as I slowly walked home, I carefully kept my parasol lowered, so that no one should see me. But I could not elude the vigilance of Mrs. Ross, who, as usual, was at her post in the doorway. Although I knew she was a dangerous woman, I rather liked her, for there was, to me, something winning in her apparent friendliness, and we had come to be quite intimate, so much so that I usually called there on my way to or from school; but now, when she bade me come in, I declined, which act brought her at once to the gate, where she obtained a full view of my swollen features.

"Laws a mercy!" she exclaimed, "what's up now? Why, you look like a toad. What's the matter?"

"Nothing much," I said, and this was all she could solicit from me.

That night she called at Mr. Randall's, and after sitting awhile, asked me "to walk a little piece with her." I saw there was something on her mind, and conjecturing that it might have some connection with me, I obeyed willingly, notwithstanding Mrs. Randall's silent attempts to keep me back. Twitching my sleeve when we were outside the gate, Mrs. Ross asked if "it were true that I cried because Dr. Clayton didn't come as he promised?"

"Why, what do you mean?" I said. To which she replied, by telling me that after I left her, she just ran in to Cap'n Thompson's a minute or two, when, who should she find there but Dr. Clayton, and when Dell told him she'd been to visit the school, he said, "Ah, indeed, I was intending to do so myself this afternoon, but I was necessarily detained by a very sick patient."

"'That explains why she cried so,' said Dell, and then," continued Mrs. Ross, "she went on to tell him how you looked out of the winder, and when she asked you if you expected anybody, you said 'No,' and then at last you cried right out in the school."

"The mean thing!" I exclaimed. "Did she tell Dr. Clayton all that?"

"Yes, she did," answered Mrs. Ross; "and it made my blood bile to hear her go on makin' fun of you, that is, kinder makin' fun."

"And the doctor, what did he say?" I asked. To which she replied, "Oh, he laughed, and said it was too bad to disappoint you, if it affected you like that, but he couldn't help it."

I hardly knew at which I was most indignant, Dr. Clayton or Dell, and when I laid my aching head on my pillow, my last thoughts were, that "if Dr. Clayton ever did come to school I'd let him know I didn't care for him — he might have Dell Thompson and welcome!"

I changed my mind, however, when early the next afternoon, the gentleman himself appeared to vindicate his cause, saying he was sorry that he could not have kept his appointment, adding, as he finally relinquished my hand, "You had company, though, I believe, and so, on the whole, I am glad I was detained, for I had rather visit you alone."

Much as I now esteem Dr. Clayton, I do not hesitate to say that he was then a male flirt, a species of mankind which I detest. He was the handsomest, most agreeable man I had ever seen, and by some strange fascination, he possessed the power of swaying me at his will. This he well knew, and hence the wrong he committed by working upon my feelings. Never passed hours more agreeably to me than did those of that afternoon. And I even forgot that I was to go home that night, and that in all probability father would come for me as soon as school was out, thus preventing the quiet talk alone with Dr. Clayton, which I so much desired: so when, about four o'clock, I saw the head of old Sorrel appearing over the hill, my emotions were not particularly pleasant, and I wished I had not been so foolish as to insist upon going home every week. The driver, however, proved to be Charlie, and this in a measure consoled me, for he, I knew, was good at taking *hints*, and would wait for me as long as I desired; so I welcomed him with a tolerably good grace, introducing him to Dr. Clayton, who addressed him as *Mr. Lee*, thereby winning his friendship at once and forever!

When school was out and the scholars gone, I commenced making preparations for my departure, shutting down the windows and piling away books, slowly and deliberately, while Charlie, who seemed in no hurry, amused himself by whipping at the thistle-tops which grew near the door. At last Dr. Clayton, turning to him, said, "And so you have come to carry your sister home, when I was promising myself that pleasure?"

Charlie glanced at my face, and its expression, doubtless, prompted his answer, "You can do so now, if you choose, for I like to ride alone."

Of course I disclaimed against such an arrangement, but my objections were overruled, and almost before I knew what I was doing, I found myself seated in Dr. Clayton's covered buggy, with him at my side. Telling Charlie "not to be surprised if he did not see us until sunset," he drove off in a different direction from Meadow Brook, remarking to me that "it was a fine afternoon for riding and he meant to enjoy it."

I hardly know whether he had any object in passing Capt. Thompson's, but he certainly did so, bowing graciously and showing his white teeth to Dell, who, from a chamber window, looked haughtily down upon me, and as I afterwards learned, made fun of my pink sun-bonnet and little yellow dotted shawl. The sight of her naturally led him to speak of her, and much to my surprise, he asked me how I liked her! I could not answer truthfully and say "very well;" so I replied that "I hardly knew her. She was very fine looking, and I presumed she was very intelligent and accomplished."

"You are a good-hearted little girl, Rose," said he, "to speak thus of her. Do you suppose *she* would do the same by you if asked a similar question?"

"Oh, no," I answered, eagerly, "she couldn't say I was fine looking. Nobody ever said that."

"If I should tell you that *I* think you better looking than Dell Thompson, what would you say?" he asked, looking under my bonnet, while, with glowing cheeks, I turned my head away, and replied, "I am sure you would not mean it. I know I am ugly, but I do not care so much about it now as I used to."

There was a silence for some minutes, and when he spoke again, it was of faces, which, without regularity of features or brilliancy of complexion, still had an expression exceedingly pleasing and attractive. "I do not say yours is such a face," said he, "for I never flatter; but I *do* say, and I mean it, too, that I like your looks far better than I do Miss Thompson's.

If I had cried then, as I wished to, I should have done a most foolish thing; but by a strong effort of the will, I forced down my tears, and changing the conversation, commenced talking on subjects quite foreign to Dell Thompson, or good looks. I found Dr. Clayton a most agreeable companion, and ere the close of that ride, he was "all the world" to me. In short, I suppose I was as much in love as a child of thirteen can well be, and when we at last reached home and I introduced him to my mother and sisters, I blushed like a guilty thing, stealing out of the room as soon as possible, and staying out for a long time, although I wanted so much to be back there with him.

"Catched a beau, hain't you? and a handsome one, too!" said Sally, applying her eye to the key-hole and thus obtaining a view of his face.

Tommy Trimmer, a little boy, five years of age, who lived near by, and who chanced to be there, overheard her, and when Dr. Clayton, who was very fond of children, coaxed him into his lap, he asked, pointing to me, "Be you Rosa's beau? Sally said you was!"

The doctor laughed aloud, referring Tommy to me for an answer, and telling him "it was just as I said."

"Rose is altogether too young to be riding round with beaux. It will give her a bad name," said grandma, when at last the doctor was gone.

No one made any answer until Lizzie, who was more of my way of thinking, said, "*You* must have had beaux early, grandma, for you wasn't quite fifteen when you were married; I saw it so in the Bible!"

Of course, grandma had nothing to offer in her own defence, save the very correct remark, that "girls now-adays were not what they were when she was young;"—and here the conversation ceased.

CHAPTER VII
DELL THOMPSON'S PARTY

One day, about three weeks after the commencement of my school, I was surprised by a call from Dell Thompson, who, after conversing awhile, very familiarly, astonished me with an invitation to visit her the next afternoon. "She was going to have a few of her friends from the village," she said, "Dr. Clayton with the rest."

Here she looked at me and I looked out of the window, while she continued, "You'll come, I suppose."

I replied that I would, after which she departed, leaving me in a perfect state of bewilderment. *I* invited to Captain Thompson's, with Dell's fashionable friends! What could it mean, and what should I wear? This last was by far the more important question; for I knew that the people of the village were noted for their fine dress, and I, of course, could not compete with them in point of elegance. Dr. Clayton too, I had heard, was rather fastidious in his ideas of a lady's dress, and my heart sank within me as I mentally enumerated the articles of my scanty wardrobe, finding therein nothing which I deemed fit for the occasion, save a white dotted muslin, which was now lying soiled and wrinkled at the bottom of my trunk. It is true, I had a blue and white lawn, neatly made and quite becoming, but my heart was set upon the muslin, and so when Mrs. Ross, with whom I was that week boarding, offered to wash and iron it, I accepted the proffered kindness.

The next morning, when I passed Captain Thompson's, I observed a great commotion in and around the house. The blinds were thrown back, and through the parlor windows I caught sight of brooms and dusters, while at intervals during the day, the scholars brought me tidings of cake, jellies, and ice-cream, said to be in progress. At precisely four o'clock I dismissed school, and taking a short cut across the fields, soon reached my boarding-place, where I found Mrs. Ross bending over the ironing-table with a face flushed, and indicative of some anxiety.

"I never see nothin' beat it," she began, holding down her hot iron and thereby making a slightly yellow spot on the dress. "I never see nothin' beat it, how this gown pesters me. It must be poor stuff, or somethin',—but mebby it'll look better on you," she continued, as she gave it a finishing touch, and then held it up to view.

And, indeed, it was sorry looking enough; some places being wholly destitute of starch, while others were rough and stiff as a piece of buckram. Common sense told me to wear the blue, but I had heard Dr. Clayton say that nothing became a young girl so well as white, and so I determined to wear it. It *would* look better on me, I thought, and with all the eagerness of a child I commenced my toilet, discovering to my great dismay that I had neither shoes nor stockings fit to wear with a muslin dress. The week previous I had taken my best ones home, where I had purposely left them, not thinking it possible for me to need them. Here then was a dilemma, out of which Mrs. Ross at last helped me, by offering to lend the articles which I lacked; an offer which I gladly accepted. Her stockings were rather coarse, having been knit by herself, but they possessed the virtue of being white, and clean, and would have answered my purpose very well, had it not been for the slippers, which were far too long for me, and showed almost the whole of my foot. Besides that, I found it rather difficult keeping them on, until Mrs. Ross suggested the propriety of stuffing the toes with cotton! This done, I donned the muslin dress, which seemed to me much shorter than when I had last worn it, inasmuch as I had the painful consciousness of being *all feet*, whenever I glanced in that direction.

But Mrs. Ross said "I looked mighty crank," at the same time fastening on my low-necked waist her *glass* breastpin, which she pronounced, "just the checker." "You orto have some gloves to wear when you get there," said she, as she saw me drawing on my brown ones, "and I b'lieve I've got the very thing," she continued, bringing from the depths of the bureau-drawer a pair of white cotton mitts, fancifully embroidered on the back with yellow and blue. These she bade me "tuck in my bosom until I got there, and on no account to lose 'em, as she had 'em before she was married!"

Thus equipped, I started for Captain Thompson's, reaching there just as the clock was striking *five*, and finding, to my surprise, that I was not only the first arrival, but that neither Mrs. Thompson nor Dell had yet commenced dressing! Fearing I had mistaken the day, I questioned the servant girl who answered my ring, and who assured me that I was right, while at the same time, she conducted me to the chamber above, where, in the long mirror, I obtained a full-length view of myself, feet and all! My first impulse was to laugh, my second to cry, and to the latter I finally yielded. No one came near me—I heard no one—saw no one, until in light flowing muslin, white silk hose, and the tiniest of all tiny French slippers, Dell Thompson sailed into the room, starting with well feigned surprise when she saw me, asking how long I had been there, and what was the matter.

Without considering what I was doing, I told her unreservedly about the shoes and stockings, pointing to my *peacock* feet as proof of what I said. With all her faults, there was enough of the woman about Dell to inspire her with a feeling of pity for me, and after forcing back the laugh she could not well help, she said kindly, "Your shoes *are* rather large, but I think, perhaps, I can remedy the difficulty."

At the same time she started to leave the room. What new impulse came over her, I never knew; but sure am I that something changed her mind, for, when nearly at the door, she suddenly paused, saying; "I know, though, you can't wear my slippers, so it's of no use trying the experiment:" adding, as she saw how my countenance fell, "I wouldn't mind it if I were you. Nobody'll notice it, unless it is Dr. Clayton, who, I believe, admires small ankles and little feet; but you don't care for him, he's old enough to be your father, and, besides that, he thinks you perfect, any way."

Her words and manner annoyed me, and for a moment I debated in my own mind the propriety of leaving at once, but I had not seen Dr. Clayton since he carried me home, and so I finally concluded to remain, thinking that I would keep my seat, and on no account stir when he was looking at me. After coming to this conclusion, I ventured to ask Dell where the rest of the company were, and was told that they were not invited until evening.

"Until evening," I repeated; "then I guess I'll go before they come, for I shall be afraid to walk home alone."

"There's a good moon," said she; adding, "You must not leave, on any account, for that will spoil all the—pleasure" she said—*fun* I now think she meant; but I could not fathom her then, and I never dreamed that she had invited me there merely to show me up before her fashionable friends, and make light of me in the estimation of Dr. Clayton.

"Come down to the parlor," she said at last, after arranging for the third time the heavy braids of her black, beautiful hair; and following her, I soon stood in the presence of Mrs. Thompson, a tall, dark, haughty looking woman, who, half arising from the sofa, bowed stiffly, muttering a few words of welcome as Dell introduced me.

Dropping into the first seat, a large willow chair near the door, I tried to act natural, but I could not; for turn which way I would, I felt that a pair of large black eyes were upon me, scanning me from my head to my *feet*; and when her linen cambric handkerchief went up to her mouth, apparently to stifle a cough, I was certain that it also smothered a laugh, which I suppose my rather singular appearance called forth. Right glad was I when both the ladies found an excuse for leaving the parlor, though I did find it rather tiresome sitting there alone until the shades of evening began to fall.

At last, when it was nearly dark, I ventured out upon the long piazza, where I had not been long, when a gentleman on horseback galloped into the yard, and in a moment I recognized Dr. Clayton's voice, as he gave his horse to the keeping of Capt. Thompson's hired man. Hastily retreating to the parlor, I had just time to seat myself in a corner where I thought I should attract the least attention, when he entered the room with Dell, whose hand I am sure he held until he saw me; then quickly dropping it, he advanced to my side, greeting me kindly, and once, when Dell's back was towards us, whispering softly; "I am so glad to find you here. I was afraid the party would prove a bore."

Just then we heard the sound of fast coming wheels, and in a moment there came round the corner a long open omnibus, drawn by four horses, and densely crowded with young people of both sexes, all seemingly shouting and laughing with all their might. I was not much used to the ways of the world then, and having been taught that it was not lady-like to be either rude or boisterous, I wondered greatly that well-bred people should conduct themselves so badly: a species of wonder, by the way, in which I now occasionally indulge. Bounding out, and adjusting their light, flowing robes, the young ladies went tripping up the stairs, still talking, laughing, and screaming so loudly, that once I started up, exclaiming, "Why, what *is* the matter!"

With a peculiar smile, Dr. Clayton laid his hand on my head in a very *fatherly* way, saying; "My little girl hasn't yet learned that in order to be *refined*, she must be rough and boisterous, and I hope she never will, for it is refreshing to find occasionally something feminine and natural."

By this time the guests were assembled in the parlor, and when I saw how tastefully they were dressed, and how much at ease they appeared, I began to wish myself anywhere but there. One by one they were presented to me, I at first keeping my seat; but when Dr. Clayton whispered to me to stand up, I did so, bending my knees a little, so as to make my dress longer, and thus partially hide my feet! But this could not be done, and like two backgammon boards they set out at right angles, with the *wads* of cotton lying up, round and hard. The young ladies had undoubtedly received a description of me, for they inspected me closely, glancing the while mischievously at Dell, who seemed to be in her element; asking me if I were not tired; telling me I looked so, and adding, aside, but loud enough for Dr. Clayton and myself to hear—"I should think she would be, for she's been here ever since five o'clock. I hadn't even commenced dressing!"

"Is it possible?" said one; while another exclaimed, "How *green*! but I suppose it's her first introduction into society, and she knows no better."

This conversation was probably not intended for me, but I heard it all, and with much bitterness at my heart I turned away to hide my tears, involuntarily drawing nearer to Dr. Clayton, as if for protection. But, for some reason or other, he did not appear now as he did when we were alone; then he was all kindness and attention, while he now evidently avoided me; seeming slightly annoyed when any of his acquaintance teased him about me, as I more than once heard them doing. In *his* nature, as in every other man's, there were both good and bad qualities, and they now seemed warring with each other; the former chiding him for deserting me when I stood so much in need of his attention, and the latter shrinking from anything which would incur the ridicule of his companions.

At last, as if his good genius had conquered, he suddenly broke away from a group of girls, and crossing over to where I was standing, offered me his arm, telling me "I must stir round and be more sociable."

I looked down at my feet, so did he, and for an instant there was a flush on his face; but it passed off, and with a word of encouragement, he led me towards the music-room, where Dell Thompson was unmercifully pounding a five hundred dollar piano, which groaned and shrieked under the infliction, while the bystanders, who had insisted upon her playing, were all talking together, seemingly intent upon seeing which could make the most noise, they or the instrument.

"Do you play, Miss Lee?" was asked me by half a dozen or more.

I had taken lessons two quarters, and I could play a few dancing tunes, marches, etc., and so I said, whereupon they insisted upon my favoring them with Money Musk, as they wanted to dance, and none of them could perform anything as *old-fashioned* as that. I looked at Dr. Clayton, who, in a low tone, asked, "Are you sure you can get through with it?"

There was *doubt* in the tones of his voice which touched my pride, and without deigning him an answer I took my seat, resolving to do my best. The set was soon formed, Dr. Clayton dancing with Dell Thompson, who remarked as he led her away—"I suppose we shall have a rare performance."

Something, I am sure, must have inspired me, for never before did I play so well; keeping perfect time, and striking every note distinctly. My audience were evidently both surprised and pleased, for they called for piece after piece, until my list was exhausted, when one of the gentlemen, more thoughtful than the ladies, suggested the possibility of my being tired.

"Perhaps she dances, too. Ask her, Bob," said a young lady, while Dell eagerly rejoined, "Oh, yes, do;" but *Bob* was forestalled by Dr. Clayton, who, for several minutes, had stood by my side, complimenting my playing, and who now asked me to be his partner in the next cotillon, his cousin having volunteered to take my place at the piano.

In my excitement I forgot my *shoes*, forgot everything, save that Dr. Clayton's eye was looking down upon me, that my hand was resting in his, and ere I was aware of it, I found myself upon the floor. I was perfectly familiar with the changes of the cotillon, but at my right was John Thompson; who, when it came his turn to swing with me, refused to take my hand, treating me with such marked insolence that I became confused, and made several mistakes, at which he laughed contemptuously. Besides this, my big shoes incommoded me; and at last, in the midst of the promenade, one of them dropped off, the *cotton-ball* rolled out, I tripped, lost my balance, and after one or two headlong plunges, fell flat at the feet of Dr. Clayton, who stood aghast with surprise and mortification. It was ludicrous enough, I know; but I do not think there was any necessity for the loud roar which was raised over my mishap; and burning with shame and vexation, I gathered myself up, and fled from the room; but not until I heard Dell Thompson say, as she picked up the shoe and passed it to Dr. Clayton, "It is Mrs. Ross's; she hadn't any of her own, which she thought suitable, and so she borrowed."

"That accounts for the *cotton-wad*," said John, dealing said wad a kick that sent it bounding past me.

Rushing up the stairs, I found my shawl and bonnet; and then, without a word to any one, started for home, minus my shoe, which I entirely forgot in my excitement. I had scarcely got outside the gate when the sound of a footstep caused me to look around, and I saw Dr. Clayton, his hat in one hand and Mrs. Ross's slipper in the other. This last he passed to me, and then without a word drew my arm within his, and for a time we walked on in silence, while I cried as if my heart would break. Coming at last to an old oak tree, under which a rude bench had been constructed, he bade me sit down; and placing himself by my side, asked me, "What was the matter?"

"You know well enough what's the matter," I said angrily, struggling to rise; but his arm was strong, and he held me fast, while he tried to quiet me, and in this he soon succeeded, for he possessed over me a power which I could not resist.

Gradually, as I grew calm, I told him all; how I believed that Dell Thompson had invited me only to ridicule me, how she had asked me to come in the afternoon, and then made fun of me for doing so; while her companions called me *green*; and that in the absence of my own slippers I had worn those of Mrs. Ross; thereby meeting with the worst catastrophe of all; to wit, the falling flat in the dance!

Here I broke down entirely, and cried out aloud; while the doctor, after one or two hearty laughs at my distress, tried again to comfort me, asking me what I cared for Dell Thompson's ridicule. "She wasn't worth minding," he said, "and no one who knows her would attach any importance to her remarks."

"But what makes her treat me so?" I asked; "I never harmed her."

For a time the doctor said nothing; but the arm, which all the time had encircled my waist, drew me still closer to his side, while he at last replied, "she is *jealous of you*—jealous because she thinks I like *the little Rose* better than I do her."

"And it's very foolish in her to think so," I exclaimed.

Again the doctor was silent, but by the light of the full moon I saw that there was a curious train of thought passing through his mind, but it did not manifest itself in words; for when he again spoke, it was merely to reply, "Yes, very foolish;" then, after another pause, he added, "and still I know of no reason why I should like her best—do you?"

"Yes," I answered quickly, "there are many reasons. She is handsome; I am homely. She is graceful; I am awkward. She is rich; I am poor"——

"She is artificial; you are truthful;" said he, interrupting me, while, without paying any heed to this remark, I continued, "she is a young lady, and I am a little girl—only thirteen."

"I wish you were older, Rose," said he, "and had seen a little more of the world."

Then followed a long conversation in which much was said, which had far better been left unsaid; for I was a warm-hearted, impulsive child, believing that I to him was what he was to me. And still he did not once commit himself, nor in what he said was there aught which could possibly have been construed into an avowal of anything save *friendship*, which was the theme upon which he rang many a change. Alas, for such friendships! They are dangerous to one's peace of mind, particularly if told beneath an old oak tree, with the silvery moonlight shining down upon you, and the soft summer air gently moving the green leaves above your head. How long we sat there I do not know; but I was the first to propose going, telling him they would miss him at the party, and wonder at his absence.

"Let them wonder then," said he; "I have no intention of returning to the house. It would be intolerable after this pleasant chat with you, so I shall just get my horse and go quietly home."

I did not then know that he had not sufficient courage to brave the jokes and jeers which he knew were sure to greet him, should he return to Captain Thompson's. Neither did I know that with his fashionable friends he would scarcely dare defend me; nor that when John Thompson once, in his presence, imitated the way in which I stumbled and fell, *he* joined in the laugh which followed; saying, though as if in apology, "that it was too bad to make fun of me, for I was quite a nice little girl."

We found Mrs. Ross sitting up for me, sleeping in her chair, while the tallow candle at her side had burned and spluttered away, until the black, crisped wick was longer than the candle itself.

"Lordy massy! doctor, is that you?" she exclaimed, rubbing open her eyes and hooking up her dress, which, for comfort, she had loosened. "I thought, mebby, you'd beau Rosa home. Come in and stay a spell. I'd as lief you'd spark it awhile in t'other room as not!"

But the doctor had no idea of doing anything so marked as that; and with a whispered good night to me, and an audible one to Mrs. Ross, he departed; just as the good lady asked me, loud enough for him to hear, "if I'd dirtied her *stockings*, lost her *mitts*, or broken her breastpin?"

CHAPTER VIII
CLOSE OF SCHOOL IN PINE DISTRICT

Whether Dr. Clayton cared for me or not, he exerted his influence in my behalf, plainly telling John Thompson that he ought to be ashamed to annoy me as he did; and dropping a few hints to Mrs. Thompson, who now tried to restrain her son; so that after the party, hostilities in that quarter nearly ceased. But the ball was in motion, and could not well be stopped; for what the Thompsons now lacked, the rest of the District made up. It was the general impression, I believe, that the scholars had learned nothing save a few pieces of poetry; and that I had done nothing but whip, scold, and cry. To all these accusations I plead guilty; and when Mr. Randall, one day, proposed to me to bring my labors to a close, I replied that "nothing could please me better," though there was a tremor in my voice as I thought how the people of Meadow Brook would laugh. Mr. Randall, probably, divined my thoughts, for he quickly rejoined, "The weather is gettin' so hot that the youngsters need a vacation. Mebby, in the fall, when it is cooler, we shall have you back."

And so it was settled that school should close the next week on Saturday, and that on Friday I should have an *examination*! This, to a teacher in Western New York, may seem strange; but those who have taught in that part of New England where I did, know that such a thing cannot well be avoided. No matter how small the school, or how inefficient the teacher may be, an examination must be held, or you at once lose *caste*; the people unanimously declaring you to be ashamed of showing how little your pupils have learned. In my case, I was rather anxious than otherwise for an opportunity to show off; for I was sure my scholars would acquit themselves creditably. I well knew they could stand up and repeat "verses," the multiplication table, the names of the fourteen counties of Massachusetts, and tell who made them, and where the sun rose, louder and faster than any other seventeen children in town! I confidently expected all the parents and friends to be there, and as my own wardrobe was rather scanty, I coaxed my sister Anna, who, though several years my senior, was still not much taller than myself, to let me wear her new black silk!

It was my first appearance in a long dress, and it troubled me greatly; but by dint of holding it up, as ladies do now-adays, I succeeded in getting to the schoolhouse, where I found my pupils arrayed in their best; Ike Ross having in his shirt bosom the selfsame glass breastpin which I had sported at Dell Thompson's party. Not wishing the spectators to lose any of the exercises, I sat in grim silence, awaiting their arrival: but my waiting was all in vain; for, with the exception of Mrs. Randall and Dr. Clayton, the latter of whom came in the capacity of Inspector, not a single individual was present! Not a parent—not a friend, nor a foe—and still, if the examination had not been held, those who stayed away would have ridiculed me, and voted my school even a worse failure than they did. So much for consistency. Parents, I think, are not sufficiently aware of the great good their occasional presence in the schoolroom will do, both to teacher and scholar; the latter of whom will almost invariably study harder and strive to have better lessons, if there is a prospect of their father or mother's hearing them recite; while the former, feeling that an interest is taken in them, will also be incited to fresh efforts for the improvement of those committed to their charge.

But not thus thought the people of Pine Hill. Satisfied that an examination was going on, they stayed at home, expressing their surprise when they heard that nobody was there, wondering what it meant, and saying "folks ought to be ashamed for not going!" As if to make amends for their neglect, Dr. Clayton, in his closing remarks, said some very complimentary things concerning my school, which he bade the children repeat to their parents; and such is human nature, that, when I had received my *Eight Dollars*, and was gone, the District, in speaking of me, said, "I wasn't the *worst* teacher, after all."

About four o'clock, there came up a thunder shower, which caused both Mrs. Randall and the scholars to hasten home. Dr. Clayton, on the contrary, was in no hurry. "It was, perhaps, the last opportunity he would have of seeing me," he said, "and he meant to improve it."

It was not very far to Meadow Brook I thought, and so I at last ventured to say.

"I know that," he replied; "but people might talk were I to call on you, and I do not wish to do anything which will affect you unpleasantly."

"I don't care what folks say," arose to my lips, but its utterance was prevented by a flash of lightning and a thunder crash, which made me shriek aloud, while I covered my face with my hands.

I shall not describe the way which Dr. Clayton took to calm my fright, for all who have passed through a similar experience can imagine it; but the remembrance of that thunder-storm lingered in my memory long after I had forgotten the night when I sat with him in the soft moonlight beneath the old oak tree. When the storm had ceased and the sun was again shining on the tree-tops at the west, he left me, placing on my hand at parting a little gold ring, on which was inscribed, simply, "Rose."

"It was the gift of friendship," he said—"nothing more;" and he wished me to wear it "for the sake of the few pleasant hours we had spent together."

I suppose it was wrong in me to accept it. I thought so then, but I could not refuse it; and remembering the fate of the one sent by Herbert Langley to Anna, I resolved upon keeping it a secret, and only wearing it when I was alone. For a long time I sat in the deserted schoolroom, while the damp air, which came through the open window, fell upon my uncovered neck and arms, nor was I reminded of the lapse of time until it began to grow dark around me; then hastily throwing on my things, I started for Mr. Randall's, wetting my feet, for I had no rubbers with me. As the result of this, when I awoke next morning I was conscious of a pain in my head, a soreness in my throat, and an aching of my back, quite as unexpected as it was disagreeable. I had taken a violent cold, and Mrs. Randall, when she saw how pale I was and how faint I appeared, said I must not go to school. George, she said, would go and tell the scholars, and I must stay there until my father came for me at night, as had been arranged the week before. To this plan I finally yielded, and all the day long I hovered over the fire, which, in the little sitting-room, was kindled for my comfort.

At night, when my father came for me, I was almost too weak to stand alone; but the excitement of riding imparted to me an artificial strength, which wholly deserted me the moment I reached home, and for many days I kept my bed, attended by *Dr. Clayton,* who accidently heard of my illness, and who came daily to see me. Grandma, who was something of a nurse, proposed several times that he be dismissed, saying he only made me worse, for I was always more feverish and restless after one of his visits! But the doctor, to whom she one day made the suggestion, said he should not leave me until I was well, and when she asked him how he accounted for my rapid pulse and flushed cheeks, whenever he was present, he very gravely replied, that "possibly my *heart* might be *affected*—the symptoms seemed much like it," adding, as he saw the look of concern on grandma's face, "but I think I can cure that, don't you, Rose?" turning to me, and taking my hand to see *how fast my pulse did beat*!

After this, grandma made no further objections to his visits. "If Rose had the heart disease, and he could cure it, he ought to do so!"

But, alas! for the heart disease, which feeds upon the smile of one who, when sure that he holds it in his grasp, casts it from him, as children do a long coveted toy, of which they have grown weary.

CHAPTER IX
PRO AND CON

On a pleasant May morning, in the spring succeeding the events narrated in the last chapter, the door of Dr. Clayton's office was locked against all intruders. The shutters were closed; while within, with his feet upon a table and his hands clasped over his head, the doctor himself was revolving the all-important question—whether it were better to offer himself at once to Dell Thompson "and have it done with," or to wait a few years for a *little girl*, who had recently crossed his pathway, leaving on his memory footprints he could not easily efface. For the benefit of any young men who may be similarly situated, we give a portion of his reasoning, as follows:

"Now, I am as positive as a man need be that I can have either of them for the asking; therefore, in a case which involves the happiness of one's whole life, it behooves me to consider the matter well. To be sure, if I follow the bent of my inclination, I am decided at once; but then, marriages of convenience sometimes prove just as pleasant as those of pure love; and so I'll go over with the *pros* and *cons* of both, deciding upon the one which has the most of the former!

"First, then, there's *Rose*, a most beautiful name. Only think how refreshing it would be after riding ten or twelve miles, visiting farmer Stubbs or widow Grubbs, to know there was a *Rose* watching for your return. Yes, her name is in her favor."

Here the hands came down from the head, and wrote one pro against the name of Rose, after which they resume their former position, and the doctor goes on with his soliloquy:

"She is frank, artless, unassuming, means what she says—in short, she is perfectly natural, and I always feel refreshed after a talk with her." (Makes *pro* number 2.) "Then she is so wholly unselfish in her affection for me—loves me so devotedly—sees no fault in me whatever—thinks me handsome, I dare say, and all that."

Here glancing at himself in a little mirror opposite, and smoothing his shining moustache, the doctor waxes eloquent on said Rose's supposed admiration for him, writing down, in the heat of his excitement two *pros*, making in all *four*! Verily, Rosa Lee, your prospect of becoming Mrs. Dr. Clayton is brightening fast. But to proceed:

"She is smart, intelligent, talented, writes poetry—and, with proper training, would perhaps make a distinguished writer. Were I sure on this point, I should not hesitate; but you can't tell what these precocious children will make; frequently they come to a stand-still."

And here, to make the matter sure, he writes against her name one *pro* for what she possibly may be, and one *con* for what she probably will not be!

"Then I love her better than anything else in the known world. I do, that's a fact; but she's young—only fourteen—and before she's old enough to marry she may change forty times, and that would kill me dead."

Puts down one pro for his own love, and one *con* for Rose's possible inconstancy.

"But she is poor—or, her father, they say, is worth only about $5,000! He already has nine children, and there's time enough for three or four more:— *thirteen* into *five thousand* makes—*Long Division*, a rule I never fancied; too poor altogether!"

And against Rose's name there is *con* No. 3, *long* and *black*, with the shadow of her four unborn brothers, who, by the way, never came in for a share of the $5,000.

"Then her family connections, I do not suppose, are such as would add anything to my influence. Good, respectable people, no doubt, but not known in the world like the Hungerfords, Dell Thompson's maternal relatives. To be sure, I once heard Rose speak of an uncle who resides in Boston, but I dare say he's some grocer or mechanic, living on a back street; while Dell's uncle, from the same city, must be a man of wealth and importance, judging by the figure his wife cuts when she visits the captain."

Here Dell received a *pro* for the Hungerford blood flowing in her veins, while Rose had a *con* for the want of said Hungerford blood.

"Dell, too, has $10,000 of her own, or rather will have, when her grandmother dies; and there are not many young men who can jump into that fortune every day. Yes, $10,000 is a decided temptation."

And lest Rose, who already numbered six, should come out in the majority, three long marks were put down against the $10,000 to be inherited at the death of a grandmother, whose name Dell bore.

"Then Dell has an air, which shows at once what she is, and no man need be ashamed of her in any place." (Mark No. 5.) "Then, again, she's handsome—decidedly so—such beautiful eyes! such small feet! and curls!"

Here a vague remembrance of certain long shoes, with wads of cotton, *versus* French slippers and silken hose, arose before the man of the world, resulting in a *pro* for the slippers, and a *con* for the cotton!

"But Dell is deceitful—high-tempered—artificial—selfish superficial—and all that! The other picture suits me best, or would, were it not for the Hungerford blood, and the $10,000. Let me see how it foots up:—Six *pros* for Dell, and the same number for Rose."

Here was a dilemma; but anon he remembered how awkwardly the last mentioned young lady looked, when she fell at his feet—and this decides the matter. He is sensitive to ridicule, very, and he could not endure the sneering remarks which an avowed attachment to her might call forth from the world of fashion; so he crosses one of the *pros* which he had written against her name, when he thought how much she admired him—and then it stands, Dell 6; Rose 5!

Thus was the die cast. Alas! for the young girl, who, that same spring morning, stole away to her accustomed haunt, the old grape-vine, whose swelling buds were not an unfit symbol of the bright hopes now springing in her glad heart. As she sits there alone, with the running brook at her feet, she thinks of him who has grown so strongly into her love; and though, in words, he has never said so, by ten thousand little acts he has told her that her affection was returned, and for his sake she wishes she was older. He has wished so too, in her presence, many a time; but as that cannot be, she resolves to spend the season of her childhood in making herself what she knows he would wish her to be, were she to share his lot in life; and then, when the lapse of years shall have ripened her into womanhood, she thinks how she can, without shame, put her hand in his, and go forth into the world satisfied, though it brought her naught but care, if he were only with her.

Alas, for thee, Rosa! A few miles to the southward, and the same sun which now shines softly down on you, looks in through a richly curtained window, and its golden rays fall on the queenly form of your rival; who, with a look of exultation on her finely cast features, listens to the words she has long waited to hear, and which have now been spoken; while he, of whom you dream, bends gently over her, *his own—his betrothed!* And still, in the very moment of his triumph, there comes up before him a pale, childish face, which, with its dreamy eyes of blue, looks reproachfully upon him. But pride and ambition weave together a veil with which hides the image from his view, bidding him forget that any other save the peerless Dell, e'er stirred the fountain of his love.

Would it be well for us always to know what is passing in the minds of our friends, whether present or absent? I think not; and still, could Rosa Lee have known what had transpired, methinks she would not have darted away so quickly as she did, when told that Dr. Clayton was coming through the gate one afternoon, about six weeks after his engagement with Dell. *Why* she ran, she could not tell, except it were, as her brother Charlie said, that "gals always run off and *spit on their hair*, when they saw their beaux coming."

Homely as this expression is, there was in this case some truth in it; for, though Rose did not *spit* upon her hair, she went to her room and brushed it, winding one or two of the rougher curls about her finger, then taking from its hiding-place the ring, his gift, she placed it upon her finger, and with heightened color went down to greet the doctor, who had come to make his farewell visit—for, four weeks from that night, Dell Thompson would be his wife. Long had he debated the propriety of seeing Rose again, conscience bidding him leave her alone, while inclination clamored loudly for one more quiet talk with her, one more walk by moonlight, one more look into her childish face, and then he would leave her forever; never again suffering a thought of her to come between him and the bride of his choice.

And for this purpose he had come; but when he saw how joyfully Rose met him, and how the bloom deepened on her usually pale cheek, his heart misgave him, and for the first time, he began to realize the wrong he had done her. But it was now too late to remedy it, he thought; and as if bent upon making matters still worse, he asked her to accompany him in a walk down the green lane, to the haunts he knew she loved the best, and where they had more than once been before. Oh, that walk!—how long it lingered in the memory of Rose, for never before had the doctor's manner been so marked, or his words so kind as when together they sat upon the moss-grown bank, beneath the spreading vine, while he talked to her of the past, of the happiness he had experienced in her society, and which he said would be one of the few green spots, to which, in the years to come, he should look back with pleasure. Then drawing her so closely to him that her head almost rested upon his shoulder, he asked of her the privilege of "once kissing her before they parted"— —he did not say *forever*, but the rustling leaves and the murmuring brook whispered it in her ear as she granted his request, shuddering the while, and wondering at the strangeness of his manner. Possibly he had it in his mind to tell her, but if so, he found himself unequal to the task, and he left her without a word of the coming event, of which she had not the slightest suspicion.

CHAPTER X
MRS. DR. CLAYTON

Although Meadow Brook and Pine District were distant from each other only four or five miles, there was between the two neighborhoods but little communication; and this, added to the fact that Aunt Sally Wright was confined to her bed, was undoubtedly the reason why the news of the approaching nuptials did not reach us until the week before the time appointed for them to take place. It was a warm sultry day in July, that Aunt Sally, who was now convalescent, sent us word that she would visit us that afternoon, if it was perfectly convenient; the little girl who brought the message, adding that "Miss Wright said Miss Lee needn't put herself out an atom, as she wan't a bit particular what she *ett.*"

Of course it was convenient, and about one o'clock she came, talkative and full of news as ever. I was suffering from a severe headache, which, during the morning, had kept me confined to the bed; but knowing how much Aunt Sally would have to tell, and feeling curious to hear it all, I went down to the sitting-room, where her first exclamation was, "Now do tell what makes you look so down in the mouth?"

I was about to tell her of my headache, when she prevented me by continuing—"But law! it's no wonder, seein' you've lost the doctor slick and clean."

A dim foreshadowing of the truth came over me, but with a strong effort, I controlled my feelings, and in a very indifferent manner, asked her what she meant.

"Now I'll give up," said she, "if you hain't heerd on't. Why, it's in everybody's mouth. They are to be married next Thursday night, at nine o'clock; and the dress is white satin, with a veil that comes most to the floor."

"Who is to be married?" asked Anna, eagerly, her interest all awakened by the mention of white satin and lace veils.

"Why, Dr. Clayton and Dell Thompson;" returned Aunt Sally. "They was published last Sunday; Andy Slosson see it himself and told me. They are goin' first out to York State, to see them great Falls, and then they are goin' to live in Boston, boardin' at some of them big taverns; and Dell has got six bran new gowns a-purpose to wear to breakfast."

Here Aunt Sally paused for breath, while Anna asked who was invited, and if it was to be a large wedding.

"I don't know how large," said Aunt Sally, "but it's pretty likely all the upper crust'll be there. *I* hain't been invited, 'cause they think I'm sick, I s'pose,—but goodness alive! look at Rosa!" she continued, pointing towards me, who, weary and faint, had lain my head upon the window-stool.

"She's got the sick headache," said Anna, while Lizzie, with a delicate tact, for which in my heart I blessed her, came up to me, saying, "I don't believe you are able to sit up; I'd go to bed."

Glad of any excuse to be alone, I left the room, going to my chamber, where I wept myself to sleep. When I awoke the sun had set, but I heard the voices of the family below, and once when I thought I caught the sound of Dr. Clayton's name, I involuntarily stopped my ears to shut out the sound. A moment after, the door of my room was softly opened, and Carrie came stealing in on tiptoe. Learning that I was awake, she advanced towards me, holding to view a note, which she said had been left there for me by Captain Thompson's hired man, and was an invitation to the wedding! It was still sufficiently light for me to see, and leaning upon my elbow, I read on a card, that Mrs. Thompson would be "at home" from eight to eleven on the evening of the 25th, while in the corner were the names of "Dr. Clayton and Dell Thompson."

There was no longer a shadow of hope!—it was all true, and he had insulted me with an invitation to witness his marriage with another! I did not know then, as I afterwards did, that the invitation was purposely sent by Dell to annoy me! For a moment I forgot my headache in my anger, but ere long it returned in all its force, and if the next day my headache continued with unabated severity, it was not without a sufficient cause, for sleepless nights are seldom conducive to one's health. Of course I did not attend the wedding, which was said to have been a brilliant affair; the bride and the table looking beautifully, while the bridegroom, it was rumored, was pale and nervous, making the responses in a scarcely audible tone of voice.

The next morning, between eight and nine o'clock, as I was on my way to school, I met the travelling carriage of Capt. Thompson, which was taking the newly married couple to the dépôt. John was driving, while on the back seat, with his arm partly around his bride, was the doctor. My first impulse was not to look at them, but this act *pride* forbade, and very civilly I returned the nod of Dell, and the polite bow of the doctor, whose face turned crimson when he saw me. A moment more, and a turn of the road hid them from my view; then seating myself upon a large flat stone, beneath a tree, where were the remains of a *play-house* built by my own hands only the autumn before, I cried out loud, thinking myself the most wretched of beings, and wondering if ever any one before had such trouble as I! As nearly as I am able to judge, I was taking my first lesson in *love-sickness*; a kind of disease which is seldom dangerous, but, like the toothache, very disagreeable while it lasts. At least I found it so, and for weeks I pined away with a kind of sentimental melancholy, which now appears to me wholly foolish and ridiculous; for were I indeed the wife of Dr. Clayton, instead of Rosa Lee, this book would undoubtedly never have been written; while in place of bending over the inkstand this stormy morning, as I am doing, I should probably have been engaged in washing, dressing, scolding, and cuffing three or four little Claytons, or in the still more laudable employment of darning the *socks* and mending the *trousers* (a thing, by the way, which I can't do) of said little Claytons' sire; who, by this time, would, perhaps, have ceased to call me "his Rose," bestowing upon me the less euphonious title of "she," or "my woman?"

But not thus did I reason then. I only knew that I had lost him and was very unhappy. Many a long walk I took alone in the shadowy woods, singing to myself snatches of love-songs, particularly the one containing the following:

"I have not loved lightly—
I'll think of thee yet,
And I'll pray for thee nightly.
Till life's sun is set."

Somehow, too, I got the impression that my heart was all broken to pieces; and this fact satisfactorily settled, I began to take a melancholy pleasure in brooding over my *early death*, and thinking how Dr. Clayton would feel, when he heard the sad news! Almost every week I was *weighed*, feeling each time a good deal chagrined to find that I was not losing flesh as fast as a person in a decline would naturally do. In this state of affairs, I one day came across a little sketch of Hannah More, in which her early disappointment was described, and forthwith I likened myself to *her*, and taking courage from her example, I finally concluded that if I could not have the doctor I could at least write for the newspapers, and some day I might perhaps be able to make a *book*. This, I thought, would amply atone for my loss—an opinion which I hold still, for if ever I do see myself in a book, and the *reviews* let me alone, which, in consideration of all I have suffered, I am sure they will do, I shall consider it a most fortunate circumstance that Dell's $10,000, in prospect, proved a stronger temptation than my father's $5,000 divided by thirteen!

CHAPTER XI
BOSTON

The bridal party had returned from the Falls, and after spending a week or more at Capt. Thompson's the doctor took down his sign, boxed up his books, pills, powders, and *skeleton,* which some called his *'natomy,* while Dell packed up her six morning gowns with hosts of other finery, and then one day in August they started for Boston; where the doctor hoped for a wider field of labor, fully expecting to be aided by the powerful influence of Mr. Marshall, his wife's uncle, whose high station in the city he never once doubted. For this opinion he had, as the world goes, some well founded reasons; for not only did Dell often quote "my Aunt Marshall of Boston," but the lady herself also managed to impress the people of Pine District with her superiority over them, and her great importance at home. Notwithstanding that she frequently spent several weeks at Capt. Thompson's, she still could not endure the country—"the people were so vulgar—'twas so dull there, and no concerts, no operas, no theatres, no star actors, no parties, and more than all, no dear, delightful old Common, with its shaded walks and velvet grass."

Of course Dr. Clayton, in thinking of her city home, fancied to himself a princely mansion on Beacon street, overlooking the "dear, delightful old Common," and it is scarcely more than natural that his heart expanded with some little degree of pride, as he saw in contemplation the dinner parties, evening parties, soirées, etc., which he confidently expected to attend at said princely mansion. At first he had entertained a faint hope that he might possibly board with his new uncle; but this idea was instantly repelled by his wife, who did not seem so much inclined to talk of her "city Aunt" as formerly. So it was decided that they should for a time take rooms at the Tremont.

It was a dark, rainy night when they arrived, and as it was cold for the season, their rooms seemed cheerless and dreary, while, to crown all, the bride of six weeks was undeniably and decidedly out of temper; finding fault with everything, even to her handsome husband, who fidgeted and fussed, brought her the bottle of hair oil instead of cologne, stepped on her linen travelling dress with his muddy boot, spit in the grate instead of the spit-box, breathed in her face when he knew how she disliked tobacco, thought of Rosa Lee, and wondered if she were ever cross ("*nervous*" Dell called it), thought not, and *almost wished*—no, didn't wish anything, but as an offset thought of the $10,000, asked Dell how *old* her grandmother was, received for an answer, "I don't know and I don't care;" after which he went down stairs and regaled himself with a cigar until informed that supper was ready. Ate all alone, Dell refusing to go down—found her in tears on returning to his room, was told that she "was homesick, and wished she'd never come." *He* began to wish so too, but said "she'd feel better by and by." Sat for an hour or more cross-legged listening to the rain, and wondering if there *was* a cure for *nervousness*; finally went to bed and dreamed of Rosa Lee and the moonlight night, when they sat under the old oak tree, and of the thunder-storm when he gave her the little gold ring.

The next morning Mrs. Doctor Clayton was all smiles, and when, with her handsome eyes, shining hair, and tasteful wrapper, she descended to the breakfast-room, she attracted much attention, and more than one asked who she was, as they turned for a second glance. Nothing of this escaped the doctor, and with a glow of pride he forgot the vexations of the night previous, and gave vent to a mental *pshaw!* as he thought of his dream; for well he knew that the little plain-faced Rosa could not compare with the splendid woman at his side. Breakfast being over, he ventured to suggest the possibility of their soon receiving a call from her aunt; but Dell hastily replied, that such a thing was hardly probable, as her Aunt had her own affairs to attend to, and would not trouble herself about them. The doctor's hands went into his pockets, and his eyes went over inquiringly to his wife, who continued speaking rapidly, as if it were a painful duty which she felt compelled to perform.

"I don't know where you got the idea that Uncle Marshall is such a great man—not from me, certainly. But got it you have, and it's time you knew the truth. He is a good, honest man, I dare say, and respectable, too; but he is not one of the *ton*, by any means. Why, he's nothing more nor less than a *tailor*, and earns his bread from day to day."

"But his wife"—interrupted the doctor—"how happens it that she supports so much style?"

"Oh, that's easily accounted for," returned Dell. "They have no children—she is fond of dress, and spends all she can get for that purpose. She was an apprentice girl and learned her trade in my uncle's shop, and it is said, sometimes helps him now when he is pressed hard."

"Why did you never tell me this before?" asked the doctor, his brow growing thoughtful.

"And why should I tell you?" answered Dell. "What did I suppose you cared whether he were a *prince* or a *tailor*. You married me, I hope, for myself, and not for my relations."

The doctor thought of the ten thousand dollars just in time to force down the answer which sprang to his lips, and which was far better to be unuttered; so, in its place, he asked, "Where do they live?"

"On a back street, some distance from here," said Dell; adding, that their house, though small, was pleasant and neatly furnished. "It is well enough in the country to have a *city Aunt* on which to plume one's self," she continued, laughingly; "but here, where she is known, I do not intend having much intercourse with her, for a *physician* and *tailor* will, of course, occupy entirely different positions. However, I must treat her, at first, with a show of politeness, and if you are so disposed, we'll go round there and call this morning."

The doctor made no objections, and ere long they were walking over the stony pavement towards R—— street, which, as Dell had said, was rather out of the way. The house, however, at which they stopped, was a pleasant little cottage, with a nicely-kept yard in front, while the parlor, into which they were shown, was quite tastefully furnished. Mrs. Marshall herself answered their ring, appearing greatly surprised when she saw them, but not more so than Doctor Clayton, who would never have recognized the dashing lady of Pine District in the plain-looking woman, who, in a cheap calico wrapper, unbrushed hair, and checked apron, now sat before him— his Aunt. And yet he could not help thinking her far more agreeable than he had ever seen her before. The truth was, that Mrs. Marshall was one of those weak-minded women who, being nothing at home, strove to make amends by "making believe" abroad; assuming everything in the latter and nothing in the former condition. Consequently, she, who in the country was proud and overbearing, affecting ignorance of the most trivial matters, was, at home, a comparatively quiet, domestic woman; doing her own work, and, aside from being a little jealous and envious of her more fortunate neighbors, generally minding her own business.

After the first flutter of meeting the doctor was over, she became herself again, and set about entertaining them to the best of her ability, inviting them to stay with her to dinner, and urging as an inducement, that she was going to have "peaches and cream for dessert." But Dell rather haughtily declined, whereupon her aunt asked "when she would come round and spend the day?" saying, "she must do so before long, or they might not be in that house."

"Not be in this house! Why not?" asked Dell; and Mrs. Marshall replied, "Why, you know, we have always rented it of *Mr. Lee*, and he talks of selling it."

Instantly the doctor thought of Rosa, and involuntarily repeated the name—"Lee—Lee"——

"Yes," said Mrs. Marshall. "He has a brother in Meadow Brook, whom you may know."

"Is he wealthy?" asked the doctor.

"Why, ye-es, I s'pose so," said Mrs. Marshall, hesitatingly, as if unwilling to admit what she could not deny. "He lives in a big house on Beacon street—keeps his carriage—and they say the curtains in the front parlor cost a thousand dollars, and there are only two windows either."

Here she cast a deprecating glance towards her own very prettily embroidered muslin curtains, which probably cost about a hundredth part of that sum. Soon after, the newly married pair arose to go, the doctor feeling, in spite of himself, a little uncomfortable, though at what he hardly knew; for he would not acknowledge to himself that he was at all disappointed because Dell's uncle was a tailor instead of a millionaire, or because Rose's uncle lived on Beacon street, and sported curtains which cost a thousand dollars. This did not in the least affect Dell. *She* was his wife, and as such he would love and cherish her, ministering as far as possible to her wants, and overlooking the faults which he knew she possessed. Thus reasoned his better nature as he rode home, unconscious that the object of his thoughts was at that very moment misconstruing his silence into disappointment, and writing against him bitter things in her heart.

It was a peculiarity of Dell's to get angry when people least expected it, and then to *sulk* until such time as she saw fit to be gracious; so when they reached the Tremont, the doctor was astonished to find her *past speaking*; neither could he by any amount of coaxing elicit a word from her for more than an hour. At the end of that time, however, her pent-up wrath exploded; and, in angry tones, she accused him of feeling sorry that he had married her, because her uncle didn't prove to be a great man as he had supposed.

"I saw it all in your face when we were in the omnibus," said she; "it is of no use for you to deny it," adding, as she burst into tears, "but you cannot regret *your* marriage more than I do mine, and you needn't feel so smart either, for your father was a poor shoemaker in Maine, and when you went to college you rang the bell in part payment of your tuition."

This was a phase of married life for which the doctor was wholly unprepared, and during the first part of his wife's speech he stood confounded, but by the time she had finished, his mind was pretty well made up to *box her ears!* This, however, he did not do, though he bade her "shut up her head," repenting the harsh words the moment they were uttered, and having manliness enough to tell her so. Winding his arm around her, he talked to her calmly and rationally until she came out of her pet, and agreed "to make up." This process we leave to the imagination of the reader, only suggesting that no one who saw the handsome, loving pair, which half an hour after went down to dinner, would have dreamed of the dark cloud which had so recently lowered on their matrimonial horizon.

Here, wishing the doctor success in procuring patients, we leave them for a time, while we go back to Meadow Brook, where our house was one day thrown into a state of unusual excitement by the arrival of a letter from Aunt Charlotte, which contained an invitation for Anna and myself to spend the remainder of the autumn and the whole of the coming winter with her in the city. "Rosa," she wrote, "could go to school, while Anna would be introduced into society."

Of course we were greatly surprised, wondering what had come over our haughty aunt, who, as the reader will recollect, once spent a Thanksgiving with us. She must have changed, we thought, or else there was some mistake about the invitation. But this could not be, for there it was in black and white, written evidently in all sincerity, while added to it was a postscript from Uncle Joseph, who also joined in the request. That, if nothing more, proved that the invitation was genuine, for there was no mistaking my uncle's peculiar handwriting, and it only remained for us to decide whether we would accept or not. Anna and myself said "Yes," at once, and after a grave deliberation in grandma's room, the same conclusion was also reached by my parents, who, after giving us abundance of good advice, (not a word of which *I* heard, as I was wondering if I should ever meet the doctor and Dell), enjoined it upon Anna, first, never to dance at the parties which she might sometimes attend; second, never to wear her dresses indecently low, as some of the city girls did; and third, not to flirt with Herbert Langley. For this last injunction they probably fancied there was little need, it being now five years since she had seen him, and as they knew nothing of the perfumed, gilt-edged notes which lay hidden in her work-box, they very naturally supposed she had forgotten him. I thought so, too, for hers was the last letter, which had been unanswered for many months, and Anna, I knew, was far too proud to care for one who had forgotten her.

Occasionally we had heard of him through others, and it was always the same story, viz., that he was going down to a drunkard's grave, as fast as daily drams and weekly sprees could carry him; but if these reports produced any effect upon Anna, it was imperceptible. She was now twenty years of age, and was a fair, delicate looking girl, whom some called *proud*, others *cold*, and a few *selfish*; but this last I deny, for though she might appear so to strangers, there was not in our whole family, if I except brother Charlie, one who would sacrifice more of their own comfort for that of another than would my sister Anna; neither was there one whom I loved better, for though she was six years my senior, she always treated me as one nearer her own age, while I looked up to her as my oracle, thinking that whatever she did must necessarily be right.

When it was decided that we were to go, the next important, and to me, most delightful task, was the looking over and fixing up of our wardrobes, which kept us busy for some time. As Anna was to go into society, she of course had nearly all the new things, and much as I loved her, I must confess to a feeling of envy when I saw the black silk, blue merino, crimson and brown delaine, etc., which were purchased for her, while I was put off with her old dresses, "made over as good as new," but when I too, was presented with a blue merino by Charlie, who was now a clerk in one of the Meadow Brook stores, all my bad feelings left me, and with great alacrity I assisted in the preparations.

It was a lovely day late in October, that old Sorrel stood at the door ready to convey us to the dépôt. This was the first time I had really left home, and when I saw the tears in my mother's eyes, and the trembling of grandma's whole body; when Juliet held me so long to her bosom; when Lizzie and Carrie stole from me a hasty kiss, and then ran off to hide their grief; when Charlie and John, who were both clerks, came down to the dépôt to bid us good-bye, affecting to be very manly, notwithstanding that their chins quivered; and when, last of all, my father's fervent "God bless you, my children," resounded in my ears, I began to have a faint idea of the bitterness there is in parting, be it but for a few months. As we expected, we found our uncle's carriage at the dépôt in Boston, and ere long we had reached his house in Beacon street.

I remember the thrill of delight which I experienced, when first I entered my Aunt Charlotte's stylish house, and felt that it was to be my home, at least for a time. Everything was in perfect order, and for an instant I looked around me in silent wonder, almost forgetting to reply to the greeting of my aunt, who, in heavy brocade and long blue streamers depending from her head, met us kindly and hoped we were well. She had changed since last I saw her, but it was more the work of care than of time. She was much thinner, and the crow-tracks around her eyes were now decidedly deep-cut wrinkles, while her hair was here and there streaked with more than one silver thread.

My uncle was still the same good-humored, pleasant man, a little afraid of his wife, it may be, but evidently master of his own house. I glanced around for Herbert, but he was not there, and when, on Anna's account more than my own, I asked for him, I was told that he was down street, but would soon be home. Ringing a bell, my aunt bade the girl who appeared, "show the young ladies to their rooms," which proved to be a large airy chamber with a bedroom, dressing-room, and closet adjoining. After a hasty toilet we again returned to the parlor, where we found a tall, richly dressed young man, whom I should never have recognized as Herbert Langley. He was much altered from when I last saw him: there was a deep flush on his cheeks, which had reached even to his nose; while the eyes I had once thought so handsome were watery and unsteady in their movement. On the whole, however, he was still what some would call good-looking. He was sitting with his back to the door, but at the sound of our footsteps he turned around, and coming towards us, welcomed us most cordially to Boston, calling us "cousins," and claiming a cousin's privilege of kissing us—me *once*, and Anna *three* times, if not four.

She was a little piqued at his neglect in answering her last letter, and wishing to show proper resentment, she drew back rather haughtily, as if wondering how he dare "take such liberties." This he readily perceived, and instantly assuming an air quite as indifferent as her own, he turned towards me, hardly noticing her again, though it was easy to see that the reserve of both was merely affectation. That evening he was gone until nine o'clock, and when he entered the parlor, I noticed on the face of my aunt the same anxious expression which I remembered having seen there, when from our sitting-room window, she watched his return. But he was perfectly sober, and with a sigh of relief, she resumed her work; while he, coming round to my side, startled me by saying that "he had just met with a friend of mine—Dr. Clayton."

"Where did you see him?" asked Anna, while I bent lower over the book I was reading; for that name had still a power to move me strongly.

"Why," answered Herbert, "Tom Wilson, an old schoolmate of mine, boards at the Tremont, where he is now lying very sick. All the old physicians have given him up, and so he has employed this Dr. Clayton, who, it seems, has been at the same hotel for six weeks or more. I called on Tom this evening, and while I was there Dr. Clayton came in. In the course of our conversation he spoke of Meadow Brook, and then, as a matter of course, I said there were now in our family two young ladies from that place. When I mentioned Rosa's name, he turned almost as white as Tom himself, and if she were not so young, I should be inclined to think there was something between them. What do you say, coz?"

Here Anna came to my aid, saying, "Why, he's a *married man*, and his wife is with him at the Tremont."

"The dickens he is!" said Herbert, looking a little puzzled. Then turning to his mother, he added, "Mother, you ought to call on this Mrs. Clayton, for if she is an acquaintance of Anna and Rosa, they will very naturally wish to see her occasionally."

"She needn't call for me," said I, quickly.

"Nor for me, for I don't know her," rejoined Anna, while with a haughty toss of her head, Aunt Charlotte replied, that "her circle of acquaintances was quite large enough now, and she'd no idea of extending it by taking in people about whom she knew nothing."

I know it was very wrong in me, but I could not help straightening up a little in my chair as I wondered what the proud Dell Thompson would say if she knew that the despised Rosa Lee was living as an equal in a family which looked down upon her and her husband as *nobodies*. I was roused from my reverie by my aunt's asking Herbert in a low tone, "how *Ada* was to-night," and glancing towards him, I fancied that said *Ada*, whoever she might be, was to him not a very pleasant subject just then, for his brow darkened visibly, while he replied, "I never once thought to inquire, but I dare say she's no worse, or she would have sent for you post haste."

There was a moment's silence, and then my aunt again spoke, "Herbert, I wish you'd do better. You know how lonely she is, and how much she must necessarily feel your neglect."

"Fudge!" was his answer, as he folded his hands over his head, and leaning back in his chair, looked straight into the astral lamp.

That night, when Anna and I were alone in our room, the former sat for a time in deep thought, saying, when I at last told her the clock was striking eleven, "I wonder who *Ada* is!"

I wondered so, too, and my interest was not at all diminished when the next morning, at the breakfast table, Aunt Charlotte said to her son, "Herbert, I shall be busy this morning making arrangements about a school for Rosa, and I wish you'd go in and see Ada, will you?"

"Yes, yes, I will," said he, rather impatiently, adding, "and if I don't find her any better, I mean to assume the responsibility of discharging that old superannuated *greeny* who attends her, and install Dr. Clayton in his place. I took quite a fancy to him, and I'm going to give him my patronage!"

"Oh, I wish you would!" I exclaimed involuntarily; for in spite of the wrong he had done me, I cherished no feeling of animosity towards him.

Then, again, I had heard that it was sometimes very difficult for a young physician to obtain much practice in a strange place with no one to help him, and I thought, perhaps, Herbert's "patronage" might be of some avail.

"I see," said Herbert laughingly, "there *has* been something, and though he is a married man, you still feel an interest in him, and want him to succeed; all right, and I'll do what I can to help him; for I verily believe he'll get Tom on his legs again in spite of what the temperance folks say about his blood's being all turned into whisky!"

At these words a shadow passed over Aunt Charlotte's face, but it was soon chased away by the next remark of Herbert, which was, "Ain't you glad, mother, I reformed before I got to be as bad as Tom? Why, girls (addressing Anna and me), I haven't drank a drop since—since—how long is it mother, since I left off"—*drinking* he could not say, so he finally added, "left off *imbibing* occasionally?"

There was a look of happiness on that mother's face, as she replied, "Almost a year."

Yes, 'twas almost a year since her son had tasted ardent spirits, and had she not good reasons for thinking he would never fall again? Assured of this fact, how proud she would have been of her only boy; for, aside from this great error, he possessed many noble, generous qualities; and during my stay in Boston, I found that, in spite of his well-known habits, he was a pretty general favorite. Oh, how lovingly my aunt looked after him when he went out, and how earnestly she watched him when he came in, and all the while she was tempting him beyond what most men could bear; for regularly on her dinner-table appeared either porter, champagne, or madeira, one taste of which would set him all on fire. But, unfortunately, she belonged to that class of fashionable people who deem the wine-bottle a necessary appendage to the dinner table, and if, in the sequel, her son should fill a drunkard's grave, would there be any just cause why, in her anguish, she should murmur at Providence for having dealt with her thus harshly? Ought she not rather to blame herself for having thus daily tempted him to sin by placing before him what she well knew was sure to work his ruin?

But to our story. We were at dinner when Herbert came in from his morning ramble, and taking his accustomed seat at the table, he said to his mother, "I called on Ada as you desired, and found her sitting up in a rose-colored dressing-gown, which she thinks very becoming to her, I know, for she sat directly opposite the mirror, and I should not dare tell how many times I caught her casting admiring glances at herself."

Aunt Charlotte frowned, while Herbert, turning to me, continued— "Miss Montrose is so much better that I don't believe I can patronize your doctor in that quarter, but I'll do something for him—break my leg, may be—or have the delirium tremens."

This species of jesting seemed to be a kind of mania with Herbert, for almost every day of his life he referred to his former habit of drinking, greatly to the annoyance of his mother, who, on the occasion just mentioned, turned slightly pale, while Anna looked down upon the carpet and sighed. Thinking this as favorable an opportunity for making inquiries concerning Ada Montrose as I should have, I asked Herbert who she was. His mother's lips moved as if she would answer the question, but ere she could speak, Herbert replied, "She's a Georgia lady, a great coquette, who is spending the winter here with a fortieth cousin. Some call her handsome, and I believe mother thinks her beautiful, but if Anna paid as much attention to her toilet and dressed as elegantly as Ada Montrose, she would, in my opinion, look far better."

'Twas the first compliment he had paid Anna since our arrival, and it brought a bright flush to her usually marble cheek; for Herbert Langley possessed a strange power over my sister, which she did not try to resist. I fancied that my aunt was not quite pleased with Herbert's comparing Miss Montrose to Anna, but ere she could frame any answer, he asked us if we would like to attend the theatre that evening. Notwithstanding my father's hostility to *circuses*, I did not remember having heard him say much against *theatres*, and so I answered quickly, "Oh, yes, Anna, let's go. I want to see what they do."

And so, with my aunt's permission, it was settled that we should go, and at the usual hour I found myself in the National Theatre, which was densely crowded, for a celebrated actress appeared that night for the last time in Boston. Perfectly bewildered, I followed Herbert and Anna to my uncle's box, which commanded a fine view of the stage, and then, when I became a little accustomed to the glare of lights and the hum of voices, which in some degree reminded me of that never-to-be-forgotten *circus* of Cousin Will memory, I ventured to look over the sea of faces, half starting from my seat as I recognized among the crowd Dr. Clayton and his wife, the latter appearing to be looking at us through what I thought resembled the dice boxes of a backgammon board tied together, but which I soon learned was an opera-glass. The doctor was paler and thinner than when I last saw him, and it was with more than one pang that I watched him as, from time to time, he cast a glance of pride at the splendid-looking woman at his side, who attracted considerable attention, and at whom, in the course of the evening, more than one glass was levelled.

Ere long my attention was diverted from them to a tall, dark, and rather peculiar-looking gentleman, who entered the box at our right. Sinking into a seat, he abandoned himself apparently, to his own thoughts, which could not have been very pleasant; for his forehead, which was high and white, seemed at times to be one mass of wrinkles, while his eyes, large, black, and deepset in his head, alternately flashed with anger and vexation. I am not much of a physiognomist, but there was in the face of the stranger something which at once attracted and riveted my attention. He was not handsome, like Dr. Clayton—nay, I am not sure but many would call him ugly, but I did not; and, somehow, I felt certain that no girl of *fourteen* had ever wept over his fickleness, for he looked the soul of honor and integrity. Gradually, too, as the play proceeded, the expression which I had at first observed passed away; his dark eyes lighted up; and when, at last, a bright smile broke over his face, I pronounced him far better looking than the doctor, who was fast losing ground in my good opinion.

The play was the "Lady of Lyons," and though I was familiar with the story, I seemed now to hear it for the first time; so fully did I enter into the feelings of the heroine, Pauline, whose distress I could not believe was feigned. All was real to me; and I can now scarcely repress a smile, as I recall to mind how I must have looked, standing there with flushed cheeks, clasped hands, staring eyes, and lips slightly apart, drinking in every word of the actress. Once Anna pulled my dress, whispering to me, "Do sit down, Rosa; they are all looking at you, and Mrs. Clayton is laughing and pointing you out to her husband."

"I didn't care for Dell Thompson, or the doctor either," and so I said, while at the same time I glanced towards the stranger, whose eyes were fixed upon me with an expression I could not fathom.

He was not making fun of me, I was sure of that; but as if there were a magnetic influence in his look, which I could not resist, I dropped into my seat, and remained motionless until the closing scene, where, with a piercing shriek, Pauline rushed into the arms of her husband. Then there came over me the same sensation which I had experienced years before in the old schoolhouse at Meadow Brook. Everything grew dark around me, and with a faint cry I fell across Anna's lap. I was not entirely unconscious, for I have a dim remembrance of being led from the heated room, the close atmosphere of which had probably helped to bring on my faintness. The cool air outside revived me in a measure, but it was the mesmeric touch of two large, warm hands which fully restored to me my faculties, and, looking up, I saw bending over me the gentleman in whom I had been so much interested. Dr. Clayton, too, was there, looking worried and anxious, but instinctively leaving me to the care of the stranger, who seemed to know exactly what to do.

"You are better now, I think," said he, gazing down upon me with his deep black eyes, and adding, with the same peculiar smile I had before observed, "Miss — —'s acting seldom receives so genuine a compliment as this. I imagine she ought to feel flattered."

At this moment a loud stamping and hallooing came to my ear, and, pulling Anna's shawl, Herbert exclaimed, "Come, let's go in again; they are calling back the dancing-girl, and I wouldn't miss it for anything. Come, Rose, you want to see it all, and we'll stand right by the door."

I felt perfectly well, and started to follow him, when something in the stranger's face arrested me, for it seemed to say, "I wouldn't go." But he did not speak, and bowing to me very politely, he walked away, while I went after Herbert and Anna, reaching them just in time to witness a part of Mlle. Lisette's dance, which seemed to me a good deal like the performance of the *Circus girl*, only "a little more so;" and I felt certain that Cousin Will, had he been there, would have pronounced her superior even to the boasted *Albany girl*!

When at last it was over, and we were again leaving the room, Dr. Clayton, as if seeing me for the first time, offered me his hand, and in a low tone expressed to me his pleasure that I was to be in the city during the winter; adding, as he cast a furtive glance towards his wife, "You'll come and see me often, won't you; for I am very lonely?"

For an instant I felt a thrill of pride, to know that there was yet aught in me which could interest *him*, but 'twas only for a moment, and then there came up before me thoughts of the stranger, and owing to some unknown influence, which I shall not attempt to explain, the doctor's power over me was from that moment at an end; and though I still liked him, it was as I would like any friend who evinced a regard for me.

Of the stranger I often thought, wondering who he was and whence he came; but no one knew, and all that I could learn was, that Herbert saw him the next morning standing on the steps of the Revere House, and chancing the same afternoon to be at the Worcester dépôt, he saw him enter the cars bound for Albany, and heard from one of the bystanders that he was a Georgian, and had probably come to Boston after "*a runaway nigger!*" Being a true born daughter of freedom-loving Massachusetts, this intelligence of course had the effect of cooling my ardor somewhat, and wishing in my heart that every one of his negroes would run away, I banished him for a time from my mind.

After many inquiries, and much consultation with her particular friend Mrs. Ashley, my aunt at last decided to send me to Madam — —'s school; while Anna, after a two weeks' siege with dress-makers, was introduced into society, where, if she was not a reigning belle, she was at least a favorite; and more than once I heard the most flattering compliments bestowed upon *her*, while it was thought to be "a pity that her sister was so *plain* and unpretending in her appearance!"

CHAPTER XII
ADA MONTROSE

Aunt Charlotte, Anna, and myself were sitting in the parlor one morning, about four weeks after our arrival in Boston, when the door-bell rang, and the servant ushered in a young lady, who I readily guessed was Ada Montrose, for there was about her an air of languor, as if she had just arisen from a sick bed. All doubt on this point was soon settled by my aunt's exclaiming, as she hastened to greet her, "Why, Ada, my child, this is a surprise. How do you do?"

The voice which answered was, I thought, the sweetest and most musical I had ever heard, and yet there was in it something which made me involuntarily shudder. I do not know that I believe in *presentiments*, but sure I am that the moment I heard the tones of Ada Montrose's voice, and looked upon her face, I experienced a most disagreeable sensation, as if, in some way or other, *she* would one day cross my path. She was beautiful— so beautiful, that it seemed impossible to detect a single fault either in her features or complexion, though there was in the former an expression which made me feel, when her eyes were fixed upon me, much as the bird must when charmed by the rattlesnake. Do what I would, I could not rid myself of the idea that she was my *evil genius*, though how in any way she, a proud southern belle, could ever affect me, a plain school-girl of fourteen, was difficult to tell. She was, as I afterwards learned, twenty-two years of age, but being rather diminutive in size, and affecting a great deal of childish simplicity, she passed for four or five years younger; and, indeed, she herself gave her age as eighteen—looking up to Anna, who was really two years her junior, as a very ancient, matronly sort of person, who was supposed to remember as far back as the flood.

Divesting herself of her warm wrappings, which she left upon the floor, and shaking out her long curls, she informed my aunt that she had come to spend the day, saying, by way of apologizing for not having sent her word, that "she had ventured to come without an invitation, she felt herself so perfectly at home."

Of course Aunt Charlotte was delighted, and after assuring her of the fact, she suddenly remembered our presence, and introduced us to the lady as "Mr. Lee's nieces from the country." Not an instant did the large brownish black eyes rest on me, for I was of little importance compared with Anna, who the Thursday night previous had made her first appearance in society, where her sweet face and fresh, unstudied manners had produced something of a sensation, which had undoubtedly reached the ear of the reigning belle. What her thoughts were as she scanned my sister from head to foot, I do not know; but as I watched her, I fancied I could detect an expression of mingled scorn and surprise that one so unassuming should awaken an interest in those who were accustomed to pay her homage. When she had satisfied herself with Anna's personal appearance, she gave me a hasty glance, and then drawing from her reticule a fanciful mat which she was crotcheting, she leaned back among the soft cushions of her chair, and commenced talking to my aunt in a very artless, childish manner, never noticing us in the least, except once when she asked me to pull the bell rope, which was much nearer to her than me. Several times I fancied she seemed to be listening for something, and when at last I heard Herbert's voice in the hall and saw the deepening flush on her cheek, I was sure that she felt more than a common interest in him.

In his usual good-natured, off-hand way he entered the room, tossing into my lap a letter from brother Charlie, and telling Anna that her *beau* hadn't yet written; then, as his eye fell upon Ada, he started back in evident surprise. Soon recovering himself, however, he said, as he took the little snowflake of a hand, which she offered him—

"Why, Ad, who knew you were here?"

"Not you, or you would have come sooner, I reckon;" said she, looking up in his face in a confiding kind of way, which brought a frown to Anna's brow.

"Maybe I shouldn't have come so soon," he replied laughingly, at the same time stealing a sidelong glance at Anna.

"Here, sit right down by me," said Miss Montrose, as she saw him looking for a seat. "I want to scold you for not calling on me oftener when I was sick. You don't know how neglected I felt. Why didn't you come, hey?"

And she playfully pulled his hair, allowing her hand to remain some time among his wavy locks. This was a kind of coquetry entirely new to me, and I looked on in amazement, while Anna, more disturbed than she was willing to acknowledge, left the room. When she was gone, Ada said, letting her hand fall from Herbert's head to his arm, "Tell me, is that the *Lee girl*, who attracted so much attention at Mrs. G——'s party?"

There was a look of gratified pride on Herbert's face as he answered, "Yes—the same—don't you think her pretty?"

They had probably forgotten my presence—Ada most certainly had, or else she did not care; for she replied, "Pretty enough for some tastes I suppose, but she lacks polish and refinement. Is she at all related to you?"

"My step-father's niece, that's all," replied Herbert, while Ada quickly rejoined in a low tone, "Then, of course, *I* shan't have to cousin her."

"Probably not," was Herbert's answer, which I interpreted one way and Ada another.

Her next remark was a proposal that Herbert should that afternoon take her out to ride; but to this he made some objection; whereupon she pretended to be angry, leaning back on the sofa and muttering that "she didn't believe he cared a bit for her, and he might as well confess it at once."

Here the dinner bell rang, and offering his arm to the pouting beauty, Herbert led her to the dining-room, where she was soon restored to good humor by my aunt, who lavished upon her the utmost attention, humoring every whim, and going so far as to prepare for her *four* different cups of black tea, which had been ordered expressly for her, and to which she objected as being too hot, or too cold—too weak or too strong. It took but a short time to show that she was a *spoiled baby*, good natured only when all the attention was lavished upon her, and when her wishes were paramount to all others.

Dinner being over, Herbert did not, as was his usual custom, return to the parlor; but taking his hat he went out into the street, in spite of his mother's whispered effort to keep him at home. This, of course, vexed the little lady, and after thrumming a few notes upon the piano, she announced her intention of returning home, saying that "she wished she had not come." At this moment the door-bell rang, and some young ladies came in to call upon Anna. They seemed surprised at finding Ada there, and after inquiring for her health, one of them said, "Do tell us Ada, who that gentleman was that came and went so slily, without our ever seeing him? Mrs. Cameron says he was from Georgia, and that is all we know about him. Who was he?"

Ada started, and turning slightly pale, replied, "What do you mean? I've seen no gentleman from Georgia. Where was he? and when was he here?"

"As much as three weeks or more ago," returned Miss Marvin. "He stopped at the Revere House, and Mrs. Cameron, who boards there, got somewhat acquainted with him."

"Mrs. Cameron!" repeated Ada, turning alternately red and white. "And pray what did she say?"

I fancied there was a spice of malice in Miss Marvin's nature; at least, she evidently wished to annoy Ada, for she replied, "She said he was *ugly looking*, though quite *distingué*; that he came in the afternoon, while she was in the public parlor talking with a lady about *you* and your engagement with Mr. Langley!"

"The hateful old thing!" muttered Ada, while Anna turned white as marble, and Miss Marvin continued—"When the lady had gone he begged pardon for the liberty, but asked her if she knew you. Of course, she told him she did, and gave him any further information which she thought would please him."

"Of course she did—the meddling widow!" again interrupted Ada; after which Miss Marvin proceeded—"Mrs. Cameron didn't mean to do anything wrong, for how could she guess that 'twould affect him in any way to know you were engaged?"

"And she told *him* I was engaged! It isn't so. I ain't," exclaimed Ada, while the angry tears dropped from her glittering eyes.

"What does that mean then?" asked Miss Marvin, laughingly, pointing at the ring on Ada's finger.

Her first impulse was to wrench it from her hand and cast it from her, but she remembered herself in time, and growing quite calm, as if to attribute her recent agitation to a different cause, she said; "I wish people would attend to their own affairs, and let mine alone. Suppose I am engaged—is that a reason why Mrs. Cameron should discuss the matter with strangers? But what else did she say? And where is the gentleman now?"

"Gone home," answered Miss Marvin, glancing mischievously at her companions. "He went the next morning, and she said he looked very much disturbed, either at your illness or your engagement, the former probably, and that is why I think it strange that he didn't stop to see you; though maybe he did."

"No, he didn't," chimed in Miss Marvin's sister, "for don't you know she said he went to the theatre?"

All this time my interest in the unknown Georgian had been increasing, and at this last remark I forgot myself entirely, and started forward, exclaiming, "Yes, he was there, I saw him and spoke with him too."

The next moment I sank back upon the ottoman, abashed and mortified, while Ada gave me a withering glance, and said scornfully, "*You* spoke to him! And pray, what did you say?"

An explanation of what I said, would, I knew, oblige me to confess the fainting fit, of which I was somewhat ashamed, and so I made no reply; nor was any expected, I think, for without waiting for my answer, Ada said to Miss Marvin, "Mrs. Cameron, of course, learned his name, even if she had to ask it outright."

"Yes, she made inquiries of the clerk, who wouldn't take the trouble of looking on the book, but said he believed it was *Field*, or something like that," returned Miss Marvin.

As if uncertainty were now made sure, Ada turned so white that in some alarm her young friends asked what they should do for her; but she refused their offers of aid, saying, "it was only the heat of the room, and she should soon feel better."

"And is it the heat of the room which affects *you*, Miss Lee?" asked one of the girls, observing for the first time the extreme pallor of Anna's face.

"Only a headache," was her answer, as she pressed her hand upon her forehead.

She was fearfully pale, and I knew it was no common thing which had thus moved her, and when not long afterwards the young ladies left us, I was glad, for I felt that both she and Ada needed to be alone. The moment they were gone Anna left the parlor, while I, frightened by the agonized expression of her face, soon followed her; but the door of our room was locked, and it was in vain I called on her to admit me, for she only answered in a voice choked with tears, "Go away, Rosa; I would rather be alone."

So I left her and returned to the parlor, where I found Ada weeping passionately, while my aunt, who had not been present during the conversation which had so affected her, was trying in vain to learn the cause of her grief.

"Nothing much," was all Ada would say, except that "she wanted to go home."

In the midst of our excitement, Herbert came in. He had repented of his ungracious refusal to ride with Ada, and now the carriage stood at the door, but she refused, saying petulantly, when urged by my aunt to go, that "if she couldn't ride when she wanted to, she wouldn't ride at all."

"Where's Anna? she'll go, I know," said Herbert, glancing around the room, and adding in a low tone, which reached my ear only, "and I'd far rather she would."

When I explained to him that she had a headache, and did not wish to be disturbed, he exclaimed, "What ails all the girls to-day. Anything the matter with you, Rose? If there isn't, put on your bonnet and I'll show you the city, for I am resolved upon riding with somebody."

As my aunt made no objection, I was soon ready and seated by the side of Herbert, in the light vehicle, which he drove himself. I think he exerted himself to be agreeable, for I never saw him appear so well before, and in my heart I did not blame my poor sister for liking him, as I was sure she did, while at the same time I wondered how he could fancy Ada Montrose. As if divining my thoughts, he turned suddenly towards me and said, "Rosa, how do you like Ada?"

Without stopping to reflect, I replied promptly, *"Not at all."*

"Frankly spoken," said he, and then for several minutes he was silent, while I was trying to decide in my own mind whether or not he was offended, and I was about to ask him, when he turned to me again, saying, "We are engaged—did you know it?"

I replied that I had inferred as much from the conversation which I had heard between her and Miss Marvin, saying further, for his manner emboldened me, that "I was surprised, for I did not think her such an one as he would fancy."

"Neither is she," said he, again relapsing into silence. At last, rousing up, he continued, "I must talk to somebody, and as you seem to be a sensible girl, I may as well make a clean breast, and tell you all about it. Ada came up here from Georgia last spring, and the moment mother saw her, she picked her out for her future daughter-in-law. I don't know why it is, but mother has wanted me to get married ever since I began to shave. I believe she thinks it will make me steady; but I am steady enough now, for I haven't drank a drop in almost a year. I should though, if Ada Montrose was my wife. But that's nothing to the point. Mother saw her and liked her. *I* saw her, and liked her well enough at first, for she is beautiful, you know, and every man is more or less attracted by that. They say, too, that she is wealthy, and though I would as soon marry a poor girl as a rich one, provided I liked her, I shall not deny but her money had its influence with me, to a certain extent. And then, too, it was fun to get her away from the other young men who flocked around her, like bees round a honey jar. But, to make a long story short, we got engaged—Heaven only knows how; but engaged we were, and then"—— Here he paused, as if nearing a painful subject, but soon resuming the thread of his story, he continued; "And then I stopped writing to Anna, for I would not be dishonorable. Do you think she felt it?"

The question was so unexpected, that I was thrown quite off my guard, and replied, "Of course, she did; who wouldn't feel mortified to have their letters unanswered?"

"'Twas wrong, I know," said he. "I ought to have been man enough to tell her how it was, and I did begin more than a dozen letters, but never finished them. Do you think Anna likes me now, or could like me, if I was not engaged, and she knew I'd never get drunk again?"

Could he have seen her when first she learned that his affections were given to another, he would have been sufficiently answered, but he did not, and it was not for me, I thought, to enlighten him; so I replied evasively, after which he continued, "As soon as I was engaged to Ada, she began to exact so much attention from me, acting so *silly*, and appearing so ridiculous that I got sick of it, and now my daily study is how to rid myself of her; but I believe I've commenced right. Can I make a confidant of you, and feel sure you'll not betray me to any one, unless it is Anna?"

I hardly knew how to answer, for if it was anything wrong which he meditated, I did not wish to be in the secret, and so I told him; but it made no difference, for he proceeded to say, "I shall never marry Ada Montrose, never; neither would it break her heart if I shouldn't for she's more than half tired of me now."

I thought of the dark stranger, and felt that he was right, but I said nothing, and he went on; "Sometimes I thought I'd go up to Meadow Brook, tell Anna all about it, ask her to marry me, and so settle the matter at once; but then I did not know but she might have grown up raw, awkward, and disagreeable, so I devised a plan by which I could find out. Mother would burn her right hand off I believe, to save me from a drunkard's grave, and when I wish to win her consent to any particular thing, all I have to do is to threaten her with the wine-cup."

"Oh, Herbert! how can you?" I exclaimed, for I was inexpressibly shocked.

"It's a way I've got into," said he, laughing at my rueful face. "And when I suggested that Anna should spend the winter here, I hinted to the old lady that if she didn't consent, I'd go off with a party of young men on a hunting excursion. Of course she yielded at once, for she well knew that if I joined my former boon companions, I should fall.

"And so we are indebted to you for our winter in Boston," said I, beginning to see things in a new light.

"Why no, not wholly," he answered; "mother consented much easier than I supposed she would. The fact is, she's changed some since she was at Meadow Brook. She's joined the Episcopal Church, and though that in my estimation don't amount to much, of course, she has to do better, for it wouldn't answer for a professor to put on so many airs."

As the daughter of a deacon, I felt it incumbent upon me to reprove the thoughtless young man, but it did no good, for he proceeded to say, "It's all true, and there's only one denomination who are sincere in what they profess, and that's the Methodist. They carry their religion into their whole life, while the Episcopalians, Presbyterians, and Baptists sit on different sides of the fence, and quarrel like fun about High Church and Low, Old School and New, close communion and open communion, and all that sort of thing. I tell you, Rose, if I am ever converted—and mother thinks I will be—I shall be a roaring Methodist, and ride the Circuit at once!"

I was unused to the world, and had never heard any one speak thus lightly of religion; but I knew not what to say, so I kept silence, while he continued, "But I am rambling from my subject. Mother *is* a different woman, if she does *read* her prayers; and as she has never known a word about my writing to Anna, she consented to her coming, without much trouble, saying she would try to make it pleasant for her, and proposing that you too should accompany her, and go to school. You can't imagine how delighted I was to find Anna what she is, and from the moment I met her in the parlor, Ada Montrose's destiny, so far as I am concerned, was decreed; that is, if I can secure your sister; and I think I shall have no difficulty in so doing, for notwithstanding her affected coolness, it is easy to see that I am not indifferent to her."

It was in vain for me to argue that he was doing Ada a great wrong, for he insisted upon saying that he was not. "She hadn't soul enough," he said, "to really care for any one, and even if she had, he would far rather commit suicide at once, than be yoked to her for life; she was so silly, so fawning, so flat!"

It was nearly dark when we reached home, and as the lamps were not yet lighted in the parlor, I went immediately to my room, where I found Anna lying upon the sofa, with her face buried in the cushions. I knew she was not asleep, though she would not answer me, until I had thrice repeated her name. Then lifting up her head, she turned towards me a face as white as ashes, while she said, motioning to a little stool near her, "Sit down by me, Rosa, I must talk to some one, or my heart will break."

Taking the seat, I listened while she told me how much she had loved Herbert Langley—how she had struggled to overcome that love when she thought he had slighted her, and how when she saw him daily in his own home, it had returned upon her with all its former strength, until there came to her the startling news that he was engaged to another. "I cannot stay here," said she. "I am going home. I have written to mother—see," and she pointed to a letter which lay upon the table, and which she bade me read. It was a strange, rambling thing, saying that "she should die if she staid longer in Boston, and that she was coming back to Meadow Brook."

"You can't send this, Anna," said I, at the same time tossing it into the grate, where a bright coal fire was burning.

At this bold act of mine she expressed no emotion whatever, but simply remarked, "I can write another or go without writing."

"And you indeed love Herbert so much?" I said.

"Better than my life—and why shouldn't I?" she replied. "He is all that is noble and good."

"Suppose he proves to be a drunkard?" I queried, looking her steadily in the face, while she answered simply, "And what then? Would that be harder to endure than a life without him?"

I know not whether the spirit of prophecy was upon me, or whether I felt a dim foreshadowing of my sister's wretched future, but from some cause or other, I proceeded to picture to her the sorrows of a drunkard's home and the utter degradation of a drunkard's wife, while she listened shudderingly, saying when I had finished, "God save me from such a fate!"

There was the sound of footsteps in the hall, and Herbert's voice was heard at the door, asking for admittance. He had often visited us in our room, and now, without consulting Anna's wishes, I bade him enter, going out myself and leaving them alone. What passed between them I never knew, but the supper table waited long for Herbert, and was finally removed, my aunt thinking he had gone out, "to see Ada, perhaps," she said, and then she asked me how I liked her, telling me she was to be Herbert's wife, and that she hoped they would be married early in the spring.

I made her no direct reply, for I felt I was acting a double—nay, a treble part, in being thus confided in by *three*, but I could not well help it, and I hoped, by betraying neither party, to atone in a measure for any deceit I might be practising. After that night there was a great change in Anna, who became so lively and cheerful that nearly all observed it, while

Herbert's attentions to her, both at home and abroad, were so marked as to arouse the jealously of Ada, who, while she affected to scorn the idea of being supplanted by "that awkward Lee girl," as she called her, could not wholly conceal her anxiety lest "the Lee girl" should, after all, win from her her betrothed husband. Something of this she told my aunt, who, knowing nothing of the true state of affairs, and having the utmost confidence in her son's honor, laughed at her fears, telling her once in my hearing, though she was unaware of my proximity, that, "however much Herbert might flirt with Anna, he had been too well brought up to think of marrying one so far beneath him."

"But he does think of it—I most know he does," persisted Ada, beginning to cry; "and I wish you'd send her home, won't you?"

I did not hear my aunt's reply, but with Ada, my own heart echoed, "send her home," for much as I liked Herbert, I shrank from the thought of committing my gentle sister's happiness to his keeping, and secretly I resolved upon writing to my father and acquainting him with the whole; but, alas! I deferred it from day to day, until it was too late.

CHAPTER XIII
THE FLIGHT

One bright morning about the middle of January, Herbert announced his intention of going to Worcester with Anna, who, he said, wished to visit the Lunatic Asylum, and as a young physician of his acquaintance had just commenced practising there, it would be a good opportunity for them to go over the building. To this my aunt made no objection, merely proposing that Ada, too, should go. Afterwards I remembered the peculiar look in Herbert's eye, as he replied "Oh fie! mother, Ada's nerves are not strong enough to endure it. She can go with me some other time."

Accordingly, when breakfast was over, Anna went up to her room to make the necessary preparations for her ride, while I stood by and gave her whatever assistance she needed. I observed that every article which belonged to her was put in its proper place, but I gave it no further heed, though I did wonder why she kissed me so often, turning back even after she had reached the door to bid me another good-bye. Slowly the day passed away and night came on, dark, cold, and stormy. Even now, as I write, I can recall to mind the gloom which pervaded my spirits, as I listened to the sound of the sleet and hail, which drove past the window, where I had watched so long for their return. Seven, eight, nine, ten, was rung from more than one church dome, and then we gave them up, for the shrill whistle of the last train on which they would be likely to come, had long since sounded in our ears.

"They must have stayed somewhere; don't you think so?" said my aunt, addressing her husband, who, manlike, was not in the least alarmed, but sat conning his evening paper, nearer asleep than awake.

"Of course they have," said he, looking up at his wife's inquiry. "I wouldn't come in this storm, if I were in their places."

That night I watered my pillow with tears, scarcely knowing why I wept, save that I felt oppressed with a sense of desolation, as if Anna was gone from me forever. The next day came and went, but it brought no tidings of the missing pair, and half unconscious of what she was doing, my aunt went from room to room, sometimes weeping and again brightening up, as she enumerated the many things which might have prevented their return. At evening, Ada came in, and my aunt immediately began urging her to spend the night. This she did willingly, seeming very anxious concerning the absence of Herbert, and feeling, I was sure, a little suspicious that I might know more of his whereabouts than I chose to tell, for once, when we were alone, she turned towards me and very haughtily asked, if "I had any idea where they were?"

"None, whatever," said I, and she continued—

"Has it never occurred to you that this Anna Lee manifested altogether too marked a preference for a gentleman whom she knew to be engaged?"

"The preference was mutual," I replied. "Herbert liked Anna, and Anna liked Herbert."

"And they have gone off to consummate that liking by a marriage," interrupted Ada.

"I do not know that they have," I returned; "but such a termination of affairs would not surprise me."

She was very pale, and there were tears in her eyes, but I thought they arose more from a sense of mortification than from any real love which she bore for Herbert Langley, and so I did not pity her as I should otherwise have done. The next morning at breakfast both she and my aunt (particularly the latter) looked weary and worn, as if neither had slept at all during the night. My uncle, on the contrary, seemed to be unmoved. He probably had an opinion of his own, but whatever it was he kept it to himself, merely saying that if the eastern mail brought no letter he would go in quest of them himself. I knew I could not study in my present excitement, and so I asked permission to remain at home. Stationing myself at the window, I watched anxiously for the return of Herod, who, as usual, had been sent to the office. He came at last, bringing his pocket full of letters, two of which were for me, one postmarked Meadow Brook, and the other Albany! With a trembling hand I tore open the latter, which was in my sister's handwriting. Glancing at the signature, my fears were confirmed, for there stood the name of "Anna Langley" in Herbert's bold dashing hand!

"*She* had refused to write it thus," he said, in a postscript, "and so he had done it for her."

The letter contained no apology from either for what they had done, but merely informed me of the fact that instead of stopping in Worcester, they had gone straight on to Albany, which they reached about six o'clock, going to the Delevan House, where in less than an hour they were husband and wife; Herbert's old comrade, Tom Wilson, accompanying them, and being a witness of the ceremony. What affected me more unpleasantly than all the rest, was the derisive manner in which Herbert spoke of Ada.

"Give her my love," he said, "and tell her not to feel too badly. I'd like well enough to marry her, too, but under the present laws a man can't have two wives, unless he joins the Mormons. Maybe I shall do that sometime, and then I'll remember *her*!"

Of his mother he wrote differently, and though there was no cringing, no acknowledgment of wrong, he spoke of her kindly and respectfully, saying, "he hoped she would love his Anna for his sake."

Of course I could not tell Ada what he said of her, neither was it necessary, for guessing the truth from my face, she came up softly behind me, and looking over my shoulder, read every word until she came to the message intended for her. Then stamping her little foot, she exclaimed passionately, "The villain, to insult me thus! As if *I*, sprung from the best blood in Georgia, would stoop to become a rival of that low-born country girl. No! By this act Herbert Langley has shown that he is all unworthy of me, and I rejoice in my escape, while I give him much joy with his highly refined and polished bride."

All my Lee temper, which is considerable, was roused, and turning towards the lady, I exclaimed, "My sister, Miss Montrose, is as good as *you*, aye, or as Herbert Langley either, and the news of her marriage with *him* will carry sorrow to our home at Meadow Brook, where they will say she has literally thrown herself away."

"Very likely," returned Ada, sarcastically. "It is quite probable that a *poor laborer* will object to his daughter's marrying into one of the first families in Boston."

"He isn't a poor laborer," I replied, "and even if he were, he *would* object to his daughter's marrying a drunkard, for such Herbert Langley has been and such he will be again."

A deep groan came from the white lips of my aunt, and for the first time since Ada's outbreak, I remembered that she was there. She did not reprove me angrily, but in trembling tones she said, "Rose, Herbert is *my* child, *my* boy, and it becomes not a girl of your age to speak thus of him in the presence of his mother."

I was humbled, and winding my arms about her neck, I asked forgiveness for the harsh words I had spoken; and she forgave me, for she meant to do right, and if sometimes she erred, it was owing more to a weakness of the flesh than an unwillingness of the spirit. In the midst of our excitement *Tom Wilson* was ushered in. He had returned in the same train which brought the letter, and had come to give us any further information which we might be desirous of knowing.

"When will Herbert come home?" was my aunt's first question, her whole manner indicating how much interest she felt in the answer.

"Not very soon," returned Tom. "He is tired of the city, he says, and besides that he wishes to avoid the unpleasant remarks his elopement will necessarily occasion."

"More like he wishes to avoid introducing his bride into society, which he knows has no wish to receive her," muttered Ada.

Tom paid no attention to this spiteful speech, but continued, "He has drawn his money from the — — Bank, and with it he intends purchasing a farm in the western part of New York."

"An admirable plan," again interrupted Ada. "That Lee girl is just calculated for a farmer's wife."

Taken alone there was nothing particularly disagreeable in the three words "*that Lee girl;*" but spoken by Ada Montrose they sounded insultingly, and every time she uttered them, I felt my blood boil, for *I*, too, was a *Lee girl*, and I was sure she included me in the same contemptuous category. As Herbert had said, I did not think the disappointment would break her heart. She was too angry for that, and I believe now, as I did then, that most of her feeling arose from the mortification of knowing that a "poor country girl," as she called Anna, was preferred to herself. For half an hour or more Tom Wilson and my aunt conversed together, she asking him at least a dozen times "if he did not think Herbert could be induced to return." At last, with quivering lips and flushed cheeks, as if it cost her pride a great effort, she said, "Of course I mean *Anna*, too, when I speak of Herbert's return. She is his wife, you say, and though I might, perhaps, wish it otherwise, it cannot now be helped, and if he only would come back to me, I should love her for his sake."

In my heart I blessed her for these words, and mentally resolved to leave no argument untried, which might bring the fugitives back. But it could not be. Herbert was decided, he said. He meant to be a farmer and live in the country, adding what he knew would silence his mother sooner than aught else he could say, "that temptations for him to drink were far greater in the city than in the country, and it was for this reason partly that he preferred living in the latter place."

And so my aunt yielded the point; but from the day of her son's desertion, there was in her a perceptible change. Far oftener was she found in the house of prayer, and less frequently was she seen in places of amusement, while more than once I heard her in secret asking that her wayward boy might be shielded from the great temptation. Alas! for thee, poor Herbert Langley, sleeping in thine early grave! There were prayers enough, methinks, to save thee; for at the old Meadow Brook home, thou wert remembered in the early morn, and not forgotten when at eve, my father knelt him down to pray. Why, then, didst thou fall ere thy sun had reached the meridian of manhood? Was it because in thine early training there was an error which no after exertions could repair? We answer, Yes. The fault was there, and little know they what they do, who set before their sons the poisonous cup, and bid them, by their own example, drink and die. How many young men, from the higher walks of life, now sleeping in the dishonored grave of a drunkard, might at this moment be filling some honorable position, had it not been for the wine or beer drinking habit acquired in childhood by their own firesides, and at their father's table? Look to it, then, you around whose hearthstones promising sons are gathered, and if in the coming years you would escape the sleepless nights, the bitter tears, and the broken hearts of those whose children walk in the path, which, sooner than all others, leadeth down to death, teach them, both by precept and by practice, to "touch not, taste not, handle not," for therein alone lieth safety.

CHAPTER XIV
TEN THOUSAND DOLLARS

Early in March, as I was one Saturday morning seated with my aunt in her pleasant, cozy sewing-room, a little boy brought me a note from Dell Clayton, in which she requested me, if possible, to spend the afternoon with her. She was sick, she wrote, unable to sit up, and what was worse than all, she was homesick and unhappy! Her aunt, she said, was out of the city, and as she had no acquaintance, she thought the sight of a familiar face would do her good.

Aunt Charlotte, to whom I handed the note, consented to my going, and immediately after dinner, which that day was served at an earlier hour than usual, I started. Long and daily walks have always been to me a luxury, and so, though I had been but a few months in Boston, I was tolerably well acquainted with most of its localities, and had no trouble in finding the once stylish, but now rather dilapidated and gloomy looking block, in one part of which Dr. Clayton was keeping house. Since the night when I met him at the theatre, I had never seen him, and all that I knew of him was that he had left the Tremont. Subsequently, however, I heard the whole history of their proceedings—partly from the doctor, partly from Dell, and partly from other sources, and as a recital of it may not be wholly uninteresting to my readers, I will give it before proceeding with a description of my call.

It seems that boarding at the Tremont was rather too expensive for a physician, whose patients were not so numerous as to be troublesome, and several times had the doctor proposed returning to his old place in Sturbridge, where everything was cheaper; but to this Dell objected, for she well knew it would be an admission that they could not succeed in Boston, and against this her pride revolted. "People at home," she reasoned, "would never know how matters really were, and as long as she could keep up an appearance of gentility and upper-ten-dom with her former friends, she should do so," preferring, like many others, almost absolute want in the city, to plenty in the country. From this, the reader is not to infer that the doctor was extremely poor; for when he first went to Boston he was worth about fifteen hundred dollars, which, in a country village, with a prudent wife, would have surrounded him with all the comforts of life, besides leaving him with something for that "rainy day," about which everybody blessed with a careful grandmother has heard more or less.

In the city, of course, it needed a great deal of money to keep up the kind of style upon which Dell insisted, and which, after all, was far from satisfying her—it was so much inferior to the elegance she saw around her; and as check after check of the doctor's little hoard was drawn from the bank to meet their expenses, while but few would get sick, or being so would send for him, his heart sank within him, and without really meaning to do so, he began to wonder "when that old grandmother would die!" Finding that he could not much longer pay the enormous bills, which were presented to him weekly at the Tremont, he decided at last upon housekeeping, and exercising in this case his own judgment, in spite of the tears, sulks, and remonstrances of his wife, he hired a house in an obscure street, where the rents were much lower than in the more fashionable part of the city. Very neatly he fitted it up, going rather beyond his means, it is true, but depending a great deal upon the fast failing health of Grandmother Barton, to set all things right.

Everything was at last arranged, and with that comfortable feeling which other men have experienced in similar circumstances, he took his seat for the first time at his own table, forgetting in his happiness that the smiling, handsome face of the lady opposite, in blue merino morning gown and clean white linen collar, had ever worn any look save that which now sat upon it. Breakfast was hardly over, when the door bell rang violently and a man appeared telling the doctor that his services were required immediately by the wealthy Mrs. Archer, who lived in an adjoining street, and who owned the entire block in which he lived.

Mrs. Archer belonged to that class of people who are always dying, first with one fancied disease and then with another, in the end, however, living much longer than those whose business it is to minister to their wants. Being freakish and whimsical, she seldom employed the same physician longer than a year, but during that time a man with limited wants was sure of a livelihood, for his services were required every day, and the remuneration for the same was so prompt and liberal as to make her patronage much sought after, particularly by new practitioners. Having taken a violent fancy to Dr. Clayton when he bargained with her for the house, she had decided henceforth to employ him, if on trial he proved to be all she wished.

The doctor was well aware of her peculiarities, and for several days past had indulged a faint hope that she might favor him with a call. This she had now done, and very eagerly he prepared to visit her. As he reached his gate, he was met by a boy who brought a telegraphic dispatch from Wilbraham, saying that *Grandma Barton was dead*! Yes, the old lady was gone, and Dell was undoubtedly the heiress of ten thousand dollars at least, and probably more, for her grandmother bore the reputation of being miserly, and rumor said that twice ten thousand was nearer the actual sum of her possessions. To ascertain the truth as soon as possible was the doctor's great desire, and as the next train bound for the east started in about two hours, he decided to go at once, though the funeral was not to take place for two or three days.

Suddenly Mrs. Archer's message occurred to him, but matters were now changed—he was *a rich man*, and as such Mrs. Archer's patronage was not of vital importance. Still it would hardly do to slight her, and rather unwillingly he bent his steps towards her dwelling. When there he appeared so abrupt and absent-minded, telling her there was nothing whatever the matter with her as he could see, that the good lady was wholly disgusted, and the moment he was gone, she dispatched the servant for another physician, who, possessing more tact, and not having recently come into the possession of a fortune, told her with a grave, concerned look, that "he never saw anything like her case—it really baffled his skill, though he thought he *could* cure her, and it would give him pleasure to try."

Of course he was employed, and just as Dr. Clayton and Dell were stepping into the omnibus, which took them to the dépôt, a note was handed to the former, saying his services were no longer needed by Mrs. Archer. Without giving it a thought, the doctor crushed the note into his pocket, and then springing into the carriage, took his seat by Dell, to whom he was unusually attentive, for she had risen in his estimation full *ten thousand dollars' worth*, and what man, for that sum of money, would not occasionally endure a cross look, or a peevish word! Not the doctor most certainly; and when on reaching the dépôt, they found that the cars would not leave for half an hour or more, he could not resist her entreaties to go with her to a jeweller's, on — — street, where the day before she had seen "such a beautiful set of cameos, earrings, bracelet, and pin to match—then, too, they were so cheap, only $50. She knew he would buy them!"

'Twas in vain for him to say that he had not fifty dollars for she replied, that "he could take it from the bank and replace it when she got her fortune;" adding, "I'll give you a hundred in place of it: so gratify me this once, that's a dear, good man."

Of course, the *dear good man* was persuaded as many an other dear good man has been, and will be again by a coaxing woman. The cameos were bought, and in the best of humor the young couple took their seats in the cars, which were soon bearing them swiftly towards the house of death. Very pleasant were the doctor's reflections as the train sped on over valley and plain: he was a fortunate, happy man, and if when they paused at the Meadow Brook station he thought for an instant of the girl Rosa Lee, her memory was to him like an idle dream, which had passed away in the *golden* beams of day. Arrived at Wilbraham dépôt, they took a carriage for the village, which is about two miles or more from the railroad.

The old brown shutters of the large wooden building, where Mrs. Barton had lived and died, were closed, and about the house there was no sign of life. But this was hardly different from what it had been during the old lady's life, for she was one who lived mostly within herself, seldom seeing company, though always sure to go whenever she was invited. Exceedingly penurious, she stinted her household to the last degree of endurance, and denied herself even the comforts of life, while her last request had been that her body might be suffered to remain in her sleeping-room, so as not to litter the parlor, or wear the carpet!

At the head of the family was Mabel Warrener, a poor young girl, who for the three years had lived with Mrs. Barton in the capacity of half waiting-maid, half companion, and to her the neighbors now looked for directions. Anxious to pay all due deference to the wishes of her late mistress, Mabel at first said, "Let the body remain where it is;" but when she reflected that "the fashionable Mrs. Clayton from Boston," with her proud husband (for so were they considered), would probably be there, she changed her mind, and the deceased was carried into the dark, damp parlor, where a fire had not been kindled for more than a year. The same was also true of the chamber above, which was designed for the doctor and his lady, the latter of whom shivered as she entered it, rather haughtily bidding Mabel, who accompanied her, "to make a fire there as soon as possible, for she was not accustomed to cold rooms, and should freeze to death."

Very meekly Mabel complied, not only with this requisition, but with fifty others, from the same source; for Dell, thinking she was now mistress of the house, took upon herself many airs, ordering this, that and the other, until the neighbors, quite disgusted, left poor Mabel alone, with the exception of the deaf old woman, who ruled in the kitchen as cook. The morning following the arrival of the doctor, Capt. Thompson, wife, and son came out from Sturbridge to attend the funeral; for though they were in no way connected with Mrs. Barton, they knew her well, and wished to pay her this last tribute of respect. Then, too, Mrs. Thompson was very desirous of seeing Dell, who was now an heiress, and as such entitled to attention. Long they talked together concerning the future, Dell telling how she meant "to fix up the old rookery for a summer residence," and inviting her sister-in-law to spend as much time with her as she possibly could. The cameos were next duly inspected, admired, tried on, and then the two went down to the room below, and turning back the thin muslin which shaded the face of the dead, gazed upon the pinched, stony features which seemed so much to reproach them for their cold-hearted selfishness, in thus planning ways and means by which to spend her hoarded wealth even before she was buried from their sight.

That afternoon there was heard a tolling bell, and a long procession moved slowly to the churchyard, where the words "ashes to ashes—dust to dust," and the sound of the hard frozen earth, rattling upon the coffin-lid, broke the solemn stillness, but disturbed not the rest of those, who, henceforth, would be the fellow-sleepers of her now committed to the grave. When the party of mourners had returned to the house, the doctor began to speak of the necessity there was for his returning immediately to the city, at the same time hinting to Capt. Thompson that "if there was a *will* he would like to see it."

Mabel Warrener, who was supposed to know more than any one else concerning Mrs. Barton's affairs, was called in and questioned, she replying that her mistress, one day, about two weeks before her death, had said to her that if, after her death, any inquiry should be made concerning her will, it could be found in the private drawer of her secretary, where was also a letter for Mrs. Clayton. Both of these were brought out, and with her handkerchief over her eyes, Dell listened while Capt. Thompson read aloud the astounding fact that the entire possessions of Mrs. Barton, amounting to $15,000, were given to Mabel Warrener, who, having had no suspicion whatever of the fortune in store for her, fainted away, and was borne from the room, as was also Dell; while the doctor, it was confidently asserted, went out behind the woodshed and actually *vomited*, so great was his disappointment! Soon rallying, however, both he and his wife declared it a fraud, accusing the still unconscious Mabel of treachery, and it was not until the lawyer who had drawn the will was produced, that they could be convinced. Suddenly remembering her letter, Dell broke it open and found therein the reasons for this most unaccountable freak. Always peculiar and naturally jealous, Mrs. Barton had felt piqued that she was not invited to Dell's wedding, which, considering that she was spending the summer in Albany at the time when it took place, was not very remarkable. Then, too, she was not consulted, and she didn't believe in doctors, they killed more than they cured; but the head and front of the offence seemed to be that instead of hiring two or three rooms and keeping house in a small, economical way, they *boarded* at the Tremont, where Dell had nothing to do but "to change her dress, eat, sleep, and *laze*"—so the letter ran—"and she

(Mrs. Barton) would not suffer a penny of her money to go for the support of such extravagance: she preferred giving it to Mabel Warrener, who was a prudent, saving girl, and would take care of it; while the paltry doctor would spend it for cigars, fast horses, patent leather boots, and all sorts of fooleries."

The letter ended with an exhortation to Dell to "go to work and earn her own living, as her grandmother had done before her."

The doctor's reflections, as he rode back to Boston, were not of the most enviable nature; and who can wonder if he *was* rather testy towards his wife, who retorted so angrily as to bring on quite a sharp quarrel, which was prevented from being heard by the roar of the machinery; and if at *Meadow Brook* he *did* think again of Rosa Lee, half fancying that 5,000 divided by 13, if shared with *her*, might be preferable to *nothing* divided by *nothing*, shared with Dell; who can blame him? Not *I*, most certainly. Wasn't he terribly disappointed? Hadn't he just lost $15,000, to say nothing of a patient, whose patronage would have insured him a living for at least a year, besides introducing him into a broader field of practice; and if the cameo earrings *were* rather becoming to the dark hair and black eyes of his wife, did that in any way compensate him for the fifty dollars which stood on the Cr. side of his bank-book? Still, I see no good reason why, after their arrival home at a late hour of the night, they should sit up for more than an hour in a cold, cheerless room, telling each other—the one that she wished she had never married him, for "he alone stood in the way of her inheritance;" while the other replied, that "but for her extravagance he should now have had $1,500 in the bank instead of five hundred."

Wretched couple! Their history is like that of many others, who marry without a particle of love, or at most, only a passing fancy. Had Dell chosen, she could in time have won the affection of her husband, but being naturally selfish and exacting, she expected from him every attention; while in return she seldom gave him aught save cross looks and peevish words, complaining that he did not treat her now as he once had done. As long as the doctor had a fortune in expectancy, he bore his wife's ill humor tolerably well, but now that hope was gone, his whole being seemed changed, and Dell was not often obliged to quarrel alone.

At last, broken in spirits, and being really sick, she had sent for me, as I have before stated. I found her in bed, propped up on pillows, her shining hair combed back, and her large black eyes seeming blacker than ever, from contrast with her colorless cheek. All her old haughtiness was gone, and the moment she saw me she stretched her arms towards me, and bursting into tears, exclaimed, "Oh, Rose, I am *so* glad you have come. I was afraid you wouldn't, for I knew your aunt was very aristocratic, and I thought she might not be willing to have you visit poor, obscure people like us."

There was much of bitterness in the last part of this speech, and it grated harshly upon my feelings; but it was like her, I knew, and she had only judged my aunt by what she well knew she should herself be in a similar position; so I took no notice of it, save to assure her that Aunt Charlotte was perfectly willing I should come, while at the same time I expressed my sorrow at finding her so unwell, and asked "what was the matter."

"Oh, nothing much," said she. "I have no particular disease, unless it be one of the mind, and that you know is not easily cured."

I made no answer to this; but after a moment's silence, I ventured to inquire for her husband. Instantly there came a bright glow to her cheek, as she replied, "Oh, he is as well as could be expected, considering his terrible disappointment."

Of course I asked what disappointment, whereupon she proceeded to narrate a part of what I have already told to my readers, withholding nearly all the points wherein she had been to blame, and dwelling with apparent delight upon the faults of her husband, who, she protested, was wholly selfish and avaricious. "I know," said she, "why he married me; 'twas for the sake of the few dollars he thought my grandmother would leave me, and now being disappointed in that, he cares no more for me than he does for *you*—no, nor half so much, for he always preferred you to me, and I wish I had let you have him, for you liked him, I know, better than I did."

As she said this, she looked me steadily in the face, as if to read my inmost soul. I felt provoked, for I now thought of my former affection for the doctor as something of which I was *a little ashamed*, and I did not much like to be reminded of it by his wife. So I ventured to say that "whatever I might once have felt for her husband, it was all over now, and I could think of no greater misfortune than that of being his wife!"

Now, I should know better than to speak thus to any woman concerning her husband, for however much she may talk against him herself, she certainly has no desire or expectation that her listener will agree with her. On this occasion, Dell grew angry at once, telling me "I needn't speak so lightly of her husband—he was good enough for anybody," while at the same time she muttered something about "sour grapes!"

I was taken quite aback, and remained silent, until she at last said, laughingly, "I don't wish to quarrel with you, Rose. Pardon any ill humor I may have manifested. I get nervous and fidgety staying here alone so much."

"Is not the doctor with you sometimes?" I inquired.

"Oh, yes; once in a great while," said she; "but he can bear the atmosphere of any other sick-room better than mine. So he's off—hunting up patients, I suppose. I tell him he gets his living that way, and a poor living it bids fair to be. Between you and me, Rose," she continued, growing excited, "he is *shiftless*, if you know what that means, and we are worth today just as much as we ever shall be."

I felt that she wronged him, and told her so, at the same time enumerating his many good qualities, while she listened, evidently better pleased than when I had spoken lightly of him. In the midst of our conversation there was a familiar step in the hall, and a moment after the doctor himself entered the room. He looked careworn and haggard; but at the sight of me, whose presence surprised him, his face quickly lighted up, and there was much of his olden manner as he took my hand and expressed his pleasure at finding me there. 'Twas but a for moment, however, for catching the eye of his wife, he became almost instantly reserved, and seating himself near a window, he pretended to be much occupied with a book, which I accidentally discovered was wrong side up! It was strange how much waiting-upon Dell suddenly needed. Heretofore she had been very quiet, saying she did not wish for anything, but now that he was there, her pillows must be turned, her head must be bathed, the window must be open and then shut, while with every other breath, she declared him to be "the awkwardest man she ever saw," saying once, "she didn't wonder he had no more practice if he handled all his patients as roughly as he did her."

After this unkind speech, the doctor made no farther attempt to please her, but left her side and returned to his seat by the window. Ere long the supper bell rang. I had not supposed it was so late, and starting up announced my intention of going home, but to this neither the doctor nor Dell would listen, both of them insisting upon my staying to tea; *she*, because she felt that common civility required it, and *he*, because he really wished it. Once out of her sight, he was himself again, and playfully drawing my arm within his, he led me to the dining-room, placing me at the head of the table, where Dell was accustomed to sit, while he took the seat opposite. As we sat there thus, I shall not say that there came to my mind no thought of what might have been, but I can say, and truthfully too, that such thoughts brought with them naught of pain; for though Dr. Clayton had once possessed the power of swaying me at his will, that time had gone by, and he was to me now only a friend, whom I both liked and pitied, for I knew he was far from being happy. Once, when I handed him his second cup of tea, he said, smiling upon me, "It makes me very happy to see you there—in that seat."

I made no answer; and, as if thinking he had said what he ought not, he immediately changed the conversation, and began to question me of my studies, etc., asking me among other things, if I went to *dancing school*. Instantly I remembered Mrs. Ross's slippers with the little *wads* of cotton, and I laughed aloud. It seems his thoughts took the same direction, for he, too, laughed so loudly that when we returned to Dell's room, she rather pettishly inquired what we found to amuse us so much, saying "she hadn't seen the doctor look so pleased since—since, well, since grandma's death," she finally added, at the same time glancing at him to witness the effect of her words.

He turned very white about the mouth, and I am quite certain I heard the word "*thunder!*" At all events, his eyes flashed angrily upon the provoking woman, who again inquired at what we were laughing. When I told her, she too laughed, saying, "Oh, yes, I remember it well, and have sometimes thought that I owe my present position to that awkward misstep of yours."

"I am very glad I fell, then," said I, rather impatiently, while I threw on my hood and shawl, preparatory to going home.

"Hadn't you better call an omnibus for her?" asked Dell of her husband, who was putting on his overshoes.

"I am going round with her myself," he answered. "I have a patient on the way," and he hurried from the room ere she could say anything further.

It was a beautiful moonlight night, and as I took his arm I recalled the time when once before we had walked thus together. I think he remembered it too, for he asked me "if I ever visited Pine District?"

"Not often," I replied; and he continued to say, that "notwithstanding that it was little more than a year and a half since he first saw me there, it seemed to him an age," adding; "and it is not strange neither, for I have passed through many trials since then."

To this I made no reply, and ere long he proceeded to speak further of himself, and of his disappointment, first with regard to his business, and next with regard to his domestic relations, which he gave me to understand were not particularly happy. Very delicately and carefully he handled the latter subject, speaking not one half so harshly of Dell as she had spoken of him. Still I felt that he had no right thus to speak to me, and so I told him.

"I know it, Rose," he returned. "I know it all; but for this once you *must* hear me, and I will never trouble you again. I committed a great error in marrying one, while my heart belonged to another—stay," he continued, as I was about to interrupt him. "You must hear me out. It is not of my love for *that other* that I would speak; but, Rose, I would know how far I have wronged you. *Did* you love me, and had I asked you to share my home, when at a suitable age, would you have done so?"

He was very pale, and the arm on which my hand was resting, trembled violently, but grew still when he heard my answer, which was, "I *did* love you, but 'twas a childish love and quickly passed away. And were you now free as you once were, I could be to you nothing save a friend."

There was a mixture of disappointment and pleasure on his face; but he replied, "I am glad that it is so, and shall now feel happier, for the hardest part of all was the thought that possibly *you, too*, might suffer."

"Not at all," I answered, adding, "it would be foolish to break my heart for one man, when there are so many in the world."

This I said with bitterness, for I remembered the time when I had wept in the shadowy woods of Meadow Brook, and if for a moment I experienced a feeling of satisfaction in knowing that what *I* suffered then, *he* was suffering now, I can only plead *woman's nature* as an apology. 'Twas but for a moment, however, and then, casting off all such feelings, I spoke to him kindly of his wife, telling him he could be happy with her if he tried, and that if he were not, it was probably as much his fault as hers. Brighter days, too, would come, I said, when his practice would not be limited to *three* patients, one of whom was too poor to pay, and another was already convalescent, while the third was in the last stages of her disease, and would need his services but a few days longer.

"You are my good angel, Rose," said he, when at last we reached my uncle's door, "and your words inspire me with courage. Come and see us often, for the sight of you does me good, and God knows how much I stand in need of sympathy. Farewell."

He pressed my hand, and hastily raising it to his lips, turned away, dreading, as I well knew, a return to the sick-room, where naught would greet him save reproachful complaints, and where the dark eyes, which had first won his admiration, would flash angrily upon him. In the hall, I stood for a time, pondering in my mind some way by which I could assist him, and I even thought of feigning sickness myself for the sake of adding another patient to his list! But this, I knew, he would easily detect, and possibly he might misconstrue my motive for so doing, and this project was abandoned, and I entered the parlor in quest of my aunt, who, I learned from one of the servants, was in her own room, suffering from a severe headache. She had taken a violent cold, which, by the next morning, had developed itself into a species of influenza, at that time prevailing in the city. Added to this was a general debility and prostration of the nerves, brought on by her recent trouble and anxiety concerning Herbert.

My uncle, who was always alarmed when she was ill, wished for medical advice; but to this she objected, as Dr. Mott, the family physician, was absent, and she knew of no other, whom she dare trust. Instantly I thought of Dr. Clayton. If she could be prevailed upon to employ him, I knew she would like him, for *I* could testify to his extreme kindness in a sick-room, and good nursing was what she most needed. When I suggested that he should be called, she at first refused; but before night, being much worse, she consented, and never had I experienced a moment of greater happiness than when I hastened to the kitchen with a message for John, who was to go immediately for Dr. Clayton. Then taking my uncle aside, I explained to him the straitened circumstances of the young physician, hinting to him, that prompt remuneration for his services would undoubtedly be acceptable.

"Yes, yes, I understand," said he; "you want me to pay him to-day."

Here we were interrupted by the ringing of the door-bell. Dr. Clayton had come, and the result was as I had hoped. My aunt was greatly pleased — he was so kind and gentle, humoring all her fancies, and evincing withal so much judgment and skill, that she felt confidence in his abilities; and when he was gone, expressed herself as preferring him even to Dr. Mott, "who," she said, "was getting old and cross."

As he was leaving the house, my uncle placed in his hand a five dollar bill, whereupon the doctor turned very red, and asked if he were not expected to call again.

"Certainly, certainly," said my uncle, who, manlike, hadn't the least bit of tact; "keep coming until Charlotte is well. I only paid you for this call to please Rosa."

Instead of the displeased, mortified look, which I expected to see on the doctor's face, there was an expression of deep gratitude, as he turned his eyes towards me; and I thought there was a moisture in them, which surprised me, for I did not then know how much that five dollars was needed: it being the exact amount requisite for the payment of the girl, who refused to remain with them another day unless her wages were forthcoming. To such straits are people, apparently in easy circumstances, sometimes reduced.

For more than a week my aunt was confined to her room, while the doctor came regularly, always staying a long time, and by his delicate attentions winning golden laurels from his patient, who was far better pleased with him than with the fussy old man, who, being always in a hurry, only stopped for a moment, while he looked at her *tongue*, felt her *pulse*, and recommended *blistering* and *bleeding*, with a dose of *calomel*, neither of which Dr. Clayton believed to be a *saving ordinance*, and indispensable to the *comfort* and recovery of his patients. By this, I do not mean anything derogatory to the good old custom of tormenting folks to death before their time, but having a faint remembrance of certain *blisters*, which, together with *cabbage leaves* and the *tallowed rags*, once kept me in a state of torture for nearly a week, to say nothing of the *sore mouth*, the *loose teeth*, and the tightly-bandaged arm, I cannot help experiencing a kind of nervous tremor at the very mention of said prescriptions.

Dr. Clayton's attendance upon my aunt was a great benefit to him, as, through its means, he became known to several of the higher circle, who began to employ him, so that by the last of May, the time when I left Boston for Meadow Brook, he had quite a large practice. For some reason or other, Mrs. Archer, too, sent for him again; and as he had now no ten thousand dollars in prospect, he succeeded in pleasing the whimsical lady, thereby securing her patronage for a year at least. Here, for a time, I leave him, while I go back to the dear old home at Meadow Brook, over which a shadow, dark and heavy, was brooding.

CHAPTER XV
THE OLD HOMESTEAD

"Meadow Brook Station! Stop five minutes for refreshments!" shouted the conductor, and alighting from the noisy, crowded cars, I stood once more in my own native town, gazing with a feeling of delight upon the sunny hills, dotted over with the old-fashioned gable-roofed houses, and upon the green, grassy meadow, through which rolled the blue waters of the Chicopee. I had not stood thus long, when a broad hand was laid upon my shoulder, and the next instant my arms were around the neck of my father, who, I thought, had changed much since last I saw him; for his face was thin and pale, while threads of silver were scattered through his soft, brown hair.

It was the loss of Anna, I fancied; and when we at last were seated in the buggy, and on our way home, I hastened to speak of her, and to tell him of the favorable report we heard of Herbert. But naught which I said seemed to rouse him; and at last I, too, fell into the same thoughtful mood, in which even old Sorrel shared, for he moved with his head down, scarcely once leaving the slow, measured walk he had first assumed. When, at last, we reached the hill-top, from which could be seen the Homestead, with its maple trees in front, and long row of apple trees, now in full bloom, in the rear, I started up, exclaiming, "Home, sweet home! It never looked half so beautiful to me before."

In a moment, however, I checked myself; for my father groaned aloud, while his face grew whiter than before.

"What is it, father," I asked; "are they sick, or dead?"

"Neither, neither," he replied, at the same time chirruping to old Sorrel, who pricked up his ears, and soon carried us to the door of our house, where I was warmly greeted by all.

And still there was in what they said and did an air of melancholy which puzzled me; and when I was alone with Lizzie, I asked her the cause why they looked so sad? Bursting into tears, she replied, "This is not our home any longer. We must leave it, and go, we don't know where—to the *poor-house*, 'pa sometimes says, when he feels the worst, and then grandma cries so hard—oh, it's dreadful!"

"And why must we leave it?" I asked; and Lizzie answered, "Pa has signed notes for Uncle Thomas, who has failed, and now the homestead must be sold to pay his debts—and they so proud, too!"

It was as Lizzie had said. Uncle Thomas Harding was my mother's brother, who lived in Providence, in far greater style, it was said, than he was able to support. Several times had Aunt Harding visited us, together with her two daughters, Ellen and Theodosia. They were proud, haughty girls, and evidently looked upon us, their *country cousins*, with contempt; only tolerating us, because it was pleasant to have some place in the country where to while away a few weeks, which, in the heated, dusty city, would otherwise hang heavily upon their hands. On such occasions they made themselves perfectly at home, and somehow or other managed to have my mother feel that she was really indebted to them for the honor they conferred upon her, by calling her Aunty, by appropriating to themselves the greater portion of the house, by skimming the cream from the pans of milk, by eating up the pie she had saved for us children when we came hungry and cross from school, and by keeping old Sorrel constantly in the harness, or under the saddle.

In return for all this, they sometimes gave us an old collar, a silk apron, a soiled ribbon, or broken parasol—and once, when my parents visited them, they sent us a trunk full of rubbish, among which was Fielding's "Tom Jones!" This my grandmother cautiously took from the trunk with the *tongs* and threw into the fire, thereby creating in me so great a desire for a knowledge of its contents, that, on the first occasion which presented itself, I gratified my curiosity, feeling, when I had done so, that my grandmother was right in disposing of the volume as she did. Dear old lady! her aversion to everything savoring of fiction was remarkable, and when not long since a certain *medium* informed me that she, my grandmother, was greatly distressed to learn that I had so far degenerated as to be *writing a book*, I thought seriously of giving up my project at once, and should probably have done so, had not another *medium* of still greater power than the first received a communication, stating that, after due reflection, my grandmother had concluded that "I might continue the story called Meadow Brook, provided I showed off my Aunt Harding and her two daughters in their true character." So, as a dutiful child, it becomes me to tell how my father, who was warmly attached to my Uncle Thomas, lent him money from time to time, and signed notes to the amount of several thousand dollars, never once dreaming that in the end *he* would be ruined, while my uncle, influenced by his more crafty wife, managed in some unaccountable way to maintain nearly the same style of living as formerly; and if his proud daughters ever felt the ills of poverty, it was certainly not apparent in the rich silks and costly furs which they continued to sport.

It was a terrible blow to us all, but upon no one did it fall so heavily as upon my father, crushing him to the earth, and rendering him nearly as powerless as is the giant oak when torn from its parent bed by the wrathful storm. The old homestead was endeared to him by a thousand hallowed associations. It was the home of his boyhood, and around the cheerful fires, which years ago were kindled on its spacious hearth-stone, he had played with those who long since had passed from his side, some to mingle in the great drama of life, and others to that world where they number not by years. There, too, in his early manhood had he brought his bride, my gentle mother, and on the rough bark of the towering maples, by the side of his own and his brothers' names, were carved those of his children, all save little Jamie, who died ere his tiny fingers had learned the use of knife or hammer. No wonder, then, that his head grew dizzy and his heart sick as he thought of leaving it forever; and when at last the trying moment came, when with trembling hand he signed the deed which made him homeless, who shall deem him weak, if he laid his weary head upon the lap of his aged mother and wept like a little child?

A small house in the village was hired, and after a few weeks' preparation, one bright June morning, when the flowers we had watched over and tended with care were in bloom, when the robins which, year after year had returned to their nests in the maple tree, were singing their sweetest songs, and when the blue sky bent gently over us, we bade adieu to the spot, looking back with wistful eye until every trace of our home had disappeared. Farewell forever to thee, dear old homestead, where now other footsteps tread and other children play than those of "auld lang syne." The lights and shadows of years have fallen upon thee since that summer morn, and with them have come changes to thee as well as to us. The maple, whose branches swept the roof above my window, making oft sad music when tuned by the autumn wind, has been cut away, and the robins, who brought to us the first tidings of spring, have died or flown to other haunts. "The moss-covered bucket which hung in the well" has been removed; the curb, whose edges were worn by childish hands, is gone; while in place of the violets and daisies which once blossomed on the grassy lawn, the thistle and the burdock now are growing, and the white rose bush by the door, from whence they plucked the buds which strewed the coffin-bed of our baby brother, is dead. Weeds choke the garden walks, and the moss grows green and damp on the old stone wall. Even the brook which ran so merrily past our door has been stopped in its course, and its sparkling waters, bereft of freedom, now turn the wheel of a huge saw-mill, with a low and sullen roar. All is changed, and though memory still turns fondly to the spot which gave me birth, I have learned to love another home, for where my blessed mother dwells, 'tis surely home to me. By her side there is, I know, a vacant chair, and in her heart a lonely void, which naught on earth can fill; but while she lives, and I know that there is in the world for me a mother and a mother's love, can I not feel that I have indeed a home, though it be not the spot where first she blessed me as her child?

CHAPTER XVI
"OUT WEST"

What a train of conflicting ideas do those two words oftentimes awaken, bringing up visions of *log cabins,* ladder stairs, *wooden latches,* fried hominy and maple sugar, to say nothing of the hobgoblins in the shape of bears, rattlesnakes, wolves, and "folks who don't know anything;" the latter being universally considered the "staple production" of every place bearing the name of "out West." Even western New York, with her hundreds of large and flourishing villages, her well cultivated farms, her numerous schools, her educated, intelligent people, and her vast wealth, is looked upon with distrust by some of her eastern neighbors, because, forsooth, her boundaries lie farther towards the setting sun, and because she once bore the title of "way out west in the Genesees."

Of course I speak only from observation and personal experience; for at Meadow Brook, ten years ago, many fears were expressed lest Anna should miss the society to which she had been accustomed; and when after the sale of the homestead, she wrote, asking me to come and live with her, I hesitated, for to me it seemed much like burying myself from the world, particularly as she chanced to mention that the schoolhouse was a *log* one, and that there were in the neighborhood several buildings of the same material. Never having seen anything of the kind, I could not then understand that there is often in a log house far more comfort and genuine happiness than in the stateliest mansion which graces Fifth Avenue or Beacon street; and that the owners of said dwellings are frequently worth their thousands, and only wait for a convenient opportunity to build a more commodious and imposing residence.

At last, after many consultations with my parents, I concluded to go, and about the middle of November I again bade adieu to Meadow Brook; and in company with a friend of my father, who was going West, I started for Rockland, N. Y., which is in the western part of Ontario county, and about fourteen miles from Canandaigua, at which place Herbert was to meet me. I had never before been west of Springfield, and when about sunset I looked out upon the delightful prospect around Albany, I felt a thrill of delight mingled with a feeling of pain, for I began to have a vague impression that possibly Massachusetts, with all her boasted privileges, could not outrival the Empire State. It was dark, and the night lamps were already lighted when we entered the cars at Albany; for we were to ride all night. In front of us was an unoccupied seat, which I turned towards me for the better accommodation of my band-box, which contained my new bonnet; and I was about settling myself for a nap, when a gentleman and lady came in, the latter of whom stopping near us, said, "Here, Richard, is a vacant seat. These folks can't of course expect to monopolize two;" at the same time she commenced turning the seat back, to the great peril of my bonnet, which, as it was made in Boston, I confidently expected would be the envy and fashion of all Rockland!

I was sitting with my hand over my eyes, but at the sound of that voice I started, and, looking up, saw before me Ada Montrose, and with her the "dark gentleman" who had so much interested me at the theatre. Instantly throwing my veil over my face, for I had no wish to be recognized, I watched him with a feeling akin to jealousy, while he attended to the comfort of his companion, who demeaned herself towards him much as she had done towards Herbert Langley. All thoughts of sleep had left me, and throughout the entire night I was awake, speculating upon the probable relation in which he stood to her: and once when it suddenly occurred to me that possibly they were married, the tears actually started to my eyes.

As the hours sped on, he said to her a few low spoken words, whereupon she laid her head upon his shoulder, as if that were its natural resting-place, while he threw his arm around her, bidding her "sleep if she could." Of course she was his wife, I said, and with much of bitterness at my heart, I turned away and watched the slowly-moving lights of the canal-boats, discernible on the opposite side of the Mohawk, along whose banks we were passing. Whether Ada liked her pillow or not, she clung to it pertinaciously until it seemed to me that her neck must snap asunder, while with a martyr's patience he supported her, dozing occasionally himself, and bending his head so low that his glossy black hair occasionally touched the white brow of the sleeping girl.

"Bride and groom," I heard a rough-looking man mutter, as he passed them in quest of a seat, and as this confirmed my fears, I again turned towards the window, which I opened, so that the night-air might cool my burning cheeks.

That night I made up my mind to be an "old maid." Nobody would ever want me I knew, I was so homely; and with calm resignation I thought how much good I would do in the world, and how I would honor the sisterhood! Very slowly the morning light came struggling in through the dirty windows, rousing the weary passengers, who, rubbing their red-rimmed eyes, looked around to see who their companions were. It was nearly noon when we reached Canandaigua, and so carefully had I kept my face hidden from view that Ada had no suspicion whatever of my presence. At Canandaigua I took leave of my companion, and stepping out upon the platform in front of the dépôt, looked anxiously around for Herbert, but he was not there. Thinking he would soon be there, I found my way to the public parlor, which for few moments I occupied alone. I had just removed my dusty bonnet, and was brushing my tangled hair, when the door opened, and I stood face to face with Ada Montrose, who started back, and for a moment evidently debated the propriety of recognizing me. Thinking she might do just as she pleased, I simply nodded, as I would to any stranger, and went on with my toilet, while throwing herself upon the sofa, she exclaimed, "Dear me, how tired I am! Do you live here?"

"Of course not," I answered; "I am on my way to visit my sister Anna, whom you perhaps remember."

She turned very red, and replied by asking if I were in the train which had just passed.

"Yes," I answered; "I occupied the seat directly behind you and—your *husband*—is it not?"

I felt that I must know the truth, and hence the rather impertinent question, which, however, did not seem to displease her in the least. Affecting to be a little embarrassed, she said, "Not my husband—yet. He came on to Boston to accompany me home, and wishing to see a friend of his, who lives here, we have stopped over one train."

I know not why it was, but her words gave me comfort; while at the same time the state of single-blessedness appeared to me far less attractive than it had a few hours before! I was on the point of asking her about my aunt, when the door again opened and there stood before us a slovenly-looking man, attired in a slouched hat, muddy pantaloons, grey coat, and huge cow-hide boots. So complete was the metamorphosis that neither of us recognized him, until he had exclaimed, as his eye fell upon Ada, "Good Heavens, Ade! How came you here?" Then we knew it was Herbert Langley!

So astonished was I that it was some time ere I found voice to return his rather noisy greeting. Try as he would, he could not conceal the fact that he was rather disconcerted at being seen by Ada in such a plight, and after a little he stammered out an apology, saying he was a *farmer* now, and lived in the country, and of course could not be expected to dress as he used in the city. This, I knew, was no excuse, and I trembled lest he might be changed in more points than one.

"How is your wife, Mrs. Langley?" asked Ada, in a mocking, deferential tone.

Instantly the whole expression of Herbert's face was changed, and there was a look of tenderness and pride in his eyes as he advanced towards Ada, and whispered in her ear something which I did not understand. Whatever it was, it made her blush, as she replied rather sneeringly, "Of course I congratulate you."

It has always been my misfortune to be rather stupid in some matters, and I had not the least idea what either of them meant, or why Herbert was to be congratulated. Possibly I might have asked an explanation, but just then the town clock struck the hour of one, and turning towards me, he said, it was time we were on our way, for the fall rains had made the roads almost impassable, and he was afraid we should not reach home before dark. "So put on your things quick," he added. "The *carriage* is all ready."

This last he said laughingly, for the carriage proved to be a long lumber wagon, such as is seldom found in Massachusetts, or at least, *I* had never seen one like it before, and it became a serious question in my mind as to *how* I was expected to enter it, there being no possible way of doing so, save by climbing over the *wheels*, which were reeking with mud. Herbert seemed to enjoy my embarrassment, for he asked me if "I didn't think I could step from the ground into the box," a distance of several feet? I was soon relieved from my difficulty by the porter, who placed before me some wooden steps, on which I mounted safely, and seated myself in the large arm-chair, which, with its warm buffalo-robes, was really more comfortable than the old-fashioned one-horse wagons of New England, though I did not think so then; and when the spirited horses, at a crack from Herbert's whip, sprang forward, while I, losing my balance, pitched over backward, I began to cry, wishing in my heart that I was back in Meadow Brook.

It was a cold, raw, autumnal day. The roads, as Herbert had said, were horrible; and as we ploughed through the thick mud, which, in some places was up to the wheel hubs, I took, I believe, my first lesson in genuine home-sickness, which, in my opinion, is about as hard to bear as love-sickness! Indeed, I think they *feel* much alike—the latter being, perhaps, a very little the worse of the two! It was in vain that Herbert pointed out to me the many handsome farmhouses which we passed, expatiating upon the richness and fertility of the soil, and telling me how greatly superior in everything New York was to New England. I scarcely heard him, for even though in all Massachusetts there was naught save the rocky hills, and sterile plains, it was *my home*, and from that spot the heart cannot easily be weaned.

Rockland is a large, wealthy town, embracing within its limits more than the prescribed rule of six miles square, while scattered through it are two or three little villages, each bearing a distinct name, by which they are known abroad. First, there was Laurel Hill, famed as the residence of certain families who were styled *proud* and *aristocratic*—to say nothing of their being *Episcopalians*, which last fact was by some regarded as the main cause of their haughtiness. Next came the "Centre," with its group of red houses, and its single spire, so tall, so straight, and so square, that it scarce needed the lettering over the entrance to tell to the stranger that *Presbyterians* worshiped there. Lastly came Flattville, by far the largest village in Rockland, and the home of all the *isms* in the known world. To the south of Flattville is a small lake, renowned for its quiet beauty, and the picturesque wildness of its shores. Bounded on three sides by high hills, its waters sleep calmly in the sunlight of summer, or dash angrily upon the sandy beach, when moved by the chill breath of winter.

On the brow of one of the high hills which overlook the Honeoye, and so near to it that the sweep of the waves can be distinctly heard in a clear, still night, stood the home of my sister. It was a huge, wooden building, containing rooms innumerable, while even the basement was large enough to accommodate one or more families. Being the first frame house erected in the town, it was of course looked upon with considerable interest, and as if to make it still more notorious, it bore the reputation of being *haunted*, and by some of the neighbors was called the "Haunted Castle."

Years before, when the country was new, it was a sort of public-house, and a young girl was said to have been murdered there, and buried in the cellar, from whence she was afterwards removed and thrown into the lake. For the truth of this story there was no proof, save the fact, that in the dark cellar there was a slight excavation, supposed to have been the grave of the ill-fated lady. All this Herbert very kindly told me, as we rode leisurely along, saying, when I asked if he believed it, "Believe it! No! Of course not. To be sure, it's the squeakiest old rattle-trap of a house that I ever saw; and were I at all superstitious, I could readily believe it haunted, particularly when the wind blows hard. But you are not frightened; are you?" he asked, looking in my face, which was very pale.

I hold that there is in every human breast a dread of the supernatural, and though I do not by any means believe in ghosts, I would certainly prefer not to live in a house where they are supposed to dwell. Still, I dared not tell Herbert so, and, consequently, I only laughed at the idea of a haunted house, saying, it was very romantic. It was after sunset when we at last turned into the long avenue, shaded on either side by forest maples, which the first proprietor of the place had suffered to remain; and as my eye fell upon the large, dark building, which Herbert said was his house, I involuntarily shuddered, for to me it seemed the very spot of all others which goblins would choose for their nightly revels. The wind was blowing from the west, and as I followed Herbert up to the door, my ear caught a dull, moaning sound, which caused me to quicken my footsteps, while I asked, in some trepidation, what it was.

"That? Oh, that's the roar of the lake. Don't you see how near it is to us, directly at the foot of the hill?" and he pointed out to me the broad sheet of water, just discernible in the gathering darkness.

A sudden gust of wind swept past me, and again I caught the low murmur. There was something human in the tone, and though for three years I almost daily heard that sound, I could never fully rid myself of the impression that it was the spirit of the murdered maiden which thus, to the swelling waves, complained of the crime long unpunished.

"Come this way, Rose," said Herbert, as I entered the narrow "entry" so common in old-fashioned houses; and following him, I was soon ushered into a large square room, where a bright wood fire was blazing, casting a somewhat cheerful aspect over the sombre, wainscoted walls of ancient make.

In one corner of the room was a bed, and on it lay Anna, who, the moment she saw me, uttered a cry of joy.

"Have you told her?" she asked of Herbert, when the first pleasure of our meeting was over.

He replied in the negative, whereupon she brought up from under a pile of pillows, coverlets, blankets and sheets, a little tiny, red-faced, wrinkled thing, to which she said I was *Aunt*! I knew, then, why Ada congratulated Herbert, and mentally chiding myself for my stupidity, I took the bundle of cambric and flannel in my arms, while Anna said, "We call him Jamie Lee, and we think he looks like you. Isn't he a beauty?"

He *did* look like me, and knowing that, I wondered at Anna's question; but where is the young mother who thinks her first born baby homely?— though his nose be flat—his forehead low—and his mouth extend from ear to ear! Not Anna, most certainly. He was *her* baby and Herbert's, and to her partial eyes he was beautiful, even though he did resemble *me*, whom but one person had ever called pretty. As for myself, I hardly knew whether to be pleased with my new relative or not. Babies, particularly little tiny ones, had never been my special delight, but on this occasion, feeling that some demonstration was expected from me, I kissed my little nephew, who returned my greeting with a wry face, and an outcry so loud that Anna, in great alarm lest he was "going into a fit," summoned from the kitchen, where she was enjoying a *quiet smoke*, Aunty Matson, who boasted of having washed and dressed two hundred and fifty babies, and who confidently expected to do the same service for two hundred and fifty more ere her life's sun was set.

Wearied with my ride, I asked permission to retire early; whereupon Dame Matson volunteered to show me the way to my room. Up the narrow stairs, which creaked at every step, and on through one gloomy room after another, she led me until, at last, we came to a chamber, lighter and more airy, which, she said, my sister had papered, painted, and fitted up for me; adding, as she set the candle upon the table and closed the window, "You ain't afraid of *spooks* nor nothin'?"

"*Spooks*" was to me a new word, and in some surprise I asked what she meant.

"Now, du tell," she replied, seating herself upon the foot of the bed. "Now, du tell a body where you was brought up, that you don't know what a *spook* is! Why, it's a *sperrit*—a ghost—and this house, they say, is full on 'em. But I don't b'lieve a word on't. S'posin' a gal was murdered near forty years ago, 'tain't likely she haunts the place yet, and then, too, she warn't none of the best of girls, I guess, from what I've heard my mother say."

The wind was blowing hard, and as Dame Matson uttered these last words, the door, which she had left ajar, came together with a bang, while from the lake I heard again the wailing cry, which, this time, had in it an angry tone, as if the maiden were indignant at the wrong done her by the old dame, whose eyes seemed to expand and grow blacker at the sound. Overcome as I was with fatigue, I could not sleep; and for hours I lay awake, listening to the rain as it fell upon the roof, and to the howling wind, which, indeed, produced the most unearthly noises I had ever heard. At last, however, nature could no longer endure, and I fell into a deep slumber, from which I did not awake until the sun was high up in the heavens, and preparations were going forward in the kitchen for dinner, which was served exactly at twelve. Greatly refreshed, I was ready to laugh at my fears of the night previous; and with childish joy, I explored every nook and corner of the old castle; finding many a rathole, which threw some light on the sounds over my head, which I had likened to the trampling of horses.

It took but a few days for me to discover that Herbert was exceedingly popular at Breeze Hill, as the neighborhood in which he lived was called. His free, social manners had won for him many friends, and made him almost too much of a favorite. At least, I used to think so, during the long winter evenings, when Anna sat with her baby upon her lap, listening for the footsteps of her husband, who, at some neighbor's fireside, was cracking the merry joke, and quaffing the sparkling cider; which, at Breeze Hill, was considered essential to hospitality. Gradually, too, as the winter wore on, my sister's eye took the anxious expression I had so often seen in my Aunt Charlotte; and sometimes, when he stayed from her longer than usual, she would steal down to the foot of the long Avenue, and there, alone, would wait and listen for her husband's coming; while the spirit from the lake would whisper sadly in her ear of the darkness and desolation hovering near. And all this time Herbert professed to be strictly temperate; and when, about the middle of March, a travelling lecturer held forth in the old log schoolhouse, thundering his anathemas against the use of all spirituous liquors, Herbert was the most zealous of all his listeners, and at the close of the lecture, arose himself and addressed the assembly, pouring out such a tide of eloquence as astonished the audience, who rent the air with shouts of "Langley forever!"

Knowing this, I was greatly surprised, after our return home, to see the young orator go up to the sideboard and drink off, at one draught, a goblet of the *porter* which had been ordered for Anna! *She* saw it, too, and for an instant her face was pressed against that of her sleeping boy; and when next the lamp-light fell upon it, I saw there traces of tears, while a faint smile played around her mouth, as she said, "I am afraid, Herbert, your audience would hardly think your theory and practice agree, could they see you now."

The words were ill-timed; for they awoke the young man's resentment, and with a flushed brow he retorted angrily, that "if porter were good for her, it was for him; he saw no difference between a drinking woman and a drinking man; except, indeed, that the former was the most despicable."

The next morning, the bottles of porter were gone from the sideboard; but out in the orchard, where the grass of an early spring was just starting into life, they lay shattered in a hundred pieces. Would, oh, would that she, the wife of little more than a year, could thus easily have broken the habits of him she loved better than her life. But it could not be; and all through the bright spring days she drooped, and faded, and struggled hard to keep from me the fatal truth; and when the warm breath of summer was over all the land; when the robins' song was heard in the maple trees; and the roses blossomed by the open door, they brought no gladness to her heart; no love-light to her eye, save when she looked upon her baby; now a playful, handsome child, the pet and idol of the house.

At last, Aunt Charlotte wrote to me, asking to be assured of her son's safety; and then poor Anna begged me not to tell that the wine-cup was his companion at morn; his solace at noon, and his comfort at night. Yielding to her entreaties, I answered evasively; and thus the shock, when it came to that mother's heart, was harder far to bear, from the perfect security she had felt. At Meadow Brook, too, they little dreamed how their absent daughter wept and prayed over her fallen husband, who, day after day, made rapid strides down the road to death; for, on her bended knees, Anna implored me to keep her shame a secret yet a little longer; and with this request I also complied, doing whatever I could to smooth the thorny pathway she was treading.

CHAPTER XVII
THE DARK MAN

The long summer days had merged into autumn, whose hazy breath floated like a misty veil over the distant hills. Slowly and noiselessly the leaves were dropping one by one from the maple trees, strewing the withered grass with a carpet of gorgeous hue. The birds had sung their farewell song to their summer nests, and were off for a warmer clime; while here and there busy hands and feet were seen gathering in the autumnal stores.

On Herbert's farm, however, there was a look of decay. The yellow corn and golden pumpkins were yet in the field; the apples lay in heaps upon the ground; the gates swung loosely in the wind; while the horses, uncared for and unfed, neighed piteously in their stalls as if asking why they were thus neglected. Alas! their master was a drunkard. Anna was a drunkard's wife; and mine a drunkard's home! It was no longer a secret there, and the old men shook their heads, while the young men sighed to think how he had fallen. Night after night we sat up for him, my sister and I lifting him from the threshold across which he would fall, and bearing him to his bed, where we would lay him beside his innocent son, whose blue eyes often opened with wonder at being thus disturbed. A night's debauch was always followed by a day of weakness and debility, in which he was incapable of exertion, and so everything seemed on the verge of ruin, when he suddenly conceived the idea of advertising for an efficient man, who would take the entire charge of affairs and relieve him from all care.

About this time I went back to Meadow Brook for a few weeks to be present at the bridal of my oldest sister. Anna, too, was urged to accompany me, but she declined, extorting from me a promise that if it were possible I would not divulge the real state of things. "Tell them I am happy and do not regret what I have done," said she, as she followed me down to the gate.

"And would that be true?" I asked, looking her in the face.

For an instant she hesitated, while her pale cheeks flushed and the tears started to her eyes; then glancing at little Jamie, whom she held in her arms, she answered, "Yes, it would be true. I do not regret it. I had rather be Herbert's wife as he is, than not to have been his wife at all."

Ah, who can fathom the depths of woman's love, and what punishment shall be sufficient for him who wantonly tramples upon it. Thus I thought as I turned away from my sister, pondering upon her words long after I reached the cars, and wondering if I should ever love as she did. Involuntarily the doctor rose up before me—a drunkard, and I his wife, and from my inmost soul I answered, "rather death than that!" Then, though I blushed as I did so, I fancied myself the wife of "the dark man," and *he* a drunkard. "Yes, I could bear that," I said, and as if to make the old adage true, that a *certain individual* is always near when we are talking about him, the car door opened and the subject of my meditations stood before me! There was no mistaking him. The same tall, manly form, the piercing eyes, the coal black hair and the same deep cut between the eyebrows. I knew him in a moment, and an exclamation of surprise escaped my lips, which, however, was lost by the rush of the cars. The seats were nearly all occupied, and as he passed down the aisle, my readers, I trust, will pardon me, if I *did* gather up the skirt of my dress and take my travelling bag upon my lap, while I myself sat nearer to the window, looking out in order to hide my face, which I thought possibly might not attract him!

"Is this seat occupied, miss?" said a heavy voice, which seemed to come from some far off region.

"No, sir," I answered, timidly, without venturing to turn my head, until I felt myself uncomfortably crowded; then I looked around, and behold! the dark stranger was sitting behind me near the door, while at my side was a man of mammoth dimensions, with immense moustaches, watery eyes, and a brandy breath flavored with tobacco!

I wanted to cry, and should probably have done so, had not my companion immediately commenced a conversation by asking "if I had come very far, and where I was going?"

He was exceedingly loquacious, and for several hours plied me with questions as to my own name—my parents—my grand-parents—my brothers—my sisters—our standing in the world—our religion—our politics, and our opinion of spiritualism, of which last he was a zealous advocate. At length just as it was growing dark, he gathered up his huge proportions, and to my great joy bade me adieu, expressing his regret at leaving me, and also assuring me that I would one day be a medium, which assumption he based upon the fact of my having admitted that sometimes when falling away to sleep I started suddenly and awoke. *This*, he said, was a *spirit shock*, and would in the end lead to great results.

About nine o'clock we stopped for refreshments, and on re-ëntering the cars, I found to my joy that the dark stranger's seat was appropriated by a son of Erin, who seemed nowise inclined to surrender it, inasmuch as he had with him his wife, baby, and bundle. This time the fates were propitious, for after looking around him awhile, the stranger asked permission to sit by me, saying he should not discommode me more than two or three hours, as by that time he hoped to reach his journey's end, a remark which gave me more pain than pleasure, for every nerve thrilled with joy at being thus near to one who, though an entire stranger, possessed for me a particular attraction. It was quite dark where we sat, and the night lamp burned but dimly, so he did not once obtain a full view of my face. He proved a most agreeable and attentive companion, opening and shutting the window just as often as I evinced an inclination to have him, holding my sachel in his lap; placing his own travelling trunk at my feet for a footstool, and offering me his fur-lined overcoat for a pillow; besides expressing many fears that I would take cold whenever the window was open. At almost every station, too, he asked "if I wished for anything," but I did not, except indeed to know whether he was yet the husband of Ada Montrose, and to obtain that information I would have given almost anything. At last I hit upon the following expedient. He made some remark about the country through which we were passing, and I replied by saying that "I believed it was not the first time he had been over that road, as, if I mistook not, I saw him in the cars with his *wife* the year before."

The wrinkle in his forehead grew deeper, and his face flushed as he said quickly, "I do not remember of meeting you before, though I *was* here last fall, but not with my *wife*, for I have none. It was my *ward*, Miss Montrose."

Nothing could have given me more satisfaction than this announcement, for if Ada were his *ward*, it explained, in a measure, his attentions to her; and as I cast stolen glances at him, I felt more and more convinced that there could be no affinity between him and the haughty, imperious girl to whom he was guardian. It seemed to me a very short time ere he arose, and offering me his hand, said he must go, adding, "We shall undoubtedly meet again, as I occasionally travel this way."

Yes, we should meet again. I felt sure of that, though how and where I could not tell.

It was nearly noon of the next day when I reached Meadow Brook, where I found my father at the dépôt, waiting to receive me. Very kindly he greeted me, inquiring eagerly after Anna and her boy, his grandson, whom he expressed a strong desire to see. "But I never shall," he said sadly, as he walked slowly beside me up the long hill which led to the village. Of

Herbert he spoke not a word, though my mother and my sisters did, asking me numberless questions, some of which I answered, while the others I managed to evade, keeping them ignorant of the existing state of things.

I found them all busied with the preparations for Juliet's wedding, which took place within a week after my return, I officiating as bridesmaid, while the groomsman was none other than my old enemy, John Thompson, now a tall young man of eighteen, and cousin to Juliet's husband. When first the plan was suggested to me I refused, for I bore him no good will; but my objections were overruled by Juliet, who told me how much he had improved, and that I would find him very agreeable, which was indeed true. He was very polite and attentive, referring laughingly to the "freaks of his *boyhood*," as he termed them, while at the same time he laid his hand upon his *chin*, caressing the beard which was there only in imagination, and even apologizing to me in a kind of off-hand way for his conduct of three years before. Of course I forgave him, and we are now the best of friends. So much for childish prejudices.

In the course of the evening I asked him about the doctor, and was told that he was still in Boston, and doing remarkably well. "And do you know," said John, "he imputes his success to *you!* I verily believe he thinks you a perfect angel! Any way, I know he likes you better than he does Dell, for he told me so in plain English, and I don't blame him either; the way she cuts up is enough to kill any man. Why, if I were in his place, I'd get a divorce from her at once, and offer myself to you!"

"I wouldn't have him," said I, quickly.

"Nor me either? Wouldn't you have me?" asked John, playfully.

"No, I wouldn't," was my reply; whereupon he laughed heartily, saying "he was glad he knew my sentiments before he committed himself;" and there the conversation ended.

After Juliet had left us for her new home, in an adjoining town, there ensued at our house a season of lonely quiet, in which we scarcely knew whether to laugh or to cry. There is always something sad in the giving up of a daughter to the care of another, and so my parents found it, particularly my father, who, broken in spirit and feeble in health, was unusually cast down. He could hardly suffer me to leave his sight for a moment, and still he seemed to take special pleasure in finding fault with whatever I did. Nothing pleased him, and gradually there returned upon me with its full force the olden fancy of my childhood, that *I* was not loved like the rest. It was a most bitter thought, wringing my heart with a keener anguish than it had ever done before; and once, the very day before the one set for my return to Rockland, my pent up feelings burst forth, and in angry tones I told him "it was useless for me to try to please him—he didn't love me and never had—and I was glad that the morrow would find me away, where he would no longer be troubled with my presence, which was evidently so disagreeable to him."

He made me no answer, but a fearful look of sorrow, which will haunt me to my dying day, passed over his thin, white face, and his hand, which was hard and brown with toil for *me*, was raised beseechingly as if to stay the angry torrent. Oh, how I repented of my harshness then, but I did not tell him so; I would wait till morning, and then, ere I left, I would seek the forgiveness, without which I well knew I should be wretched, for something told me that never in this world should we meet again.

Next morning when I awoke, the sun was shining brightly in at my window, and hurrying on my clothes, I descended to the dining-room. In silence we gathered around the breakfast table, and then I saw that my father was absent. "Where was he?" I asked, and was told that having business in Southbridge, a town several miles distant, he had left early, telling my mother to bid me good-bye for him. All my good resolutions were forgotten, and again I said hastily, "I think he might at least have bidden me good-bye himself, and you may tell him so."

"Hush, Rose, hush," said my mother. "Your father isn't the man he was before we left our old home. He is broken down, and it may be you have seen him for the last time."

"It is hardly probable," I answered, and with a swelling heart I bade my mother adieu; but I left no message which would tell my father how much I repented of my rashness.

Upon his grave the tall grass is growing—howling storms have swept across it—wintry snows have been piled upon it—the summer's mellow sunlight has fallen around it—flowers have blossomed and faded—changes have come to us all—and still I have never ceased to regret that last interview with my father, or to mourn over my distrust of his love for me.

CHAPTER XVIII
THE DEATH OF THE DRUNKARD

During my journey back to Rockland, I did not again meet with the stranger, although I looked for him at every station, and when at last I stepped from the cars at Canandaigua, I must confess to a feeling of disappointment. I had expected Herbert to meet me, but he was not there. I was just wondering what I should do in case he failed to come, when my attention was attracted towards a tall, athletic-looking young man, who was inspecting my trunk, which stood upon the platform. Fearful lest my best clothes should be carried off before my very face, I started quickly forward, demanding what he was doing with my baggage.

The stranger stood up, and fixed upon me a pair of singularly handsome, hazel eyes, which had in them an expression so penetrating that I quailed beneath them; while at the same time there swept over me a strange, undefined feeling as if somewhere in a dream, perchance, I had met that glance before.

"Are you Miss Lee?" he asked, and the tones of his voice thrilled me like an echo of the past.

I replied in the affirmative; and without once taking his eyes from my face, he said, "I am Henry Watson, Mr. Langley's hired man. He sent me for you, and the wagon is at the other door."

Mechanically I followed him to the place designated, and then, as if I had been a feather, he took me in his arms and placed me in the wide chair, wrapping the buffalo-robes around me, and in various ways seeing that I was comfortable. He did not seem to me like a hireling, for his language was good, his manners gentlemanly, and ere we were half-way to Breeze Hill I was very much prepossessed in his favor, except, indeed, that he would look at me so much. He was quite talkative, asking me of my parents, of my brothers, and appearing much gratified when I told him how well Charlie was doing as clerk in a dry goods store in Worcester.

"And Mr. Langley is only your cousin by marriage?" he said at last. "Have you any other male cousins?" he asked.

"I had a boy cousin once," I said, "but he is probably dead, for we have not heard from him in six long years."

Forgetful that Mr. Watson was to me an entire stranger, I very briefly told him the story of "Cousin Will," who returned not with the vessel which bore him away, and who had deserted the ship at Calcutta. For many days they searched for him in vain, and at last left him alone in that far off land, where he had probably met an early death.

"He must have been a wild boy, and I dare say you felt relieved to be rid of him," said Mr. Watson, who had appeared deeply interested in my story.

"Yes, he was wild," I replied, "but I liked him very, very much, and cried myself sick when he went away."

Again the stranger's eyes fell upon me with a look I could not fathom. I grew uneasy, and was not sorry when about sunset we turned into the long, shady avenue which led up to the house. As if by magic, a wondrous change had been wrought in my absence; for everything around the building wore an air of neatness and thrift, which betokened that there was now a *head* to manage and direct. Herbert, too, was perfectly sober, while Anna's face was far happier than when I last saw her. The cause of this she explained to me the first moment we were alone. Herbert had signed the pledge! Had become a sober man, and all through the exertions of Mr. Watson, whom she pronounced an angel in disguise. And, truly, his influence over Herbert was wonderful; for never did an anxious mother watch over her sickly child more carefully than Mr. Watson watched over his employer, shielding him from temptation, and gently leading him in the path of rectitude; until the wine-flush on his cheek gave way to a hue of health; the redness of his eyes was gone, and conscious of the victory he had achieved, he stood forth again in all the pride of his manhood, sober, virtuous, and happy.

Such was the state of things, when, early in April, we received invitations to attend a wedding party at the house of Judge Perkins, whose broad acres and heavy purse of gold had purchased for him a fair young girl, just his eldest daughter's age! It was to be a splendid affair, for all the *élite* of Rockland were bidden, and, as a matter of course, *I* forthwith commenced looking over my wardrobe, and declaring I had nothing to wear! Anna, on the contrary, did not seem at all interested, and when I questioned her for her indifference, she replied, "What if they have *wine*, and Herbert should drink?"

"They wouldn't have wine," I told her, for Judge Perkins was a staunch temperance man, and it was not probable that he would do anything so inconsistent with his profession.

After a time she became convinced that her fears were groundless, and began with me to anticipate the expected pleasure. Henry Watson was not invited, but he carried us to the door, going himself to the hotel to wait until we were ready to return. Just as he was leaving us he whispered a few words to Herbert, who replied, gaily, "Never fear for me. Judge Perkins isn't the man to throw temptation in my way."

Ah, would it had been so! Would that the sparkling champagne, the ruby wine, and the foaming ale had not graced that marriage feast, for then, perchance, *one grave* at least would not have been made so soon, nor the widow's weeds worn by my sister ere the bloom of youth had faded from her brow.

I saw her cheek pale as we entered the supper-room, but when amid the din and uproar which succeeded the drawing of the corks, Herbert stood firm to his pledge, refusing to drink, though urged to do so, the color came back to her face, and her eye proudly followed her husband, whose easy manners made him a favorite, and who, with ready tact, moved among the guests, doing far more towards their entertainment than the master of the house himself. He was standing near the bride, a beautiful young creature, with a sunny face and radiant smile. Diamonds were wreathed in her shining curls, and shone upon her snowy arms, while the costly veil almost swept the floor, and enveloped her slight form like a misty cloud. Very affable and polite had she been to Herbert, and now as he approached her, she took from the table two goblets of wine, and passing one to him, said, "Mr. Langley, I am sure, will not refuse to drink with *me*, the bride?"

To refuse would have seemed uncourteous; and so, with a hasty glance at his wife, he drank the health of the lovely woman, who, in an angel's guise, unconsciously tempted him to ruin. Involuntarily, Anna gasped as if for breath, while she started quickly forward to stay the rash act; but she was too late, and with a faint moan of anguish, she turned away to hide her tears. One taste awoke the slumbering demon, and set his veins on fire; and when at midnight Mr. Watson came for us, he took the insensible man in his arms and placed him in the wagon, beside the weeping wife, whose fond hopes were now wrecked for ever.

From that time Herbert made no further attempt at reform, but night after night, came reeling home, sometimes singing a bacchanalian song, and again rending the air with curses, until at last poor Anna learned to tremble at the sound of his footsteps; for he daily grew more and more violent and unmanageable, defying every one save Mr. Watson, who possessed over him a singular power. Thus the spring and summer passed away, and when the autumn came few would have recognized the once handsome Herbert Langley in the bloated creature, who, weak and feeble, lay all day long in bed, begging for "brandy—more brandy" to fan the flame which was feeding upon his vitals. Sometimes in his fits of frenzy he would spring upon the floor, and shriek for us to save him from the crawling serpents, which, with forked tongues and little green eyes, hissed at him from all parts of the room. Again he would say that the spirit of the murdered maiden was before him, whispering to him unutterable things concerning the drunkard's home beyond the grave, while goblins of every conceivable form beckoned him to come and join their hideous dance.

Once, when he was more quiet than usual, he said to me, "Rose, do you remember what I once told you about my mother's joining the church and reading her prayers?"

I replied in the affirmative, and he continued—"Do you know I'd give the world, were it mine, if I could hear her pray for me once more. It would cool my scorching brain, and if I dare pray for myself, I know I should be healed; but I cannot, for the moment I attempt it, there are legions of imps who flit and grin before my face, while one, larger and more unseemly than the rest, shouts in my ears, 'Lost, lost, to all eternity!' there—look, don't you hear it?" and, shivering with fright, he covered his head with the bed-clothes.

But I heard nothing save the heaving swell of the waves, and the sullen roar of the lake, which came in through the open window, seeming to his disordered imagination an accusing spirit from another world. At last looking up timidly and speaking low, as if fearful of being overheard, he said, "Is there a Prayer Book in the house?"

I answered in the affirmative. Raising himself upon his elbow, and glancing fearfully around, he continued, "Bring it quick, while they are away, and put it under my pillow. Who knows but it may operate like a spell!"

I complied with his request, and brought the book, which he placed under his head, saying, "There—now I can pray, and God won't let them mock me, will he, think?"

I could only weep as he folded his long white hands one over the other, and said reverently the prayer taught him years and years before, commencing with—

"Now I lay me down to sleep," etc.

As if the words, indeed, had a soothing power, he almost instantly fell into a deep sleep, from which he awoke refreshed, and better than he had been for several days. They said he could not live; and though it was a painful task, Anna wrote to his mother apprising her of his danger, and bidding her hasten, if she would see him again.

During the few remaining weeks of his life he was subject to strange fancies. For a time the Prayer Book beneath his pillow had the effect of keeping him comparatively quiet; but, anon, it lost its power, and one day he awoke with a fearful shriek. The imps, as he called them, had again returned, and were mockingly taunting him with the victory he vainly imagined he had obtained.

"Keep off, ye devils!" he shouted, drawing the volume from beneath his pillow, and holding it to view. "Keep off; for, see, this book is full of prayers, which my mother has said. *My mother!* Do you hear? Ha! They laugh at the idea, and well they may. Had she learned to pray sooner, I might not have been the vile thing that I am. But *she* taught me to *drink. She* set the example; so go to *her* with those horrid faces, besmeared with the smoke of the pit."

There was a bitter groan, and then the wretched woman, his mother, fell half fainting upon a chair. She had just arrived, and eager to see her boy, had entered the room in time to hear what he said. He knew her in a moment, and starting upright in bed, exclaimed, "Woman, look—this is your work— the result of your example. There was a time, long ago—how long ago it seems—but there *was* a time, I say, when I loathed the very smell of the liquors, which daily graced our table. By little and by little that loathing was overcome. *You* drank and called it good; and what one's mother says is true. So I, too, tasted and tasted again until here I am, Herbert Langley, husband of Anna Lee, ruined body and soul—body and soul! What do you say to that, mother?"

He sank back upon the bed exhausted; while Aunt Charlotte, who had swooned entirely away, was taken from the room. The shock was too great for her, and for two days she did not again venture into his presence. The next time, however, that she saw him, his mood had changed, and winding his feeble arms around her neck, he wept like a child, asking her to take from his heart the worm which was knawing there. Oh, how I pitied the heartbroken woman! for I well knew she would gladly have lain down her life could that have saved her son. For three days longer he lingered, and then there came the closing scene, which haunted me for months.

He had been restless during the night, muttering incoherently, and occasionally striking at the fancied shapes which surrounded him; but towards morning he grew more violent, and at last with a shriek which chilled my blood, he sprang from the bed, and pointing towards the window, whispered, "Hark! Don't you hear it?—*music from the infernal regions!* They are come, every demon of them, for me. It's a grand turnout. There! Don't you see them with their flaming eyes looking through the windows, and that shriveled hag, whose hair is curling snakes! See! She beckons me with her bony claws, and says I am to be *her* son. Do you hear that mother? *Her son!* Go back!" he shouted, leaping towards the window. "You don't get me this time. I won't die yet. Give me the Prayer Book, and let me hurl it at her head—that'll settle her, I reckon."

He would have gone through the window, had not Mr. Watson taken him in his arms and borne him back to the bed, where he held him fast, soothing him as best he could by assuring him there were no such unearthly objects in the room as he supposed.

"I know it," said Herbert, for a moment comparatively rational. "I know what it is. It is DELIRIUM TREMENS, and I know what causes it, too; shall I tell you?"

Mr. Watson nodded, and Herbert continued: "*Cider, beer, wine, brandy*— DEATH: that's the programme which keeps the fire of hell eternally burning. Where is my boy—Anna's boy and mine?" he asked after a pause.

"Do you wish to see him," asked Mr. Watson.

"See him? Yes. I want to do one good deed before I die. *I would kill him*— murder my only child, and send him to Heaven, where rumsellers never go—where women, with witching eyes and luring words, never tempt men to drink. Bring him in: why do you loiter?" turning to Anna. "Is it that you would have him live to be the wreck I am—to curse the mother who bore him and the day he was born! Bring him quick, I tell you, for time hastens, and in the distance I hear the clank of the hag's footsteps."

"Oh, Herbert, Herbert, my poor husband," was all Anna could say, as she wound her arms around his neck and laid her colorless cheek against his fevered brow.

In a moment he grew calm, and drawing her to his bosom, his tears fell like rain upon her face, while he called her his "wounded dove," and asked her forgiveness for all he had made her suffer. "You will live with mother when I am gone," he said. "You and Jamie. God forbid that I should harm our beautiful boy; but I would see him once more. Don't be afraid," he added, as he saw her hesitate. "I will not hurt him."

Disengaging herself from her husband's embrace, Anna glided from the room, to which she soon returned, leading little Jamie, now two years of age. Very lovingly the dying man looked upon his son, and then laying his shaking hand upon the golden curls, he said, "God keep you, my boy, from being what I am; and if a drunkard's blessing can be of any avail, you have mine, my precious, precious child."

"Would you like to kiss him?" asked Aunt Charlotte; to which he replied, "No, no; I am too polluted to touch aught so pure. But take him away," he continued, growing excited. "Take him away, for the demon on my pillow is again whispering of murder."

Hastily the wondering child was taken from the room, and then Herbert fell into a disturbed slumber, in which he seemed to be holding converse with beings of another world, inquiring of them if they had enough to drink, and chiding the rich man for asking *water*, when he might as well call for *brandy*!

About noon he awoke and inquired for me. With some trepidation I approached him, for his eyes were those of a madman; but he meditated no harm, and only asked if I supposed that the Prayer Book laid upon the outside of his pillow, where the hag could see it, would have the effect of keeping her away.

"Perhaps so," I said, at the same time placing it so that his heavy brown hair fell partially on it.

"Now, will some one pray—mother, you?" and his eyes turned imploringly towards the half crazed woman, who essayed to pray for the departing spirit.

"That'll do—that'll do," he exclaimed, interrupting her. "It's of no use spending your breath for me. It's too late—too late—so the hag says, and she's coming again, with myriads on myriads of fiends; but they can't hurt me as long as this is here," and his hand clutched convulsively for the book which lay beside him.

"The hymn book—the hymn book—bring that too," he gasped, while a cold perspiration stood thickly upon his forehead.

It was brought and placed on the opposite side of his head.

"'Twon't do—'twon't do," he sobbed. "All the hymns Dr. Watts ever wrote can't help me, for they come nearer and nearer, as wolves hover round their prey. Is there no help, no escape?" he cried, with the energy of despair; adding, as a sudden look of joy lit up his ghastly features, "Yes— the Bible! Strange I have not thought of that before. The Bible will keep them at bay. Bring it, Anna, quick, for they are almost here."

She obeyed; and grasping the word of God eagerly in his hands, he laughed aloud, saying, "Now, do your worst, ye fiends incarnate. The Bible will save me."

There was a moment of perfect silence; and then, with a groan so full of anguish that I involuntarily stopped my ears to shut out the fearful sound, the Bible was loosed from the clammy hands, which for a brief instant fought fiercely in the empty air, and then dropped lifeless at his side.

Herbert was dead!

At the foot of the garden, near the long avenue where the shadow of the maple trees would fall upon his grave, and the moan of the lake be always heard, we buried him; and then, the broken-hearted Anna, widowed thus early, went back to her accustomed duties, performing each one quietly and gently, but without a smile upon her white, stony face, or a tear in her large mournful blue eyes. Aunt Charlotte, too, utterly crushed and wretched, went back to her city home, having first won a promise from Anna that in the autumn she would follow her. And then we were left alone with our great sorrow, wholly dependent, as it were, upon Mr. Watson, for support and counsel.

There had always been about him a mystery I could not fathom, and greatly was I surprised when one evening, a week after Herbert's death, he asked me to go with him to his room, as there was something he wished to tell me. I complied with his request, and was soon seated in the large willow chair near the table on which lay many works of our best authors, for he possessed a taste for literature, and devoted all his leisure moments to study. Drawing a seat to my side, he said, taking my hand in his, "Rosa, what do you think I am going to tell you?"

I tried to wrest my hand from his grasp, for the unwonted liberty angered me. But he held it fast, smiling at my fruitless endeavors, and after a moment continued: "Why do you try to remove your hand from mine? I have held it many a time, and I have a right so to do—a *cousin's* right. Look at me, Rosa, don't you know me?"

Involuntarily I started to my feet, gazing earnestly upon him, then with a cry of joy I threw my arms around his neck, exclaiming, *"Cousin Will! Cousin Will!"*

It was indeed he, come back to us when we had thought of him as dead. A few words will suffice to tell his story. Perfectly disgusted with sea life, he had deserted at Calcutta, where he kept himself secreted until the vessel sailed. But it was not his wish to remain there long, and the first time an English ship was in port he offered to work his passage to Liverpool. The offer was accepted, and while we were mourning over his supposed death he was threading the smoky streets of London, doing sometimes one thing and sometimes another, but always earning an honest livelihood.

"Never, for a moment," said he, "did I forget your family, but I have fancied they were glad to be rid of me, and hence my silence. When at last I returned again to New York, I went one day to a reading-room, where I accidentally came across Mr. Langley's advertisement, and something prompted me to answer it in person. If I had ever heard of him before, I had forgotten it; consequently I neither recognized him nor his wife, who has changed much since I saw her; but when I accidently heard them speak of "Rosa," and "Meadow Brook," my curiosity was roused, and I became aware of the relationship existing between us. Why I have kept it a secret so long I can hardly tell, except that there was about it, to me, a kind of pleasing excitement, and then, too, I fancied that Mr. Langley would not so well bear restraint and direction from me if he supposed me an interested party; but *he* has gone, and concealment on that score is no longer necessary. I have told you my story, Rosa, and now it is for you to say whether I am again received and loved as the "Cousin Will" of olden time."

He was a big, tall man, six feet two inches high, while I was a young girl scarcely yet seventeen; but notwithstanding all this, I threw my arms around his sun-burnt neck and kissed his sun-burnt cheek as I had often done before. This was my answer, and with it he was satisfied.

After leaving his room I went directly to my sister, to whom I repeated the strange story I had heard. She was pleased and gratified, but her faculties were too much benumbed for her to manifest any particular emotion, though as time wore on I could see how much she leaned upon him and confided in his judgment. It seemed necessary for her to remain in Rockland through the summer, and as she would not consent to my leaving her, I was rather compelled to stay; although almost weekly there came to us letters from home urging our return, and at last, near the middle of September, we one day received a letter from Charlie, which, owing to some delay, had been on the road two whole weeks. In it he wrote that our father had failed rapidly within a few days and we must come quickly if we would again see him alive, adding that he talked almost constantly of *Rose*, asking if they thought she would come.

Oh, how vividly I recalled the past, remembering with anguish the harsh words I had uttered when last I saw him. It was true I had once written, imploring pardon for my fault, and Lizzie, who answered my letter, had said "Father bade me say that you were freely forgiven;" but still I felt that I could not let him die until I had heard my forgiveness from his own lips. It was impossible for Anna to accompany me, and, as William would not leave her, I started alone, my heart filled with many dark forebodings, lest I should be too late.

CHAPTER XIX
THE DEATH OF THE RIGHTEOUS

All around the house was still; while within, the children and the neighbors trod softly as they went from room to room, and their faces wore an anxious, troubled look, as if they already felt the presence of the *shadow* hovering near. The heavy brass knocker was muffled, and the deep-toned churchbell across the way no longer told the hours of 12 and 9, for at each stroke the sick man had turned upon his pillow, and moaned as if in pain. So when the Sabbath came the people went up unsummoned to the house of God, where they reverently prayed for him, who was passing from their midst, and who, ere another week rolled round, would be "where congregations ne'er break up, and Sabbaths never end."

For many days he had lain in a kind of stupor from which nothing roused him save the rush of the engine as it swept across the meadow at the foot of the hill. Then he would start up, asking eagerly if "they had come, Anna, Rose, and Jamie." Much he talked of the absent ones, and as day by day went by and still they came not, he wept like a little child, as he said to his wife, "I shall never see them more."

"And if you do not," she asked, "what shall I tell them?"

For a time he lay as if her question was unheard—then opening his eyes he answered, "Tell Anna, my stricken one, that there is for her a balm in Gilead; that whom the Lord loveth he chasteneth, and though the waters through which she is passing be deep and troubled, they shall not overflow, for the everlasting arms are beneath her."

"And Rosa, have you no message for her?" asked my mother as he ceased speaking.

"Oh, Rosa, Rosa," he answered quickly, "Tell her—tell her everything—but not here—not in this room. She thinks I do not love her, and when she comes and finds me gone, go with her to my grave. She will believe you if you tell her there how dear she was to me, and how, through the long weary nights before I died, I wept and prayed for her that she might one day meet me in the better land. I never meant to love one child more than another, but if I did—tell her she was my pride, the one on whom I doted.

She thought me cold and unfeeling, because I stayed not to bid her adieu that morning. Ah, she did not know that with the first dawn of day I stole up to her chamber to look on her once more for the last, last time. There were tears on her cheek, I kissed them away; tell her that, and perchance her heart will soften towards her poor old father."

From that time he sank rapidly, and one bright September day, near the hour of sunset, it was told in Meadow Brook that he was dying. On such occasions, in a small country village, the liveliest sympathy is felt; and now those who knew and loved him spoke to each other softly and low, while even the little children ceased their noisy play upon the common, and with a timid, curious glance towards the open windows of the sick room, hastened home, where they kept closely at their mother's side, wondering—asking of her what death was, and if she were sure that he, the dying one, would go to Heaven.

Meantime, the sun was almost set, and as its last golden rays fell upon the face of the sufferer, a radiant smile lit up his features, and he exclaimed aloud, "'Tis the glorious light of the Eternal shining down upon me. Do not weep, mother. We shall not be parted long," he continued, as he felt upon his forehead a tear from the grey-haired, wrinkled woman, on whose bosom his head was pillowed, just as it had been, long, long ago, when first a tender babe he lay in that mother's arms. To her it seemed not long, and yet it was fifty years since he was lent to her, and now, when God would have his own again, she said submissively, "Thy will be done." Once before had a great sorrow fallen upon her, leaving her henceforth to walk alone, and then her soul had well-nigh fainted beneath the blow, for she was younger far by many years. But now she was old, and already she heard the roar of the deep dark river on whose very banks she stood, and down whose swift current her first born was floating; so she stifled her own grief, for, as he had said, she knew it would not be long ere they met again.

"Where is Fanny?" he asked, and his arms closed fondly around his wife.

It mattered not that time and care had dimmed the lustre of her eye, and robbed her cheek of its girlish bloom; to him she was beautiful still, for through weal and woe she had been faithful to her marriage vow, and now the bitterest pang of all was the leaving *her* alone.

"The God of the widow and the fatherless watch over and keep you all so that at the last, when I ask for my children, there shall not one be missing," he said, as his arms unclosed, and then, with a low, wailing moan, the *mother* bent over the white face of her son, so that the *wife* might not see the fearful change which had come upon it, for *my father was dead!*

You who have kept with me while I described the death scene of the unfortunate Herbert, and of my sainted father, can you not—do you not say, "Let me die the death of the righteous, and let my last end be like his?"

Lonely and desolate was the home at which I arrived one day too late, for they had buried him, and there was naught left to me of my father save the lock of hair which they severed from his head as he lay in the coffin. Yes, he was gone; but so long as life and being endure, so long shall fond remembrances of him linger in my memory, and if at the last I meet him in the better world, will it not be in a measure the blessed influence of his dying message, which has led the wanderer there?

CHAPTER XX
GOING SOUTH

After the first shock of our sorrow was over, the question arose as to what we were to do in future for our support. Grandma was already old, while mother was not so young as she had been once, and neither could do much towards their own maintenance, which necessarily would devolve upon us their children. It had ever been a pet project of mine to go South as a teacher, and when one day in looking over a Boston paper I accidentally came across the advertisement of a Georgia lady, Mrs. A. D. Lansing, who wished for a private governess, I resolved at once to apply for the situation, greatly fearing lest I might be too late.

I was not, however; for after waiting impatiently for a few weeks, I received a letter from the lady herself, who, after enumerating the duties I was expected to perform and the branches I was to teach, added, in a P. S.: "Before making any definite arrangements with Miss Lee, Mrs. Lansing wishes to be informed if, either by her *friends* or *herself*, she is considered pretty, as a person of decidedly ordinary looks will be preferred."

"Spiteful, jealous old thing!" exclaimed Lizzie, who was looking over my shoulder, "I wouldn't stir a step."

But I thought differently. My curiosity was roused to know the cause of her strange freak; and then, too, six hundred dollars per year would amply atone for any little peculiarities in my employer. So I answered her letter forthwith, assuring her that neither my friends nor myself had ever been guilty of calling me pretty—in short, I was decidedly homely, and trusted that on that point at least I should please her.

"What a fib, Rosa," said Charlie, when I told him what I had written. "You know you are not homely. You used to be, I'll admit; but you are far from being so now. To be sure, you are not what many would call handsome, but you are decidedly good-looking. You've got handsome eyes, splendid hair (and he pulled one of my short, thick curls by way of adding emphasis to his words) and your complexion is not one half so sallow and muddy as it used to be. Depend upon it, this 'Mrs. Angeline Delafield Lansing, of Cedar Grove' will think you have deceived her."

"Nonsense!" I replied, seating myself at the piano, which was now my constant companion, Mrs. Lansing having written that she was very particular about music.

Now, to tell the truth, I was *not* very much of a performer, but looking upon the South very much as I did upon the far West, I fancied that a small amount of showy accomplishments would pass for the real coin. Still I determined to play as well as possible, and so week after week I practised, until, when I had nearly given up all hopes of ever hearing from the lady again, I one day received a letter bearing the W—— post-mark, and containing a check on a Boston bank for money sufficient to defray my expenses. There were also a few hastily written lines, saying that "Mrs. Lansing considered our engagement as settled, but she should not expect me until the latter part of April, as she could not immediately get rid of her present governess, a *painted, insipid* creature from *New York*, and the veriest humbug in the world."

"A sweet time you'll have of it with madam," said Charlie, "and once for all I advise you to give up going. Why, only think, April there is hotter than pepper, and of course you'll take the fever and die."

But I was not to be persuaded. The "sunny South" had for me a peculiar fascination; and then, too, there was another reason which, more than all others, prompted me to go. Georgia was the home of the *dark man*, as I called him, and though there was hardly a probability of my ever meeting him there, such a thing was still possible, and like Longfellow's Evangeline, who, on the broad Mississippi, felt that each dip of the oar carried her nearer to her lost Gabriel, so each day I felt a stronger and stronger conviction that somewhere in the southern land I should find him.

In the meantime, Anna had been with us for a few weeks, but greatly changed from the Anna of former times. Listlessly she moved from room to room—never smiling, never weeping, and seldom speaking unless she were first addressed. To her, everything was dark, deep night, and such a gloom did her presence cast over us all, that though we would gladly have kept her with us, we still felt relieved when she left us for a home in Boston, where little Jamie soon became the idol of his grandmother, whose subdued cheerfulness had ere long a visible effect upon Anna. Cousin Will, too, had visited us, and after spending a short time had sailed with brother John for California, promising himself a joyous future, when he should return with money sufficient to purchase the old homestead, which he said should be mother's as long as she lived.

It was a cold, dark, snowy morning in the latter part of April, when I at last started on my journey. The surface of the ground was frozen hard, the trees were leafless and bare, while but few green things gave token that spring was with us. It is not strange, then, that I almost fancied myself in another world, when after a prosperous sea voyage I one morning went on shore at Charleston, and first breathed the soft, balmy air of the South. Dense and green was the foliage of the trees, while thousands of roses and flowering shrubs filled the air with a perfume almost sickening to the senses. From Charleston to Augusta was a wearisome ride, for the cars were crowded and dirty, and there was to me nothing remarkably pleasing in the long stretches of cypress swamps and pine barrens through which we passed.

It was late in the evening when we reached the town of C——, from whence I was to proceed to W——, by stage. It was a most beautiful night; and for hours I watched the soft moonlight as it glimmered among the trees which lined either side of the narrow road, and whose branches often swept against the windows of our lumbering vehicle. It was long after sunrise when we arrived at W——, but so thickly wooded is the country around, that I obtained not a single glimpse of the town until I suddenly found myself "thar," as the driver said, dismounting and opening the door of our prison-house. The hotel into which I was ushered, would, perhaps, compare favorably with our country taverns at the North; but at each step I took, I felt a more and more painful consciousness that *home*, my home, was far away.

After shaking the dust from my travelling dress, and slaking my thirst from the big gourd shell (my special delight), which hung by the side of a bucket of cool water which stood on a little stand in the parlor, I inquired for some one who would take to Mrs. Lansing my card, and thus apprise her of my arrival. The landlord immediately summoned a bright, handsome mulatto boy, who, after receiving my orders, and favoring me with a sight of his ivories, started off bare-headed, and for that matter bare-bodied too, for Cedar Grove, which the landlord pointed out to me in the distance, and which, with its dense surroundings of trees, looked to me delightfully cool and pleasant. After waiting rather impatiently for an hour or more, a large, old-fashioned carriage, drawn by two rather poor-looking horses, stopped before the door. It belonged to Mrs. Lansing; and the footman, jumping down from the rack behind, handed me a note, in which the lady begged me to come directly to her house, saying she was herself indisposed, or she would have come down to meet me, and also adding, that if I would excuse her she would rather not see me until supper-time, when she hoped to feel better.

At the extremity of Main street, we turned in at a ponderous gate, and after passing through two or three fields or lawns, stopped at last in front of Cedar Grove, which stood upon a slight eminence overlooking the town. In perfect delight I gazed around me, for it seemed the embodiment of my childish dreams, and involuntarily I exclaimed, "This is indeed the sunny, sunny South." It was very beautiful, that spacious yard and garden, with their winding walks on which no ray of sunlight fell, so securely were they shaded, by the cedar and the fir, the catalpa, the magnolia, and the fig tree, most of them seen now by me for the first time in all their natural beauty, reminded one so forcibly of Eden. The house itself was a large, square building, surrounded on three sides by a piazza, which I afterwards found was the family sitting-room; it being there that they congregated both morning and evening. The building had once been white, but the paint was nearly all worn off, and it now presented a rather dilapidated appearance, with its broken shutters and decayed pillars, round which vines and ivy were twining. The floors within were bare, but scrupulously clean; while the rooms lacked the costly furniture I had confidently expected to see.

Scarcely was I seated in the parlor, when I heard a sweet, childish voice exclaim, "She's in *thar*—she is," while at the same time a pair of soft, blue eyes looked through the crevice of the door, and then were quickly withdrawn, their owner laughing aloud as if she had accomplished some daring feat, and calling out, "I seen her, Hal—I did. And she don't look cross neither. You dassn't peek in thar, dast you?"

They were my future pupils, I was sure; and already my heart warmed towards them, particularly her with the silvery voice, and I was just thinking of going out to find them, when I heard a light footstep on the stairs, and the next moment a tall, dark-eyed girl, apparently fourteen or fifteen years of age, entered the room, introducing herself as Miss Lina Lansing, and welcoming me so cordially that I felt myself at once at home.

"Mother," said she, "is indisposed, as I believe she wrote you, and has sent me to receive you, and ask what you would like."

I had scarcely slept a moment the night previous, so I replied, that if convenient, I would go immediately to my room. Ringing the bell, she summoned to the room a short, dumpy mulatto, whom she called Cressy, and who, she said, was to be my attendant. Following her up the stairs, I was ushered into a large, airy chamber, which, though not furnished with elegance, still contained everything for my comfort, even to a huge *feather bed*, the sight of which made me wipe the perspiration from my face.

"Shall I wash missus' feet first, or comb her har," asked the negress, pouring a pitcher of water into a small bathing tub.

This was entirely new to me, who had always been accustomed to wait upon myself, so I declined her offers of assistance, telling her, "I preferred being alone, and could do everything for myself which was necessary."

"Laws, missus!" she answered, rolling the whites of her eyes, "'taint no ways likely you can bresh and 'range all dat ar har," pointing to my thick and now somewhat tangled curls. "Why, Miss Lina's straighter dan a string, an' I'll be boun' she never yet tache a comb to it herself."

With some difficulty I convinced the African that her services were not needed, and staring at me as if I had been a kind of monstrosity, she left the room, the door of which I bolted against any new intruder. The windows of my chamber looked out upon the garden, where now were blossoming roses and flowers of every possible hue and form. A little to the right, and about a quarter of a mile away was, another building, larger and more imposing than that of Mrs. Lansing, while a great deal of taste seemed to be displayed in the arrangement of the grounds. As nearly as I could judge, it stood upon a little hill, for the trees appeared to rise regularly one above the other, the fir and the cedar forming the outer boundary; while, as I afterwards learned, the inner rows consisted of the graceful magnolia, the wide-spreading catalpa, the beautiful china tree, and the persimmon, whose leaves in the autumn wear a most brilliant hue, and present so fine a contrast to the dark green of the pine and the fir. Very, very pleasant it looked to me, with its white walls just discernible amid the dense foliage which surrounded it, and for a long time I stood gazing towards it wondering whose home it was, and if the inmates were as happy as it seemed they might be.

At last, faint with the fatigue of my journey and the odor of the flowers, which, from the garden below, came in at the open window, I threw myself upon the lounge (feather bed looking altogether too formidable) and was soon fast asleep, dreaming of Meadow Brook, of the white house on the hill, and of the *dark man*, who, I thought, told me that it should one day be my home. When at last I awoke, the sun was no longer shining in at my windows, for it was late in the afternoon, and the fiercest heat of the day was past. Springing up, I commenced dressing with some trepidation, for I expected to meet the mistress of the house at supper-time. My toilet was nearly completed when I heard in the hall the patter of childish feet, while a round, bright eye was applied to the key-hole. It was the same which had looked at me in the parlor, and anxious to see its owner, I stepped out of the door just as a fairy creature with golden curls started to run away. I was too quick for her, however, and catching her in my arms, I pushed back the clustering ringlets from her brow, and gazing into her sunny face, asked her name.

Raising her white, waxen hand, she did for me the office I had done for her, viz. pushed back *my* curls, and looking in my face, answered, "Ma says it's *Jessica*, but Lina, Hal, and Uncle Dick call me *Jessie*, and I like that a heap the best. You are our new governess, ain't you?"

She was singularly beautiful, and yet it was not so much the regularity of her features, nor the clearness of her complexion which made her so. It was the light which shone in her lustrous blue eyes, which gave her the expression of an angel, for such she was—an angel in her southern home, which, without her would have been dark and cheerless. Her brother, whom she called *Hal*, was three years older, and not nearly so handsome. He was very dark, and it seemed to me that I had seen a face like his before; but ere I could remember where, a faint voice from the piazza, which faced the east and was now quite cool, called out, "Halbert, Halbert, come here."

"That's ma," said Jessie, getting down from my arms. "That's ma— come and see her," and following her, I soon stood in the presence of Mrs. Lansing, who was reclining rather indolently in a large willow chair, while at her back was a negress half asleep, but appearing wide awake whenever her mistress moved.

She was a chubby, rosy-cheeked woman, apparently thirty-five years of age. Her eyes were very black, and she had a habit of frequently shutting them, so as to show off the long, fringed eyelashes. On the whole, I thought, she was quite prepossessing in her appearance, an opinion, however, which I changed ere long; for by the time I reached her, there was a dark cloud on her brow, evidently of displeasure or of disappointment. Still she was very polite, offering me her jewelled hand, and saying, "Miss Lee, I suppose. You are welcome to Georgia then;" after an instant, she added, "You don't look at all like I thought you would."

I was *uglier* than she expected, I presumed, and the tears started to my eyes as I replied, "I wrote to you that I was very plain, but after a little I shall look better; I am tired now with travelling."

A strange, peculiar smile flitted over her face, while she intently regarded me as if to assure herself of my sanity. I was puzzled, and in my perplexity I said something about returning home, if my looks were so disagreeable. "They were used to me there, and didn't mind it," I said; at the same time leaning my head against the vine-wreathed pillars, I sobbed aloud. Lithe as a kitten, little Jessie sprang up behind me, and winding her arms around my neck, asked why I cried.

"Did ma make you cry?" she said. "Uncle Dick says she makes all the governesses cry."

"Jessica, Jessica, get down this moment," said the lady. "I did not intend to hurt Miss Lee's feelings, and do not understand how I could have done so. She is either acting a part, or else she strangely misunderstands me."

I never acted a part in my life, and, somewhat indignant, I wiped away my tears and asked "what she meant."

There was the same smile on her face which I had noticed before, as she said, "Do you really think yourself ugly?"

Of course I did. I had never thought otherwise, for hadn't I been told so ever since I was a child no larger than Jessie, and the impression thus early received had never been eradicated. Thus I answered her, and she believed me, for she replied, "You are mistaken, Miss Lee, for however plain you might have been in childhood, you are not so now. Neither do I understand how with those eyes, that hair and brow, you can think yourself ugly. I do not believe you meant to deceive me, but, to tell the truth, I am disappointed; but that cannot now be helped, and we'll make the best of it."

Perfectly astonished, I listened to her remarks, giving her the credit of meaning what she said, and for the first time in my life, I felt as I suppose folks *must* feel who think they are handsome! After this little storm was over, she evidently exerted herself to be agreeable for a few moments, and then rather abruptly asked me how old I was.

"Not quite eighteen!" she repeated in some surprise. "Why I supposed you were *twenty-five* at least! Don't you think she looks older than *Ada*?" turning to Lina, who answered quickly, "Oh, no, mother, nothing like as old. Why, I shouldn't think her over seventeen at the most."

Now among my other misfortunes I numbered that of "looking old as the hills," so I didn't care particularly for what they said, though it struck me as rather singular that Mrs. Lansing should thus discuss me in my presence; but this thought was lost in the more absorbing one as to *who* the *Ada* could be of whom she had spoken. Possibly it was Ada Montrose, though I ardently hoped to the contrary, for well I knew there was no happiness for me where she was. Thinking it would be on a par with the questions put to me, I was on the point of asking who *Ada* was, when we were summoned to supper, which consisted mostly of broiled chickens, strong coffee, iced milk, egg bread, and hoecakes, if I except the row of sables who grouped themselves around the table, and the *feather girl*, whose efforts to keep awake amused me so much that I almost forgot to eat. We were nearly through when a handsome mulatto boy entered and handed a letter to his mistress, which she immediately opened, holding it so that the address could be read by Halbert, who, after spelling it out, exclaimed, "That's from Uncle Dick, I know!"

"Is he coming home?" asked Jessie, dropping her knife and fork, while even Lina, who seldom evinced much interest in anything, roused up and repeated the question which Jessie had asked.

"Yes. He is in New York now," said Mrs. Lansing; "and will be here in a week."

"Good!" exclaimed Halbert.

"Oh, I'm right glad," said Jessie, while Lina asked if *Ada* was with him.

"No," returned Mrs. Lansing. "She is still in Paris with her cousin, and will not return until autumn."

"I'm glad of that," said Lina, to which Hal rejoined, "And so am I. She's so proud and stuck up, I can't bear her."

"Children, children," spoke Mrs. Lansing, rather sternly, at the same time rising from the table.

It was not yet sunset; and as soon as we were again assembled upon the piazza, Halbert and Jessie, who were never still, asked permission to "run up to Uncle Dick's, and tell the servants he was coming home."

Mrs. Lansing made no objection; and then they proposed that I should accompany them. Feeling that a walk would do me good, I turned towards Mrs. Lansing, for her consent. It was given, of course; but had I known her better I should have detected a shade of displeasure on her face.

"You had better go too," said she to Lina; but Lina was too listless and indolent, and so we went without her, little Jessie holding my hand, and jumping instead of walking.

"Eva's mighty lazy," said she, at last; "don't you think so!"

"Who's lazy?" I asked; and she replied—

"'Thar, I done forgot again, and called her *Eva*. Her name is Evangeline, and we used to call her Eva, until mother read a bad book that had little Eva in it, and then she called her Lina."

"'Twan't a bad book, neither," exclaimed Halbert, stopping suddenly; "Uncle Dick said 'twan't; but it made mother mad, I tell you, and now when she gets rarin' he calls her *Mrs. St. Clare.*"

I needed no one to tell me that it was "Uncle Tom," to which he referred, but I said nothing except to chide the children for their negro language.

"I know we talk awful," said Jessie, brushing her curls from her eyes. "Uncle Dick says we do, but I mean to learn better. I don't talk half like I used to."

I could not help smiling in spite of myself upon the little creature bounding and frisking at my side. *Uncle Dick* seemed to be her oracle, and after looking around to make sure that no one heard me, I asked "who he was?"

"Why, he's Uncle Dick," said she; "the bestest uncle in the world;" while Halbert added, "He's got a heap of money, too; and once, when ma thought I was asleep, I heard her tell Lina, that if he didn't get married it would be divided between us, and I should have the most, 'cause I'm named after him, Richard Halbert Delafield Lansing, and they call me *Hal*, for short. I told Uncle Dick what mother said, and I tell you, he looked blacker'n a nigger; and somehow, after that he took to ridin' and foolin' with Ada, wonderfully."

As yet everything with me was comparatively conjecture. I did not know positively that the *Uncle Dick* of the children was the "*dark man*" of Rosa Lee; but the answer to my next question would decide it, and half tremblingly was it put. "Who is this Ada. What is her other name?"

"*Ada Montrose*, and she lives with us. Uncle Dick is her guardian," said Halbert, throwing a bit of dirt at the negro boy who accompanied us, and who returned the young gentleman's salute with interest.

I was satisfied, and did not wish to hear any more. I should meet him again, and tinged as my temperament is with a love of the marvellous, I could not help believing that Providence had led me there. By this time we had reached "Sunny Bank," as it was very appropriately called, and never before had I seen so lovely a spot. The grounds, which were very spacious, were surrounded on all sides by a hedge of the beautiful Cherokee rose, and, unlike those of Cedar Grove, were laid out with perfect taste and order, Mr. Delafield, as I afterwards learned, had spent much time at the North, and in the arrangement of his house and grounds, he had not only imitated, but far surpassed the style of the country seats which are so often found within a few miles of our eastern cities. For this he was in a measure indebted to Dame Nature, who at the South scatters her favors with a lavish hand, sometimes beautifying and adorning objects far better than the utmost skill of man could do. The gate at the entrance of Sunny Bank was a huge wooden structure, having for its *posts* two immense oak trees, around whose trunks the graceful ivy twined, and then hung in fanciful festoons from several of the lower branches.

As I had supposed, the house itself stood upon a slight elevation, and the walk which led up to it was bordered on either side by the mock orange, whose boughs, meeting overhead, formed an effectual screen from the rays of the sun. The building, though fashioned in the same style as that of Mrs. Lansing, was much larger, and had about it a far more stylish air. Much of the furniture had been brought from New York, Halbert said; adding that "all the floors were covered with matting in the summer, and elegant Turkey carpets in the winter."

In the rear of the house were the cabins of the negroes, who were lounging idly about, some on the ground, some in the doors, and some stretched at full length upon the back of the piazza, evidently enjoying the cool evening breeze. At sight of us, they roused up a little, and when Halbert, after announcing that I was Miss Lee, the new governess, further informed them that their master was coming home in a few days, they instantly gathered round us, evincing so much joy as to astonish me, who had heretofore looked upon a southern slaveholder as a tyrant greatly dreaded by his vassals.

"You must like Mr. Delafield very much," I ventured to remark to one old lady, whose hair was white as wool.

"*Like* Mass'r Richard!" said she, rolling up her eyes. "Lor' bless you, miss, *like* don't begin to 'spress it. Why, I farly worships him; for didn't I tend him when he was a nussin' baby? and hain't these old arms toted him more'n a million of miles?"

Here her voice was drowned by the others, all of whom united in declaring him the "berry best mass'r in Georgy." This did not, of course, tend in any way to diminish the interest which I felt in the stranger; and, ere I was aware of it, I found myself anticipating his return almost as anxiously as the negroes themselves.

It was dark when we reached Cedar Grove; and as there was company in the parlor, I went immediately to my room. I had not been there long, however, when a servant was sent up, saying, that "Mrs. Lansing wished me to come down and play."

This was an ordeal which I greatly dreaded; for, from what I had seen of Mrs. Lansing, I knew she would criticise my performance closely; and fearing inability to acquit myself at all creditably, I trembled violently as I descended to the parlor, which was nearly full of visitors.

"Miss Lee, ladies," said Mrs. Lansing, at the same time motioning towards the music-stool as the seat I was expected to occupy.

There was a film before my eyes as I took my post and nervously turned over the leaves of a music-book; which, by the way, was wrong side up, though I didn't know it then! I have heard much of *stage fright*, and sure am I. that never did poor mortal suffer more from an attack of that nature than did I during the few moments that I sat there, trying to recall something familiar, something which I knew I could play. At last, when the patience of the company seemed nearly exhausted, I dashed off at random, playing *parts* of two or three different tunes, changing the key as many times, using the load pedal when I should have used the soft, and at last ending with the most horrid discord to which my ears ever listened. The audience were, undoubtedly, thunderstruck, for they spoke not for the space of a minute; and, with a feeling of desperation, I was about to make a second effort, hoping thereby to retrieve my character, when Mrs. Lansing said, in a cold, sarcastic voice, "That will do, Miss Lee; we are perfectly satisfied." Then, turning to a haughty-looking young lady who sat by the window, she continued: "Come, Miss Porter; you certainly can't refuse to favor us, *now*."

With a very consequential air, for which I could not blame her, Miss Porter took my place, and, without any apparent effort, killed my poor performance outright; for she executed admirably some of the most difficult music. When she had finished, the ladies rose to go, Mrs. Lansing following them to the door, and whispering (I know she did) something about "her being humbugged again."

When she returned to the room, I stole a glance at her face, which was very red, and indicative of anything but good will towards me. I felt the hot tears rising, but when, with a bang, she closed the piano, and turning towards me, demanded "how long I had taken music lessons," I forced them back, and answered promptly, "five quarters."

"Only five quarters!" she repeated, in evident amazement. "Why, Lina has taken *three years*, and she wouldn't consider herself competent to *teach*, even were she *poor*, and obliged to do so."

The latter part of this speech I did not fancy; for even if a person *is* poor, and obliged to work, they do not often like to be taunted with it; at least, *I* didn't, but I couldn't help myself. I was at the mercy of Mrs. Lansing, who proceeded to say, that "she had often been deceived by Northern teachers, who thought to palm themselves off for better scholars than they really were; and now she had almost come to the conclusion that they were not so well educated as the majority of Southern girls."

"I, at least, never intended to deceive you," said I; "I told you in my letter that I was *not* an accomplished musician, and still you consented to employ me."

Here I broke down entirely, and wept passionately, telling her, in broken sentences, that "however mortifying it would be, I was willing to go back, if she wished it."

At this point, little Jessie, who all the time had been present, came to my side, and winding her arms around my neck, said, "You sha'n't go home. We like you, Hal and me, and you sha'n't go—shall she, Hal?"

Thus appealed to, Hal took up my cause, which he warmly defended; telling his mother "she made every governess cry, and told them they didn't know anything, when they *did*, for Uncle Dick said so, and *he* knew; and that, as for music, Miss Lee played a *heap* better than Lina, because she played something *new*—something he never heard before."

"Nor any one else," muttered Mrs. Lansing, while Hal continued, "Uncle Dick says, the best teachers sometimes don't play at all, and Miss Lee sha'n't go home."

Very faintly, I repeated my willingness to do so, if Mrs. Lansing thought best; to which she replied, "I will deal fairly with you, Miss Lee. I am disappointed in your musical abilities, and if I find that your are deficient in other things, I shall be obliged to dismiss you; but for a few days I will keep you on trial."

"Uncle Dick won't let you send her away, I know," said Hal; and this, I am inclined to think, determined her upon getting rid of me before his return.

Still, I was ostensibly *upon trial*, and whoever has been in a similar situation, will readily understand that I could not, of course, do myself justice. With Mrs. Lansing's prying eyes continually upon me, I really acted as though I were half-witted; and by the close of the second day, I myself began to doubt the soundness of my mind, wondering why the folks at home had never discovered my stupidity. Continual excitement kept my cheeks in a constant glow, while the remainder of my face was quite pale, and several times, in their mother's presence, the children told me "how handsome I was!" This annoyed her—and on the morning of the third day, she informed me that she would defray my expenses back to Massachusetts, where I could tell them I was *too young* to suit her; adding, that I might as well go the next morning. This was a death-blow to my hopes; and so violent was the shock, that I could not even weep. Hal and Jessie were furious, declaring I should not go; and when I convinced them that I must, they insisted upon my teaching that day, at all events.

To this I consented; and as Mrs. Lansing had now no object in watching me, she absented herself from the schoolroom entirely, leaving me to do as I pleased. The consequence was, that my benumbed faculties awoke again to life, everything which, for the last ten days, I seemed to have forgotten, came back to me; while even the children noticed how differently I appeared.

CHAPTER XXI
UNCLE DICK

The day was drawing to a close. The children's lessons were over, the last I was to hear. Their books were piled away awaiting the arrival of my successor, and at my request I was left in the schoolroom alone—alone with my grief, which was indeed bitter and hard to bear, for I knew that injustice had been done me, and most keenly I felt the mortification of returning home in disgrace. Very beautiful to me seemed that fair south land of which I had dreamed so oft, and I felt that I could not leave it.

Through the open window I heard the shouts of the children, but I did not heed them, nor observe that throughout the entire house there seemed to be an unusual commotion. An hour went by, and then in the hall I heard the voice of Jessie, and the words she uttered sent an electric thrill through my nerves, and brought me to my feet, for they were, "Come this way, Uncle Dick. I reckon she's in the schoolroom."

The next moment he stood before me, the *dark man*, scanning me curiously, but still without anything like rudeness in his gaze.

"Uncle Dick's come. This is him," said Jessie, leading him towards the spot where I stood.

A bright beautiful smile broke over his strongly marked features, and I felt as if a gleam of sunlight had shone for an instant over my pathway. Taking my hand in his, he bade Jessie leave us, as he wished to see me alone. She started to obey, but ere she reached the door, she turned back and asking him to stoop down, whispered in his ear, loudly enough for me to hear, "I want you to like her."

"Of course I shall," he replied, and again that smile broke over his face.

I did not expect him to recognize me, for with the exception of the night at the theatre he had never fairly seen my features, and still I was conscious of a feeling of disappointment when I saw that he evidently had no suspicion of ever having met me before. When I spoke, however, and he heard the sound my voice, he started and looked me more fully in the face; but whatever his thoughts might have been, he seemed to be satisfied that he was mistaken, and seating himself at my side, he commenced conversing with me as familiarly as if he had known me all my life. Gradually our conversation turned upon *books*, and ere I was aware of it I passed through what I now know to have been a pretty thorough examination of all the branches which Mrs. Lansing had wished me to teach, but so adroitly was the whole thing managed that it seemed like a quiet, pleasant talk, though I *did* wonder at his asking so many questions. *French*, was the last subject discussed, and here I was at fault, for my pronunciation I well knew was bad, although Mr. Delafield, who was himself a fine French scholar, told me it was quite as good as the majority of the Americans who had neither lived in Paris, nor had the advantage of a native teacher.

"You play, I believe. I would like to hear you," he said at last, laying his hand on my shoulder, as if he would lead me to the parlor.

Instantly the blood rushed to my face, for since the night of my disgrace I had not touched the piano, neither did I wish to again. So I tried to excuse myself, and when he insisted, I finally said, with my eyes full of tears, "Please excuse me, sir, for I can't play. I failed before your sister, and I shall do the same before you."

"No you won't," he replied, at the same time drawing my arm within his and leading me towards the door. "You have nothing to fear, Miss Lee, and if you acquit yourself half as creditably here as you have elsewhere, I shall be satisfied."

A faint perception of the truth began to dawn upon me, and I looked up at him so earnestly that he stopped and smiling down upon me, said, "You have taught a district school in New England, I believe?"

"Yes, sir," I answered.

"And you were examined, of course?"

"Yes, sir, and got a certificate, too," I said eagerly.

"I presume you did," he continued, "and if necessary I can give you another, for I have been doing nothing more or less than trying to find out how much you know. As I have before hinted, I am perfectly satisfied, and unless you leave from choice, you will remain at Cedar Grove."

He spoke as one having full authority to do as he pleased, and I instinctively felt that though nominally Mrs. Lansing was mistress there, *he*, in reality, was the leader, the *head*, whose bidding every one obeyed. The change from utter despondency to almost perfect happiness, was too great, and withdrawing my hand from his arm, I sat down upon the stairs and cried like a child, while he stood, looking down upon me and thinking, I dare say, that I was a very foolish girl. At last, when I thought his patience was nearly exhausted, I wiped my eyes, and starting up, said, "You have made me very happy, Mr. Delafield, for I could not have borne the disgrace as being sent home as incompetent. I can play for you now, or for Mrs. Lansing either."

And the result proved that I was right, for I exceeded my own expectations, and was astonished at myself.

"Angeline," said he, in a slightly commanding voice, as that lady looked curiously in at the door, "Angeline, come here;" and she crossed over to his side, where he detained her by placing his arm around her waist.

For a moment then I wavered, for though I could not *see*, I could *feel* the haughty gaze of the large black eyes, which I knew were bent upon me.

"You have done well, Miss Lee," he said, when at last I arose from the instrument, at the same time playfully touching my cheeks, which were burning with feverish excitement.

That night, after I had retired to my room, Halbert and Jessie came to the door, requesting permission to come in. I admitted them, when Jessie, jumping into my lap, said, "Oh, I'm so glad you are going to stay. Hal says so."

"Yes," put in Hal, "Uncle Dick told me that you mustn't be sent away, for you were a heap better scholar than she had represented you to be."

"Perhaps it will not be as Mr. Delafield says," I remarked; and Hal quickly rejoined, "Yes it will; ma does just what he tells her to do; and then, too, he *pays* the governess, for I heard him say so, and he told her if you were dismissed 'twas the last one he'd hire. And he said she must treat you better than she did Miss Rawson, for you were very young, and little things hurt your feelings, and when Ada came home, she mustn't domineer over you, for he wouldn't allow it. Oh, I like Uncle Dick. Don't you?"

The moonlight was streaming across the floor, but it did not reveal the blush which deepened on my cheek as I faintly answered "Yes," bidding him at the same time not to tell of it, for I began to feel afraid of the boy's loquacity. That night I dreamed of "Uncle Dick," whose name was the last which sounded in my ears when I fell asleep, and the first of which I thought when I awoke in the morning. As I was dressing, I heard little Jessie on the piazza, singing in her childish way, "*I love Uncle Dick, I do, and so does Hal, and so does Mis-ses Lee!*"

"Who told you *that*, Pussy?" asked a voice which I recognized as Mr. Delafield's, and very nervously I listened for Jessie's answer, which was, "Oh, I know she does. Hal asked her didn't she like you, and she said she did."

"Rather early to avow a preference, I think. I shouldn't wonder if a Miss Rawson performance were to be enacted a second time," said another voice, which I knew to be that of Mrs. Lansing, who had joined her brother upon the piazza.

"Angeline," said Mr. Delafield, somewhat sternly, "don't be foolish. If Halbert asked Miss Lee if she liked me, wasn't it the most natural thing in the world for her to say 'Yes.' I do wish you'd rid yourself of the impression that every girl who looks at me is in love with me, or that I am in love with every lady to whom I choose to be polite."

"Do you think Miss Lee pretty?" asked Mrs. Lansing, without paying any attention to his last remark.

Up to this point I could not well help overhearing their conversation, for I was arranging my hair before the mirror which stood near the window; but now there was no longer any necessity for my remaining there, and I resolutely walked away, though I would have given much to have heard his answer. He had gone home when I went down to the breakfast-room, where I found Mrs. Lansing, who greeted me rather coldly, and appeared slightly embarrassed. I had purposely donned my travelling dress, for though Mr. Delafield had said I was to stay, I felt that she too must do the same ere I had a right to remain. The sight of my dress seemed to annoy her, for it brought to her cheeks two bright red spots which grew deeper all the while we were at breakfast. When it was over, and the children had gone out, I very composedly asked her "how long before the stage would call for me."

Turning her flashing black eyes upon me, she said, "Do you mean to insult me, Miss Lee? The stage has been gone an hour. I supposed you knew you were to remain."

"Mr. Delafield intimated as much," I answered; "but my engagement was with *you*, not *him*, and until I hear from you that I am expected to stay, I do not of course feel at liberty to do so."

She brightened up perceptibly, and after saying something about Richard's meddling in *her* affairs, replied, "I presume you were embarrassed when you first came, and so could not appear to advantage; and as my brother thinks you are a tolerably fair scholar, I have decided to keep you."

I bowed in acquiescence, and she continued. "There is something, however, which I must first say to you; but as this is not the proper place, you will go with me to my room."

I complied with her request, and closing the door, she began with a long preamble as to the proper way for a young lady to conduct herself in the presence of gentlemen, especially those who were every way her superiors. "For instance," said she, "there's my brother Richard, who is rather noted for his familiar, affectionate manner towards the ladies. As long as he confines himself to his equals I do not so much mind it, but when he lavishes his attentions upon my governesses, I think it wrong, for he might, you know, raise hopes which of course could never be realized Now, Miss Rawson was a very silly girl who thought herself beautiful, and ere I was aware of it she was deeply in love with Richard. Of course, he cared nothing for her, even if he did play with and caress her. It is his way, and he means nothing by it. Then, too, Miss Rawson *was* rather handsome, and Richard has always been a passionate admirer of beauty. He used to say, when he was younger, that he never could love a woman who was not beautiful, and I've sometimes thought that the sight of a pretty face completely upset him. For this reason I prefer having a plain-looking governess. Miss Rawson was far too pretty, and after my trouble with her I determined to employ none but ugly ones. This is why I wrote to you concerning your personal appearance, which is, I am sorry to say, so much more prepossessing than I had reason to suppose. Still I do not apprehend any difficulty, provided you are always reserved and distant in Richard's presence, and decline any attentions he may occasionally offer you. Miss Montrose, of whom you have heard us speak, will probably be home this summer, and then his time will be occupied with her. I do not think he will ever marry any one, but if he does, it will undoubtedly be Ada. I won't detain you longer," she added, as she saw me try to suppress a yawn; "I won't detain you any longer than to warn you once more against being as silly as Miss Rawson was—the foolish thing—only think of it, my governess in love with my brother, and *he* a *Delafield!*"

It *was* very absurd, I thought; and mentally resolving not to fall into a like error, I repaired to the schoolroom, where in due time I was joined by the children, little Jessie bringing me a beautiful bouquet, which she said "Uncle Dick had arranged for me."

Feeling anxious to please Mrs. Lansing, my first impulse was to send the flowers back, but upon second thoughts, I concluded that this would not come under the head of "attentions," and so all the morning they stood in the tiny vase, which Halbert brought to hold them, all except one rose-bud which Jessie selected from the group, and twined among my curls. This at the dinner-table attracted the watchful eye of my employer, who, without any apparent motive, casually remarked upon its beauty, saying, "It looked like a species of *rose* which grew in her brother's garden," and adding that "she did not know as there were any of that kind on her grounds."

I blushed crimson, while Jessie answered, "It didn't grow here. *Uncle Dick* brought it to her with a heap more."

Casting upon me a frowning glance, Mrs. Lansing said, "Seems to me you have forgotten the conditions on which I kept you."

This was the first I had heard of *conditions*; but so anxious was I to retain my situation, that I resolved to please her at all hazards, and stammering out that "Jessie put it in my hair," I tore it from among my curls and threw it upon the floor. Then, as soon as dinner was over, I went up to the schoolroom, and removing the bouquet from the vase, threw that too, from the window. Very wonderingly, little Jessie looked up in my face, asking "why I did it," and if "I didn't love flowers."

"Very, very much," I answered; "but your mother don't want me to keep them."

That afternoon he came to visit us "officially," he said, and when I saw his winning manner, and how much of sunshine he brought with him, I did not wonder that one as susceptible as Miss Rawson was represented to be, should have fallen in love with him. But with *me* it was different. *I* had been warned against his pleasant, affectionate ways; and so, when in conversing with me and Lina, he threw his arm around her waist and laid his hand carelessly upon my shoulder, I moved quickly away, while I was sensible of a deepening flush upon my face. He seemed puzzled, and for an instant looked inquiringly at me, as if to ask a reason for my conduct. He was showing Lina a book of engravings, and after a while called me to look at a picture which he thought was particularly fine. I complied with his request, and wishing to see more, took a seat at his side, when either purposely, or from force of habit, he threw his arm across the back of my chair. The action reminded me of Dr. Clayton, and I was feeling somewhat annoyed, when looking up, I met the haughty eyes of Mrs. Lansing, who was passing the door, and had stopped to look in. This of course embarrassed me, and hardly knowing what I did, I said rather angrily, "You will oblige me, Mr. Delafield, by taking your arm from my chair. It does not look well."

"Certainly," said he, instantly removing it; "I was not before aware that it was there," and a very peculiar smile was perceptible about his mouth, as he, too, caught sight of his sister, who, with an approving nod for me, passed on.

I could have cried with vexation, for I feared he would think me very prudish, and I knew well enough that his familiarity was only the promptings of an unusually kind and affectionate nature. After staying a few moments longer, he arose to go, saying as he turned towards me, "Jessie gave you my flowers, I suppose."

"Yes sir," I replied, while my face again grew scarlet. "They were beautiful, and I thank you very much."

"I am glad to hear it," he continued, looking me steadily in my eyes. "I thought perhaps, you did not like them when I found them on the walk, withered and dried by the sun."

I was trying to think what to say by way of apology for thus treating his gift, when little Jessie came to my relief, by saying, "She didn't like to throw 'em away, but ma didn't want her to keep 'em."

"Ah, yes. I understand it now," said he, adding in an undertone, as he shook my hand, in accordance with the southern custom of bidding good-bye: "I hope, Miss Lee, you will exercise your own judgment in such trivial matters as that."

That night I cried myself to sleep, half wishing I had never come to Cedar Grove, for I knew Mrs. Lansing would prove an exacting, unreasonable mistress; and when Ada came home, my situation, I thought, would be anything but agreeable; while, worse than all the rest, was the fear that I had displeased Mr. Delafield, and appeared very ridiculous in his eyes. Supposing he had put his arm on my chair, was that any reason why I should get angry and speak to him as I did? It was his way, and as he had said, he was not himself aware of what he was doing. Of course, then, he would think me very foolish, and would ever after treat me with coolness and indifference. How then was I surprised, when the next morning, in the presence of his sister, he handed me a much larger and handsomer bouquet than the one of the preceding day, saying, as he did so, "I want you to keep this and not throw it away, as you did my other one."

Mrs. Lansing's face, which had been unusually placid and serene, now looked cloudy and disturbed; but she said nothing; neither did she ever again make any allusion to the flowers which so frequently came to me from Sunny Bank. One reason for this might have been that she was otherwise perfectly satisfied with the conduct of her brother, which, by the way, was *not* wholly satisfactory to me! It is true, he was very polite, very kind; but there was about him a reserve which I could not understand, for after that little affair in the schoolroom, he never treated me with the same familiarity which marked his deportment towards the other young ladies, who came to the house. He did not like me, I said, and the thought that I was disagreeable to *him* made me very unhappy. To be sure, he was almost constantly at Cedar Grove, where he spent most of the time in the schoolroom, "superintending us," he told his sister, who, believing me rather inefficient, made no objection to his supposed supervision of Lina's studies. He did not often talk much to me, but I frequently met the earnest gaze of his piercing dark eyes, particularly when little Jessie sat in my lap, listening to my instructions; and once when Herbert asked him for "a copy,"—something beginning with "R," he wrote "Rosa Lee, Meadow Brook, Massachusetts." Still he disliked me—I was sure of that; and though I did not then know why it was, the impression that I was to him an object of aversion made me unhappy, and almost every day I cried, while Mrs. Lansing more than once told me that "she did not believe the South agreed with me, for I was not half so *plump* and *rosy* as when I first came."

About this time, too, a Miss Dean, from the village, who had evinced quite a liking for me, told me, confidentially, that Mr. Delafield and Ada were certainly engaged; adding, that "it was sometimes sickening to see them together"—a fact I could not doubt, knowing him as I did, and remembering Ada's demeanor towards Herbert when they were engaged. From the same source, too, I learned that Mr. Montrose and the elder Mr. Delafield had been warm friends; and that the latter, who died when both Mrs. Lansing and Richard were quite young, had committed them to the care of Mr. Montrose, who was to them the kindest of fathers until the time of his death, which occurred a few years after Mrs. Lansing's marriage, when Richard was just of age. To *his* guardianship, therefore, as to that of a brother, had Mr. Montrose left his daughter, then a beautiful girl of seventeen; and since that time she had lived with Mrs. Lansing, who, though she appeared to love the young orphan, still opposed her marriage with her brother; not from any aversion to Ada, but because she did not wish Richard to marry at all, as in case he did not, his property would, in all probability, fall to her children, she being the only heir. When I asked her why Mr. Delafield was worth so much more than Mrs. Lansing, she replied, that the elder Mr. Delafield, in his will, had left two-thirds of his property to his son, bequeathing the other third to his daughter, whose husband had wasted nearly the whole in his extravagant manner of living. Cedar Grove, too, she said, was mortgaged to Richard for more than it was worth, and it was wholly owing to his forbearance and extreme generosity that Mrs. Lansing was enabled to support her present style of living. This, she said, aside from Mrs. Lansing's hope that her children would one day inherit her brother's wealth, was a sufficient reason why she wished him to remain a bachelor, as the presence of a wife at Sunny Bank would, in all probability, lessen his liberality towards herself. Miss Dean, who seemed to be well posted, also told me that, in case Mrs. Lansing saw her brother was determined to marry, she would, of course, prefer that he should marry Ada, who was quite a favorite, inasmuch as she had money of her own, and was connected with one of the first families in South Carolina.

All this I believed, and when I saw how anxious Mrs. Lansing appeared for Ada's return, and how much interest Mr. Delafield, too, seemed to take in her, I felt sure that matters were at last amicably arranged, and that, for once, rumor was right in saying that Sunny Bank would, in the autumn, be graced by the presence of a mistress. Latterly, Mr. Delafield had been making some repairs, and only a few days before, when I chanced to be there with Jessie, he had taken me through his library into a little, pleasant, airy room, which he was fitting up with great elegance.

"This," said he, laughingly, "I design as the boudoir of *Mrs. Delafield*, when I shall be fortunate enough to boast such an appendage to my household; and as a woman's taste is supposed to be superior to that of men, I want your opinion. How do you like it? Do you think it would suit *my wife*, if I had one?"

Of course he meant *Ada*, and in fancy I saw her reclining upon the luxurious lounges, or gazing out upon the vine-wreathed piazza, and wealth of flowers, which greeted my view when I looked from the large bay window. For an instant I dared not trust my voice to speak, and when at last I did so, I am sure it must have trembled, for he came to my side and looked me earnestly in the face, while he smiled at my answer.

"It ought to suit her, unless her home heretofore has been Paradise."

After that I had not the least doubt of his engagement with Ada, and I began seriously to think of going back to Meadow Brook to take charge of a select school, which was about to be opened there. I had now been in Georgia about four months, and one night I went down to the pleasant summer-house at the foot of the garden. It was a beautiful moonlight night and the air was almost oppressive with the sweet fragrance of the flowers. Why I went there I hardly know, only I fancied I could better make up my mind as to my future course, if I were alone and in the open air. "Nobody likes me here," I said to myself, as I took a seat within the arbor, "nobody but Halbert and Jessie. Mrs. Lansing is freaky and cross. Lina, selfish and indifferent, while Mr. Delafield thinks only of Ada's return, which I so much dread, and to be rid of meeting her, I will go home before she comes." So I decided that on the morrow, I would make known my determination to Mrs. Lansing, who I fancied would be glad, while Mr. Delafield would not be affected either way. *I* was nothing to *him*—he was nothing to *me*—so I reasoned, and then I made plans for the future, just as other maidens of eighteen have done, when their heart was aching with a heavy pain, whose cause they did not understand. I should never marry—*that* was a settled point—I should teach school all my days, and by the time I was twenty-five (it seemed a great way off then) I should have a school of my own,

"Lee Seminary" I would call it, and I had just completed the arrangement of the grounds, which somehow bore a strong resemblance to those of Sunny Bank, when I was roused from my reverie by the sound of a footstep, and in a moment Mr. Delafield stood at the entrance of the summer-house. He evidently did not expect to find me there, for he started back at first, and then, hoping he did not intrude, came to my side, saying, "A penny for your thoughts, Miss Lee, provided they are not as gloomy as your face would indicate."

"You can have them for nothing," I returned, elevating my eyebrows, and drawing down the corners of my mouth as if I felt that in some way he had injured me.

"You are *blue* to-night, and have been so for several days. What is the matter?" he asked, at the same time throwing his arms around my waist with his olden familiarity.

Quickly remembering himself, however, he withdrew it, saying as he did so, "I beg your pardon, Miss Lee. I am so in the habit of taking such liberties, that I forgot myself!" and he moved off a little distance. I could have cried with vexation, for though it might have been improper, I was perfectly willing to sit there with his arm around me! It might have dispelled all idea of the "Lee Seminary" of which I was to be Principal! But he gave me no such opportunity, and folding his arms as if to keep them in their place, he continued, "But tell me, Miss Lee, what *is* the matter. You do not seem yourself?"

It was perfectly proper for me to tell him, I thought, and very deliberately I unfolded to him my plan of returning home within a week of Mrs. Lansing were willing, which I was sure she would be, as she had never been quite satisfied with my acquirements. When I had finished speaking, I turned towards him, not to see what effect my words had produced, for I had not the most remote idea that he would care. Great then was my surprise, when I saw the blank expression of his face, which looked darker than ever. Starting up, he walked two or three times rapidly across the little arbor, and then resuming his seat, said gently, "Have you been unhappy here, Miss Lee?"

I could hardly repress my tears as I told him how much I liked the south land, and how I should hate to leave it.

"Why then do you do so?" he asked; and I answered "I can do more good at home; nobody likes me here."

He came nearer to my side, as he said, "Nobody likes you! oh, Rose, there is *one* at least who more than likes" — —

It was the first time he had ever called me *Rose,* and it thrilled me with an indefinable emotion; but so impressed was I with the idea of his engagement with Ada, that I never dreamed of interpreting his words, as I now think he meant I should; and ere he could say more, I interrupted him with, "Yes—little Jessie loves me, I know, and when I think of her, I would fain stay."

Still nearer to me he came, as he said, "And think you Jessie is the only one who loves you?"

If ever Mrs. Lansing's belief that I was *non compos mentis* was verified, it was then; for with the utmost stupidity I answered, "Why, no; *Halbert* likes me, but both he and Jessie will forget me when I am gone, and learn to love another."

I think he was quite disgusted; for with a slight gesture of impatience he changed his manner and in a very businesslike way began to reason the case with me, urging a great many reasons why I should not leave; the most potent one with me, being the fact that *he* wanted me to stay—"he would miss me very much," he said, "for he liked my society—it was a pleasure to talk with me, for he was sure I meant what I said; I was natural—truthful— so different from most of the young ladies (of course he excepted Ada), and then, too, it seemed as if he had known me always, or at least, had met me before, for my voice was familiar."

I could not tell him of our meeting in Boston, but I saw no harm in reminding him of the night, when for a few hours I was his travelling-companion, and so to his last remark, I answered, "We have met before, in the cars between Utica and Albany."

In some surprise he looked earnestly at me a moment, and then said, "Is it possible? Why have you never mentioned it before?"

"Because, sir," I replied, "I did not suppose you would remember me."

He appeared thoughtful for a time, and then again, looking closely at me, said, "I did not, I believe, get a glimpse of your features then, and still it seems as if I had seen them before—or something like them. At all events, I sometimes dream of a childish face, which must resemble you as you were a few years ago."

Once I half determined to remind him of the little girl who fainted at the theatre; but ere I did so, he continued, "When I met you in the cars, if I mistake not, you spoke of Miss Montrose. Did you ever see her? but of course not," he added, ere I had time to reply. I cannot tell why I shrank from acknowledging my slight acquaintance with Ada, but I did, and for a moment I said nothing; then thinking it would be wrong to give him a false impression, I said, "I can hardly say that I am acquainted with Miss Montrose; but I have met her several times at my uncle's in Boston, where I spent the winter, four years ago."

Again he bent forward as if to scan my face, while he replied, "Indeed! Were you in Boston then? It is strange Ada never spoke of you, or you of her before. Was there a misunderstanding between you?"

"Oh, no," I answered quickly; "she was a fashionable young lady, and I a mere school-girl; so, of course, we knew but little of each other."

"What was your uncle's name?" he inquired; and I answered "Lee," noticing the while, how the shadow which had settled upon his face at the mention of Boston, passed gradually away.

For a moment he was silent, and then rather abruptly, he asked, "Did you like her?"

I remembered the time when Dr. Clayton had asked me a similar question concerning Dell Thompson, and now, as then, I answered evasively, that "I hardly knew her—she was very beautiful and accomplished."

Here he interrupted me by saying, "I did not ask if you thought her *beautiful*. I asked if you liked her."

I felt a little annoyed, for I thought he had no right thus to question me, and forgetting that she was to be his wife, I replied, "*No sir, I did not like her. Neither do I think she liked me, or my sister who was with me; and this is one reason why I wish to leave before her return.*"

I supposed he would be offended at hearing me speak thus of her, but he was not; he merely smiled as he answered, "Ada has many faults, I know, but I do not believe your situation will be less pleasant on account of her presence. If it is, just state the case to me. I am competent to manage it, I believe; besides that, it is uncertain how long she will remain at Cedar Grove."

He commenced plucking at the green vine-leaves which grew above my head, while I turned my face away to hide my emotions; for of course, when Ada left Cedar Grove, it would be as his bride, I thought, and was surprised when he continued, "The cousin with whom she is travelling in Europe, has won from her a half promise that she will spend next winter with her in New Orleans, and if so she will leave in October; so you see, she can't annoy you long; and now you must promise me not to leave us unless she prove perfectly disagreeable."

There is not, I believe, the least coquetry in my nature, and I replied frankly that I would stay.

"You have made me very happy, Miss Lee," said he, rising up and laying his hand upon my head, just as a *father* might caress his child, for he was thirty-one and I was eighteen!

That night I pondered long upon what he had said, recalling every word and look, and at last, when a ray of light faintly glimmered upon my *befogged intellect*, I hid my face in the pillow, lest the moonlight, which shone around me, should read thereon the secret thought which I scarcely dared to harbor for a moment. Could it be possible that *he* loved me, and but that for my unaccountably stupid blunder in thrusting first Jessie and then Halbert in his face, he would have told me so! But no—it was impossible. He was probably engaged to Ada. *She* was beautiful and rich—*I* was homely and poor. It could not be. And then, my reader, did I first awake to the consciousness of how much I loved him; and how, when he was wedded to another, the world would be to me naught but a dreary blank. Anon, I remembered my former affection for Dr. Clayton, and then I grew calm. I had outgrown that, I said, and in all probability I should outlive this, my second heart-trouble. So, falling back upon the "Lee Seminary" as something which was to comfort me in my lone pilgrimage, I fell asleep and dreamed that Mr. Delafield's children, amounting in all to a *dozen*, were every one placed under my special charge!

CHAPTER XXII
ADA

She was now daily expected, the vessel in which she had sailed having landed at New York, and numerous preparations in honor of her arrival were in progress at Cedar Grove, where she was evidently regarded as a person of consequence. The best chamber in the house was appropriated for her use; Mr. Delafield himself taking much interest in the arrangement of its furniture, and bringing over each morning fresh bouquets of flowers, which, in costly vases, adorned the apartment. Every one seemed anxious and expectant, save Jessie and Halbert, the former of whom did not wish her to come, as she took up so much of "Uncle Dick's" time, while the latter openly avowed his dislike, saying, he wished she'd stay in Europe always.

As for myself, though there was no particular reason why I should do so, I dreaded her arrival, and when at last, word came to the schoolroom that she was in the parlor, and the children must come down to see her, I stole out into the garden, in order that I might put off the interview with her as long as possible. I knew I must meet her at the supper table, and so after a time I went up to my room to dress, donning a plain white muslin, which I had often been told became me better than aught else I could wear. Before my toilet was finished, little Jessie came in and insisted upon twining among my curls a few simple buds, which, she said, looked "mighty nice," adding, as she stepped back a pace or two to witness the effect, "I think you are a heap prettier than Ada; but Uncle Dick don't, 'cause I asked him, and he said 'Of course Ad was the handsomest.' Hal says how he's her beau, and I reckon he is, for he kissed her like fury!"

"He kisses everybody, don't he?" I asked; and she replied,—

"Mighty nigh everybody but *you*. I never seen him kiss *you*, and when I asked him why, he said you wouldn't let him—won't you?"

"It wouldn't be *proper*," I said, smiling down upon the little fairy, who, poised on one foot, was whirling in circles, and then looking up into my face, with her soft dreamy eyes.

At that moment the supper bell rang, and bounding away, she left me alone. For full five minutes I waited trying to summon sufficient courage to go down, and at last chiding myself for my weakness, I started for the dining-room. My footsteps were light, as they evidently were not aware of my approach, for they were talking of me, and as I reached the door, I heard Jessie, who was giving Ada a description of her teacher, say, "Why she's the properest person in the world, for she won't even let Uncle Dick kiss her."

"Somewhat different from Miss Rawson," said Ada, joining in the general laugh; at the same time lifting her large, languid eyes, she saw me, and started slightly, I fancied, as she recognized me.

She had changed since I saw her last, and her face now wore a weary, jaded look, while the dark circle beneath her eyelids told of late hours and heated rooms.

"Miss Lee—Miss Montrose," said Mrs. Lansing, and the proud Ada bowed haughtily to the humble governess, who with heightened color took her accustomed seat at the table.

"You have seen each other before, I believe," said Mr. Delafield, looking curiously at both of us, while Mrs. Lansing, in much surprise, exclaimed, "Seen each other! Where, pray?"

I waited for Ada to answer, and after staring at me a moment, she replied, quite indifferently, "Miss Lee's face does seem familiar, and if I mistake not, I met her *once or twice* in Boston"—and this was all she said, if I except a glance, half entreating, half threatening, which she threw at me from beneath her long, drooping eyelashes. This glance I did not then understand, but I now know it to have been prompted by a dread lest I should tell of her engagement with Herbert Langley, and thus betray her to Mr. Delafield, to whom, it seems, she had positively denied the whole, solemnly assuring him that there had never been between them anything more serious than a mere friendly acquaintance. When, therefore, she saw me, her fears were awakened, and knowing that I had her *secret* in my possession, she looked upon me with suspicion and dislike, while I, wholly unconscious of her feelings, had not the least intention of ever speaking of the past, unless circumstances should render it necessary. But of this she was not aware, and that night, in the privacy of her room, she communed with herself as to the best means of counteracting anything which I might say concerning her conduct in Boston, deciding at last that the surest way of accomplishing her object was to brand me as a person whose word could not be trusted! And this she deemed an easy task, inasmuch as no one there had ever seen or heard of me before. Strange, too, as it may seem, there was mingled with her distrust of me a slight shade of jealously lest Mr. Delafield should in any way notice me. True, I was a poor obscure girl, earning my daily bread, and on no point could I compete with her save one, and that was age, I being, as she well knew, eight or nine years her junior. To be old and unmarried was with her almost a crime, and as year after year passed on, leaving her still Ada Montrose, her horror of single blessedness increased, while at the same time she seemed to look upon those much younger than herself as almost her enemies, especially if they came between her and Mr. Delafield, who, as the world goes, was at the age of thirty-one more likely to choose a girl of eighteen than one of twenty-seven. This, then, was my fault. I was young and had also in my possession a secret which she did not wish to have divulged, for well she knew that one as upright and honorable as Mr. Delafield would despise a woman who could stoop to a falsehood as she had done.

"No, it shall not be!" said she, as she sat alone in her room with her face resting upon her hands; "it shall not be! I will thwart her and she shall never triumph over me, as did her pale-faced sister, but for whom I might now have borne the title of Mrs. instead of trembling lest some one should ask how old I am!" And the proud belle felt a pang of envy towards my poor widowed sister whose heart was buried in the grave of her unfortunate husband.

Not that she (Ada) had ever cared particularly for Herbert Langley, but women of the world sometimes bestow their hand where the heart cannot be given, and thus might she have done had not circumstances prevented, for she had then no hope of ever winning her guardian.

Here, ere we proceed farther, it may be well to relate briefly her past history, going back to the time when on his death-bed her father had not only given her to the charge of Mr. Delafield, but had also made a request that, if it were consistent with his feelings, Richard would one day make her his wife. As we have said elsewhere, Mr. Delafield was a great admirer of beauty, and when he looked upon the exceedingly lovely face of the youthful Ada, and thought of her as a lonely orphan, his heart was touched, and he found no difficulty in promising to protect her, and also to make her his wife, if, upon a more intimate acquaintance, he found her all he could wish her to be. That he did not find her thus was proved by the fact that nearly ten years had elapsed since her father's death, and she was Ada Montrose still, while he, as he grew older, seemed less likely to find any one who fully came up to his standard of excellence, beauty, in reality, now being of minor importance, notwithstanding his sister's assertion that he would never marry one who had not a pretty face.

Upon this point, however, Ada had some doubts; for if beauty were what he desired, she still possessed it to an uncommon degree, and it did not seem to move him in the least. Rumor, indeed, said they were on the eve of marriage, but she knew better, for never yet had he really told her in earnest that he loved her. It is true that years before, when she first came a weeping orphan to Cedar Grove, he had devoted himself to her entirely, feeling, perhaps, a little proud of his *ward*, to whom he sometimes talked of *love*, or hinted vaguely of the time when she would be his bride, as they wandered together beneath the whispering pines, which grew around his home, and once, when she was in Boston, he had actually made up his mind to offer himself immediately and take her to Sunny Bank as its mistress. To this resolution he was urged by her cousin, a strong-minded woman, who, in visiting at Cedar Grove, had labored to impress upon him the sense of the duty he owed not only to her father but to Ada herself, who was represented as loving him devotedly, and who was said to have made a vow never to marry unless it were her guardian. Very artfully, too, did Mrs. Johnson insinuate that her illness, of which they had heard, had its origin in "hope deferred which maketh the heart sick."

The knowledge that a beautiful girl loves you—nay, is dying for you, is sufficient, I suppose, to touch the feelings of men less susceptible to female charms than Richard Delafield, and acting upon the impulse of the moment, he started off without, however, leaving any word as to his destination. Arrived in Boston, he went to the Revere House, where, as we know, he casually heard of Ada's engagement with Herbert Langley. To say he was not disappointed would hardly be just, for his self-pride was touched in knowing that Ada had given her affections to another, and that other not a very worthy object, if the word of his gossiping informer was to be trusted. Too much displeased even to see her, he had left the city immediately, declaring that he would never again think of marriage with any one.

As the reader will remember, Ada heard of him through one of her acquaintance, and from something her cousin had written, she half guessed the nature of his visit. Accordingly on her return to Georgia she several times in his presence laughingly referred to the gossiping story, which, she said, some of the Bostonians got up concerning her and a *millionaire*, positively denying it, and wishing people would let her alone! But all this was to no purpose. Mr. Delafield's impulse had subsided, and though his manner towards her was always kind, affectionate, and brotherly, he never spoke to her of love or marriage, except sometimes to ask her teasingly if "if they were not both of them almost old enough to get married."

Still she did not despair, for of his own accord he had accompanied her and her cousin to Europe, whither he had always intended to go, and though he had left them some months before, Mrs. Johnson was willing to leave Paris, where Ada's beauty attracted much attention from the polite Frenchmen, she would not believe he was at all weary of *her*, but rather, as he had said, that his *business* required his immediate return to America.

Latterly Mrs. Lansing had in a measure espoused her cause, and knowing, as she did, of the recent repairs at Sunny Bank, said by Richard to be for the benefit of his bride, she began again to entertain sanguine hopes of eventually becoming Mrs. Delafield, provided the *governess* did not, by her foolish tattling, mar her prospects.

Such, then, was the state of affairs when I was the burden of Ada's thoughts, as she sat alone in her room on the first night after her return home. For a time she mused with her face in her hands, then lifting up her head and throwing back the silken tresses, which fell over her brow, she gazed long and earnestly at herself in the opposite mirror.

"Yes, I am fading," she said at last, "and each year my chance for winning him grows less, and if this *Lee girl should* tell, it would take from me every shadow of hope—but it shall not be. I can prevent her foolish tattling from doing me harm, and I will."

Then the better nature of Ada Montrose whispered to her of the great wrong she was meditating against a poor, defenceless girl, who as yet had never injured her, and for a moment she wavered.

"If I only knew she would never tell," said she; "but she *will*, accidentally if not intentionally. Low-bred people like her are always bold, and as she becomes better acquainted with me, she may possibly say something to me about Herbert in the presence of Mr. Delafield, who will question her, perhaps, and thus learn the whole. So I'll be prepared. She's nothing but a poor governess, and *my* word will be preferred to hers, provided I first give her the character of a deceiver."

On awaking next morning her resolution was partially shaken, and might, perhaps, have been given up entirely, if, in looking from her window, she had not seen a sight which awoke within her the demon *jealousy*, by whose aid she could do almost anything. The *governess* had arisen early, as was her usual custom, and gone forth into the garden, where she came unexpectedly upon Mr. Delafield, who, after expressing his pleasure at meeting her, very quietly drew her arm within his own, and then walked with her several times through the garden, casting often admiring glances towards the drooping figure at his side, who, trembling lest the Argus eyes of Mrs. Lansing were upon her, would fain have been left alone. All this Ada saw, and as she thought how different was his manner towards Rose from what it had ever been towards her, a sudden light flashed upon her. She had not lived twenty-seven years for nothing, and like Dicken's woman with the "mortified bonnet," she knew the signs, and with a sinking heart, she exclaimed, "Is it possible that he *loves* her?"

The thought was maddening, and now strengthened tenfold in her purpose of working the young girl evil, she went forth into the garden to meet them, nodding coldly to Rosa, and bestowing her sweetest smile upon her guardian, who wound his arm around her waist and playfully kissed her forehead—a liberty he would not dare to have taken with Rose, who, thinking that of course she was not wanted, made an effort to withdraw her hand. But Mr. Delafield's arm was strong, and he pressed it closely to his side, at the same time giving her a look which bade her stay, notwithstanding that Ada two or three times hinted to her the propriety of going.

"Why don't you ask Miss Lee about your Boston friends?" said Mr. Delafield, when they had taken a few turns in silence.

Ada tossed her head scornfully, and replied, "I don't think I had any acquaintances in common with *Miss Lee*, unless, indeed, it were her *old aunty;*" and with a little hateful laugh she leaned across Mr. Delafield, and asked, "How is she? Richard, you would like to know."

I was provoked at her manner, but I answered civilly that my aunt was well, adding, as one would naturally do, "Herbert Langley, I suppose you know, is dead."

The news was unexpected, and coming as it did, it produced upon her a singular effect, blanching her cheek to a marble whiteness, while her lips quivered spasmodically. Mr. Delafield was startled, and stopping short, demanded of her what was the matter.

"Oh, nothing much," she answered, recovering her composure, and pressing her hand upon her side, "nothing but an ugly pain, which is gone now. I have felt it often lately," and her face looked as unruffled and innocent as if she really thought it was the truth she had uttered.

I knew she told a falsehood, but Mr. Delafield did not, and leading her to the summer-house, which was near, bade her sit down, while he made minute inquiries concerning the pain, asking how long since she first felt it, and saying he would speak to Dr. Matson the first time he came to Cedar Grove, adding that a *blister*, he presumed, would help it!

"Oh, mercy!" she exclaimed, again growing pale. "You make too serious a matter of it."

But he did not think so—he was very tender of her, as a brother would be of his orphaned sister; and knowing that her mother had died of consumption, he watched narrowly for the first indications of that disease in her. Just then little Jessie came bounding down the walk, saying that "breakfast was ready," and leading her by the hand, I returned to the house, followed by Mr. Delafield and Ada, the latter of whom made some remark concerning my *gait*, which she pronounced "wholly *Yankee* and *countrified*."

"And *graceful*," rejoined Mr. Delafield, at the same time telling her he did not like to hear one female speak disparagingly of another.

Ada bit her lip with vexation, and when she took her seat at the table, she was evidently not in the best of humors. At Mrs. Lansing's invitation her brother remained to breakfast, and I could not perceive that he was any more polite to the beautiful lady in elegant French muslin on his right, than he was to the plain-looking girl in a shilling calico on his left. Indeed, if there was a difference, it was in favor of the latter, with whom he conversed the most, addressing her as if she had at least *common sense*, while towards Ada he always assumed the trifling, bantering manner which he seemed to think was suited to her capacity.

Breakfast being over, I started for my room, accidentally dropping upon the stairs a handkerchief, which had been given me by Anna, and which had her name "Anna Lee" marked in the corner. In honor of Ada's return, there was no school that day, and as the morning advanced and the heat in my chamber grew oppressive, I went with my book to the sitting-room, and took a seat by an open window, where I soon became so absorbed in reading as not to observe Mrs. Lansing and Ada, who came out upon the piazza and sat down quite near me, but still in such a position that neither of us could see the other. After a time they were joined by Mr. Delafield, and then for a moment I thought of stealing quietly away, but thinking my remaining there could do no harm, I resumed my book and forgot my neighbors entirely, until my attention was roused by the sound of my own name.

It was Mrs. Lansing who spoke, and she asked, "What kind of folks are those relatives of Miss Lee?"

"Oh, about *so so*," answered Ada, and Mrs. Lansing continued, "And she was then at school? I believe."

"*At school!*" repeated Ada, apparently in much surprise. "Mercy, no! Why, she was a grown up woman, as much as twenty-two or twenty-three years old."

"There, I thought so," answered Mrs. Lansing, who the reader will remember had, at my first introduction, taken me to be twenty-five. "I thought she must be more than eighteen, didn't you, Richard?"

"*Eighteen!*" repeated Ada. "It isn't possible she calls herself eighteen. She dare not do it in my presence. Why, she had been a teacher, I don't know how long, and, besides that, 'twas said that she had once been engaged to a Dr. Clayton, who, for some reason, jilted her, and was then a married man as much as thirty years old. *Eighteen*, indeed. I'd like to hear her say so."

I was confounded, but supposing she had mistaken me for Anna, my first impulse was to go out and tell her so, but fearing lest she should think I had intentionally listened, my second thought was to go away where I could hear nothing further, and then, when Mrs. Lansing questioned me, as I felt sure she would, I fancied it would be an easy matter to exonerate myself from the falsehood Ada had put upon me. I had reached the hall, and was half-way up the stairs, when Mr. Delafield, who had arisen and was walking back and forth on the piazza, espied me, and called me back.

There was a troubled look on his face, and fixing his piercing black eyes upon me as if he would read my inmost thoughts, he said with something of bitterness in the tones of his voice, "I *did* think I had found *one* female who, on all occasions, spoke the truth; but if what Ada has said is true, I am mistaken; though why *you* (and his hand involuntarily clutched my arm) or any other woman should stoop to a falsehood, or seek to deny her age, be she a hundred or less, is a secret which Heaven knows, perhaps, but I do not."

I felt my face flush with indignation, and turning towards Ada, who, not having expected a scene like this, was very pale, I said, "It is not necessary, Miss Montrose, for you to repeat what you have asserted concerning me, for I accidentally overheard it, and I thank Mr. Delafield for giving me an opportunity to exonerate myself from the charge you are pleased to bring against me."

"Been listening," muttered Mrs. Lansing.

"Silence, Angeline. Go on, Rose," interrupted Mr. Delafield, in a voice which we both obeyed, she resuming her needlework, while I continued, "I had taken my seat by the open window ere you and Miss Montrose came out here, and not thinking it necessary to leave, I remained, without, however, hearing a word of your conversation until I caught the sound of my name. Then, indeed, my senses were sharpened, and I heard Miss Montrose's statement, which I am sure she would never have made were she not laboring under a mistake."

Here Ada, who was not in the least prepared for the occasion, began to stammer out something about "letting the matter drop—she did not wish to harm me, and had said what she did inadvertently, without ever dreaming of making trouble. She didn't see why Richard wished to make it such a serious matter, for she was sure *she* didn't care whether I were *forty* or *eighteen*."

"But *I* care," he said, grasping my arm still tighter, "*I* care to have justice done. I have supposed Miss Lee to be frank, ingenuous and truthful, and if what you assert is true, she is the reverse, and should suffer accordingly, while on the contrary if she be innocent, she shall have an opportunity of proving herself so."

By this time Ada had collected her scattered senses, and resolving to brave the storm she had raised, replied, "Certainly, Miss Lee has a right to clear herself if she can, and prove that she *is* really *Rose* instead of *Anna* Lee."

"*Rose* instead of *Anna*! What do you mean?" thundered Mr. Delafield, while *I* was too much astonished to speak.

Ada was not very *deep*, and in all her plotting she had never thought how easy it would be for me to prove the falsity of her assertion by writing home; so with the utmost coolness she replied, "I mean this:—there were *two Lee girls* living at the house of their uncle where I occasionally visited: one was *Anna*, a young lady of twenty-two or twenty-three, the other was *Rose*, a school-girl of fourteen or fifteen. The oldest of these two I have every reason to believe stands before us—at least *this*, which I found upon the stairs, would indicate as much," and she held to view the handkerchief which I had dropped and had not missed.

Glancing at the name, Mrs. Lansing said, "I have observed a similar mark upon several of her garments, and rather wondered at it."

This was true, for Anna had dealt generously with me, giving me many of her clothes, some of which bore her full name, while others had merely the initials. I was about to tell of this, when Mr. Delafield prevented me by asking if I could prove that I was what I represented myself to be, and that I was a mere school-girl when I saw Miss Montrose in Boston.

"Yes, sir, I can," I answered firmly; "by writing home, I can prove it, if in no other way. But Miss Montrose knows better than to confound me with *Anna*, whom she surely has reason for remembering."

Fearful lest her darling secret was about to be divulged, Ada roused up and in a tone of angry defiance, answered, "Yes, I have reason for remembering you, for you did me good service by taking off my hands a worthless, drunken fellow, about whom the Bostonians were annoying me. I thank you for it, Miss Lee, and only wonder how you could suppose I would forget you. I recognized you the moment we met at the table, but I did not then dream of your calling yourself *eighteen* when you are certainly *twenty-six*!"

I was confounded and remained speechless, while with renewed strength my accuser continued, "Perhaps you will deny having been a teacher at that time, when according to your statement you were only fourteen."

"No," I answered, "I do not deny that; I *had* taught, but I was only *thirteen* when I did so, as any one at home will testify."

"Thirteen! how improbable!" exclaimed Mrs. Lansing, while Ada continued, "And what of your engagement with Dr. Clayton. I heard it from the lips of your aunt; but perhaps she told me a falsehood?" and she looked maliciously at me, while with a stamp of his foot Mr. Delafield said sternly, "Ada, you have no right to question her of that."

"But I am glad she did," I said, "for as I live, I have never been engaged to any man."

"Nor in love with one either? Will you say you were never in love with Dr. Clayton?" persisted Ada.

It was a cruel question, but I could not deny it, and I remained silent, while I cowered beneath the burning gaze of Mr. Delafield, who still held me fast, but who now loosened his hold, and slightly pushing me from him, leaned against the pillar, with folded arms, and dark, lowering brow, while Mrs. Lansing and Ada exchanged glances of triumph. They had by my silence gained a partial advantage over me, but as long as I felt the clasp of Mr. Delafield's hand, I was strong to defy them. Now, however, that had failed me, and girl-like I began to cry, telling them "they could easily test the whole matter by writing either to Boston or Meadow Brook."

This alternative had not occurred to Ada before, but now she readily saw how easily I could prove my innocence, and as she met Mr. Delafield's inquiring glance, she turned very pale and laid her hand upon her side as if the *pain* had returned.

"Rose," said Mr. Delafield, "you would hardly wish for me to write to Meadow Brook were you guilty, and as you seem willing that we should do so, I am inclined to hope that Ada may be mistaken. Come, stand by me (and reaching out his hand he drew me to his side) and tell me all the particulars of your acquaintance with Miss Montrose, and also about that sister with whom you are confounded, and you (turning to the other ladies) are not to speak, until she is through, when Ada can make any correction or explanation necessary."

It was an act of justice which I owed to myself, I knew, and wiping my eyes, I was about to commence, when Ada, rising up, said mockingly, "With the Hon. Judge's permission I will leave, as I do not wish to hear the falsehoods which I am sure will be uttered."

Again Mr. Delafield's long arm was extended, and catching Ada, as she was passing, he drew her to his side, where he held her firmly, saying, "It looks suspicious, Ada, that you are not willing to hear Miss Lee's defence. You have, either by mistake or design (the former, I hope), preferred against her serious charges, and you *must* listen to her explanation. Commence," he added, looking down upon me, and in a firm, unfaltering manner I told both my story and that of Anna, who, I said, had eloped with Herbert Langley and was now a broken-hearted widow, living with his mother in Boston.

At this part of my narrative Ada's hand was pressed convulsively on her side, while with parted lips and pale cheeks she leaned forward, looking at me anxiously; but when she saw that I did not speak of her ever having been engaged to Herbert, the color came back to her face, and with a sigh of relief she listened more composedly, nodding assent when I referred her to our meeting at the dépôt at Canandaigua, and faintly admitting that "she might have been mistaken. I looked so much like Anna that 'twas not impossible."

This I knew was false, but I did not contradict her, and proceeded with my story, until suddenly recollecting the incident at the theatre, I turned to Mr. Delafield and asked "if he remembered it?"

He thought a moment, and then the arm, which had gradually been winding itself about my waist, clasped me to his side, while he exclaimed, "Remember it? Perfectly, and *you* are that little girl. They called you Rose;—and this is why your face has puzzled me so much. I see it all now. You *are* innocent, thank Heaven," and the hand, which, heretofore, had held Ada fast, now rested caressingly upon my head and parted back my curls, as he said, more to himself than to me, "and you have remembered *me* all this time." Then, turning towards Ada, he said sternly, "We will hear you now."

Ada was caught in her own snare. She had thought to prevent me from doing her injury by branding me as a *liar*, and now that I was proved innocent, it filled her with confusion, and she remained silent until Mrs. Lansing came to her aid by saying, "I do not think Ada meant to do wrong; she probably mistook Rose for her sister, hence the blunder."

This gave Ada courage, and crossing over to me, she took my hand, begging my forgiveness and saying "she *had* been mistaken—she certainly did not mean to do me so great a wrong, and she hoped I would forget it and try to look upon her as my friend, for such she would henceforth be."

I was not quite verdant enough to credit *all* that Ada said; but I replied I was willing to forgive her, and when she asked permission to *kiss* me, so that the reconciliation might be perfect, I offered no resistance, though I did not return the compliment, for which I think Mr. Delafield felt gratified—at least I read as much in his face. During the progress of my story Ada had alternately turned red and white, particularly at the points where I touched upon Herbert. This did not escape the observation of Mr. Delafield, and suspecting more than Ada thought he did, he half seriously, half playfully asked her "why she had evinced so much feeling whenever Mr. Langley's name was mentioned."

Instantly the color left her face, which wore a livid hue, and her hand went up to her side as if the cause of her agitation were there, while with a half stifled moan, she said, "Oh, oh!—the pain!"

Of course Mrs. Lansing asked what she meant, and Ada, in answering her, managed to dwell so long upon "the horrid pain, which she feared would become chronic," that Mr. Delafield could not reasonably expect an answer to his question. Still, I think, he was not satisfied, and when I saw the mischievous look in his eye, as he told her "she must *certainly* be *blistered*," I fancied that he, too, understood her as I did.

That afternoon we were again assembled upon the piazza, Mrs. Lansing, Ada, and myself, the former nodding in her large willow chair, while the latter sat upon a little stool at my feet, and with her elbow upon my lap was looking up into my face with the childish simplicity she knew so well how to assume. She was just asking me to assure her again of my forgiveness when Mr. Delafield joined us, and coming up behind me leaned over my chair, while he handed to Ada a little oblong package, saying, "I was in the village just after dinner, and seeing the Dr. I asked him about *your pain*. As I expected, he prescribed a *blister*, and at my request he prepared one, which you are to apply at night when you go to bed!"

I could not see him, but I absolutely pitied poor Ada, who began to realize that the way of the transgressor is hard. The tears started to her eyes, while with a look of dismay, she exclaimed, "Oh, Richard, how could you? I never was blistered in my life. It will kill me. I can't do it,"—and she cried aloud.

Very gently, Mr. Delafield soothed her, telling her that so far from "killing her," it would certainly "cure her," he knew it would, and he insisted upon her trying it. At last, as an idea, perfectly natural, under the circumstances, dawned upon her mind, she looked up very submissively at him and said, "To please you, I'll try it; though the remedy, I think, is worse than the disease."

I hardly know whether he had any faith in her words—*I* certainly had not, and when next morning she came down to breakfast in a loose wrapper, with a very languid look, I could not bring myself to ask her concerning the *blister*, which the livelong night had drawn nicely—on the back of the *fire-board*, in her room! As I expected, Mr. Delafield soon made his appearance, and after inquiring how his prescription worked, and if it had pained her much, he said, looking towards neither of us, "How would you like to ride on horseback with me out to Mr. Parker's plantation? I have business there, and do not wish to go alone."

"Oh, charming!" exclaimed Ada, jumping up and clapping her hands in a manner but little suited to a blistered side; "that will be grand, and I can wear my new riding-dress, which fits so nicely."

"Why, Ada, what do you mean?" said Mr. Delafield, with great gravity. "My invitation was intended for *Miss Lee. You* can't, of course, think of riding on horseback with a *blister.* You must have forgotten it!" and his keen eyes rested upon her face with a deeper meaning than she could fathom.

She turned very red, and for an instant, I think, half resolved to acknowledge the deception she was practising. But Richard Delafield was one who despised a falsehood, and she dared not confess to him her error, so she turned away, saying with a feigned indifference which illy accorded with the expression of her face, "Surely, I forgot all about it."

Alone in her room, however, she shed tears of anger and mortification as she saw us ride off together, and thought of the happiness from which she was debarred by a fancied blister, which had never come in contact with her flesh. But whether it drew upon her side or the fire-board, it in a measure wrought the desired cure, for seldom again did Ada attempt to deceive her guardian. Would it not be well if more of our modern young ladies should be blistered for the same disease that afflicted Ada Montrose.

It was nearly dark when we returned, and Mrs. Lansing and Ada were in their accustomed places upon the piazza, the latter holding an open letter which she had that afternoon received from her cousin Mrs. Johnson, who was spending some time in Mobile, and who wished Ada to join her there, before going on to New Orleans. They were evidently discussing the matter, and when we came up, Ada handed the letter to Mr. Delafield, bidding him read it and tell her what to do. Hastily running it over, he said, "Go, by all means: you have never seen Mobile, and it will be a good opportunity."

"But I have been thinking of giving up my visit to New Orleans," she continued in a kind of beseeching tone; "Mrs. Lansing had rather I'd remain with her this winter."

It was not so dark as to prevent me from seeing the expression of Mr. Delafield's face, and I fancied the proposition did not altogether please him. She evidently thought so too, for rather pettishly she added, "but if you wish to be rid of me, of course I'll go."

"Ada! How foolish!" he said, sternly. "I've often heard you express a desire to spend a winter in New Orleans, and now that an opportunity is presented, I think you had better accept it. I shall be there a part of the time, perhaps all," he added; and then *I* turned away lest *my* face should betray what was passing within.

"And will you go with me to Mobile?" Ada asked of him, as a child would ask her father.

"Certainly," he answered; "I do not propose letting you go alone. But how is that side? I'd almost forgotten to ask."

"It has pained me a good deal," said she, "but Martha dressed it nicely this afternoon, and it feels much better. I'm so glad you made me apply it, now the worst is over, for I believe it will do me good!"

She spoke with every appearance of candor, and much as it surprised him, Mr. Delafield was, I thought, partially, if not wholly, convinced that what she said was true, and that he had suspected her of more than she deserved; for his manner towards her changed, and as if trying to make amends, he devoted himself to her entirely for the remainder of the evening, telling her where they would go when they were in New Orleans, and laying many plans for her pleasure. Once in his zeal he thoughtlessly threw his arm around her waist, but she instantly shrank back, saying, "don't— don't—you hurt!"

This convinced him thoroughly, and I slept and woke twice that night ere the sound of their voices ceased upon the piazza, where their long interview was kept in countenance by Mrs. Lansing, who sat up until he left, and then patting Ada's cheek, told her she thought "her prospects were brightening."

I thought so, too, and there was a shadow on my heart, when I saw how much they were together during the few weeks which elapsed before her departure for Mobile. It is true he was still kind to me as of old; and whenever he found that Ada, by word or look, had slighted me, he always managed to let her know how much he disapproved her conduct, so that in his presence she was usually polite, though she could not quite conceal the fact that I was to her an object of dislike.

It was nearly the middle of October, when Ada finally left us for Mobile, accompanied by Mr. Delafield, who, in bidding us good-bye, said we need not be surprised if he did not return in several weeks. I consider it to be my misfortune that my face generally betrays all I feel, and with his physiognomic powers he could not fail to see the effect which his words produced upon me, for well I knew how lonely Cedar Grove would be without him; and when after he was gone, little Jessie climbed into my lap, and laying her head upon my shoulder wished "Uncle Dick never would go away," I mentally responded to the wish. The whole household seemed more or less affected; Mrs. Lansing was cross; Lina careless; Halbert fretful; and Jessie unhappy—while I began to be haunted with my old project of returning home; and I should, perhaps, have proposed it to Mrs. Lansing, had it not been that, at the close of the fifth day, we were greatly surprised at Mr. Delafield's unexpected return. He didn't like Mobile, he said, and would much rather be at home.

Numerous were the questions asked by Mrs. Lansing concerning Ada and the pain in her side, which last, Mr. Delafield said, had left her entirely, owing, he believed, to the timely application of the blister. He was deceived, I thought, and I must confess to a slight feeling of gratification at an occurrence which thoroughly convinced him of his mistake. One night, a few days after his return, old Hagar, his head cook, came over to Cedar Grove, groaning with rheumatism, which she termed "a misery in her back." Lina, to whom her complaints were made, listened a while, and then opening an old paper-box which stood under the table, drew forth a *plaster*, which she said she "had done found in Miss Ada's room, on t'other side the fire-board, oncet when she was clarin' the fire-place."

As Ada was gone she thought there was no harm in appropriating it to herself, which she accordingly did, laying it carefully away until it should be needed. The recital of Hagar's aches and pains reminded her of it, so she urged it upon the old negress, assuring her it must be good, or white folks would never use it! With many thanks Hagar hobbled home, applied her plaster, and went to bed! But, alas! for the expected relief, which came only in burning sensations and stinging pains, eliciting many a groan from the poor old lady, who heroically bore it until morning, when she found herself unable to perform her accustomed duties.

For a long time Mr. Delafield waited for his breakfast, which was at last served up by Hagar's daughter, who gave such a deplorable account of her mother's condition that the moment breakfast was over he went himself to the cabin, where he found the old lady moaning over her blistered back, which she said, "was a heap harder to bar than the rheumatics."

A few words explained the whole, for Hagar never concealed aught from her master, and so she gave the history of her *plaster*, which now lay upon the hearth in the ashes, where she had thrown it. Quick as thought the truth burst upon Mr. Delafield, who laughed so long and loud, that Aunt Hagar, thinking that he was making light of her misfortunes, began to cry, saying she "never thought Mars'r Richard would poke fun at her misery."

"Neither am I making fun of you," said he, adding further, by way of atoning for his error, that for the remainder of the week she should be freed from all household service, and devote her whole time, if she liked, to her aching back.

This had the effect of restoring Aunt Hagar to good humor, and in the midst of her thanks, Mr. Delafield returned slowly to the house, thinking that when a habit of deception is once firmly fixed, it required more to cure it than a blister applied to the fire-board!

CHAPTER XXIII
DR. CLAYTON

Rapidly, and to me very happily, did the winter pass away, for it was enlivened by the presence of Mr. Delafield, who was with us so often, that it became at last a serious debate among the blacks as to whether Cedar Grove or Sunny Bank were really his home. More than once, too, was it whispered in the village, that little *Rosa Lee*, plain and unassuming as she was, had stirred in the heart of the "stern old bachelor" a far deeper feeling than Ada Montrose had ever been capable of awakening. And sometimes *she*, foolish child that she was, thought so too, not from anything he said, neither from anything which he did; indeed, it would have been hard for her to tell *why* her heart sometimes beat so fast when he was near, for though his manner was always kind and considerate, he never spoke to her of *love*—never appeared as he had once done in the summer-house, when she gave him such silly answers!

And still, occasionally, Rosa dared to hope that her love was returned, else why did each day find him at her side where he lingered so long, saying to her but little, but watching her movements, and listening to her words, as he would not have done had she been to him an object of indifference. Not naturally quick to read human nature, Mrs. Lansing was wholly deceived by her brother's cold exterior, and never dreaming how in secret he worshiped the humble girl she called her governess, she left them much together. Why then did he never speak to her of the passion which had become a part of his being? Simply because he, too, was deceived. Once, indeed, he had essayed to tell her of his love, and dreading lest his affection should not be returned, he was the more ready to construe her evasive replies into a belief that it was indeed as he feared. Then, too, her shy, reserved manner, while it made him prize her all the more, disheartened him; for not thus was he accustomed to being treated, and with that jealousy which seems to be the twin sister of love, he ofttimes thought he read aversion and distrust, when there was, on Rosa's part, naught save a fear lest he should discover her secret, and despise her for it. Added to this was the remembrance of what Ada had said concerning her former engagement with Dr. Clayton. True, Rosa had denied the engagement, but when charged with having loved him she had remained silent; thus proving the story correct. And if she loved him when a child, was it not probable that she loved him still, married man though he was. He had heard of such things, or, at least, he had read of them in books, and for many days Mr. Delafield's brow was literally tied up in knots, while he tried to solve the question as to "whether, having loved once and been deceived, Rosa Lee could love again."

At last he decided that possibly she could, and his mind was fully made up to talk with her upon the subject, when an unexpected arrival blasted his hopes at once, and darkened the glimmering sunlight which was dawning upon his horizon. It was a dark, rainy night, toward the last of April, that I sat with the family in the pleasant little sitting-room. As usual, Mr. Delafield was with us, and this evening he was reading aloud from Longfellow's wonderful poem. He was just in the midst of Hiawatha's wooing, and I fancied there was in the tones of his voice a softer cadence as he read,

> "Hand in hand they went together,
> Through the woodland and the meadow,
> Left the old man standing lonely
> At the doorway of his wigwam,
> Heard the falls of Minnehaha
> Calling to them from the distance,
> Crying to them from afar off,
> Fare thee well, oh, Laughing Water."

Scarcely had the last words left his lips when a heavy tread upon the piazza and a loud ringing of the bell startled us, for it was not often that we were favored with visitors on such a night as this. Zillah, the colored girl, hastened to the door where she found a stranger, who, stepping into the hall, asked, "if Miss Rosa Lee lived there."

Starting from my chair, I turned very white, for I recognized the voice of *Dr. Clayton,* who the next moment stood before me! I forgot the past—forgot that he had been my lover—forgot that Richard Delafield's eyes were upon me—forgot every thing except that he had come from dear New England—had breathed the air of my native hills—had heard the sound of my mother's voice—and had brought me undoubtedly tidings of that mother's welfare. Springing forward with a cry of joy I took his extended hand, nor shrank away when, with unwonted tenderness, he stooped to kiss my lips, low whispering as he did so, *"Dear Rosa."*

Then, indeed, I blushed, for I knew he had no right to call me thus, but the next moment it was forgotten, and with something of pride in my manner, I presented him to Mrs. Lansing and Mr. Delafield, the latter of whom greeted him rather coldly, and after a few words of common courtesy, bade us good night, but not until he had learned what, until that moment, was news to me, viz. that Dell Clayton had been dead nearly six months! As he passed me on his way out, he said so low that no one else could hear him, "Fare thee well, oh, Laughing Water," referring to the line he had last read. There was a deep scowl upon his dark face, and as I gazed upon him, I could not help wondering if it were thus the old man looked, when from his lonely wigwam door he watched the departing footsteps of his daughter.

"Come again to-morrow, uncle Dick," said little Jessie, following him into the hall; but he made her no answer, save his accustomed good-bye kiss, and I soon heard his heavy tread as he strode down the winding walk and out into the open field, muttering to himself, as I afterwards learned:

"And she will follow where he leads her,

Leaving all things for the stranger."

Yes, Mr. Delafield was jealous—terribly jealous of Dr. Clayton, the nature of whose business he readily divined, though I did not, and nothing was further from my mind than the thought that he intended honoring me with a chance of becoming Mrs. Clayton 2d. And yet it was this alone which had brought him to Georgia, he taking the precaution to send on in advance a letter, in which he had made known his wishes, and asked for a return of the affection which, for five long years, he said, had never known one moment of abatement, even though another had slept upon his bosom as his wife. But *she* was gone, and in her place, he would see blooming, he said, the *Rose* he had loved so long. Owing to some detention, this letter had failed to reach me, hence I was wholly unprepared for the scene which followed when, at last we were left alone. Well skilled in the *signs*, Mrs. Lansing had purposely retired, not long after her brother's departure, while I, suspecting nothing, made no objection when Dr. Clayton took his seat upon the sofa at my side. I was talking to him of Anna, and from speaking of her, and poor Herbert's death, it was an easy transition to Dell, of whom he spoke kindly, nay, even affectionately, as he told me of her last days; how much she suffered, and how gentle she became, never chiding him, in the least, for a thing unskillfully done, but seeming satisfied with everything, and loving him at last with a love which, had it been earlier born, would have shed happiness over his comparatively cheerless life. Then he told me of the little child, not yet three years old, whom he had called "Rosa Lee," and gently pushing back my curls, and gazing down into my face, he said, "It is a fancy of mine, perhaps, but I love to think she looks like you, who should have been her mother."

With all my stupidity, I understood him then, and blushing crimson, I moved away to the end of the sofa, while he continued, "What did you think of my letter? You received it, I suppose?"

I had received no letter, and so I said; whereupon he proceeded to tell me its contents, a part of which the reader already knows. Utterly confounded and powerless to move, I sat motionless, while, with his arm around me, he went over with the past, recalling to my mind, with a vividness which made it seem real again, the time when first he had found me weeping in the sombre old schoolroom, away to the northward; the night when, with the soft moon-beams falling around us, we sat together beneath the tall oak tree, while I laid before him my childish griefs; and, lastly, the many pleasant hours we had whiled away together, listening to the sound of the running brook, which ran past the twining grape-vine, whose broad leaves had rustled above our heads.

"On these occasions, Rose," said he, "did nothing ever tell you how much you were beloved?"

"Yes," I answered bitterly, my woman's nature rousing up as I remembered the times to which he referred. "Yes, and what did it avail me, even though I was beloved? Ambition proved the stronger attraction of the two, and you wedded another. You, who, now that other has gone, would talk again to me of love; but Rosa Lee is no longer a child to be deceived, and you mistake her strangely, if you fancy you can cast her off and take her up again at will."

Here, overcome with emotion, I burst into tears. My words and manner misled him, for in them he saw only resentment for his former treatment; and this inspired him with hope that the feeling I once cherished for him could again be nourished into life. Very tenderly, then, he talked to me, and, as I listened, a numbness crept over my heart, for I knew he was in earnest now, and I felt that it was not the Dr. Clayton of old—the fickle, selfish man of the world—with whom I had to deal, but Dr. Clayton purified, and made better by the trials through which he had passed—a noble, true-hearted, and upright man—who now laid at my feet the love which I knew had always been mine. Very earnestly he implored forgiveness for the wrong he once had done me, saying that for it he had been terribly punished, inasmuch as he had suffered far more than I. And still he breathed no word of censure against his erring wife, who, he said, was perhaps more sinned against than sinning, and who, when the last great agony was upon her, had whispered in his ear, as her white, clammy hand rested on the flowing curls of little Rose, "Her mother, I know, will be she whose name she bears, and I am willing it should be so."

"And was she not right?" he continued, drawing me closer to his side. "Will you not be the angel of my home, the mother of my child?"

And then again he told me how much I had been loved; how he had striven in vain to cast me from his heart, when it was madness and sin to keep me there; and how, when his horizon had been darkest with want and care, there was still in the distance a ray of sunlight, the remembrance of me, which had kept his soul from fainting. And now that it was right for him to speak to me of love, would I not listen and give him an opportunity to atone for the wrong he had once done me? He paused for my reply. There was silence in the room, and I counted each pulse of my beating heart as it throbbed with the intensity of my excitement.

"Will not my darling answer me?" he said, and I felt his breath upon my cheek, his lips upon my brow.

Not thus could I sit and tell him what duty bade me say. So I moved away, and standing up before him, I said, slowly, and distinctly, "Dr. Clayton, I loved you once, but the time has gone by, the love has died out, and I would not awaken it if I could."

There was a firmness in my manner, a decision in the tones of my voice, which startled him more than what I said, and with a faint cry he too arose, and coming to my side, said, "God forgive you, Rose, for the cruel words you have uttered, but you cannot be in earnest."

And then, with the firelight flickering over his pale face, he plead with me "to think again, to revoke what I had said, and not to send him away utterly hopeless and wretched. The love I had felt for him once, though chilled and dormant now, *would bloom* again, for *he* could bring it back to life, and I must be his; he could not live without me. I need not decide then, that night," he said, "he would give me time," and again he pressed for my answer, which was the same as before; for, much as I pitied him, there was between us a *dark shadow*, and the substance of that shadow bore the form and features of *Richard Delafield*!

Sinking into a chair, he laid his head upon the table, while, burying my face in the cushions of the sofa, I wept bitterly, stealing occasional glances towards the bowed form which, in its despair, gave no sign of life. There was no acting there, for it was the grief of a strong man which I saw. Without, the storm had ceased; the wind had died away, and the rain no longer beat against the casement; but within, there raged a wilder storm of human passions, and as it swept over me in its full force, I cried, mentally, "Ought I thus to deal with him? I loved him once, perhaps I could do so again. I would at least try." And, rising up, I glided noiselessly to his side. He did not hear me, and, for a time, I stood gazing down upon him, while I thought of all he had suffered, and of his love for me, which I could not doubt. The shadow no longer stood between us; it was gone, and, strengthened by its absence, I laid my hand upon his shoulder. He shuddered as if it had been a serpent's touch, but when I whispered in his ear, "Look up, I have something to tell you," he raised his head, disclosing to my view a face over which years seemed to have passed since last I had looked upon it.

"I will try," I said, "but give me one day for reflection, and to-morrow night you shall have your answer."

As the clouds are dispersed by the soft rays of the sun, so the shadows passed from his brow at my words, and clasping me in his arms he wept over me, as Heaven grant I may never see man weep again.

The fire on the hearth had long since gone out. The lamp was burning dimly, and the moon-beams came faintly in through an eastern window ere I bade him good night, and sought the solitude of my room, where my resolution almost instantly gave way, for the *shadow* was there, and in its presence I felt I would rather die than wed a man I did not love.

"Oh, for a female friend with whom to counsel in my need," I said, as I nervously paced the room.

I thought of Mrs. Lansing. She was a woman—she had been kind to me of late, and after a few moments' reflection I determined to ask her advice. This being settled, I fell into a disturbed sleep, from which I did not wake until the bell was ringing for breakfast. I met him at the table, and my heart beat fast when I saw how anxiously he scanned my haggard face.

"You are sick this morning," he said, when at last we were alone.

Taking my hand he felt my quickened pulse, and continued, "This must not be. Calm yourself down, for I would not wish you to answer me under all this excitement."

Soon after this he left me, going down to the hotel where he had first stopped on his arrival at W——. As soon as he was gone I sought an interview with Mrs. Lansing, to whom I confided the whole story of my former love for Dr. Clayton, and of my feelings now, asking her to tell me as a friend what I should do. I did not dare look her in the face while I was talking, and when I had finished I waited with downcast eyes for her answer, which was characteristic of a woman who had never known what love was, save as she felt it for her children.

"Do! Why, marry him of course. I should not hesitate a moment, for 'tis not every girl in your circumstances who has an offer like that. He seems to be a perfect gentleman,—is certainly very fine looking—is refined, polished, highly educated, and has a good profession. What more can you desire?"

"*Love* for him," I replied; and she continued, "Pshaw! *That* will come soon enough, depend upon it. There are many happy marriages where one of the parties had at first no particular affection for the other, as I myself can testify. I *respected* Mr. Lansing, when I married him, but I did not *love* him, and our union was, I am confident, far happier than three-fourths of those where *love* is the ruling motive, for in nine cases out of ten they grow sick of each other as faults and peculiarities are brought to light, of whose existence they had never dreamed. Take your own case for an example. Suppose you had married Dr. Clayton when you fancied him so much, you would undoubtedly have been disgusted with him by this time, whereas, now that you know he is fallible, you can safely link your destiny with his, feeling sure that in good time the love you once had for him will return."

I knew there was some truth in this argument, but it failed to convince me, and I remained silent until Mrs. Lansing startled me with, "You do not of course love another?"

I was taken by surprise, and without a thought of the result, I answered "I do."

"And that other?" she continued, fixing her eyes upon me.

I know not what possessed me, but a power I could not resist impelled me to answer, "Is your brother."

She did not send me from her presence with scorn and loathing as I thought she would. Nay, she did not even speak, but for a time stood mute with astonishment. As I now recall that scene, I understand her better, and I know that the *truth*, just as it was, dawned upon her mind, and suggested the falsehood which she uttered.

Coming closely to me, she said, "I cannot see why it is that all my governesses have fallen in love with my brother, yet such is the case. I *did* think, Miss Lee, that you were an exception, but I find I am mistaken, which surprises me greatly, inasmuch as he has never paid you the slightest attention, and even if he had, I do not understand how you could think him in earnest. For years the world has looked upon his union with Ada as sure, and though for certain reasons I have sometimes opposed it, I am anxious for it now, and it is well that I am, for I suppose it is a settled thing."

I held my breath for fear I should lose a single word of what she should say next. Perhaps she was unused to falsehoods. Be that as it may, her voice trembled slightly and she spoke hurriedly as she said, "They are engaged, and have been ever since she went to Mobile, and they will probably be married next autumn; hence, you see that the love you have presumed to feel for him would be useless, even were you his equal."

She started to leave me, but turned back while she said, "I trust that what I have told you will be kept a secret, for Richard does not wish to have the matter discussed."

I nodded assent, and the next moment I was alone with my sorrow, which was far easier to bear now that uncertainty was made sure. So long as there remained a lingering hope that my love for Mr. Delafield might possibly be reciprocated, I shrunk in horror from marrying another. But now that hope was swept away, for I never thought of doubting Mrs. Lansing's word, and a kind of torpor crept over me, suspending for a time both my judgment and my will.

"I will marry Dr. Clayton," I said, and with that decision came a feeling of gratified pride as I thought I should thus prove to Richard how little I cared for him!

Ah, I knew not then that the heart I coveted enshrined no image save that of "Rosa Lee," for whom Richard Delafield would almost have lain down his life, so great was the love he bore her. He had readily divined the object of the stranger's visit, and the thought that it might be successful was terrible. All the night long he, too, had been sleepless, pacing the length and breadth of his spacious halls and murmuring occasionally as, peering out into the darkness, he saw the glimmering light from the windows of Cedar Grove, "Oh, Rose, Rose, how can I give you up!"

Perhaps I am superstitious, but I cannot help fancying that as often as these words rang out on the midnight air, the *shadow* was over and around me. But alas! it faded and I was left to do the rash act I meditated. With the coming of morn Mr. Delafield grew calm, for he had resolved upon an interview with Rosa Lee, who, if it were not too late, should know how much he loved her, and perhaps (his heart thrilled with joy as he thought it), perhaps she might yet be won from that fancy of her childhood. But first he would if possible, learn from his sister how far matters had progressed. He had seldom imparted to her his secrets, but he would speak to her now, for he could not keep silent.

She was seated at her work in her own room, when he entered, and with a feeling of alarm at his pale, haggard face, she started up, asking if he were ill. Motioning her aside, he said, abruptly, "It's of no use, Angeline, to deceive you longer. I love Rosa Lee, and if it were not for this accursed doctor, I should tell her so at once. Do you know aught of his attentions? Has he come to seek her for his wife?"

Mrs. Lansing had now a double part to perform. The falsehood she had told to Rosa, made it necessary that she should tell another to her brother, which she did more readily, for her proud nature revolted at the thoughts of receiving her governess as her sister-in-law. So, thinking any means excusable which would prevent so disgraceful a catastrophe, she answered with well feigned surprise, "I am astonished at you, brother—astonished that a Delafield should stoop so low as to think of wedding a girl like Rosa Lee. You cannot, I think, be in earnest; but if you are, I am rejoiced that I have it in my power to tell you there is no hope. I have just left Miss Lee, who has made me her confident, asking if I thought it would be contrary to all rules of propriety for her to marry Dr. Clayton so soon after the death of his wife. It seems he has always preferred her, and could you have heard her tell how much she loved him, I am sure you would have no hope of winning her, even were she your equal."

The wicked woman paused, trembling at her own wickedness; while her brother, burying his face in his hands, groaned aloud. It was an hour of bitter trial, for Rosa Lee alone had touched his heart, and could he give her up just as he had found how dear she was to him? For a time the selfish nature of the man prevailed, and then there came a moment of calmer reflection: if Rose loved another, would it be right for him to mar her happiness by intruding upon her his affection? Should he not rather rejoice in knowing that *she* was happy with the man she had chosen, and if, henceforth, the world to him was dark and cheerless, might he not occasionally gather a gleam of comfort from knowing that no shadow was across *her* pathway! Thus he reasoned, and when his sister ventured at last to say, "You will not be foolish enough to talk with her," he answered, "No—no—of coarse not;" then, with no visible sign of the fierce storm which had swept over him, save the extreme pallor of his face, he arose, and with a firm tread went back to his home, unconscious of the tear-wet eyes which followed his retreating footsteps, as from her window Rosa Lee watched him with a despairing heart and benumbed faculties.

Not again that day was Cedar Grove gladdened by his presence, and when next morning he came as was his wont, I was the betrothed of Dr. Clayton, who, with joy beaming in every look, sat by my side, talking to me of the pleasure we should experience in our projected European tour, for we were to visit the Old World, and he wished our marriage to be consummated at once, so we could sail the last of June. In a measure I had dealt candidly with him, frankly acknowledging that the love I had felt for him in childhood was gone, but saying, as was true, that I respected him—yes, *liked* him, and if he was satisfied with that, I would be unto him a faithful wife, hoping that the affection of former years might ere long awake again in my heart. And he was content to take me thus, blessing me for the utterance of words which had made him so happy.

Involuntarily I shrank from him, for I knew I was undeserving of such devotion, and my conscience smote me for withholding from him the knowledge of my love for Richard Delafield. But that was a secret I could not reveal, so I kept it to myself, and with a kind of apathetic indifference listened while he depicted in glowing colors the joyous future which he saw before him when I should be indeed his *wife*. He was going to New Orleans on business, which would detain him for three or four weeks, and on his return he asked that the ceremony might be performed, and I go with him to Meadow Brook as his bride.

"No, not so soon," I exclaimed. "Leave me my freedom a little longer;" but he only smiled as he waived aside every objection and won from me a promise that if Mrs. Lansing were willing, we would be married there as soon as he should return from New Orleans, whither he would start the next night.

Either by design or accident, Mrs. Lansing herself at that moment entered the room, apologizing for the intrusion by saying she wanted a book which lay upon the piano. Having secured the volume, she was about leaving, when, glancing at the doctor, she playfully remarked upon the happy expression of his face, saying, she should judge his suit was progressing, and adding that he had her good wishes for his success. Emboldened by her familiarity, Dr. Clayton at once preferred to her his wish that we might be made one under the shadow of her roof; we would make no trouble, he said, as we wished for no display, simply a quiet ceremony at which no one should be present save herself, her children, and her *brother*!

At the mention of *him* I started as if smitten by a heavy blow, for I thought, "I cannot in *his* presence give myself to another;" and I used all the arguments of which I was mistress to induce Dr. Clayton to defer our marriage until we reached Meadow Brook. But to this neither he nor Mrs. Lansing would listen. Glad, that I was thus out of her way, the latter seemed unusually kind, offering to give me a bridal party as a "testimony of her respect." Thus was I silenced, while they arranged the matter as they pleased, it being finally decided that the wedding was to take place immediately after the doctor's return, as he had first proposed. So overcome and bewildered was I with the exciting scenes through which I had passed, that, strange as it may seem, I slept soundly that night, dreaming towards day-break that I stood on the deck of a noble vessel, gazing upon a most glorious sunset, which, however, had less charms for me than did the man at my side, whom I called my husband, and whom I loved again as I had done long ago, when with my face buried in the grass beneath the old grape-vine I had wept over his inconstancy.

With the remembrance of that dream still haunting me, it was quite natural that I should in the morning meet Dr. Clayton with more cordiality of manner than I had yet evinced towards him. Quickly perceiving the change, he said, as he kissed my brow, "My Rose is learning to love me, I see."

And for a brief moment I, too, fancied that he was right—that I *should* love him—nay, that I was beginning to love him, when suddenly in the doorway appeared the form of one, the very sight of whom curdled my blood for an instant and then sent it bounding through my veins! It was Mr. Delafield. He had nerved himself to see me, to stand face to face with his rival, and bravely did he meet the trial, bowing courteously to Dr. Clayton and smiling kindly down upon me as he bade me good morning. I glanced at him once and saw that his eyes were riveted upon the plain band of gold, which encircled my fourth finger, confirming the truth of what he had just heard from his sister. At last, as if he would test his strength to the utmost, he took my hand and said, as he slowly twirled the ring, which was rather large, "And so you are going from us?"

I could not answer, nor was it needful that I should, for without waiting a reply he placed my hand in that of Dr. Clayton, and continued, "As a brother commits a dear sister to the care of another, so commit I to your care my Northern Rose, charging you to watch tenderly over her, for 'tis not every one who winneth such a treasure."

This was all he said; the next moment he was gone, and when, Dr. Clayton, drawing me to his side, told me how he would treasure up the words of *my friend*; I involuntarily shrank away, for the *shadow* was again around me, and turn which way I would, it whispered to me of another *love*— another *heart*, which I fain would have called my own.

That night Dr. Clayton left us, and the very morning after his departure we were surprised by the appearance of Ada, who came unexpectedly to us all. "She was tired of living with that old fidgety Mrs. Johnson," she said, "and would rather come home." Much as Mrs. Lansing liked Ada, she would rather she had stayed away until I was gone, for she was in constant dread lest the falsehood she had told me concerning her brother's engagement should in some way be betrayed. But there was no help for it, and as one *sin* always calls for another, so she must now conjure up something with which to meet the emergency. Accordingly, Ada was told that "somehow or other I had received the impression that she was engaged to Mr. Delafield, and that it was as well to let me think so; for though I probably liked Dr. Clayton well enough, she (Mrs. Lansing) fancied that I liked her brother better, and that if I supposed there was the slightest chance of winning him, I would not hesitate to discard the doctor."

Very readily Ada fell in with the views of Mrs. Lansing, who proposed further that they should continually ring in my ears the praises of my affianced husband, of whose virtues Ada was supposed to have heard from Mrs. Lansing; while at the same time, I was to be interested as much as possible in the preparations for my wedding, which was to be quite a grand affair, and to which many of the village people were to be invited. And so the days wore on, during which I could hardly be said to exist, so little did I realize what was passing around me. I dared not think, for if I did, the tumult of thought which crowded upon me seemed turning my brain to fire, and when each morning I awoke from an unrefreshing slumber, it was always with the thought, "What is it? This load which oppresses me so?" — then, as the stern reality came up before me, I would bury my face in the pillow and ask that I might die, and thus escape the living death which awaited me, and which was now but a week or two in the distance.

CHAPTER XXIV
THE CRISIS

It was the night before the one appointed for the bridal, and in the solitude of her chamber, a young girl wept in the utter hopelessness of despair. At the morrow's early dawn *he* would be there to claim her as his bride, and though he was noble and good, there was in her heart no answering chord of love, and she knew that without such love their union would be unholy. Earnestly, and with many tears had she striven to awaken again the deep affection she had felt for him in the time gone by, but it could not be, and shudderingly she thought of the long weary years when she should be an unloving wife, bearing a crushed and aching heart, wherein was enshrined the memory of one, of whom it would soon be a sin to think.

On the table at her side lay her bridal dress, the gift of Richard Delafield, who, without a shadow on his brow, or a wavering in the tones of his voice, had asked her to accept it as a token of the *esteem* he should ever feel for her! Alas, poor Rose, as your tears fell like rain upon the orange wreath which seemed to mock your woe, how little did you dream of the anguish it cost the donor to say to you the words he did, or that your sorrow was naught compared to his, for *you* could weep, while to him this privilege was denied, and his was the hard task of enduring in silence the burning pain which no tear-drop came to moisten.

Slowly the hours of night wore away, and as the moon rose higher and higher in the heavens, her rays fell upon the bowed form of Rosa, who, with clasped hands and bloodless cheeks, sat just where first we saw her— praying—weeping—thinking, and praying again, until at last there came over her troubled spirit, a calm, which ere long, resolved itself into a fixed determination. "She would tell him all—how she loved Richard Delafield, and how, though that love were hopeless, she could not call another her husband." And he would release her—she knew he would. "But if he should not?" seemed whispered in her ear. For an instant her heart stood still, and then she answered aloud, "I will not do this great wickedness and sin against both God and man."

It was strange how calm this resolution made her. Rising up from the crouching posture she had assumed in the first abandonment of her grief, she walked to the open window, where she stood gazing out upon the starry sky, until at last, sick and faint with the sweet perfume of the night air, she turned away, and shuddering, she knew not why, sought her pillow. It was now the first of June, and in that southern clime the air was already hot, sultry, and laden with disease. For two weeks a fearful epidemic, whose nature the oldest physicians did not understand, had been raging in the towns adjoining, and many who in the morning rose up full of life and vigor, were in the evening no longer numbered among the living, so rapid was the work of death. In great alarm the terrified inhabitants had fled from place to place, but the destroyer was on their tract and the "brain fever," as it was termed, claimed them for its victims.

As yet, there had been no cases in W——, but the people were in daily dread of its arrival, and a feeling of gloom pervaded the village. Mrs. Lansing, on the contrary, though usually alarmed, even at the mention of a contagious disease, expressed no fear, and went on with the preparations for the party, unconscious of the dark cloud hovering near. But when on the morning succeeding the night of which we have spoken, she heard, in passing Rosa's door the sound of some one talking incoherently, while at the same time a negro girl came rushing out, exclaiming, "The Lord help us—young Miss has now got the brain fever, and gone ravin' mad," she fled in wild alarm to the farthest extremity of the building, and gathering her frightened children together, with Ada, around her, she called to the terrified servants from the window, bidding them go for her brother and tell him as he valued his life not to venture near the infected room, but to hasten with all speed to her. And there, trembling, weeping, and wringing her hands in fear, the selfish, cold-hearted woman stayed, while parched with fever and thirst, the suffering girl lay moaning in her pain; now asking for water to cool her burning brain, and again clasping her thin, white hands convulsively upon her brow, as if to still its agonized throbbings.

But one there was who did not forget. In her excitement Mrs. Lansing failed to notice the absence of little Jessie, who going fearlessly to the bedside of her beloved teacher, gently bathed the aching head, and administered the cooling draught, while with childish love she kissed the ashen lips, and smoothed back the long tresses which floated over the pillow. In the hall below there was the sound of footsteps, and the bridegroom's voice was heard, asking for his bride, but his cheek blanched to a marble whiteness when told that she was dying in the chamber above. In a moment he had her in his arms—his precious Rose—dying—dying—he believed, for he, too, had heard of the strange disease, and he thought there was no hope. With a bitter cry, he bent over the unconscious girl, who knew him not, for the light of reason was obscured and darkness was upon her vision.

"*Can* nothing be done? Is there no help?" he exclaimed wildly, and little Jessie, awed by his grief, answered, as she laid her soft, white hand on Rosa's forehead, "*God can help her*, and maybe Uncle Dick can. I mean to go for him," and gliding noiselessly from the room, she was soon on her way to Sunny Bank, looking, with her golden curls floating over her bare white shoulders, as is she were indeed an angel of mercy.

Alone in his library sat Richard Delafield, his arms resting upon the table, and his face buried in his hands. All the night long he had sat there thus, musing sadly of the future when *she* would be gone, and he should be alone. Why had she crossed his path—that little, humble girl, and why had he been permitted to love her so madly, or to dream of a time when he could call her "*his own, his Rose, his wife.*" Again and again he repeated those words to himself, and then as he thought whose she would be when another sun should have set, he groaned aloud, and in despairing tones cried out, "How can I give her up!"

The sun had risen, and, struggling through the richly curtained window, fell upon his bowed head, but he did not heed it. He was sleeping at last, and in his dreams another than Dr. Clayton had claimed Rose for his bride, even Death, and without a tear he laid her in her coffin, and buried her where the soft sighing cedar and the whispering pine would overshadow her grave. From that dream he was roused by Jessie, who shrieked in his ear, "Wake, Uncle Dick, and come. Miss Lee is dying with the fever, and there is nobody to help her."

For a time the selfish part of Richard Delafield's nature gained the ascendant, and he said aloud, "Thank God! Rather thus than the bride of another."

Still this feeling did not prevent him from action, and with a firm step and composed manner he went with Jessie to Cedar Grove, going immediately to Rosa's chamber, where, for a moment, he stood appalled at the scene before him. She had fearfully changed since last he saw her, for the disease had advanced with rapid strides, and now utterly insensible, and white as the wintry snow, she lay with her head thrown back, and her lips apart, while her hands nervously picked at the bed-clothes around her! Many a time had Dr. Clayton heard that this was a sure omen of death, and though he had ever laughed at it as an old woman's whim, he shuddered now as he saw it in *her*, and bowing his head upon the pillow, he wept like a child. For a moment Richard Delafield stood gazing upon the apparently dying girl and the weeping man, who seemed wholly incapable of action; then rousing himself, he went in quest of the black women, commanding them in a voice they dared not disobey to come at once to the sick-room. He had heard that nothing but violent and continual perspiration had as yet been of any avail in such extreme cases, and calmly giving orders to that effect, he himself assisted while the hemlock and the bottles of hot water were applied, then, administering a powerful tonic, he bade Jessie go for her mother, while he took his station at the bedside to watch the result.

Quieted in a measure by the cool demeanor of his companion, Dr. Clayton, too, arose, and after hurriedly pacing the room, resumed his post, and there on each side of Rose they stood, those two men, the one with his fair handsome face stained with tears, praying earnestly that she might live; while the other, with dark, lowering countenance and wrinkled brow, stood with folded arms, and firmly compressed lips, struggling to subdue the evil passion which whispered, "Let her die! There will be a comfort in weeping over her grave, and knowing that she sleeps there in all her maiden purity."

In the meantime Jessie had been missed, and a servant dispatched to find her. But this the woman failed to do as she was then at Sunny Bank, and Mrs. Lansing was about venturing to go in quest of her, when she appeared with her uncle's message, saying, "she knew Miss Lee was dying, she looked so dreadfully."

"Jessie—child," screamed the affrighted Mrs. Lansing, shrinking from the little girl as if she had been a loathsome thing, "*Have* you been there—in the room?"

Without any attempt at concealment, Jessie told what she had done, and when her mother exclaimed, "You are a dead child," she answered fearlessly, "I am not afraid to die."

Just then the negro, who had been sent to the village for the family physician, returned, bringing the news that the fever had broken out there the night before, and that in one family two were already dead, while a third was thought to be dying. In the utmost dismay, Mrs. Lansing now announced her intention of leaving the place at once and fleeing for safety to her brother's plantation, which was distant about twelve miles.

"And leave Miss Lee alone? oh, mother!" said Jessie, beginning to cry, while Halbert, frightened as he was, remonstrated against the unfeeling desertion.

But Mrs. Lansing was determined—"she couldn't help her at all if she stayed," she said. "And the colored women would do all that was necessary; it wasn't like leaving her alone with Dr. Clayton, for there were a dozen able-bodied females in the house to wait upon her."

"And if she dies?" suggested Jessie; but her mother would not hear to reason, and urged on by Ada, who was no less frightened than herself, she ordered out the travelling carriage, which soon stood before the door.

She would fain have had her brother accompany her, but she knew it was useless to propose it. Still she would see him before she went, and her waiting-maid was sent to bring him.

"I'll go. Let me go," said Jessie, and ere her mother could detain her, she was half-way there.

Entering the room on tiptoe, she gave her uncle her mother's message, and then stealing up to Rose, wound her arms round her neck, and laying her soft, warm cheek caressingly against the white, thin face of her teacher, wept her last adieu. They would never, never meet again, for ere the summer flowers were faded, *one* would be safely in the bosom of the Good Shepherd, who would lead her in green pastures, and beside the still waters of the better land.

"Bury her under the tall magnolia, a little ways from father," was Jessie's last injunction to Dr. Clayton, whose tears burst forth afresh, for not till then had he thought how he must leave her alone in that far south land—many miles away from her native hills, and that to him would be denied the solace of weeping over her early grave.

It was in vain that Mr. Delafield attempted to dissuade his sister from going. She would not listen, for their lives, she said, were all endangered by remaining in town, and as several other families were going to leave, she should follow their example—then bidding him hasten to them the moment Rose was dead, she entered her carriage and was driven rapidly away, followed by Halbert and two or three negroes on horseback. Unfeeling as this proceeding seemed to Richard, he still experienced a sensation of relief at the absence of the family, and thinking they would probably be safer at "The Pines" than at Cedar Grove, he returned to the chamber above, where Rose still lay, in the same deathlike unconsciousness, perfectly still save when a movement of the head, or a faint moan, told how she suffered. Everything had been done for her which could be done, and now there was naught for them to do but to wait and watch, which they did in perfect silence—Dr. Clayton, with his head bowed upon the pillow, while Mr. Delafield leaned against the wall, with compressed lips, and eyes dark as midnight, fastened upon the white, still face before him.

The clock in the hall struck the hour of eleven, and then, with a feeble moan, the sick girl withdrew her hand from beneath the covering, and when the stern man took it within his own he forced back an exclamation of joy, for it was moist with perspiration! There was hope, and his first impulse was to tell the good news to his companion, but the demon, which all the morning he had hugged to his bosom, whispered, "not now—let him suffer yet a little longer!" Soon, however, casting this thought aside as unworthy of him, he said, "Look up, Dr. Clayton, she is better. She may live. *See!*" and lifting the damp hair from her brow, he pointed to the dewy drops which stood thickly upon it.

"Thank Heaven!" was Dr. Clayton's exclamation, and bending down, he said, "Rose, my precious Rose—she will live, and *you* have saved her," he continued advancing towards the dark statue, whose hand he pressed to his lips. "To you the credit is due, for you *worked* when despair had rendered me powerless to do, but now I am strong. I am myself again, and if I have any skill it shall be exerted in her behalf."

There was a curl on Richard Delafield's lip—a blur before his eyes, and an icy chill at his heart, which prevented him from answering. Bitter were the thoughts which crowded upon him, and which he strove to put away. If she lived, would it not be in a measure owing to the efficient means he had employed—and why should *he* wish to save her? Would he not rather see her dead? It was an evil spirit which counselled with him thus, but ere long the noble nature of Richard Delafield conquered, and when at last her eyes unclosed, and turned towards Dr. Clayton, whose name she breathed, asking for her bridal dress, he looked on calmly while his rival kissed her again and again, telling her she should yet wear it and be his bride, but when he saw how she shuddered at these words, feebly answering, "No, no. Have they not told you that I cannot be your bride, for another has come between us?" a thrill of joy ran through his frame, but soon passed away as he thought it was merely the vagary of a disordered mind.

All that day and night they stood over her, applying the remedies said to be most efficient in cases of the kind, and when the next morning came she was unquestionably better, though still in great danger from a tendency of the disease to the lungs, which, however, was less to be feared than its return to the brain. Very carefully and tenderly they watched her, and had not Mr. Delafield been blinded by her supposed love for another, he must have seen how much more readily she took things from him than from Dr. Clayton, following him with her eyes whenever he moved away, and seeming much more quiet when he was at her side. By the close of the third day she was nearly free from the brain fever, but much fear was felt by Dr. Clayton lest it should assume the typhoid form, which it did ere long, and then for three weeks she raved in wild delirium, driving Richard Delafield from her presence, shuddering when he came near, and begging of Dr. Clayton, whom she called her brother Charlie, "to send the black man with his ugly face away."

This state of affairs was almost intolerable to Richard, who, if he had loved Rose before, felt that she was tenfold dearer to him now, and so, though he dared not come in her sight when awake, he watched by her when she slept, standing over her hour after hour, and enduring with almost superhuman strength the care which Dr. Clayton could hardly be said to share, so absorbed was he in grief at the thoughts of losing her at last. Thus the days wore on until her frenzy abated, and she sank into a state of apathy from which nothing could rouse her, not even the sight of Richard Delafield, from whom she no longer shrank, but for whom she seemed to have conceived a kind of pity, asking him sometimes "if he hated her because she did not love him, and telling him how hard she had tried to do so, but could not, and that he must go away and leave her alone!" And all this while it never occurred to him that she fancied *he* was Dr. Clayton, though he *did* marvel at her never mentioning her affianced husband, in whose arms she would fall asleep, and whose hand she would kiss, calling him Charlie, and asking if he had come to carry her home.

Matters were in this state when one day, towards the dusk of evening, he was surprised by the appearance of Halbert, who said that the *cholera*, had broken out at the Pines, and he must come immediately, adding further, that his mother and Ada had both had it, that several of the blacks were dead, and that the man, who two days before had been sent to Cedar Grove, had died upon the road. Greatly alarmed for the safety of his people, Mr. Delafield started at once for the Pines, whither, in another chapter, we will follow him.

CHAPTER XXV
THE ANGEL OF THE PINES

The unexpected arrival of their master's sister and her cortége at "The Pines," as Mr. Delafield's plantation was called, produced quite a sensation among the blacks, who hastened to receive their guests with many demonstrations of joy, rather more affected than real, for Mrs. Lansing was not very popular with them. Halbert and Jessie, on the contrary, were general favorites among the servants, who thought them little less than angels, particularly Jessie, who, with her sweet, young face, laughing eyes, and wavy hair, flitted like a sunbeam from cabin to cabin, asking after this old Aunty, or that old Uncle, and screaming with delight when in one hut she found *three babies*, all of an age, and belonging to the same mother, who boasted of having given to her master "fifteen as likely girls and boys as there were in Georgy."

As yet the triplets had no names, but the arrival of the family suggested a new idea to Hannah, who, seating herself by Jessie, proposed that they be called, "Richard Delafield, Ada Montrose, and Jessie Lansing."

With the first and last the little girl was well pleased, but she objected to the middle name, and taking one of the infants upon her lap, she told the story of her beloved teacher, who was dying at Cedar Grove, and asked that the child she held might be called for her. So, baptized by Jessie's tears, which fell like rain upon its dark and wrinkled face, the babe was christened "Rosa Lee."

The house which Mrs. Lansing termed her country residence (for she always spoke of her brother's possessions as her own), was a large, double log building, containing nothing very elegant in the way of furniture, but still presenting an air of neatness and comfort; for *Aunt Dinah*, who had charge of it, prided herself upon keeping it neat and clean, as her master was likely to come upon her at any time without warning, and she liked to impress him with her rare qualifications as housekeeper. With Mrs. Lansing, however, she was less pleased, but still as the sister of "Mars'r Richard," she was entitled to consideration, and now in high turban, and all the dignity of her position, the old lady bustled about from room to room, jingling her keys, kicking the dogs, cuffing the woolly pate of any luckless wight who chanced to be in her way, and occasionally stooping down to kiss little Jessie, who, being of rather a domestic turn, followed her from place to place, herself assisting in spreading the supper table, which, with its snowy cloth, corn cake, iced milk, hot coffee, and smoking steaks, soon presented a most inviting aspect.

Relieved of their fears and thinking themselves beyond the reach of danger, Mrs. Lansing and Ada gave themselves up to the enjoyment of the hour, talking and laughing gaily, without a thought of the sick girl they had left behind, and who that night was to have been a bride. Once, indeed, when after sunset they were assembled upon the rude piazza, Ada spoke of her, wondering if she were *dead*, and how long it would be ere Dr. Clayton would marry another! Such is the world, to which Ada formed no exception, for how often do we hear the future companion of a broken-hearted man selected, even before the wife of his bosom is removed forever from his sight!

For a long time Mrs. Lansing sat there with Ada and her children, talking on indifferent subjects and occasionally congratulating herself that they were beyond reach of the fever, unless, indeed, Jessie had contracted it by her foolish carelessness! On her lap rested the little golden head of the child, who was humming snatches of "The Happy Land," a favorite song which her uncle had taught her, and which she had often sung with her teacher, asking numerous questions concerning the better world, where

> "Saints in glory stand,
>
> Bright, bright as day,"

and wondering if, when she died, Jesus would take her there to sing,

> "Worthy is our Saviour King."

Very naturally, now, her thoughts reverted to her governess, and as she listened to the whispering wind sighing through the trees, she fancied it was the voice of Rose bidding her, "come to the Happy Land." Sweet little Jessie, it was the voices of angel children, which you heard thus calling through the pines; for from their shining ranks one beauteous form was missing, and they would fain allure it back to its native sky.

Come I now to the saddest part of my story. Beneath the evergreens of the sunny South is a little mound, over which the shining stars keep watch, and the cypress spreads its long green boughs, while the children of the plantation, dark browed though they are, tread softly near that grave, which they daily strew with flowers, speaking in low tones of "the Angel of the Pines," as they term the fair young girl, who passed so suddenly from their midst. It was now nearly five weeks since Mrs. Lansing had fled from the pestilence which walked at noonday, and though it had in a measure abated in the village, there were still frequent cases, and she would not have deemed it safe to return, even if typhoid fever, which she feared nearly as much, had not been in her own house. So there was no alternative but to stay, uncomfortable though she was, for the weather was intensely hot, and she missed many of the luxuries of her home. Still it was healthy there, and this in a measure reconciled her to remain. Occasionally, it is true, she heard rumors of the cholera, on some distant plantation, but it seldom visited the pine regions—it would not come there; she was sure of that; and secure in this belief, she rested in comparative quiet, while each day the heat became more and more intense. The sun came up red, fiery, and heated like a furnace; the clouds gave forth no rain; the brooks were dried up; the leaves withered upon the trees, while the air was full of humming insects, which at night fed upon their helpless, sleeping victims.

At the close of one of these scorching, sultry days, Mrs. Lansing and Ada sat upon the piazza, panting for a breath of pure, cool air. At the side of each stood a negro girl, industriously fanning their mistresses, who scolded them as if they were to blame, because the air thus set in motion was hot and burning as the winds which blow over the great desert of Sahara. As they sat there thus, an old man came up from the negro quarters, saying "his woman done got sick wid the cramps," and he wished "his mistis jest come down see her."

But Mrs. Lansing felt herself too languid for exertion of any kind, and telling Uncle Abel that she herself was fully as sick as his wife, who was undoubtedly feigning, she sent him back with a sinking heart to the rude cabin, where his old wife lay, groaning aloud whenever the *cramps*, as she termed them, seized her. Scarcely, however, had he entered the low doorway, when a fairy form came flitting down the narrow pathway, her white dress gleaming through the dusky twilight, and her golden hair streaming out behind. It was little Jessie, who, from her crib, had heard her mother's refusal to accompany Uncle Abel, and, stealing away unobserved, she had come herself to see Aunt Chloe, with whom she was quite a favorite.

Unaccustomed as Jessie was to sickness, she saw at a glance that this was no ordinary case, and, kneeling down beside the negress, who lay upon the floor, she took her head upon her lap, and gently pushing back, beneath the gay turban, the matted, grizzly hair, she asked where the pain was.

"Bress de sweet chile," answered Chloe, "you can't tache me with the pint of a cambric needle whar 'tain't, and seems ef ebery jint in me was onsoderin' when de cramp is on."

As if to verify the truth of this remark, she suddenly bent up nearly double, and rolling upon her face, groaned aloud. At this moment a negro, who had gained some notoriety among his companions as a physician, came in, and after looking a moment at the prostrate form of Chloe, who was now vomiting freely, he whispered a word which cleared the cabin in a moment, for the mention of *cholera* had a power to curdle the blood of the terrified blacks, who fled to their own dwellings, where they cried aloud, and praying, some of them, "that de Lord would have mercy on 'em, and take somebody else to kingdom come, ef he must have a nigger anyway."

Utterly fearless, Jessie stayed by, and when *John*, or as he was more familiarly known, "Doctor," proposed going for her mother, she answered, "No, no; Uncle Abel has been for her once, but she won't come; and if she knows it is cholera, she'll take me away."

This convinced the "Doctor," who proceeded to put in practice the medical skill which he had picked up at intervals, and which was considerable for one of his capacity. By this time, a few of the women, more daring than the rest and curious to know the fate of their companion, ventured near the door, where they stood gazing wonderingly upon the poor old creature, who was fast floating out upon the broad river of death. It was a most violent attack, and its malignity was increased by a quantity of unripe fruit which she had eaten that morning.

"Will somebody make a pra'r?" she said, feebly, as she felt her life fast ebbing away. "Abel, you pray for poor Chloe," and her glassy eyes turned beseechingly towards her husband, who was noted at camp-meetings for praying the loudest and longest of any one.

But his strength had left him now, and kissing the shrivelled face of his dying wife, he said, "'Scuse me, Chloe; de sperrit is willin', but de flesh part is mighty weak and shaky like. Miss Jessie, you pray!" he continued, as the child came to his side.

"Yes, honey, pray," gasped Chloe; and, kneeling down, the little girl began the Lord's Prayer, occasionally interspersing it with a petition that "God would take the departing soul to heaven."

"Yes, dat's it," whispered Chloe; "dat's better dan all dem fine words 'bout kingdom come and daily bread; dey'll do for white folks, but God bress old Chloe, de thing for niggers to die on."

"Sing, honey, sing," she said, at last; and, mingled with the lamentations of the blacks, there arose on the evening air the soft notes of the *Happy Land*, which Jessie sang, bending low towards Chloe, who, when the song was ended, clasped her in her arms, and calling her "a shining angel," went, we trust, to the better land, where bondage is unknown, and the slave is equal to his master.

Loud and shrill rose the wail of the negroes, increasing in violence when it was known that into another cabin the pestilence had entered, prostrating a boy, who, in his agony, called for Jessie and mas'r Richard, thinking they could save him. Late as it was, Mrs. Lansing, Ada, and Lina, were still upon the piazza, which was far more comfortable than their sleeping-room, where they supposed both Halbert and Jessie were safely in bed. They were just thinking of retiring, when suddenly the midnight stillness was broken by a cry so shrill that Mrs. Lansing started to her feet, asking what it was.

From her couch by the open door, Aunt Dinah arose, and going out a few rods, listened to the sound, which seemed to come from the negro quarters, whither, at her mistress's command, she bent her steps. But a short time elapsed ere she returned with the startling news that, "the cholera was thar—that Chloe was dead, and another one had got it and was *vomucking* all over the night dress of *Miss Jessie*, who was holdin' his head."

Wholly overcome with fright, Mrs. Lansing fainted, and was borne to her room, where, for a time, she remained unconscious, forgetful of Jessie, who stayed at the quarters long after midnight, ministering to the wants of the sick, of which, before morning, there were five, while others showed symptoms of the rapidly spreading disease. As soon as Mrs. Lansing returned to consciousness, she sent for Jessie, who came reluctantly, receiving her mother's reproof in silence, and falling away to sleep as calmly as if she had not just been looking upon death, whose shadow was over and around her.

Early the next morning, a man was sent in haste to Cedar Grove, which he never reached, for the destroyer met him on the road, and in one of the cabins of a neighboring plantation, he died, forgetting, in the intensity of his sufferings, the errand on which he had been sent; and as those who attended him knew nothing of Mrs. Lansing's being at the Pines, it was not until the second day after the appearance of the cholera that she learned the fate of her servant. In a state bordering almost upon distraction, she waited for her brother, shuddering with fear whenever a new case was reported to her, and refusing to visit the sufferers, although among them were some who had played with her in childhood; and one, an old grey-haired man, who had saved her from a watery grave, when on the Savannah River she had fallen overboard. But there was no place for gratitude in her selfish heart, and the miserable creatures were left to die alone, uncheered by the presence of a pale face, save little Jessie, who won her mother's reluctant consent to be with them, and who, all the day long, went from cabin to cabin, soothing the sick and dying by her presence, and emboldening others by her own intrepidity.

Towards sunset, Mrs. Lansing herself was seized with the malady, and with a wild shriek, she called on Ada to help her; but that young lady was herself too much intimidated to heed the call, and in an adjoining room she sat with camphor at her nose and brandy at her side, until a fierce, darting pain warned her that she, too, was a victim. No longer afraid of Mrs. Lansing, she made no resistance when borne to the same apartment, where for hours they lay, bemoaning the fate which had brought them there, and trembling as they thought of the probable result.

On Mrs. Lansing's mind there was a heavy load, and once, when the cold perspiration stood thickly upon her face, she ordered Jessie and Dinah from the room, while she confessed to Ada the sin of which she had been guilty in deceiving both her brother and Rose.

"It was a wicked falsehood," said she, "and if you survive me, you must tell them so, will you?"

Ada nodded in token that she would, and then, thinking her own conscience might be made easier by a similar confession, she told how she had thought to injure Rose in Mr. Delafield's estimation, and also of the blister, which had drawn on Hagar's back instead of her own! This done, the two ladies felt greatly relieved, and as the cholera in their case had been induced mostly by *fear*, it began ere long to yield to the efficient treatment of Dinah, who to her housekeeping qualities added that of being a skillful nurse. Towards morning they were pronounced decidedly better, and as Jessie was asleep and Dinah nodding in her chair, Mrs. Lansing lifted her head from her pillow, saying to Ada, "If you please, you needn't tell what I told you last night, when I thought I was going to die!"

Ada promised to be silent, and after winning a similar promise from Mrs. Lansing, they both fell asleep, nor woke again until the sun was high up in the heavens. So much for a sick-bed repentance!

That day was hotter and more sultry than any which had preceded it; and about the middle of the afternoon little Jessie came to Dinah's side and laying her head upon her lap complained of being both *cold* and *tired*. Blankets were wrapped around her, but they brought to her no warmth, for her blood was chilled by approaching death, and when at dusk the negroes asked why she came not among them, they were told that she was dying! With streaming eyes they fell upon their knees, and from those humble cabins there went up many a fervent prayer for God to spare the child. But it could not be; she was wanted in heaven; and when old Uncle Abel, who had also been ill, crept on his hands and knees to her bedside, calling upon her name, she did not know him, for unconsciousness was upon her, and in infinite mercy she was spared the pain usually attendant upon the disease.

Almost bereft of reason and powerless to act, Mrs. Lansing sat by her child, whose life was fast ebbing away. In a short time all the negroes, who were able, had come to the house, their dark faces stained with tears and expressive of the utmost concern, as they looked upon the little girl, who lay so white and still, with her fair hair floating over the pillow and her waxen hands folded upon her bosom.

"Sing to me, Uncle Dick," she said, at last, "sing of the Happy Land not far away;" but Uncle Dick was not there, and they who watched her were too much overcome with grief to heed her request.

Slowly the hours wore on, and the spirit was almost home, when again she murmured, "Sing of the Happy Land;" and as if in answer to her prayer, the breeze, which all the day long had been hushed and still, now sighed mournfully through the trees, while a mocking-bird in the distance struck up his evening lay; and amid the gushing melody of that wondrous bird of song and the soft breathing notes of the whispering pines, little Jessie passed to the "Happy Land," which to those who watched the going out of her short life, seemed, indeed, "not far away."

With a bitter cry the bereaved mother fell upon her face and wept aloud, saying, in her heart, "My God, my God, why have I thus been dealt with?"

In the distance was heard the sound of horses' feet, and ere long her brother was with her, weeping as only strong men weep, over the lifeless form which returned him no answering caress. She had been his idol, and for a moment he, too, questioned the justice of God in thus afflicting him.

"Jessie is gone, Rosa is going, and I shall be left alone," he thought. "What have I done to deserve a chastisement like this?"

Soon, however, he grew calmer, and saying, "It is well;" he tenderly kissed the lips and brow of the beautiful child, who seemed to smile on him even in death; then going out among his people, he comforted them as best he could, dropping more than one tear to the memory of those who they told him were dead, and who numbered eight in all. At a short distance from the house was a tall cypress where Jessie had often sported, and where now was a play-house, built by her hands but a few days before. There, by the light of the silvery moon, they made her a grave, and when the sun was up, its rays fell upon the pile of earth which hid from view the sunny face and soft blue eyes of Jessie, "the Angel of the Pines."

CHAPTER XXVI
RETURN

For nearly a week after Jessie's death, Mr. Delafield remained at the Pines, doing whatever he could for the comfort of his servants, and as at the end of that time the disease had wholly disappeared, he returned to Cedar Grove, accompanied by his sister and Ada, who had learned by sad experience that the dangers from which we flee, are oftentimes less than those to which we go. They found Rose better, but still quite low, and as the fever had not entirely left her, neither Mrs. Lansing nor Ada ventured near her room, but shut themselves in their own apartment, where the former received the sympathy of her friends, which in this case was truly sincere, for Jessie was universally beloved and the tidings of her death carried sorrow to many hearts.

Over Dr. Clayton a change had come. The hopeful, happy expression of his face was gone, and in its place was a look of utter hopelessness which at first roused Richard's fears lest Rose should be worse, and in much alarm he asked if it were so.

"No, no," answered the doctor, while a shadow of pain passed over his handsome features; "she will live."

Then hurrying to the window he looked out to hide his tears from him whom he knew to be his rival, and who, now that he was unobserved, bent over the sleeping Rose, kissing her wasted cheek and mourning for her as he thought how she would weep when she learned the fate of her favorite. Oh, could he have known the whole, how passionately would he have clasped her to his bosom and held her there as his own, his darling Rose! But it was not yet to be, and he must bide his time.

She had seemed greatly relieved at his absence, and on the second day after his departure, she called Dr. Clayton to her side, fancying him to be her brother Charlie. Taking his hands in hers, she told him the whole story of her trials; how she had tried to bring back the old affection of her childhood, but could not because of the love she had for Richard Delafield.

"Oh, Charlie," she exclaimed, "he would forgive me, I know, if he knew how much I suffered during those terrible days, when I thought of giving my hand without my heart. The very idea set my brain on fire and my head has ached, oh, so hard since then, but it's over now, for I conquered at last, and on the night before the wedding, I resolved to tell him all, how I could not and would not marry him. But a dark cloud, which seemed like the rushing of mighty waters, came over me, and I don't know where I am, nor what has happened, only *he* has been here, hanging like a shadow over my pillow, where sat another shadow tenfold blacker, which he said was death; but grim and hideous as it was, I preferred it to a life with him, when my whole soul was given to another. He, too, was here occasionally, and in his presence the shadow grew less and less, while his voice called me back from the deep darkness in which I was groping. Once, when I was almost home, so near that I heard the song which little Jamie sings—Jamie, who died so long ago—he laid his cool hand upon my forehead, which was wet with the waters of the rolling river, and I heard him say to some one, 'Look up; she is better, she will live.' The next moment he was gone, but I struggled with the waves and floated back to the shore, where, though I could not see him, *his* hand was stretched out to save me, and for a time he stood between me and Dr. Clayton, who, when he thought nobody heard him, whispered in my ear, 'my bride—my own.' But from my inmost soul I answered, 'Never, never,' while I looked again towards the river which is still in sight, though slowly receding from view."

She paused a moment and then continued: "When I am dead, Charlie, you must tell him how it was, and ask him to forgive and think with pity of poor little Rose, who would have loved him if she could. If he will not listen—if he still persists in marrying me, tell him I would rather die ten thousand deaths than wed a man I do not love, and then his pride will come to his aid. But not a word of this to Mr. Delafield, Charlie, never let *him* know how I loved him. My affection is not returned, and he would despise me—would never visit my grave or think with pity of one who died so far away from home."

Then followed a message for the loved ones of Meadow Brook, but this Dr. Clayton did not hear. Perfectly paralyzed, he had listened to her story until his reason seemed in danger of leaving him, and long ere she had finished he knew he must give her up—but not to *death*; and as Richard Delafield had done, so he, in this his hour of bitter trial, felt how much rather he would see her in her coffin than the wife of another. Then in his ear the tempter whispered, "Why need these things be? She is not yet out of danger. A little relaxation of care on your part, and Richard Delafield will never call her his."

Only for a moment, however, did Dr. Clayton listen, and then laying his head upon the pillow beside that of Rose, who, wearied with her story, had fallen asleep, he wept as he had never wept before, not even when he saw creeping over her the shadow of death. Turn which way he would, there was naught before him save the darkness of despair; and as wave after wave broke over him, his mind went backward to the time when she might have been his—when he could have gathered her to his bosom—and in piteous accents he cried aloud, "My punishment is greater than I can bear."

But as the fiercest storm soonest expends its fury, so he ere long grew calm and capable of sober, serious thought. Rosa Lee was very dear to him, and to have possessed her love, he would have given almost everything; but as that could not be, ought he to stand in the way of her happiness? He knew she was deceived, for he remembered many things he had seen in Mr. Delafield, which, though he had not thought of it then, convinced him now that her affection was reciprocated; and should he not tell her so, and at the same time disclose to Richard the true state of affairs? Rosa's quiet, unobtrusive, and rather reserved manner had misled Richard, no doubt, or he would long ere this have declared his love.

"Yes, God helping me, I *will* do right," he said aloud, clasping his hands over his feverish brow. "I will watch by her until *his* return, and then committing her to his care I will leave her forever."

There was a movement at his side—Rose was dreaming, and she uttered the name of *Richard*, while, with a shiver, the doctor stopped his ears and shut out the hated sound. In a moment she awoke and asked for water. It was brought, but he no longer supported her in his arms—no longer smoothed back the tangled curls from her brow, or kissed her white lips. "She is not mine, and it were wrong to caress her now," he thought, and his tears fell upon her face as he laid her gently back upon the pillow. Wonderingly she gazed upon him, and lifting her hand, wiped his tears away, asking why he wept.

"Heaven help me from going mad," he exclaimed aloud, as he walked to the window, where for a long time he stood, trying to school himself for the part he was to act.

He succeeded at last, and never did a tender brother watch more carefully over a darling sister than did he over her during the few days which elapsed ere Mr. Delafield's return. He was alone with her when he came, and with comparative calmness he greeted his rival, who, as we have before stated, was surprised at the change in his looks.

That night, in the solitude of his chamber the doctor penned two letters; one for Rose and the other for Richard. In substance, the contents of each were much the same, for he told them all he had heard from Rose, and how, though it broke his heart to do so, he had given her up. "Deal very, very gently with her," he wrote to Mr. Delafield, "for never was there a purer, gentler being, or one more worthy of your love than she. Then take her, and when your cup is overflowing with happiness, think sometimes of one, who, henceforth will be a lonely, wretched man."

The letters being written he put them away until such time as he should need them. Once he thought to talk with Richard face to face, but this he felt he could not do; so one morning about a week after the return of the family to Cedar Grove, and when Rose was out of danger, he pressed a burning kiss upon her forehead, and placing the letters on the little dressing bureau where they would attract the immediate attention of Mr. Delafield, who, he knew would soon be there, he went in quest of Mrs. Lansing, whom he bade good-bye as composedly as if no inward fire were consuming him. In much surprise, she asked why he left them so abruptly, and he replied, "something which has recently come to my knowledge makes it necessary for me to go."

"You will of course return ere long for Miss Lee," continued the lady, who had no suspicion of the truth.

"If *I* do not come I shall send her brother as soon as she is able to be moved," said he. "She does not know that I am going, for she would not understand me if I told her, so I leave it with you to tell her when you think she will comprehend it."

Then leaving a few directions as to how she must be treated, he hurried away, never looking back, and turning into a side street when in the distance he saw Mr. Delafield coming towards him. Half an hour afterward and the puffing engine, which now each day thundered into town, was bearing him away from a place whither he had come for a bride, and from which he bore only a crushed and aching heart. Scarcely had he left Rose's chamber when a colored woman entered it to "set it to rights" as was her daily custom. She was near-sighted, and going up to the dressing-bureau, carelessly brushed off the letter directed to Richard! Falling behind the bureau, it lay concealed from view, while the negress proceeded with her duties, unconscious of the mischief she had done!

In great surprise Richard heard of Dr. Clayton's sudden departure. "There must be something wrong," he thought, though what he did not know. Going up to Rosa's chamber, he found her still asleep. The room was in order—the servant gone, and on the bureau lay the letter which soon caught his attention. Glancing at the superscription he saw it was for Rose, and thinking to keep it safely until she could understand its contents, he placed it in his pocket; then taking a book, he sat by her bedside until she awoke. She was apparently better, but an unnatural brightness of her eyes told that her mind was still unsettled. So he said nothing to her concerning the doctor's desertion, but himself ministered to her wants.

In the course of a few days Mrs. Lansing was induced to visit her. This she did more willingly, for Rose had loved her little Jessie; she would weep bitterly when she knew she was dead; and the proud nature of the haughty woman gave way to the softer feelings, which often prompts a mother to take a deeper interest in whatever was once dear to a lost, a precious child. So casting aside her nervous fear, she at last went frequently to the sick-room, her own white, delicate hands sometimes arranging the tumbled pillow or holding the cooling draught to the lips of her formerly despised governess—despised, not for anything which she had done, but because it was hers to labor for the bread she ate.

CHAPTER XXVII
LIGHT

It was early morning. The windows of my room were open, admitting the fresh, cool air, which had been purified by one of those terrific thunder storms, so common in a southern clime. For many weeks I had lain there in a state of unconsciousness, save at intervals when I had a dreamy realization of what was transpiring around me. The physician who was called in Dr. Clayton's stead had more than once hinted of continued insanity, citing similar cases which had come under his observation; but in spite of his opinion, I, that bright August morning, awoke from a refreshing sleep, with perfectly restored faculties. At first I thought I was alone, for there was a deep stillness in the room, and from the hall below I distinctly heard the ticking of the clock, reminding me of the time, years ago, when once before I had hovered between life and death. Now, as then, I experienced the delicious feeling of returning health, but I missed the familiar faces of my friends, and as I thought how far I was from home, and all who loved me, I said aloud, "I am alone, alone."

"Not alone, Rosa, for *I* am with you," answered a deep voice near, and the next moment the dark form of Richard Delafield bent over me.

Eagerly scanning my face, he said, "Do you know me?"

"Yes," I answered. "Mr. Delafield." Then as a dim remembrance of the past came over me, I lifted my head and looked around the room for one who I knew had not long since been there.

Divining my thought, he said very gently, as if the announcement would of course give me pain, "He is not here, Rosa. He was obliged to go home, but I dare say he will soon return—meantime I will take care of you. Don't feel so badly," he continued, as tears of *genuine joy* at Dr. Clayton's absence gathered in my eyes.

I could not tell him the truth, and when I next spoke it was to ask him concerning my illness, how long it had been, etc.

After telling me all that he thought proper, he took the letter from his pocket, and said, "Dr. Clayton left this for you. Have you strength to read it now?"

"Yes, yes," I replied eagerly, at the same time stretching out my hand to take it.

There was a blur upon my eyes as I read, and I pitied Dr. Clayton, who had thus laid bare to me his wretchedness, but mingled with this was a feeling of relief to know that I was free. He told me what he had written to Mr. Delafield, and when I came to that portion of the letter, I involuntarily uttered an exclamation of delight, while I glanced timidly towards him. *But he made no sign.* The letter which would have explained all was safely lodged behind the bureau, and with a gloomy brow he watched me while I read, interpreting my emotions into the satisfaction he naturally supposed I would feel in hearing from my lover. With me the revulsion was too great, for I fancied I saw in the expression of his face contempt for one who had presumed to love him, and bursting into tears, I cried and laughed alternately, while he tried to soothe me; but I would not be comforted by him—he hated me, I knew, and very pettishly I told him at last "to let me alone and go away—I was better without him than with him," I said, "and he would oblige me by leaving the room."

The next moment I repented my harshness, which I knew had caused him pain, for there was a look of sorrow upon his face as he complied with my request. But I was too proud to call him back, and for the next half hour I cried and fretted alone, first at him for making Dr. Clayton think he loved me when he didn't, secondly, at Dr. Clayton for meddling with what didn't concern him, and lastly, at myself, for being so foolish as to care whether anybody loved me or not! At the end of that time Richard came back. The cloud had disappeared, and very good-humoredly he asked "if I had got over my pet, and if I wanted anything."

I did not, but wishing to make amends for my former ill humor, I asked him *to shut the windows,* which he did, opening them again in less than five minutes, and fanning me furiously, I was "so hot and fidgety." For several hours he humored all my whims and caprices, and then, as he saw I was tiring myself out, he began to exercise his authority over me, telling me once, I remember, "to lie still and behave, or I would make myself worse!"

Intimidated by his voice and manner, I sank down among my pillows, nor stirred again until I awoke from a sweet sleep into which I had fallen. This time he was gone, but Mrs. Lansing was with me, and the tones of her voice seemed unusually kind as she addressed me. Richard again came in, bearing a beautiful bouquet, which he presented to me "as a peace offering," he said, "for having scolded me so in the morning."

Before night I was so much better that Ada, Lina, and Halbert came in to see me, each expressing their pleasure at my convalescence. But one there was who came not to greet me, and at whose absence I greatly marvelled. She had ever been the first to meet me in the morning, and the last to leave me at night. Why, then, did she tarry now, when I wished so much to see her? Alas, I did not know that never again would her home be gladdened by the sunshine of her presence, for it was Jessie whom I missed—Jessie for whom I longed—straining my ear to catch the sound of her ringing laugh, or bounding footsteps.

At last, as the day wore on and she did not come, I asked for her and why she stayed so long away.

Wringing her hands, Mrs. Lansing exclaimed, "Tell her, Richard, I cannot. It will kill me. Oh, Jessie, Jessie!"

But I had no need for further knowledge. I saw what I had not before observed, viz., the mourning garments of those around me, and in tears of anguish, I cried, "My darling is dead!"

"Yes, Jessie is dead," answered Richard. "We shall never see her again, for she is safe in the Happy Land, of which you so often told her."

I could not weep. My sorrow was too great for tears, and covering my face I thought for a long, long time. "Why was it," I asked myself, "that always when death had hovered near me, *I* had been spared, and another taken," for, as in the case of Jessie, so had it been with brother Jamie—they had died, while I had lived, and with a fervent thanksgiving to Heaven, which had dealt thus mercifully with me, I prayed that it might not be in vain.

Gradually, as I could bear it, Mr. Delafield told me the sad story—how she had hung fearlessly over my pillow when all else had deserted me—how she had come for him—and how naught but her mother's peremptory commands had taken her from my side. As he talked, there came back to me a vague recollection of a fairy form, a seraph I thought it to have been, which, when the dark river was running fast at my feet, had hovered near, whispering to me words of love, and bidding some one bury me beneath the tall magnolia. Then he told me how she had stood like a ministering spirit by the rude couch of the poor Africans, who, with their dying breath, had blessed her, calling her "The Angel of the Pines." From her head he himself had shorn her beautiful shining curls, one of which he gave to me, and which I prize as my most precious treasure; for often as I look upon it, I see again the little gleeful girl, my "Georgia rose," who, for a brief space, dwelt within her fair southern home, and was then transplanted to her native soil, where now she blooms, the fairest, sweetest flower of all which deck the fields of heaven.

The shock of her death very naturally retarded my recovery, and for many weeks more was I confined to my room. About the middle of October, Charlie, whose coming I had long expected, arrived, bringing to me the sad news that death had again entered our household, that by my father's and Jamie's grave was another mound, and at home another vacant chair, that of my aged grandmother, whose illness, he said, had prevented him from coming to me sooner, adding further that they had purposely kept her sickness from me, fearing the effect it might have. Of Dr. Clayton he could tell me but little. He had not visited Meadow Brook at all, but immediately after his return to Boston, he had written to them, saying I was out of danger, and Charlie must go for me as soon as the intense heat of summer was over. This was all they knew, though with woman's ready tact, both my mother and my sisters conjectured that something was wrong, and Charlie's first question after telling me what he did, was to inquire into the existing state of affairs between me and the doctor, and if it were my illness alone which had deferred the marriage.

"Don't ask me now," I replied, "not until we are far from here, and then I will tell you all."

This silenced Charlie, and once when Mr. Delafield questioned him concerning Dr. Clayton, and why he, too, did not come for me, he replied evasively, but in a manner calculated still further to mislead Mr. Delafield, who had no suspicion of the truth, though he fancied there was something wrong. In the meantime he was to me the same kind friend, ministering to all my wants, and with a lavish generosity procuring for me every delicacy, however costly it might be.

One day Charlie, with his usual abruptness, said to me, "Rose, why didn't you fall in love with Mr. Delafield. I should much rather have him than a widower?"

The hot blood rushed to my cheeks as I replied quickly, "He is engaged to Miss Montrose. They were to have been married this fall, Mrs. Lansing said, but the marriage is, I presume, deferred on account of their recent affliction. At least I hear nothing said of it."

"If I am any judge of human nature," returned Charlie, "Mr. Delafield cares far more for *you* than for Miss Montrose, even if they *are* engaged. But then you are poor, while she is rich, and that I suppose makes the difference."

I knew Mr. Delafield too well to suspect him of mercenary motives in marrying Ada, and so I said, "He loved her, of course, and it was natural that he should, for though she had some faults, he probably saw in her enough of good to overbalance the bad."

And still I could not help thinking that, as Charlie had said, his attentions to me were far more lover-like than they were towards her. But then I fancied that his kindness was prompted by the pity which he felt for me, a young girl so far from home. Thus the days wore on, leaving me deceived—and him deceived, while the letter still lay behind the bureau!

At last the morning dawned on which I was to say good-bye to the scenes I loved so well. I was to leave the "sunny South," with its dark evergreens, its flowering vines, its balmy air. I was to leave *him*, who, ere the next autumn leaves were falling, would take to his beautiful home a bride. Then I thought of little Jessie's grave, which I had not seen, and on which my tears would never fall, and taking from its hiding-place the tress of shining hair, I wept over that my last adieu. It was later than usual when Mr. Delafield appeared, and as he came in I saw that he was very pale.

"Are you sick?" I asked, as he wiped the perspiration from his face.

"No, no," he hurriedly answered; at the same time crossing over to a side table, he poured out and drank two large goblets of ice water.

Then resuming his former seat near me, he took my hand, and looking me earnestly in my face, said, "*Rose*, shall I ever see you here again?"

Before I could answer, Ada chimed in, "Of course we shall. Do coax the doctor to bring you here sometime, and let us see how you bear the honors of being madam!"

Instantly the earnest look passed away from Mr. Delafield's face, and was succeeded by a scowl, which remained until the carriage which was to take me to the dépôt was announced. Then the whole expression of his countenance changed, and for a brief instant my heart thrilled with joy, for I could not mistake the deep meaning of his looks as he bent over me and whispered his farewell.

"God bless you, Rose," he said. "*My Rose* I once hoped to call you. But it cannot be. Farewell!"

There was one burning kiss upon my lips, and the next moment he was gone.

"Are you going to the dépôt?" asked his sister, as he was leaving the room.

"No, no, no," he replied, and then as Charlie again bade me come, I rose bewildered to my feet, hardly realizing when Mrs. Lansing, Ada and Lina bade me adieu.

Halbert went with me in the carriage, and together with Charlie looked wonderingly at me, as I unconsciously repeated in a whisper, "*My Rose* I once hoped to call you. It is *Ada* who stands in the way," I said to myself, and covering my face with my veil, I wept as I thought of all I had lost when Richard Delafield offered his heart to another. He *did* love me. I was sure of that, but what did it avail me. He was too honorable to break his engagement with Ada, so henceforth I must walk alone, bearing the burden of an aching heart.

"Oh, I have loved you so much," said Halbert, winding his arms about my neck—"loved you as I shall never love another teacher," and the boy's tears flowed fast as he bade me good-bye.

One parting glance at Cedar Grove, one last lingering look at Sunny Bank, one thought of Jessie's grave, and then the hissing engine shot out into the woods, leaving them all behind. Leaning back on Charlie's arm and drawing my veil over my face, I thought how impossible it was that I should ever visit that spot again.

In the meantime a far different scene was being enacted in the apartment I had just vacated. Scarcely had the whistle of the engine died away in the distance, when a troop of blacks, armed with boiling suds and scrubbing-brushes, entered my chamber for the purpose of cleaning it. They had carried from it nearly every article of furniture, and nothing remained save the matting and the bureau, the latter of which they were about to remove when they were surprised at the unexpected appearance of Mr. Delafield, who could not resist the strong desire which he felt to stand once more in the room where *Rose* had spent so many weary weeks. For a moment the blacks suspended their employment, and then Linda, who seemed to be leading, took hold of the bureau, giving one end of it a shove towards the centre of the room. The movement dislodged the long lost letter, which, covered with dirt and cobwebs, fell upon the floor, at her feet. She was the same woman who, weeks before, had carelessly knocked off the letter, which she now picked up and handed to Mr. Delafield, saying, as she wiped off the dirt, "It must have laid thar a heap of a while, and now I think on't, 'pears like ever so long ago, when I was breshin' the bureau, I hearn somethin' done drap, but I couldn't find nothin', and it must have been this."

Glancing at the superscription, and recognizing the handwriting of Dr. Clayton, Mr. Delafield broke the seal, and read! From black to white—

from white to red—from red to speckled—and from speckled back again to its natural color, grew his face as he proceeded, while his eyes grew so dazzlingly bright with the intensity of his feelings that the negroes, who watched him, whispered among themselves that he "must be gwine stark mad."

His active, quick-seeing mind took in the meaning of each sentence, and even before he had finished the letter he understood everything just as it was—why Rose had appeared so strangely when she read Dr. Clayton's letter to herself, and realized perfectly what her feelings must have been as day after day went by and he still "*made no sign.*"

"But she is mine now, *thank Heaven!* and nothing shall take her from me," he exclaimed aloud, unmindful of the presence of the negroes, who, confirmed in their impression of his insanity, looked curiously after him as he went down the stairs, down the walk, and out into the street, proceeding with rapid strides towards the dépôt.

CHAPTER XXVIII
THE CHASE

The railroad which passed through W—— was only a branch of the main route leading to Charleston, and consequently there were but two passenger trains each way per day; and as Mr. Delafield's great object now was to reach Charleston before the boat in which Rose was to sail should leave the landing, it seemed impossible for him to wait until night, for not until then was the next train due. Suddenly he remembered that the express train left Augusta about four o'clock P. M. It was now ten, and he could easily reach it in time for the cars, provided there had been no change in the time table. To ascertain this, therefore, he hastened to the dépôt, where to his dismay he learned that the train left Augusta at *two*.

But with him to will was to do. Flying rather than walking back to his house, he called out Bill, his coachman, startling him with the inquiry as to whether it would be possible, with his best horses, a span of beautiful dappled greys, which were valued at a thousand dollars, to drive to Augusta in less than four hours.

Besides being naturally lazy and unwilling for exertion of any kind, *Bill* was also remarkably tender of said greys, who were his pride, and whom he had named *Fred* and *Ferd*. On hearing his master's inquiry, therefore, he looked perfectly aghast, and diving both hands into his matted wool, by way of illustration undoubtedly, replied, "Mighty tough scratchin', I can tell you, mars'r. Them ponies hain't been driv, only what I've ex'cized 'em for health, for better'n a month, and to run 'em as I'd hev to run 'em, would kill 'em stone dead. No, mars'r, can't think on't for a minit," and as if this were conclusive, and his word the law, Bill stuffed his hands into his bagging trousers, and was walking quietly away, when Mr. Delafield stopped him, saying, "I shall try it at all events. So get out the carriage immediately, and mind you are not over five minutes doing it. Ask some one to help you, if necessary—ho, Jack," and he called to a ragged mulatto boy who was doing nothing, and bade him assist Bill in harnessing the horses.

Rolling his white eyes in utter astonishment at what seemed to him the folly of his master, Bill began to expostulate, "Lor, mars'er, you kill" — —

"Silence, and do as I bid you," said Mr. Delafield, in a tone which Bill thought best to obey, and sauntering off to the stables, he brought out the ponies, who pranced and pawed the ground, while he admired their flowing manes and smooth shining coats.

Then seeing Jack standing near, ready to help, he haughtily ordered him away, saying, "Nobody but myself is fit to tache these critters. They'd know in a minit if a low-lived nigger like you came a near."

Nothing loth, Jack walked off, while Bill proceeded leisurely to harness the beautiful animals, talking to them as if they were intelligent beings, and telling them, "never to fear—they wan't a gwine to be druv to Gusty in two hours, and no sich thing. Bill sot on the box, and 'twas nothin' to mars'r, who was lollin on the cushions inside."

At this point he was startled by the voice of Mr. Delafield, who, having hastily packed a few articles in his portmanteau, and written a line to his sister, had come out to superintend in person the movements of his servant, whose peculiarities he perfectly understood.

"So ho," said he, "you mean to cheat me do you?" at the same time signifying his intention of having the horse go as fast as he liked.

"The Lord help Fred and Ferd then, for Bill can't," was the mental ejaculation of the negro as he saw the fire in his master's eye and knew he must be obeyed.

Still he managed to be as slow as possible, insisting that "Ferd allus had to drink two buckets and a half, or he wan't wuth a dime," adding in a conciliatory tone, that "with two buckets and a half in him he'd run like lightnin'."

Very impatiently Mr. Delafield waited for the disappearance of the requisite amount of water, consulting his watch, counting the minutes, and at last remarking that it took Ferd a wonderful while to drink.

"That's 'case he's sich a 'strordinary beast every way," answered Bill, who for some little time had been holding an *empty* bucket to the horse's mouth.

He was going to replenish a third time when his master ordered him back, telling him he could wait no longer; with another glance at his watch, he entered the carriage, while Bill, loudly lamenting the half bucket, without which Ferd would surely die, mounted the box, where he spent quite a while in comfortably disposing of his long, lank limbs and in adjusting his palmleaf hat.

"Go on, you rascal," shouted Mr. Delafield, beginning to lose his temper; and gathering up the reins, Bill whistled to the spirited animals, who dashed off at a far greater speed than their driver thought was at all conducive to their well being.

"Hold on dar, Ferd! Stop dat foolin', will you, Fred! Easy dar, both on you, for you come mighty nigh histin' me off de box!"

This last was said quite loud for the benefit of Mr. Delafield, who, perceiving that their speed had slackened, for they were well trained and readily obeyed Bill's voice, called out, "Drive faster, I tell you. Give them the ribbons, and let them run."

"Lor' a'mighty," answered Bill, now coming to a dead halt in order that his master might be better impressed with what he said. "You don't understand hoss flesh. At this rate you kills 'em in less than no time. Ferd never 'ill stan' it with them two buckets of water, 'case you see how shakin' him up dis way dey'll get bilin' hot and nobody can live with bilin' water in 'em."

Provoked as he was, Mr. Delafield could not repress a smile at the subterfuges of Bill to spare his horses, but he bade him drive on, saying, however, that he need not drive them at the top of their speed immediately, as they would be more likely to give out, "but after a mile or two," he continued, "put them through with the *whip* if necessary."

"Lor' mars'r," answered Bill from the box, without moving an inch, "I never tache them with a whip in de world. Fred would jump clar out of his skin. All dey want to make 'em kill deyselves is a loose rein and a whistle— so."

Suiting the action to the word, he whistled long and loud, whereupon the horses started forward as if a volley of artillery had been fired at their heels, while mingled with the roll of the wheels, Mr. Delafield heard the distressed Bill, saying. "Whoa, dar, Ferdinand, can't you whoa when I tell you. Think of the bilin' water, and keep easy. Come Frederic, you set him a 'xample. That's a good boy, no 'casion for all dis hurry, if we misses one train we catches another. All de same thing. We ain't chasin' a runaway gal' as I knows of."

After a little he succeeded in stopping them, and for the next ten or fifteen minutes they proceeded on rather leisurely, and Bill was beginning to think his master had come to his senses, when he was startled with the stern command, "Let them run now as fast as they will. Don't check them at all until we reach the dépôt."

Accordingly, for a mile or so the horses rushed on at headlong speed, Bill sympathizing with them deeply and mentally promising himself "to tend 'em mighty keerful to pay for this."

At last, when he thought it safe to do so, he held them in, taking the precaution, however to say aloud, "Get along dar, Ferd—none your lazy tricks here when mars'r's in sich a hurry. Can't you get along dar, I say. An' you Fred, wake up yer bones to de merits of de case."

But if in this way he thought to deceive the resolute man inside he was mistaken. Perceiving that their speed was considerably slackened, and hearing Bill loudly reproach the horses for their laziness, Mr. Delafield softly opened the carriage door, and leaning out, learned the cause of the delay. Bolt upright upon the box, with his brawny feet firmly braced against the dash-board so as to give him more power, sat Bill, clutching the reins with might and main, for the horses' mettle was up and it required his entire strength to keep them from running furiously! All this time, too, the cunning negro kept chiding them for their indolence in moving so slowly!

"Bill," said Mr. Delafield, sternly, "stop the carriage instantly."

"Lord a massy, mars'r," exclaimed the frightened Bill. "You almost skeered me off de box. Ferd won't get along no how. I tells him and I tells him how you'r in de hurry—don't you mind how I keeps telling him to get along, I reckons he wants dat t'other half bucket of water."

"I understand you perfectly," said Mr. Delafield, alighting from the carriage, and to the utter astonishment of Bill, mounting the box and taking the reins in his own hands. "I understand your tricks, and for the rest of the way I shall drive myself!"

Rolling his eyes wildly in their sockets, the crest fallen Bill folded his arms and resigned the horses to their fate, saying mentally, "I shall war mournin' for 'em, I shall, and he may help hisself."

Over rough and stony places—over smooth and sandy roads—over hills, over plains—through the woods, through the swamps, and through the winding valleys, on they sped like lightning, the excited horses covered with foam, their driver stern, silent and determined, while poor Bill, with the perspiration streaming down his shining face, kept up a continued expostulation, "Now, mars'r, for de dear Lord's sake, stop 'em 'fore dey draps down dead. Look at de white specks all over Ferd's back—he'll never stan' it without dat t'other half bucket. You kills 'em sartin, and dar goes a thousand dollars, smack and clean."

But Bill's entreaties were all in vain, and his distress was at its height, when fortunately his thoughts were diverted in another channel. At a sudden turn of the road a gust of wind lifted the old palmleaf from his woolly head, and carried it far away. "Now, dear Mars'r," said Bill, laying his hand on that of Mr. Delafield, "you'll sartin let 'em breathe while I picks up my hat, 'case you see how'll you look gwine into town wid a barheaded nigger. In de Lord's name, stop," he continued, as he saw in his master no signs of relenting.

Glancing over his shoulder Mr. Delafield saw the hat away over the fields, and quietly taking a bill from his pocket and placing it in the negro's hand, he replied; "That will buy you five such hats."

"Yes, but de hosses, lor' a mighty, de hosses!" exclaimed Bill almost frantically, "Don't you see Ferd is gwine to gin out?"

Mr. Delafield feared so, too, and more to himself than to his servant, he said, "perhaps the cars will be behind time, they usually are."

Without considering the consequences, Bill answered, "No they won't; case I hear how they hired a tarin' Yankee for an *engine*, and he drives all afore him—gits ahead of de time and all dat."

The next minute he repented a speech whose disastrous effects he foresaw, and he was about to deny it as a fabrication of his own brain, when his master, who really saw signs of lagging in the nervous, fiery Ferd, said, "Bill, you have a peculiar whistle with which you spur up the horses—make it now; Ferd has run himself almost down."

"De Lord have massy on us," groaned Bill, wiping away a tear; then, as Mr. Delafield repeated his order, he said, in a whining tone, "Can't, mars'r, no how; case you see my throat is dreffle sore, ridin' barheaded so in the breeze which you kicks up—can't, no how."

"But you must," persisted Mr. Delafield.

Bill still refused, until at last, as they approached the town, they heard a heavy, rumbling sound. It was the roll of cars in the distance, and starting up, Mr. Delafield seized the negro by the shoulder and in thunder tones called out, "Whistle."

"Lord, mars'r I will, I will," gasped Bill, terrified at the fiery gleam of his master's eye, and from his mouth there issued a most unearthly sound, which mingled with the shriek of the fast coming engine, urged on the jaded horses to one more desperate effort.

A few more mad plunges and they reached the dépôt, covered with foam and frothing at the mouth, just as the train was moving slowly away. With one pitying farewell glance at his dying greys, Mr. Delafield exclaimed, "Cut the harness instantly," and then with a bound sprung upon the platform, which he reached just as Bill called after him in mournful accents, "Ferd's dead, mars'r, Ferd is," while, mingled with the roar of the machinery he caught the faint echo of something about "t'other half bucket of water!"

But little cared he for that. Rosa Lee was to be overtaken, and to accomplish this, he would willingly have sacrificed every horse of which he was owner, even were they twice as valuable as the dappled greys.

So, wishing him a successful journey, and leaving him on the same seat with a Yankee peddler, who saw him when he came up and "*guessed* he was after a runaway nigger," we return for a moment to Bill, who with tears streaming from his eyes, patched the struggles of Fred until the noble animal was dead, bringing him water which he vainly coaxed him to drink, while the bystanders, who crowded around, asked him innumerable questions as to why they drove so fast and where his master was going.

To the first Bill could not reply, but to the last he promptly answered, as he patted the remains of the departed Ferdinand, "Gwine to the *devil*, in course! Whar you spect a white man to go, what treats hosses in dis kind of style, won't let 'em hev all the water dey wants and drives 'em till dey draps dead in der tracks."

The story of the half bucket was duly rehearsed, Bill firmly believing that if Ferd had drank it, he would undoubtedly have lived "dis minit and been as spry as a cricket. But now he's dead and Fred, too," continued the negro, as the latter ceased to move. "Sich another span of hosses, that ain't in all Georgy," and laying his black face upon the neck of the insensible Ferd, the negro cried like a child.

"There is one comfort, at least, my boy," said a gentlemanly looking man, who stood near and who knew Mr. Delafield, "your horses didn't suffer, for they were too much excited."

This in a measure consoled Bill, who, wiping his eyes, asked what he was to do with them, saying he "never could dig thar grave."

"My negroes shall do it for you," answered the stranger, and in a short time several stalwart men were busy in an adjacent field making a grave for the dappled greys, which they carefully buried, while on a stump, with his head resting on his knees, sat Bill as chief mourner.

"I wish I knew a prar," he whispered to himself, "for if ever hosses 'sarved it they do;" but the rude African had never prayed since he was a little child, and thinking himself too old to begin now, he rose up from the stump, just as his companions, having finished their task, were beginning to ridicule his bare head, telling him he must have an unkind master, judging from his own appearance and the sad fates of the horses, while one of them advised him to run away.

This was touching Bill in a tender point, for though he had loved the horses much, he loved his master more, and he would not hear him censured; accordingly he retorted petulantly that "thar warn't a better master in all Georgy than mars'r Dick, nor a richer one neither,—and 'twan't nobody's business if he killed five hundred horses—he could afford it—'twan't as though he was poor and owned nothin' but a few *low trash* like the 'Gusty niggers!"

This insinuation the "Gusty niggers," chose to resent as an insult, and a regular negro fight ensued, in which Bill, being the weaker party, came off rather badly beaten, his face being scratched in several places, while his pants received a huge rent, which in no wise tended to improve his personal appearance. Matters being at last amicably adjusted, the victorious party returned home, while Bill, who had frequently been in Augusta with his master, wended his way to a hatter's shop, where he soon made himself the owner of a second-hand beaver, which at his request was ornamented by a weed of crape as a badge of mourning for his favorite steeds. Then seeing that the carriage was safely stowed away, he started on foot for home, stopping at the negro quarters of almost every plantation to relate his wonderful adventures. As he was perfectly trusty and faithful, he was always allowed to carry a pass by his good natured master and thus he found no difficulty in his journey, which he took quite leisurely, never reaching Sunny Bank until the close of the second day after the one on which he had left it.

In the meantime Mr. Delafield, with closely knit brows and compressed lip, his usual look when he was in deep thought, sat musing of the time when Rosa Lee would be his wife, while at his side the Yankee peddler, with his basket of essence carefully stowed under the seat, was casting curious glances at his companion, whose history he was desirous of knowing. But there was something in Mr. Delafield's appearance which forbade familiarity, so for once the loquacious Yankee was silent.

They were now about half-way between Augusta and Charleston and going at great speed, when suddenly at a short curve there was a violent commotion—the passengers were pitched forward and backward, while the engine plunged down a steep embankment, throwing the train from the track and dragging after it the baggage car, which in some way became detached from the rest. The new "Yankee engineer" was a daring, reckless fellow, who at the North had been discharged for carelessness, and had come to try his fortune at the South. Fortunately no one was seriously hurt except Mr. Delafield, whose injuries were simply *mental*, as he knew this accident would probably detain them for many hours. In a perfect storm of excitement he stalked up and down the track, asking the conductor every few minutes how long it would probably be before they could go on, and at last growing so dark in his face that the Yankee, after looking over his essence basket and finding but few of his bottles broken, ventured to say, "Now, *Squire*, don't git mad at a feller for askin' a sassy question, but I raley du want to know if there ain't a little atom of black blood in you?"

"Very likely," answered Mr. Delafield; while the Yankee, now that the ice was broken, continued to ply him with questions, which, though very annoying to the haughty Southerner, tended to relieve in a measure the tediousness of waiting.

The sun had long been set and the stars were shining brightly ere they were able to proceed, and it was after midnight when they at last reached Charleston. Driving immediately to the lauding, Mr. Delafield to his great joy found that the steamer bound for New York still lay at the wharf and would not start until morning. But was Rosa Lee on board? That was a question which puzzled him, and as there was no way of satisfying himself until morning, he sat down in one of the state rooms and rather impatiently awaited the dawn of day.

The hurry—the confusion—and the excitement of starting was over. We were out upon the deep blue sea, and from the window of my state-room I watched the distant shore as it slowly receded from view, and felt that I was leaving the land of sunlight and of flowers. Notwithstanding the fatiguing journey of the previous day, I was better this morning than I had been for many months before, for I had slept quietly through the night.

An hour or two after breakfast Charlie came to me with a very peculiar expression on his face and asked me to go upon deck, saying the fresh breeze would do me good. I consented willingly, and throwing on my shawl and a simple Leghorn flat which had been of much service to me at Cedar Grove, and which Mr. Delafield had often said was very becoming, I went out with Charlie, who led me to the rear of the boat, where he said we were not so liable to be disturbed. Seating me upon a small settee he asked to be excused for a few moments, saying I should not be long alone. The motion of the boat produced a slight dizziness in my head, and leaning my elbow upon the arm of the settee I shaded my eyes with my hand and sat lost in thought until I heard the sound of a footstep.

"It was Charlie," I said, so I did not look up, even when he sat down by my side and wound his arm around me, wrapping my shawl closer together, oh, so gently! "Charlie is very tender of me since my sickness," I thought, and much I loved that he should thus caress me. It thrilled me strangely, bringing back to my mind the night when I sat in the vine-wreathed arbor, where I should never sit again.

For a moment there was perfect silence and I could hear the beating of Charlie's heart. Then leaning forward and removing my hand from my eyes, he pressed a kiss upon my lips and whispered as he did so, "*My own Rose!*"

Once, when I was apparently dying, the sound of that voice had called me back to life, and now with a cry of joy I sprang to my feet and turning round, stood face to face with *Richard Delafield*, who, stretching his arms towards me, said, "Come to my bosom, Rose. Henceforth it is your resting-place."

The shock was too much for me in my weak state. A faintness stole over me, and if I obeyed his command, it was because I could not help it!

When I returned to consciousness, Richard's arms were around me, and my head was resting upon his bosom, while he whispered to me words which I leave to the imagination, as I dare not give them to the world, lest he (*Uncle Dick* I call him) should be angry in his way, and I have learned to be a very little afraid of him since that morning when on board the steamer Delphine we sat and talked together of the past.

Wonderingly I listened while he told me how long he had loved me—how once he had thought to tell me of his love, but the manner in which I answered his leading question disheartened him, for he feared his affection was not returned—how it had filled his heart with bitter grief when he saw me about to marry another—how his sister had deceived him or he should have spoken to me then—and how in a moment of temptation when he stood over my pillow he had asked that I might die, for he would far rather that death should be his rival than a fellow man. Then as he thought how near I had been to the dark valley he shudderingly drew me closer to his side and told me how he had wondered at Dr. Clayton's leaving me so abruptly and how sometimes when a ray of hope was beginning to dawn upon him, it had been chilled by my manner, which he now understood.

"You cannot conceive," said he in conclusion, "what my feelings were yester morn when I bade you adieu, nor yet can you comprehend the overwhelming delight I experienced when I read that letter and felt that you would at last be mine."

When he had ceased to speak I took up the story and told him of all my own feelings, and that nothing would ever have induced me to think for a moment of becoming Dr. Clayton's wife, but the belief that he was engaged to Ada, a story which I told him his sister affirmed when I went to her for counsel.

"And so Angeline played a double part," said he, sighing deeply; "I never thought she could be guilty of so much deception, though I have always known she was averse to my marrying any one."

Of Ada he said that never for a moment had he been engaged to her. "She is to me like a sister," said he, "and though I know she has many faults, I am greatly attached to her, for we have lived together many years. She was committed to my care by her father and I shall always be faithful to my trust. And if, dear Rose, in the future, circumstances should render it necessary for her to live with us, shall you object? She cannot harm you now."

He had talked to me much of his love, but, not a word before had he said of my sharing his home at Sunny Bank, so I rather coquettishly answered, "You talk of my living with you as a settled matter, and still you have not asked me if I would."

A shadow for a moment darkened his face, and then with a very quizzical expression he made me a formal offer of himself and fortune, asking me pointedly if I would accept it—and—and, well, of course, I did what my readers knew I would do when I first told them of the *dark man* at the theatre—I said *yes*, and promised to return with him to Sunny Bank as soon as my health would permit, which he was positive would be in a very few weeks, for he should be my daily physician, and "love," he said, "would work miracles."

Thus you see we were engaged—*Richard and I!*

CHAPTER XXIX
HUMAN NATURE

The sun had set on Cedar Grove, and together on the broad, airy piazza sat Mrs. Lansing and Ada, rather impatiently waiting for Richard, whom they had not seen since he left them so abruptly in the morning. Greatly relieved at the absence of one whom she had in a measure dreaded as a rival, Ada began to hope that the conquest of her guardian would now be a comparatively easy matter, and as she knew the effect which a pretty face and a becoming dress had upon him, she had spent a great deal of time upon this evening's toilet, and looked unusually young and handsome in her pale blue tissue, with her soft curls falling over her white uncovered neck.

That day she had talked a long time with Mrs. Lansing, who had not only expressed her willingness to receive her as a sister, but had also promised to do whatever she could to forward the matter. Believing Mrs. Lansing to have far more influence over her brother than she really had, Ada began to entertain hopes of soon becoming a bride, and when she thought no one could see her, actually wrote upon a card, "Mr. and Mrs. R. Delafield," just to see how it would look! It looked well, she thought, and smoothing from her brow a frown which had been caused by her finding among her waving tresses a long white hair, she went down to the piazza to await Richard's coming.

"He has not been here since morning, and I am sure he'll come to-night. You know he has latterly been a most constant visitor," remarked Mrs. Lansing.

"Yes, but possibly the attraction which kept him so much here is gone," faintly suggested Ada.

"Fie!" returned Mrs. Lansing, with a toss of her head. "I know Richard better than that, and though he may at one time have felt a slight interest in Miss Lee, I am positive 'tis nothing serious, or lasting. Only think of it, Richard Delafield marry my *governess*, a poor *schoolmistress*! What *would* his fashionable acquaintance in Augusta and Charleston say, setting aside our friends in New Orleans!"

And on the proud woman's face there was a sneer at the very idea of her brother's thus disgracing himself.

"Hark! I do believe he's coming," said Ada, as she heard approaching footsteps, and she had just time to adjust her skirts gracefully when there stood before her, not Mr. Delafield, but the servant to whom had been intrusted the note for Mrs. Lansing.

This the negro had entirely forgotten until it was recalled to his mind by the continued absence of his master, whose return they had confidently expected before night. Taking the note from his hand, Mrs. Lansing hastily glanced at its contents, and then, with an exclamation of surprise, handed it to Ada, who turned deathly pale as she saw her new-born hopes crushed at once and forever; and if now she clasped her hand upon her side, the action was not feigned, for a pain, which blistering could not heal, was indeed there—the pain of wounded pride at seeing a humble, obscure girl preferred to herself. For several minutes not a word was spoken, and then Mrs. Lansing, who knew it would not be politic to quarrel with her brother, said, "I am astonished at Richard's proceedings, but I suppose there is no help for it, and we may as well make the best of it. Miss Lee ain't the worst girl in the world. She had many friends in the village—was well educated, and with a few lessons from us on some points of etiquette she may do very well."

"Us," angrily retorted Ada. "When I teach Dick Delafield's wife etiquette I shall be older than I am now."

"And that you would not care to be;" said Mrs. Lansing, a little sarcastically.

She was a woman, who, if essential to her own interest, could turn with every breeze, and though she was not pleased with her brother's choice, she did not deem it advisable to provoke his anger by quarrelling about it, for when once roused, but few could cope with his resolute, determined spirit. Then, too, Rosa Lee was yielding and generous, and would not object even if her husband should bestow half his fortune upon his sister; so after all it might be better to have her the mistress of Sunny Bank than one like Ada, who was more selfish and wanted everything for herself. Thus Mrs. Lansing reasoned, coming at last to feel quite amiably disposed towards Rosa Lee, whom she fully intended to manage in her own way, and she was about making up her mind to write a kind, sisterly letter to said Rosa, when her attention was attracted by a loud sobbing, and looking round she saw Ada weeping violently.

As well as she could love any one, Ada had loved her guardian, and the knowledge that he was now lost to her, overcame her for a time, and covering her face with her hands, she cried aloud. Mrs. Lansing had never really loved in her life, so she could not appreciate the feeling, and she made no effort to soothe the weeping girl who that night wet her pillow with bitter tears, and who next morning looked weary, pale and old, as she languidly took her seat at the breakfast table. Still Ada was not one to love very deeply, and as on this occasion her pride was touched rather than her heart, she ere long grew calm, and with Mrs. Lansing wisely resolved to make the best of it. Then, too, there arose the very natural desire to conceal from Richard that she had ever cared for him, and to do this she thought she must *pretend* to be pleased with his choice. Accordingly when Mrs. Lansing wrote to her brother, Ada inclosed a gilt-edged note, in which she congratulated him upon his intended marriage, telling him she had foreseen it from the first, and ended by sending her love to "*Rose.*" Thus, because she thought it would be for her interest, did Mrs. Lansing deem it best to change her tactics, while Ada was too proud to evince any open hostility, though in her heart she hated the future bride and lamented the fatality which had decreed that she should be rivalled by "both of those Lee girls."

CHAPTER XXX
"THE SOUTHERN PLANTER'S NORTHERN BRIDE."

Over the New England hills the hazy light of a most glorious Indian Summer was shining, while the forest trees, in their gorgeous array of crimson and gold, lifted their tall heads as proudly as if they heard not in the distance the voice of coming sorrows, and the sighing of winter winds. The birds had flown to their southern home where I fondly hoped to meet them, for I was to be a bride—Richard's bride—and the day for my bridal had come. We had been everywhere—Richard and I—all over the old Meadow Brook farm, sacred to me for the many hallowed associations which clustered around it, and very, very dear to *him* because it was my childhood's home. So he told me when we stood for the last time beneath the spreading grape-vine, and I pointed out to him the place where years before I had lain in the long green grass and wept over the fickleness of one who was naught to me now, save a near friend.

Together we had sat in the old brown schoolhouse,—he in the big arm chair, and I—but no matter where *I* sat when I told him of the little romping girl with yellow hair, who had there first learned to con the alphabet and to trace on the gaily colored maps the boundary lines of Georgia, little dreaming that her home would one day be there. Then when I showed him the bench where I had lain when the faintness came over me, he wound his arm closer around me,—though wherefore I do not know. Together too, we had gone over the old farmhouse, he lingering longest in the room where I was born, and when he thought I didn't see him, gathering a withered leaf from the rose bush which grew beneath the window, and which I told him I had planted when a little girl.

Every woman, young and old, in the neighborhood and in the village had seen him, either face to face or from behind the folds of a muslin curtain, some calling him "black and ugly," while others pronounced him "splendid," and all I believe united in saying that, "Rosa Lee had done wonders, considering she had no great amount of beauty to do it with!"

Once, when a remark like this came to Richard's ear he smiled quietly and said, "Rosa Lee is beautiful to me, for though her face may lack perfect regularity of features and brilliancy of complexion, she has beauty of a higher order, a beauty of the mind, which is seen in her laughing blue eyes and sunny smile."

Thus you see, my reader, that Richard thought I was handsome, while strange as it may seem there were others who said so too, and even I was sensible of a thrill of pride, such as I suppose conscious *beauties* feel, when I stood up before the mirror and saw how well I looked in my bridal dress of satin and lace—*his* gift, but not the same which he had purchased for me some months before. At first I had proposed wearing the one intended for Dr. Clayton's bride, but Richard would not suffer it, so I gave it to Lizzy, who, as soon as *John Thompson* was of age, which would be in January, would probably have need of it! This same John was to be our groomsman and much he amused Richard by telling him of the tall, hateful boy who had once been a terror to a little schoolma'am thirteen years of age, who now, with a heightened bloom upon her cheek and a strange light in her eye, stood waiting the summons to the parlor below. It came at last and as I laid my hand on Richard's arm he imprinted a kiss upon my lips, "the last," he said, "he should ever give to Rosa *Lee*."

Of what came next I have only a faint remembrance. There was a rustling of satin upon the narrow stair-case, down which Lizzie and I went a little in advance of Richard and John Thompson, the latter of whom said something in a low tone about *hoops* and the space they occupied! this remark shocked *me* inexpressibly, but Richard didn't seem to mind it at all. As we passed the front door, the cool night wind (for it was evening) blew over my face, reminding me of the South, it was so soft and balmy. When we entered the parlor, I was conscious of a goodly number of eyes fixed upon me, and as I crossed over to a vacant spot under the looking glass I heard more than one say in a whisper, "Isn't she pretty?" meaning Lizzie, I suppose! Then a man, whom I recognized as the new Episcopal clergyman (I believe I've never said that Richard was an Episcopalian) stood up before us and said something about *"You Richard*—and *You Rose,"* after which Richard placed a ring upon my finger squeezing my hand a very little as he did so. Then followed a short prayer, in which I fancied the minister made a mistake in our names, inasmuch as he spoke of *Isaac* and *Rebecca* instead of *Richard* and *Rose!* This being done I glanced at the bridegroom. There was no scowl upon his forehead now, and I could see the light shining out all over his face as he bent down and gently whispered *"my wife!"*

This dispelled the clouds at once, and as guest after guest crowded around, offering their congratulations, while Charlie and John Thompson vied with each other in repeating my new name, I began to realize that I was no longer Rosa Lee, but *Mrs. Richard Delafield.*

CHAPTER XXXI
SUNNY BANK

For a few days we lingered at my mother's fireside, and then, with the fall of the first snowflake, we left for our southern home; Richard promising my mother, who was loth to give me up, that when the summer birds came back and *roses* were blooming again by the door, he would bring his *Rose* to breathe once more the air of her native hills. We stopped at New York, Philadelphia, Baltimore and Washington, and it was not until the holidays were passed that we landed at last at Charleston and took the cars for W — — which we reached about dark.

With a loud cry of joy, *Bill*, who was waiting for us, welcomed back his master, and then almost crushing my fingers in his big black hand, said, with a sly wink, which he meant should be very expressive, "I know, now what mass'r kill dem hosses for!" at the same time making some apology for the really sorry looking animals he was compelled to drive in the place of the deceased Ferdinand and Frederic. As we drove through the town I could not help contrasting my present feelings with those of the year before, when I thought I was leaving it forever. Then, weary, sick and wretched, I had looked through blinding tears towards Sunny Bank, which was now my home, while at my side, with his arm around me, was its owner—my husband.

"You tremble, Rose," said he, as we drew near the house, and he bade me be calmer, saying the meeting between myself and his sister would soon be over.

But it was not that which I dreaded. It was the presentation to his servants, to whom I bore the formidable relation of mistress, and for whose good opinion I cared far more than I did for that of the haughty Mrs. Lansing. Something like this I said to Richard, who assured me that his household would love me because I was *his* wife, if for no other reason, and thus I found it to be. As we drove into the yard, we were surprised at seeing the house brilliantly lighted, while through the open windows forms of many persons were seen moving to and fro.

In a displeased tone of voice Richard, said, "It is Angeline's work, and I do not like it, for you need rest, and are too much fatigued to see any one to-night, but I suppose it cannot be avoided. Ho, Bill," he called to the driver, "who is here?"

"Some de quality," answered Bill, adding that "Miss Angeline done 'vite 'em to see de bride."

"She might at least have consulted my wishes," said Richard, while my heart sank within me at being obliged to meet strangers in my jaded condition.

Mrs. Lansing, it seems, had in her mind a new piano for Lina, their present one being rather old-fashioned, and as the surest means of procuring one she thought to please her brother by noticing his bride. So, in her zeal, she rather overdid the matter, inviting to Sunny Bank many of the villagers, some of whom were friendly to me and some were not, though all, I believe, felt curious to see how the "Plebeian Yankee" (thus Ada termed me) would demean herself as the wife a southern planter.

Dusky faces, with white shining eyes, peered round the corner of the building as the carriage stopped before the door, and more than one whisper reached me. "Dat's she—de new Miss, dat mars'r's liftin' so keerfully."

Upon the piazza stood Mrs. Lansing, her face wreathed in smiles, while at her side, in flowing white muslin, were Ada and Lina, the former of whom sprang gaily down the steps, and with well feigned joy threw herself into the arms of her guardian, who, after kissing her affectionately, presented her to me, saying, "Will Ada be a sister to my wife?"

"Anything, for your sake," answered Ada, with rather more emphasis on *your* than was quite pleasing me.

Mrs. Lansing came next, and there was something of hauteur in her manner as she advanced, for much as she desired to please her brother, she was not yet fully prepared to meet me as an equal. But Richard knew the avenue to her heart, and as he placed my hand in hers, he said, "For the sake of Jessie you will love my bride, I am sure."

It was enough; Jessie was forgotten by many who had wept bitterly when first they heard the sad news of her death, but in the mother's heart there was an aching void, and as if the gentle, blue-eyed child were pleading for me from her little grave, the proud woman's eyes were moist with tears as she said, "Yes, for Jessie's sake do I l——" she paused, for with that sacred name upon her lips even *she* could not utter a falsehood and say, "I love you," so she qualified it, and after a moment continued, "I will learn to love you, Rose, for such I know would be our angel Jessie's wish."

From Lina I expected no demonstration. She was too selfish, too listless to care for any one, so when she coolly shook my hand and called me *Mrs. Delafield*, I was quite satisfied, particularly as the next moment Halbert caught me round the neck, shouting out a noisy, but genuine welcome to his "Aunt Rose," and telling me "he was mighty glad I'd come back to stay for good."

"You have quite a party," said Richard to his sister as we entered the spacious hall, I shrinking behind him so as to hide myself from the curious eyes which I knew were scanning my dusty travelling dress.

"Only a few friends, who I thought would be glad to meet Miss Lee—I beg pardon—your wife," she hastily added as she saw the gathering frown upon his brow.

With a look in his eye which made her quail, he said, "Never make that mistake again, Angeline." (And she never did!) "Rose is too much exhausted to appear in the parlor to-night," he continued, as we entered my room—*our room*—the pleasant, tasteful apartment, which I once thought had been fitted up for Ada. "You ought to have had more tact than to invite company on the first night of my arrival—when you must have known how weary Rose would be. She don't look like herself, so pale and way-worn," he continued, himself removing my bonnet and tenderly stroking my aching head.

Nothing would please Ada better than to present me just as I was, pale and jaded, with dark rims beneath my eyes, induced by the severe headache from which I was really suffering. It would show her own charms to greater advantage, she thought, as she glanced at an opposite mirror and saw the contrast between us.

"Oh, Richard," she said pleadingly, "pray don't object to her going down, it wouldn't be polite, and then they are all dying to see her."

"Why then didn't they, some of them, improve the opportunity when she was here before, and *on show* every day," said Richard, moodily.

And Ada, forgetting herself, answered in a low tone, "Why, that's plain enough, Mrs. Richard Delafield is a very different personage from Miss Lee, *gov*"——

"*Ada!*" sternly interposed my husband, "Never a remark like that in my presence."

"Why, Uncle Dick," said Ada, smothering her anger and winding her white arms around his neck, "how you frighten me. I didn't mean anything, only I do want Rose to go down, so much, can't you, dear?" and she turned towards me.

With her, I felt that it would hardly be polite to refuse, so I replied that "after a cup of tea and half an hour's rest, I would try to do so."

Supper was brought to our room, the servant almost touching her knees to the floor, so low was her obeisance to the "New Miss." As I have once before remarked, my head was aching dreadfully, and as I looked at the soft, downy pillows which lay piled upon the snowy bed in the adjoining room, I thought how much rather I would throw myself among them, than join the gay company below. But it could not be, and with something like *tears* in the sound of my voice, I asked Richard to send up my trunks.

Closely inspecting me for a moment, he answered. "There is no necessity for you to dress. You look well enough just as you are, and you must not fatigue yourself any more. I shall get you excused in a little while, and sometime after you are thoroughly rested, Angeline shall give a large party at her own house, where you'll have an opportunity to display all the '*fixins*,'" and he laughed, thinking, I suppose, he had said something smart.

My dress was a dark blue merino, trimmed on the basque and sleeves with black velvet. It fitted neatly, and was, I knew, unusually becoming; so after arranging my curls and donning a clean linen collar, I took my husband's arm and went down to the drawing-room, where I found about forty people assembled. With a few of them I was already acquainted, while the majority were only known to me by sight; for though I had often seen them at Cedar Grove, they had not thought it worth their while to notice a mere governess. Now, however, as Ada had said, matters were changed, and Richard Delafield's wife could not be slighted with impunity. Consequently I was for a time overwhelmed with compliments and attention; some with whom I had never before spoken, expressing their delight at seeing me back again, while others said that a *bride* was just what was wanting to give éclat to the winter gaieties.

Close to my side kept Ada, assuming a kind of patronizing manner and answering for me whenever she thought the conversation beyond my depth. Of course she threw me quite in the shade, and in a measure she had her reward, for she, as well as I, heard a lady, a stranger in W——, say, "How much more beautiful Miss Montrose is than the bride. I wonder Mr. Delafield did not prefer her."

There was a look of exultation on Ada's face as her eyes met mine, but it passed away as we heard the answer made by Miss Porter, a lady whom Ada thought exceedingly aristocratic. "Yes," said she, "Miss Montrose is rather pretty, but she is fading fast, and I suppose Mr. Delafield preferred the freshness of youth to the decay of beauty, and for my part, I approve his choice, and think her a very pretty little creature."

I glanced at my husband—he, too, heard the remark and it pleased him, I knew, while Ada crossed over to the opposite side of the room and I saw her no more, for Richard soon asked for me to be excused; a request which the company readily granted, saying, "I must of course be tired."

It was late when Richard came up to our room, and I saw in a moment that something was the matter, for his face wore the dark, hard look it sometimes did when he was disturbed. I did not then ask the cause of his annoyance, but afterwards I learned that the moment the guests were gone, Ada, whose feelings were a good deal ruffled, not only at the attention I had received, but also at the remark of Miss Porter, commenced censuring my husband for having suffered me to appear in the drawing-room in my travelling dress. "'Twas an insult to the company," she said, "and they could excuse it on no other grounds save the supposition that I was entirely ignorant of etiquette in any form. I didn't blame her so much," said she, "for I suppose she didn't know any better, but I was astonished at *you*."

Ada had quite forgotten herself, or else she misunderstood the man with whom she had to deal. Very quietly he listened, but the storm was gathering within, and when she had finished, it burst upon her with a vengeance; he bidding her never again, either in his presence or the presence of any one, say aught disparagingly of his wife. "Her actions shall not be questioned by you," said he, "and you *shall* treat her with deference, for in every respect she is your superior, save that of *age*, and there, I admit, you have the advantage."

This decided the matter at once, for Ada was afraid of him, and though she could not conceal her dislike from me, she was in his presence always kind, considerate and sometimes even affectionate in her demeanor towards me, coming at last to call him "Uncle Dick," in imitation of Halbert, and *me* "Aunt Rose," particularly if there were any strangers present.

The morning following my arrival I was formally presented to the servants, who received me with many demonstrations of joy, the older portion "bressin' de Lord they had lived to see Mars'r Richard look so happy and peart like as he did with the new Miss." Only one eyed me at all askance, and that was Aunt Hagar, the housekeeper, who saw in me a rival—one who would henceforth wear jingling at her belt the huge bunch of keys, which for so long a time had been to her a badge of honor. Then, too, the old lady, like my other new relatives, had some fears "that Miss Rose didn't 'long to the quality, and that Mars'r Richard had done histed hisself down a peg or so by marryin' one who was brought up in de free states, whar dar warn't nary nigger to fotch 'em a drink of water or fan when de sun was roastin' hot."

With a look of injured dignity, which made the steeple of a turban on her head tremble, she undid from her waist the bunch of keys, and offering them to me, said, "I 'spects these are yourn now."

I drew back, for to me there was nothing pleasing in the idea of being disturbed every time a lump of sugar, a piece of coal, or a pan of flour was wanted, so I said, "If my husband is willing I'd rather you'd keep them yourself, as I know you are trusty."

Hagar's face brightened perceptibly and I am induced to think she forgot in a measure my misfortune in having been born in a *free state*! At all events I have not now a more devoted servant than Hagar, who declares me to be a "perfect lady," and who has more than once ventured the *treasonable remark*, that "if all de Free State folks is like Miss Rose, she'll be boun' she'd like to live thar!" Regularly each morning she comes to me and asks "what Miss would like for dinner," and regularly each morning "Miss" answers, "Dear me, Hagar, I don't know; get what you like:" feeling confident the while that the programme is already made out and that any material suggestion from me would be superfluous. So much for mistress and slave.

With his usual generosity, my husband made all of the negroes presents in honor of his marriage; offering for Bill's acceptance a silver watch, which he had purchased for him in Charleston. Taking the timepiece in his hand, Bill examined it attentively, held it to his ear, put it in his pocket, looked at the key, and then handing it back to his master, said, "no 'fence, mars'r, but if you please thar's somethin' I'd like better."

"Very well, what is it?" asked Richard; and Bill answered, "Why, you see, Mars'r, how dem hosses, Fred and Ferd, has never had proper 'spect showed to thar memory. To be sure, I wars a weed on my hat and I 'fused to gine in de dance t'odder night, but that's nothin'. Ferd had too high blood in him to keer for an ole nigger's mournin', and what I wants is for you *to paint de stable black*, and that I reckons will show 'em proper 'tention. What do you say, Miss Rose?"

As the horses had fallen in my cause, I readily espoused Bill's project for the novelty of the thing, if nothing else; and should any one of my readers visit Sunny Bank, which I wish they may, they will see the stables wearing a hue as dark as Bill himself, who has now a pair of iron-greys, which he calls "Richard" and "Rose," notwithstanding that both are of the masculine gender. These, particularly the latter, are the pride of Bill's heart, and when the year of mourning has expired, he intends, he says, to have the stable painted "yaller," that being the color of a young girl who has lately made sad havoc with his affections!

Here I may as well say that Mrs. Lansing managed until she procured the desired piano, which came in company with another, a much nicer one, on the front of which was inscribed "Rose, from her husband." In return for her brother's gift, Mrs. Lansing made a large party, where I had an opportunity of wearing my bridal dress, together with a costly set of diamonds, which I found upon my table, when I went up to make my toilet. It did not need the simple word "Richard" on a bit of paper to tell me whence they came, and the tears started to my eyes when I thought how kind he was, while I was conscious of a glow of pride, when I saw *little Rosa Lee* flashing with diamonds, which encircled her arms and neck, and shone among the curls of her hair. Bertha, my tasteful waiting maid—for I am getting quite southernized—pronounced me beautiful, as she gave the finishing stroke to my toilet, while one, for whose judgment I cared still more, and who all the time had been conning his evening paper, apparently oblivious to the presence of white satin, point lace, orange flowers and diamonds, responded, "Yes, Bertha, your young mistress *is* beautiful."

Dress does make a vast deal of difference in one's looks, and if that night two-thirds of the three hundred *particular* friends, whose hands I shook, pronounced me "beautiful, handsome, charming, lovely," and all that, it was owing chiefly, I think, to the fitness of my robes, and the brilliancy of my diamonds. These last were the subject of much remark, they being the finest which had ever been worn in W——, Ada *very good-naturedly* saying, "she hoped my good fortune wouldn't quite turn my head!"

Mrs. Lansing's party was followed by many more, and ere I was aware of it Mrs. Richard Delafield was quite a belle—what she said, what she did, and what she wore being pronounced *au fait* by the fashionables of W——. Upon all this Ada looked jealously; never allowing an opportunity to pass without speaking slightingly of me, though always careful that Richard should not know of it. In his presence she was vastly kind, sitting at my feet, calling me "Aunty," and treating me as if I had been twenty years her senior. At first she spent much more of her time at Sunny Bank than was at all agreeable to me, and I was not sorry when a little incident occurred which in a measure tended to keep her away. She had always been in the habit of treating my husband with a great show of affection, and now that he was, as she said, "an old married man," she seemed to think it no matter how much she caressed him. Even *I* dared not seat myself upon his knee as coolly as she would, and her temerity troubled me, particularly as I knew it was annoying to him. This I must have manifested in some way, for one morning, when as usual she entered our room without knocking, and perched herself on Richard's knee, he pushed her off, saying, half in earnest, half in jest, "Don't act so foolish, Ada, you make me sick, for now that I have Rose to pet me I can easily dispense with your caresses, which are rather too much of a good thing."

Ada was angry, and with a little hateful laugh, she said, turning to me, "*jealous*, I suppose, and have read your better half a lecture on propriety. When *I* marry, I trust I shall have faith enough in my husband's love for me, not to care even if he does chance to look at some one else."

I knew Richard would vindicate my cause, so I remained silent while he answered, "You do Rose injustice, for never have we exchanged a word concerning the manner you have assumed towards me, and which I should suppose your own sense of propriety would condemn. Were you my wife, 'twould be different."

"Your wife," interrupted Ada, with bitter scorn, "I am not your wife, thank fortune, neither did I ever aspire to be, and I have yet to see the man whom I would for a moment think of marrying."

There was not the slightest cause for this speech, but Ada was angry; and, as if to exasperate her still more, Richard coolly asked, "Didn't you think of marrying *Herbert Langley* when you engaged yourself to him?"

He had heard the whole story at Meadow Brook, but this was the first time he had hinted it to Ada, who turned very pale and without another word left the room, going back to Cedar Grove, where for three weeks she pouted and cried alternately. At the end of that time, however, she concluded it better to "make up" so she wrote a note to us both, asking *my* pardon for her rudeness and begging my husband to forgive her for the many falsehoods she had told concerning her engagement with Herbert, which she now frankly confessed. Of course we forgave her, and as she was not one who remembered anything long, she soon began to visit us as of old, though she no longer sat on my husband's knee, or wound her arms around his neck. His rebuke did her good, and she profited by it, while the fact that he was fully aware of the deception she had practised tended to humble her, and on rainy days, when Richard was necessarily away from home, I found her quite an agreeable companion.

Thus the winter and spring passed away, and my mother's letters began to grow urgent for my return, but for various reasons Richard did not think it advisable for me to under take so long a journey, and as Sunny Bank was all the world to me, I very cheerfully consented to wait until another season ere I visited my New England home. About this time I was again seized with my olden desire for authorship, induced in a measure by my knowing how much Mrs. Lansing reverenced anything which savored of a book-writer. To be an *authoress*, then, and make her proud to own me as her sister, was a subject over which I grew pale and "nervous," Richard said, while the negroes called me "fidgety" and wondered "what done ailed Miss Rose." At last, after many wakeful nights and restless days, after sick headaches, nervous headaches, and all kind of headaches, the plan was marked out for a story. *I* would be the heroine myself and give to the world as much of my history as I thought proper, and if I failed—if no railroad, steamboat, or stagecoach passenger ever pointed me out as "the woman who wrote that book," or if my publishers "respectfully declined" another bearing my signature, I thought I should still have the satisfaction of knowing I had tried to benefit the world, and I felt almost sure that in Meadow Brook at least there were people stupid enough to buy my book and possibly to like it, just because little Rosa Lee, who used to climb fences and hunt hen's eggs with them in her childish days, had written it. So, one sunny morning in June, when my husband had left me to be gone for two weeks, I shut myself up in my room, donned a loose wrapper, tucked back my curls, opened my writing desk, took out a quire of foolscap, and had just written "MEADOW BROOK," when the bell rang and Bertha announced "a lady in the parlor." With a deep sigh, as I thought how "WE writers disliked to be disturbed," I arranged my curls, resumed my cambric morning gown, and went down to receive my visitor, telling her that I was *very* well, that the weather was *very* warm, that I expected to be *very* lonely without my husband, that her bonnet was *very* pretty, that I didn't think negroes as annoying and hateful as she did, after which she took her leave; and I went back to my room, this time locking the door and writing the first chapter of my book before the bell rang for dinner.

To Bertha I imparted my secret, reading to her each page as I wrote it, and though she was not, perhaps, the most appreciating auditor one could have, she was certainly the most attentive and approving. It is true she objected to my describing myself as such a homely child. "Jest tell de truffe and done wid it," she said; whereupon I assured her that I *had* told the truth, and then she suggested that in order to make amends for my ugliness I should represent myself as having been "peart like and smart." So, if the reader thinks I have made myself too precocious, the fault is chargeable to Bertha, for I did it to please her!

For two weeks I wrote, scarcely allowing myself a moment's rest, and Bertha, who, when she saw how it wore upon me, began at last to expostulate. "Thar wasn't no 'casion," she said, "to kill myself, when thar was heaps 'o niggers kickin' round under foot, and if miss 'sisted on writin' a book, why didn't she make some dem lazy critters do it for her!"

At the end of two weeks Richard returned, asking me as he looked in my face "what was the matter, and how I had spent my time?"

Before I could answer, Bertha, who was quite incensed against my book, said, "she's done writin' a spellin' book, or somethin', and sits up 'most all night. I tell her how 'twill kill her, but she pay no 'tention!"

The secret was out, and with many blushes I plead guilty, and producing my manuscript, watched Richard while he read it. Over the first chapter, where he thought I was going to die, he cried—or that is, tears came to his eyes; the third he skipped partially, the next entirely, and the next and the next (I hope the reader has not done likewise); but when he found Dr. Clayton he read every word, his forehead tying itself up in knots, which, however, cleared away the moment he came upon himself at the theatre, though I believe he didn't feel much complimented by my description of his personal appearance!

There, just as *he* was introduced, the story ended, and fortunate was it for me that it did so, for he declared I should not write another word after I got through with him; and I promised that I wouldn't, mentally resolving that it should be some time before I reached that point. This then, my reader, is the reason why I said no more of him, when first I presented him to your notice, but left him for a while in mystery. I knew Richard was anxious to hear what *did* become of himself, and I fancied that if I wrote considerable before I said anything very definite of him, he would be more likely to let me finish the book, as he would not wish me to waste so much paper for nothing! And the sequel proved that I was right. Regularly each day I wrote, Richard always stopping me the moment he thought I was tired, and invariably breaking me off in the wrong place, so if there should be any parts of my story which do not join together smoothly, you may know it was there that Richard took my pen from my hand, or hid the inkstand.

Towards the middle of August, invitations came for us to attend a large wedding in Charleston. I was exceedingly anxious to go, having heard much of the bride, who was a distant relative of my husband, and though both he and Mrs. Lansing raised every conceivable objection to my leaving home, I adroitly put aside all their arguments, and ere Richard fully realized that he had been coaxed into doing something he had fully determined not to do, we were rattling along in a dusty Charleston omnibus towards one of the largest hotels, where rooms had been engaged for us. The morning after our arrival, I went into the public parlor, and as I seated myself at the piano I saw just across the room, near an open window, a quiet, intelligent-looking lady, apparently twenty-six or twenty-seven years of age, and near her sporting upon the carpet, was a beautiful little girl, with flowing curls and soft dark eyes, which instantly riveted my attention, they were so like something I had seen before.

At the sound of the music she came to my side, listening attentively, and when I had finished, she laid one white, chubby hand on my lap and the other on the keys, saying, "please play again, *Rose* like to hear you."

"And so your name is Rose?" I answered, "Rose what?"

"*Rosa Lee Clayton*, and that's my new *ma*," she replied, pointing towards the lady, whose usually pale cheek was for an instant suffused with a blush such as brides only wear.

I knew now why I had felt interested in the child. It was the *father* which I saw looking at me through the eyes of brown, and taking the little creature in my arms, I was about to question her of her sire, when an increasing glow on the lady's cheek and a footstep in the hall told me he was coming!

The next moment he stood before me, Dr. Clayton! his face perfectly unruffled and wearing an expression of content, at least, if not perfect happiness. I was conscious of a faintness stealing over me, but by a strong effort I shook it off, and rising to my feet, I offered him my hand, which he pressed, saying, "This is indeed a surprise, Rose—I beg your pardon, Mrs. Delafield, I suppose?"

I nodded in the affirmative, and was about to say something more, when another footstep approached, and my husband's tall figure darkened the doorway. For an instant they both turned pale, and Dr. Clayton grasped the piano nervously; but the shock soon passed away, and then as friend meets friend after a brief separation, so met these two men, who but the year before had watched together over my pillow, praying, the one that I might live, and the other that I might die.

Wonderingly the little girl looked up into her father's face, and pulling the skirt of my dress, said, "Who is the lady, pa? with the pretty curls so much like mine?"

Never before, I believe, did I like Dr. Clayton as I did at that moment when I saw the deep tenderness which broke over his features as he took his daughter in his arms, and pressing his lips to her forehead, answered, "It is *Rosa Lee*, my child, the lady for whom you were named."

"Don't you love her, pa? *I* do," she asked, stretching her little fat arms towards me.

I glanced at my husband—his brow was dark as midnight. I looked at Dr. Clayton, there was a slight quivering of his lips, while his wife was pale as a water lily, and then I burst into a merry laugh, in which the gentlemen soon joined, though it would have puzzled us all to have told at what we were laughing.

After a few words of explanation as to why we were there, Dr. Clayton suddenly remembered himself, and leading me towards the lady, introduced her as "My wife, Mrs. Clayton." She had been living in Florida with a cousin, at whose house they were married, about two weeks before, and they were now on their way to Boston, stopping for a few days in Charleston to see the city. I found her a very quiet, sensible woman, but as different from Dell Thompson, or Rosa Lee, as a person well could be, and I was wondering to myself how it was possible for a man to love so many people of opposite temperaments, when she said something about New England, and I asked if she were ever there.

"Oh, yes," she answered, "I was born there, in Wilbraham, Mass. I was living with the grandmother of the first Mrs. Clayton at the time of her death."

In a moment it all came to me; Dell had told me of *Mabel Warrener*, who had inherited her grandmother's fortune, and now she sat there before me, Mrs. Clayton 2d. Surely the freaks of fortune are wonderful! Naturally refined and intelligent, Mabel had employed a part of her money in giving herself a good education, graduating at Mount Holyoke Female Seminary, and going thence back to her home in Wilbraham, which she had fitted up with much taste, and where she was living when Dr. Clayton met her on his return from Georgia. Of her then he only thought as of a pleasant, agreeable woman; but when time, absence, and my marriage had softened the keenness of his disappointment, he often found his thoughts wandering towards the fair Mabel, who, upon inquiry, he learned had gone to Florida. Rose needed a mother, and he needed a wife; so, after an interchange of letters, he one morning started with his little girl for the "land of flowers," where neither sickness, nor death, nor yet a Richard Delafield, came between him and his bride. They seemed very happy, for after a little Dr. Clayton recovered his equanimity, and appeared perfectly natural.

Not a word, however, did he say of the past, or in any way allude to Georgia, except once when he asked me if I did not think *Rose* resembled Jessie in a measure. I had thought of the same thing, though Rosa's eyes were darker and her hair more of a chestnut brown. She was a sweet little creature, and if anything could have reconciled me to being the wife of Dr. Clayton, it would have been the fact that she was my daughter. But as I contrasted the two men, as my eye fell on Dr. Clayton's handsome face and curly locks, and then rested on the dark features and raven hair of Richard, I felt that in him there was more of the true, the noble man, and my heart warmly approved me for the choice I had made.

Nearly all the morning we sat there talking on indifferent subjects, and when dinner was over, Mrs. Clayton came to my room, staying a long time, and gaining fast in my good opinion, when I saw how kind and friendly she was. She had heard the whole story, for she told me so, holding little Rose upon her lap and smoothing her silken curls.

"We cannot all love the same person," she said in conclusion; "and I am so glad you refused him, for otherwise he would not have been my husband;" and her quiet eyes lighted up with a look of happiness which plainer than words could express told me that she had brought to Dr. Clayton no divided affections.

At the making of my toilet for the wedding she was present, aiding Bertha greatly by her own tasteful suggestions, and when at last I was dressed with perfect childish simplicity, she ran for her husband "to come and see if I didn't look pretty."

"Mrs. Delafield was always pretty to me," was the doctor's answer, and that was all he said.

They were to leave early next morning before I would be up, and so when the carriage was announced, we went to bid them good-bye.

"May I kiss your wife?" asked the doctor of my husband, as he held my hand.

"Certainly, sir," answered Richard, "an even exchange is always fair," and instead of once, *he* kissed the blushing Mabel twice, which of course gave Dr. Clayton liberty to do the same by me.

Suddenly remembering something which I had left in my room, I went up for it, and on my way back glanced into the parlor, occupied by Dr. Clayton. He was seated upon the sofa by the side of his wife, around whose waist his arm was affectionately thrown, while partly on his lap and partly upon that of her step-mother was little Rose, her long eyelashes drooping sleepily over her eyes of brown. It was a beautiful tableau, and whenever I think of Dr. Clayton now, it is as I last saw him, happy and contented, for he has not only won a most excellent wife, but also secured that $10,000 after all!

CHAPTER XXXII
NOVEMBER 25TH

Dear Reader,

Just one year ago to-night the orange wreath and bridal veil were twined among my curls, and with a loving heart I stood up before the man of God and took upon myself the vows, which made me Richard's forever. The orange flowers are faded now, and the bridal veil looks soiled and worn; but the sunlight of happiness which shone upon me when first he called me his wife has grown brighter and brighter as each day has unfolded to me some new virtue which I knew not that he possessed when, he became my husband.

No shadow, however slight, has ever fallen between us, for though he has a fiery temper and an indomitable will, they are both under perfect control, and so much confidence have I in his love for me, that should I ever in any way come in collision with his temper or his will, I have faith to believe I could bend the one and subdue the other. Every comfort and luxury which affection can dictate or money procure has been gathered around me, until my home seems to me a second paradise.

The fervid heat of summer has passed, and the hazy light which betokens the fall of the leaf has come. On the northern hills, they say, the November snows have already fallen, but we are still basking in the soft sunlight of a most glorious autumn; and as I write, the south wind comes in through the open window, whispering to me of the fading flowers, whose perfume it gathered as it floated along. Just opposite me, in a willow chair, with her head buried in a towering turban of royal purple, sits Juno, a middle aged woman, nodding to the breeze, which occasionally brushes past her so fast that she lazily opens her eyes, and with her long-heeled foot gives a jog to the *rosewood crib*, wherein lies sleeping a little tiny thing which was *left* here five weeks ago to-day. Oh, how odd and funny it seemed when Richard first laid on my arm a little bundle of cambric and lace, and whispered in my ear, "Would you like to see our baby?" She is a great pet, and should this book never reach so far as Georgia, Mrs. Lansing, I am sure, will like me all the same, for her words and manner have been very kind since the morning when I said to Richard, "We will call our baby *Jessie*."

So Jessie was she baptized, Mrs. Lansing's tears falling like rain on the face of the unconscious child, which she folded to her bosom as tenderly as if it had indeed been her own lost Jessie come back to her again. Upon Ada the arrival of the stranger produced a novel effect, overwhelming her with such a load of modesty that she kept out of Richard's way nearly two weeks, and never once came to see me until I was sitting up in my merino morning gown, which she had embroidered for me herself. Ada has a very nice sense of propriety!

But little more remains for me to say, and that I must say briefly. I am determined to finish my story, and as my husband for the first time since my illness has left me alone for an hour or two, I am improving the opportunity, having first bribed Bertha to bring me my writing materials, by promising her a dress which she has long coveted.

The royal purple turban by the window has become somewhat displaced by the strong west wind, and now wide awake, begins to grumble at "Miss Rosy's *impudence* in 'xertin' herself to write trash which is of no kind o' count, and which no *human* will ever read."

I hope her prediction is a false one, for I have lately conceived the idea of devoting the entire proceeds of this book to the benefit of *Rosa Lee*, who, of course, has no part in the $10,000 which her father has married!

There is a rustling in the crib—the baby is waking, and at my request Juno brings her to me, saying as she lays her on my lap, "She's the berry pictur' of t'other Jessie," and as her soft blue eyes unclose and my hand rests on her curly hair which begins to look golden in the sunlight, I, too, think the same, and with a throbbing heart I pray the Father to save her from the early death which came to our lost darling—"Jessie, the angel of the Pines."

Rose Delafield.